RESTLESS HAWKE

A SECOND GENERATION HAWKE FAMILY NOVEL

BILLIONAIRES OF NEW ORLEANS: THE HAWKE FAMILY SECOND GENERATION
BOOK 6

GWYN MCNAMEE

RESTLESS HAWKE
© 2025 Gwyn McNamee

Cover Model: Cole; Photographer: Wander Aguiar

Cover Design: Michelle Johnson at Bluesky Design

Editing: Stephie Walls at Wallflower Edits

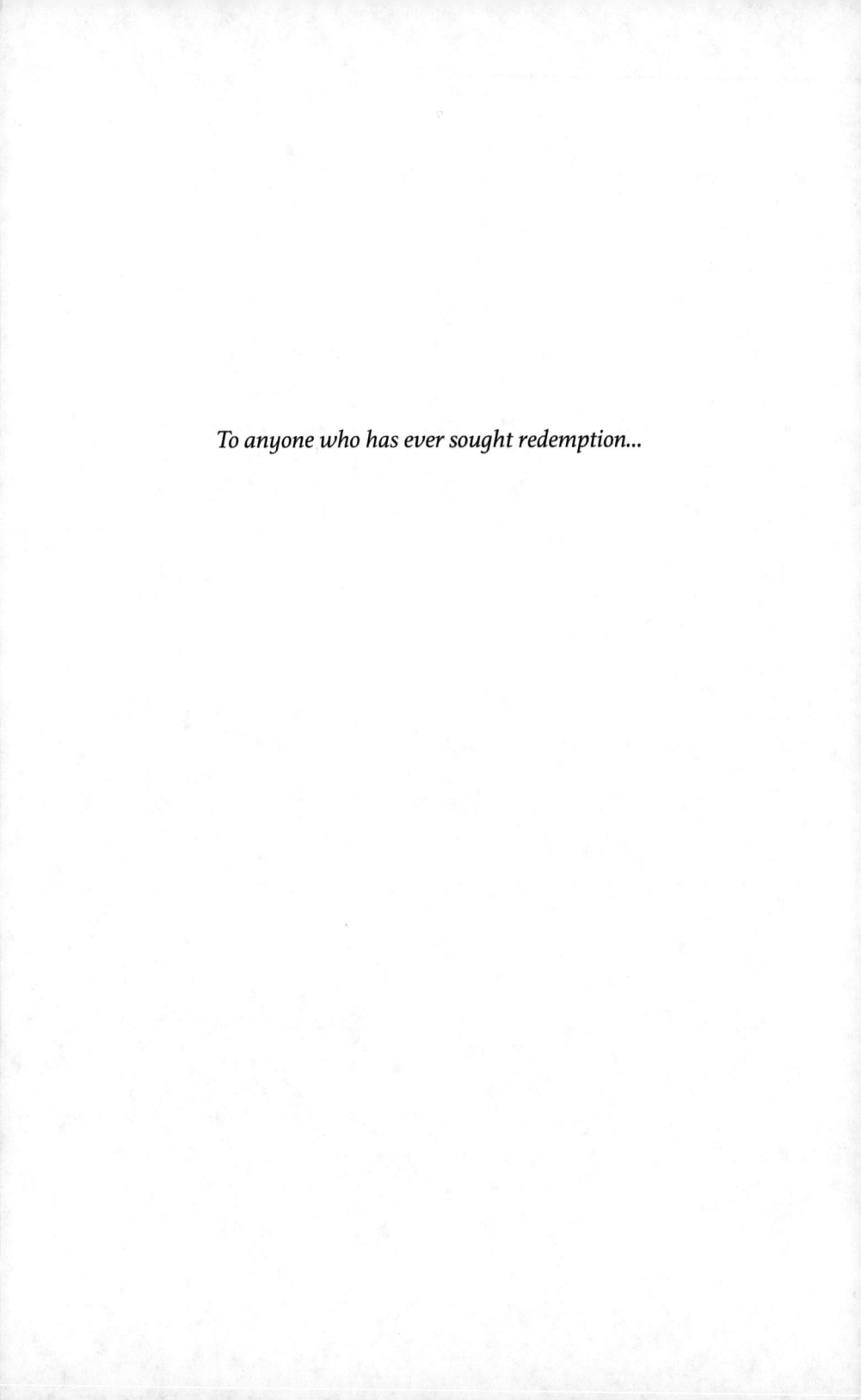

To anyone who has ever sought redemption...

HAWKE FAMILY TREE

THE HAWKE FAMILY
Antonia and Sam "The Savage" Hawke

SAVAGE COLLISION

Savage Hawke & Danika Eriksson
|
Kennedy Hawke

STONE SOBER

Stone Hawke & Nora Eriksson
/ \
Isaac Hawke   Coen Hawke

TAINTED SAINT

Solomon "Saint" Clarke & Caroline Brooks
/ \
Pope Clarke   Bishop Clarke

TORTURED SKYE

Skye Hawke & Gabe Anderson
/ \
Atlas Anderson   Astrid Anderson

BUILDING STORM

Storm Hawke (Matthews) & Landon McCabe
/ \
Angelina Matthews   Alessandra McCabe

STEELE RESOLVE

Luca "Steele" Abello & Byron Harris
|
Jude Harris-Abello (ad)

1

COEN

*Y*ou have to be ruthless to win—and losing isn't an option.
Nothing but complete focus will bring victory.
Watch everything like a hawk waiting to swoop in on its prey.
Never blink.
Never react.
Never give away anything your opponent can use.
Never hand them the rope with which to hang you...

Those words echo through my head—sound advice given by a man who certainly knows how to win.

He did it for decades in the courtroom, protecting the Hawkes from any manner of threat—and God knows there have been too many to even count. But when Dad offered Isaac and me those sage words of wisdom when we were just little boys, still learning the ways of the world and what it meant to have the Hawke-blue eyes and name, he never could have anticipated I'd be using them to face down an opponent across a felt poker table rather than a counsel's table in some New Orleans courtroom.

Expectation meet harsh reality.

The man who almost gave his life for the Hawkes on multiple occasions never wanted this for his sons. That advice was meant to help us get somewhere in life. Somewhere that would bolster the family name and help establish our dominance.

Instead, I'm here after not only failing every single person I care about but also betraying them in the worst way possible.

That acrid taste of it has lingered in my mouth since the moment I placed the bet against Atlas, and it has only gotten worse in the three weeks since fight night and the wedding.

I've tried to keep the fact that I'm now the ultimate pariah out of my head while I play.

I've *tried* to follow Dad's advice and forget everything I did, how badly I wounded them, how exposed everyone is now that I've opened the door to a monster...

Play.

Be a rock.

But it feels more like I'm Sisyphus, rolling a boulder of unbearable weight up a steep hill only to have it crashing back down on me—over and over and over and over...

Be ruthless.

There isn't any other option.

Because at this point, it's in my hands—the future of *all* the Hawkes.

I'm the one who betrayed their trust.

I'm the one who put myself into this position by ending up in bed with a man like Satriano. It doesn't matter that I didn't know it was him when I placed my bet. The result is the same.

A very dangerous man has a stranglehold on me—on *us*—because I made the shittiest decision of my life.

Yet the *money* isn't even really the issue.

And *that's* what made me run from the wedding.

Run from New Orleans.

Run from the Hawkes.

What I owe is nothing compared to the retribution Satriano seeks in exchange for what Atlas did. That knockout sealed my fate—and put his life as well as that of *every* single member of the family in mortal jeopardy.

One punch set Satriano back *billions*.

And he doesn't want it repaid in cash.

He wants it repaid in *blood.*

Owning a Hawke means controlling all of us, and he knew precisely what he was doing when he asked Atlas to throw that fight. If he had, Satriano would have made bank and had Atlas in his pocket. If he didn't, Satriano would own me *and* Atlas. It was a win-win for the man who now controls the New Orleans underworld. And a loss-loss for the Hawkes.

That's why *this* is so important—sitting here now, winning this game, buying some time and goodwill.

My single remaining opponent checks his cards for the tenth time. Casually. A mere glance, as if he couldn't care less what he holds.

An act.

The same one I perform every time I play.

After more than six hours at the table, it's down to the two of us—all the other players who started out around this felt have dropped away. With everyone one, my odds of walking away with the massive pile of chips increases.

Fifty-fifty odds aren't bad.

I would feel a lot more confident about my chances, except so far, I haven't picked up his tell.

Everyone has one—except me.

I've trained myself not to fidget, how to hold my cards to ensure my hands stay steady and relaxed, how to look at them so that my pupils don't dilate and facial features don't reveal anything.

A decade of perfecting the art in high-stakes games.

Since the first time I sat at a table, I knew this was where I belonged.

Not behind the bar at the club or running one of the dozens of other Hawke businesses throughout town.

Definitely not with Dad in the courtroom.

That has always been Isaac's domain, where he wants to be and where he excels. But for me, it has always been *here*—at a table like this—with cards in my hand and nothing standing between me and that purse except one man or the occasional woman.

Only now, I'm not playing for myself.

I'm playing for all of *them*.

To say I'm sorry. To supplicate myself at their feet and beg for forgiveness the only way I know how. And to protect them from what will come if I don't try to fix things.

If that's even possible...

Jake "the Snake" Nelson finally looks up at me and pushes his massive pile of chips to the center. "All in."

He didn't have to do that.

He could have placed a bet that would have protected some of that money so, if he loses, he won't walk away empty-handed.

He did it for a reason.

And now I'm finally seeing his tell.

Jake is a bravado player, relying on a big bet to shake me.

But he doesn't understand who he's dealing with.

I didn't come to Atlantic City to walk away with anything but the win.

Calling, I shove in the rest of my chips, while fighting the smirk that wants to pull at my lips...and lay down my cards.

A collective gasp goes up around me from those watching the game.

My opponent flinches, then sets his cards on the felt with a scowl.

Those two aces in his hand, the one in the flop, and the final the dealer pulled as the river probably made him very comfortable, but it can't beat my king-high straight flush.

Fuck yes.

I needed this win badly.

Some days, the cards just aren't in your favor—something "The Snake" is feeling right now, and a lesson I learned the hard way.

The losing streak that got me to this point almost destroyed everything.

And it still might...

A flash of green catches the corner of my eye, and, for the first time since the opening hand was dealt, I glance toward the crowd gathered around to watch the end of the game.

The casino lights reflect off the iridescent fabric of the slinky, curve-hugging emerald dress, but the woman wearing it has already turned away, a long cascade of dark hair falling down her exposed back.

She disappears into the throng so quickly that I almost wonder if I imagined her perfect ass and wide hips...

"Sir?"

Shit.

I shake my head to clear it and refocus on the table and what's mine.

My biggest win since I fled New Orleans.

After weeks of chasing down private games in backrooms and casino tournaments with spots open, winning some and losing others, this finally feels like that little glimmer of hope I've been searching for—a chance that I might be able to pay back what I owe Satriano and save the Hawkes.

The casino host inclines his head at the chips as Jake shoves away from the table in a huff. "Congratulations, sir."

I release a long, steady breath and sit back in my chair, finally allowing some of the tension I've been hiding to uncoil from my body. "Thank you."

"Your winnings will be deposited into your account via wire transfer, as per the usual process."

"Excellent. Thank you, Bobby." Inclining my head in thanks, I toss a few $1,000 chips to the dealer. "Thanks for the good cards."

Some people are superstitious.

They won't play with certain dealers.

Won't even approach a table if someone they don't like is sitting behind the deck.

I've never believed in superstitions like that.

You win because you're good and because the cards are in your favor. You lose because the cards aren't or because you fucked something up and didn't follow Dad's rules.

But what happened over the last six months to put me in this position in the first place wasn't *that*.

It was bad luck, pure and simple.

Different dealers, different casinos, different poker tournaments, different private games held in dark rooms, each time a loss. Loss after loss after loss, like repeated stabs to the heart, compounding the pain and damage.

That bet against Atlas was supposed to stop the bleeding, get me back everything I had lost. Instead, it only twisted the knife deeper.

This pile in the middle of the table is another small dent in what I owe Satriano.

Two million out of ten.

That number still shocks me at times.

Ten million...

All to fund that downward spiral I set myself on, always believing I would win it back. Always so confident that the horrible slide would eventually level out. Always so sure I could secure the next big win and then act like none of it had ever happened.

Fuck was I an idiot...

I push up from my chair and step away from the table.

All I want after a game like that is a stiff drink and to fall into bed.

The lights and sounds of the casino assault me the moment I step out of the poker room. Thousands of people fill the floor, many completely oblivious to the fact that they've been sucked in by quicksand that will suffocate them and wring them dry.

Most don't have the skill to survive in a place like this.

The games are designed to lose.

And the house always wins.

Which is why poker has been my game.

I prefer my opponents to have names and faces, to be able to read them for all the little tells, knowing the deck isn't already stacked against me the way it is with any other casino game. And normally, I would prefer to celebrate a win properly—with a strong drink and a warm, willing body under me.

But I shouldn't stay any longer than necessary.

The more time I spend here, the greater the chance one of the Hawke spies will get word to the family about where I am, and if they interfere, everything will become even more of a shitstorm than it already is. So, going back to my comped suite upstairs, packing, and heading out to the next game is the wisest plan.

I make my way past the central bar toward the guest elevators when that same flash of shiny green catches my eye again.

My steps falter, and I pause to examine the back of the woman sitting alone at the bar, sipping lazily from a martini glass.

Slender shoulders taper down to a stunning ass hugged in the skin-tight, shimmery emerald fabric.

I *should* keep walking.

I *should* leave.

But I want to celebrate.

And one night here with her would be worth any risk that staying in one place for too long might pose.

One night...or maybe two.

Because even though I haven't seen her face yet, those lush curves and the way her body swayed when she walked away earlier are enough to tell me I won't get enough of *her* in the hours we have left before tomorrow morning.

ALLEGRA

THE SHARP ACIDITY of my cosmopolitan makes my lips purse as I swallow, but I relish the heat that spreads through my body the moment it hits my stomach, my shoulders relaxing slightly.

Damn. I needed this...

It's been too long of a day.

Too much time being "on" and not relaxing.

But I immediately tense again as the stool next to me slides back and my skin prickles from a heated gaze raking over me.

I've always known when someone's eyes were on me, when I was being watched. It's something I learned to use to my advantage at a very young age. And it has served me well.

"Glenfiddich, forty-year, double, neat."

His deep voice rumbles across the tiny space between us.

Assertive.

Almost commanding.

This is a man who knows exactly what he wants and likely demands perfection from everyone around him to obtain it.

A little shiver rolls through me.

I know this kind of man.

Been *warned* about his type.

Learned a long time ago not to get involved with anyone who oozes that type of confidence that borders on arrogance.

Arrogance is very rarely—if ever—warranted. Men merely wear it as a shield against the things and people in the world they're intimidated by or as a badge of honor they haven't earned.

Which means the man seated beside me with the voice that was enough to get a physical response from me with only a few words isn't anyone to trifle with.

He is used to getting his way, and I need to prepare myself for what is undoubtedly coming mine.

Because he didn't choose the seat beside me by accident...

The bartender turns away to make the requested drink, and I continue to stare down into my cosmo, running my finger along the rim of the glass lazily. Disinterested despite my new neighbor's gaze continuing to heat my skin.

He accepts his glass from the bartender. "Thank you."

Out of my peripheral vision, I catch the glint of the lights off the tumbler as it moves up to his lips, but I keep my focus anywhere but him. I won't give him that satisfaction—at least, not that easily.

Make him wait.

Make him sweat.

He takes a slow sip before he sets it down and releases a contented sigh, like that single taste of the expensive scotch was *precisely* what he had been waiting for all day.

I know the feeling...

I've been waiting, too.

"Strong drink..." I continue to glide my fingertip along the rim of my glass, my long, crimson nail almost dipping into the pink liquid. "Bad night at the slots?"

The leather on his stool creaks slightly as he swivels toward me, and the scent of smoke and something crisp and briny, almost like the ocean on a beautiful summer day wafts over me.

It draws my focus away from my drink, and I finally turn my head slowly to look at him.

A lazy grin spreads across his perfectly formed lips—lips that look like they could perform any number of sins and do it devilishly well.

Warm, Caribbean-blue eyes that call for me to dive into them and swim forever assess me carefully, roaming from my hair down to meet my gaze for a brief second, then over my bright-red lips, my exposed cleavage, the shimmering green of my dress, and finally the leg slipping out of the high slit that leaves very little to the imagination and promises the same kind of sin his mouth does.

The longer his appraisal takes, the more I have to fight the urge to squirm.

Heat ripples over my skin everywhere his gaze touches, but I force myself to remain unaffected.

I didn't expect those eyes.

Or that look.

Attention like this from men rarely rattles me.

There are times I even relish it and bathe in the power I can hold over the weaker sex that is controlled by what's between their legs.

But this feels...different.

In a way I am not wholly comfortable with.

Finally, his focus returns to my face again, and he smirks. "No, actually. Why do you ask?"

I shrug nonchalantly and take another sip of my drink. "It isn't every day you see somebody walk up to a bar and order something that costs more than $500 per pour. I thought maybe you were drowning your sorrows."

He tilts his glass toward me, a light chuckle filling the space between us and sending goosebumps skittering across my skin. "If I had just lost a bunch of money, would I have ordered a $500 scotch?"

A grin fights to pull up my lips. "I guess that's true." Matching his movement, I tilt my glass his way. "Touché."

His long, elegant fingers tighten on his scotch, and he brings it to his mouth again and enjoys another sip, never taking his gaze off mine. As he pulls the glass from his lips, he leans closer. "And what are *you* doing sitting here, drinking alone?"

Those warm azure eyes sparkle with mischief and heat, longing to keep me company in a way that would require privacy.

I trail my finger through the condensation forming on the martini glass, scanning the casino floor around us. "Just enjoying people-watching."

He nods slowly and follows my gaze. "This is a good place for that." Another sip. That intense focus swings back my way. He considers me for a moment and tilts his head toward the high-stakes poker room. "Is that what you were doing over at the table earlier? People-watching?"

Shit.

This man never looked up.

Never *once* gave any indication he saw me there, but apparently, he doesn't miss much, even when his unnerving focus is elsewhere—like on winning that massive pool of chips.

I allow my shoulders to rise slightly and fall, trying to appear disinterested and unrattled at being caught. "Something like that."

He rests his left forearm on the bar, leaning back a bit and watching me with a knowing glint in his eyes. Almost like he can see what really lies under this dress and the makeup I have all over my face. As if all of it might as well not exist. "I have a pretty good idea what you were doing."

Raising a brow, I turn toward him on the stool, my leg slipping even farther out from the slit, revealing almost my entire thigh. If I opened my legs even a fraction of an inch, he would know I'm not wearing anything under this. "Do you?"

His eyes sweep over me.

The skin-tight dress.

All the exposed flesh.

My collarbone...

Breasts...

And he's undoubtedly picturing my back that he saw when I walked away earlier and again when he came in and sat down.

A knowing grin plays at his lips, and that confidence I heard earlier in his voice resonates from him. "You were looking for your next mark."

I try not to let my back stiffen at the implication, but my shoulders tighten at what he so casually laid out. "You think I'm a hooker?"

He snorts, then takes another drink before he sets down his glass and leans closer. "A stunning woman like *you*, in a dress like *that*, *alone*, at a place like *this*, hanging out near the high-stakes room and then the *bar*?" He twirls his finger around in the air. "My family's in the business—casinos, not hookers—and I know a professional when I see one."

A professional...

I allow my lips to curl up into a saccharine-sweet smile that has lured many men to unsuspecting danger like a siren's call. "What if I *am* a professional?" My gaze travels over the bar around us—all the open seats along it on either side, the more casual, comfortable, lounging chairs and couches set up all along the wall behind us—then I lean toward him. "You chose the seat next to me, already suspecting what I was. So, what does that say about your intentions?"

The grin he offers sends heat blazing through my veins. "Care to find out?"

More than I should...

I snort and take the final sip of my drink, setting the empty glass on the bar and inclining my head toward the bartender. "You can close my tab."

My new *friend* beside me raises a brow. "Tab? You don't have somebody buying you drinks?"

Like a mark hoping to take me up to their room?

He really does think I'm a hooker.

Holding his gaze, refusing to look away, I shake my head. "Despite what you think, no. I really did come here to have a drink and to people-watch."

At least the man has the decency to flinch.

It's finally sinking in what a mistake he's made, and he doesn't seem like the type of man who makes them often.

Or who likes doing it...

The bartender slides the bill to me, and I scribble my name and room number on it, ensuring my bar neighbor can't see what I write before I return it. "Thank you."

I climb off my stool and step back from the bar, but the man with zero sense and blue eyes that would be easy to drown in reaches out and wraps his hand around my upper arm, stopping me from walking away.

Callouses graze across my skin and send a shiver of awareness through me.

He doesn't *look* like the kind of man who would have rough fingers and hands.

He's too clean and polished.

He screams money and lots of it.

And right now, he's begging for forgiveness with those damn gorgeous eyes of his.

Any humor that once lived in his gaze and the tilt of his lips fades. "I'm sorry, for what it's worth. I didn't mean to insult you."

I offer a mirthless laugh, pursing my lips and squaring my shoulders. "No, you just thought I was a hooker."

His eyes soften even more, warming in a way that is *far* too inviting. "Truly. I'm sorry. What's your name?"

"Why would I give you that?" I raise a brow. "Why would I give you anything?"

The perfectly square jawline that goes with all the other insanely Adonis-like features tenses. "Because I don't get distracted at the poker table, and I was when I saw you earlier…"

Something flutters in my chest.

Hot.

Dangerous.

I lean down to brush my lips against his ear. "Then, it is rather unfortunate that you had such a low opinion of me."

When I pull back, his eyes have darkened, now swirling like a hurricane is forming at the center. "I know places like this, and the best way to lose what you just won at the table is to bring a professional up to your room and get trick-rolled. I was trying to be careful."

Despite the repeated insult of thinking I was a working girl, I grin at him. "Were you?" I raise my brows. "Because, as we've already established, you *chose* the seat next to mine, knowing full well what you thought I was. I think you like the danger. The fact that it's forbidden and could cost you everything." I lean even closer, ensuring my lips graze his ear. "You thrive on it."

His back stiffens slightly, but the interest still controls his gaze when I pull away, keeping it locked on me. "You're really not going to give me your name?"

Shaking my head, I tug out of his hold, those callouses skating roughly over my skin as I prepare to make my exit. "What's the point?"

I don't wait for him to try to argue.

It wouldn't matter if I did.

Nothing he could say would get me to stay or to reveal the information he so eagerly seeks.

My heels click on the marble with each step I put between us.

I don't look back, even though I can feel his gaze locked on me as I descend the two steps from the central bar and make my way out onto the casino floor.

And I don't bother fighting the full-blown grin that pulls up my lips as I disappear into the crowd and walk away from him for the second time...

Confident he's following and memorizing my every move.

Just like he did when I dropped the bait at the poker table earlier.

2

ONE WEEK LATER

COEN

The elevator doors slide closed, sealing me into the obscenely opulent space. Pleasant instrumental music floats over the speakers. So different from what they play in the casinos in the States. Like everything in Monaco, the music screams luxury and is meant to help enhance the entire experience.

But even the soothing notes can't undo the dark mood that has settled over me and locked itself in tight since the moment I woke this morning in the plush bed, in the lavish suite with the glittering view of the Mediterranean.

It only gets worse.

Every second.

Every minute.

Every hour.

Every single fucking morning I climb out of whatever hotel bed I've slept in.

Every damn day.

The longer I'm away from New Orleans and the Hawkes, working to make amends and protect them from Satriano...the knife in my heart only drives in deeper.

Twists harder.

Hurts more.

Like the serrated edge is catching on something vital and tugging with each inch it goes in until I'm fully impaled.

I press my hand over the spot as the elevator continues to drop, along with my stomach. And that feeling in my gut doesn't have anything to do with the tournament I'm about to play or how important it is that I win.

The realization that I've been lucky to make it another week without them finding me has been weighing heavily on me since I left Atlantic City. Even putting a vast ocean between us hasn't cured the need to look over my shoulder constantly.

I won't be able to hide forever...

The only reason I was even able to sneak away and get out of New Orleans during the wedding reception was because everyone was so preoccupied with the hotel opening and celebrating Cass and Kennedy's big day.

Otherwise, Dad would've had me locked in my condo with Gabe, Saint, and probably even Bishop, armed at my door every fucking minute to ensure: one—that I wouldn't leave, and two —that Satriano wouldn't come for me.

Because we all knew it was inevitable.

I did them a favor by leaving, by staying hidden as I try to right my wrongs by calling in every favor and using every connection I've made at the various casinos over the years to get into games and pay for their silence to the family about it.

But it's only a matter of time before my luck runs out and someone who knows they're looking for me sees me and spills where I am. And once that happens, the plan I have to get this runaway train under control will come to a screeching halt when they drag me back kicking and screaming—and make things *worse.*

The elevator stops its descent, and the doors glide open.

All the hairs on the back of my neck stand on end.

That same paranoia settles over me again—at the least opportune time.

Just as I'm about to walk into and sit down at a tournament that could be worth millions, exactly what I need to make a dent in my debt to Satriano.

I step out onto the casino floor and release an annoyed sigh. The last time I was in Monte Carlo, it was under much more pleasant circumstances. But I won't be able to enjoy the amenities or the potential company when I can't shake the feeling that I've run out of time.

As soon as the tournament ends, I have to go.

If I keep moving and am careful about it, maybe I can buy more time. Four weeks haven't been enough. Not nearly when I must wait for the big games and tournaments to make any kind of difference. When I am trying to *prove* my usefulness to the man who holds all the cards.

I make my way toward the room where the tournament is taking place, and the casino host sees me coming, his smile brightening. "Good morning, sir."

"Anton." I incline my head toward him and let my eyes sweep over the other players already gathering. "Are we prepared to start?"

I never arrive early.

Prefer to be the last, when possible.

Not because I want to make an entrance, but because the longer I stand around, waiting for the other players to show, the greater the chance everyone has to try to size me up. And though I'm familiar with most of the players on the circuit who have enough money to compete at this level, there are always a few outliers—folks I've never played against. Especially away from the States.

And that always makes the games so much more interesting.

And *dangerous.*

Anton smiles and glances over my shoulder into the main casino. "We're waiting on one more player, but if you'd like to take your seat..."

He motions toward the chair in the center of the table directly across from the dealer, exactly where I always like to be —where I can see everyone and read them but can also gauge at least what the first half of the players might be holding before I place my bets.

I slowly make my way over, casually lowering myself into the chair as the others still milling around take their seats as well.

The guy next to me leans over, almost bumping me with the brim of his cowboy hat, and offers me his hand. "Hey, there. Butch Kavanaugh."

I stare at him.

American, too.

And too dumb to comprehend I'm not here to make friends.

I look away without taking his hand.

He's one of the few American players I don't know and have never faced, which means he's new blood.

That could be a very good thing or it could be disastrous. Having an untested player in a game like this could throw off the entire balance of the table. But if he's green, he may also make more mistakes and get out early, which means more money on the felt right away and less competition throughout the day.

Butch shakes his head and huffs, holding up his hands defensively. "Geez, all right then..."

He's offended by my brush-off, but that's good.

It means he's emotional.

And emotional players give it *all* away.

With a $500,000 buy-in, things will undoubtedly get testy, especially because Ned Fairbanks is playing today. He sits at the far end to my right, back ramrod straight.

Impassive.

For now.

But I know what lies beneath it.

The man's unstable—shockingly so—and when he loses, you don't want to be within a ten-foot radius of him, which is why I prefer to avoid any tournaments he'll be at.

Today is an exception—one I had to make in order to ensure I'm utilizing every opportunity presented to me. Missing a single tournament could make the difference between paying Satriano back quickly or his demanding it in blood from someone else in the family, like Atlas or Wren.

I shudder, picturing how happy she looked the moment he dropped to his knee at the reception and proposed. Not because I am not happy for them—I had a hard time keeping tears at bay. Because I couldn't handle it if anything bad happened because of me. And while Atlas may have chosen to stand against his demands by refusing to throw that fight, he never would have been in the position to *have* to if it weren't for me.

And I'm the only thing standing between them having a happy future with their unborn child and the monster lurking under the crib, waiting to strike.

That same monster haunts my dreams and waking hours, but I can't dwell on it when I should be concentrating on the upcoming game.

Don't give them the rope with which to hang you...

Our dealer appears, standing on his side of the table, hands behind his back, waiting to be called to his seat once our final player arrives and settles into the single empty chair on the left end of the table.

Next to me, Butch drums his fingers on the table, the annoying incessant sound already starting to irk everyone, given the dirty looks they toss him. He finally seems to catch on and pulls up his hand. "Sorry, just anxious to get playing."

You and me both.

Once I'm in the zone, there'll be no getting me out of it, but these few minutes before the first hand is dealt are always the worst—like Dad said they were when you were walking into a courtroom that first day of trial.

Right now, staring at a potential jury pool sounds a lot nicer than owing a mobster...

Maybe I should have gone to law school.

Giorgio Nikolaou smirks from my right at Butch's comment. "I heard you cleaned up in Atlantic City last week."

My back stiffens at his lightly accented words, but I try to stay casual. Giorgio and I have always been civil, but when the Greek sits at the same table, I know I'll have strong competition.

The fact that he's been keeping tabs on me doesn't sit well. Acid climbs my throat, and I force myself to relax my hands out of the fists they've become on my lap.

Even if no one can see them, that doesn't mean they can't read the tension building in me with Giorgio's comment.

"Where'd you hear that?"

His smirk grows, his green eyes sparkling with mischief and something else—maybe the knowledge that he was able to throw me off for a split second, something he's *never* done at the table before. "The Hawkes aren't the only one with connections, you know."

Believe me, I do.

The Nikolaou family is to Athens what Satriano now is to

New Orleans. Which is why I don't fuck with him or even speak to the man outside these tournaments.

I grunt and nod at him, unwilling to engage in the conversation about my win—or the fact that I've been dodging the Hawkes. I would rather no one know where I am, especially not a man who can obviously pull strings and isn't afraid to use his knowledge to his advantage and my *dis*advantage.

If he can find me, they can, too.

A vise starts to tighten around my chest, squeezing tightly.

Nothing but complete focus will bring victory.

Never give away anything your opponent can use.

I force air into my lungs. Force every muscle in my body to unwind and relax. Force that nagging feeling in the back of my mind to stay buried until the final cards are dealt.

Panic later.

Play now.

Anton's eyes suddenly widen toward the door.

Butch crosses his arms over his chest, looking perturbed and ready to tear into our final player. "Finally..."

Hurried steps sweep into the room, but I don't even bother looking until whoever it is finally settles at the table and the dealer takes his spot.

Anton spreads out his hands. "Welcome, players. I will now remind everyone of the rules of the tournament that were already sent to you..."

He recites the laundry list I'm more than familiar with, given how many of these I've played over the years, then walks around and sets our chips in front of each of us based on our buy-ins to secure our seats at this invite-only table.

I follow his hand until he reaches the final player and sets them on the felt—my eyes finally landing on the person we have been waiting for.

My breath catches as those shimmering silvery-gray eyes meet mine from the other end of the table.

Fuck.

One corner of her bright-red lips twitches an acknowledge-ment, but that's all I get as whatever Anton prattles on about gets washed away by the whooshing of blood in my ears.

Fuck. Fuck. Fuck. Fuck. FUUUUUUCK.

I was *right.*

She *was* sizing me up—scoping out her mark. But it wasn't because she's a hooker and she was attempting to get me to take her to bed so she could rob me. That woman *knew* she'd be sitting at this table with me in Monaco and wanted to memo-rize any tells or weaknesses I might have.

She's a player—and from the look she's giving me, a deadly one.

I am so fucked.

ALLEGRA

THE INTENSE, startled look on his face is enough to make me feel like I've won even before the first card has been dealt, but I still fight a deeper smirk that might give me away to my opponents.

I settle into my seat and prepare to play at a table full of rich, arrogant men. Not that it's any different than ninety-five percent of the other tournaments I've participated in. For the most part, this is still very much a man's game—despite a few very talented women who have managed to break into the poker circuit—which gives me a tremendous upper hand.

It allows me to use all my assets, and I am more than willing to do it if it means winning.

They all watch me carefully.

Ogling me.

Assessing me.

Sizing me up.

Most of them—if not all—wonder what the fuck I'm doing here.

Furrowed brows, tense mouths, and narrowed gazes give them away.

It throws them off their game, puts them on edge, to have someone like me sitting at the felt. A young, beautiful woman with exposed skin is the type of distraction they don't want. But only my friend from Atlantic City seems to be truly *shaken* by my arrival.

He does his best to try to hide his reaction. The tensing of his shoulders. The stiffening of his spine. The way he swallows thickly, his Adam's apple bobbing in his lightly tanned neck. The way he shifts in his chair that seems to have suddenly gotten very uncomfortable for him.

There's nothing better than seeing your opponent off balance before the game starts. Watching grown men who pride themselves on not having tells and being able to control their reactions squirm from one single look or a half-smile is enough to prove why it was so easy for sirens to ensnare them and bring them to their watery graves.

Always have the upper hand...

Something taught to me at a very young age and a mantra I have always tried to remember over the years. It's served me well. Gotten me through some very hard times and situations that others might have found overwhelming.

I've kept my wits about me.

Held my own even when surrounded by powerful men with sinister intentions.

Today is no different. There may not be a *physical* threat at the table. But the one in his eyes shouldn't be ignored.

I was right in my assessment of him in Atlantic City. He is used to getting his way. Used to people following his commands and coming out on top.

He is used to having the upper hand—and I already have it when it comes to him.

Anton moves around the table, introducing each of the players. "Coen Hawke..."

Hearing his name finally has him shaking his head and clearing away the startled trance that seemed to have settled into place the moment he saw me. But his eyes don't return to their typical warm Caribbean-water coloring. They stay hard and sharp as ice, as if he thinks he can somehow wield it at me from across the felt.

When Anton reaches me, he inclines his head and grins at me. "And finally, Ms. Allegra Knight."

I offer a sweet smile to all the players, making sure to meet each and every gaze at the table to show them I'm friendly and not appear threatening. Most of them will probably buy it, will think I'm in over my head and that they can stomp all over me.

Good.

Let them underestimate me.

It makes for so much more fun when I wipe the floor with them.

I likely take far too much joy in the prospect, and I've certainly celebrated destroying these types of men—both at the tables and elsewhere—but it's hard not to enjoy it when I understand how men think and *what* they think of me.

There is *nothing* as satisfying as seeing an arrogant prick fall from the pedestal he's placed himself on.

And there will be a *lot* of tumbles today.

Starting with Coen Hawke.

I settle back and wait as the dealer calls for the blinds and the first cards hit the table.

Quick hands reach out to snatch them up, like the longer they sit on the felt might somehow change what's printed on the other side. I don't even look at mine, instead taking the opportunity to watch each of the other players check theirs.

Starting across from me, I move around the table, but when I make it to Coen, his eyes are locked on me, not his cards, which remain untouched like my own.

His cool, accusatory gaze narrows on me slightly, but I break it and continue to the other players between us on this side.

Talk to me...

I've spent weeks researching each and every one of the players around this table—after using my many charms to get the list of who would be participating in the tournament—but it doesn't mean there won't be surprises from them.

Tells I didn't pick up on in my earlier scouting.

Strategies I may have missed.

I need to keep my head cool, stay focused on the game, and avoid looking at Coen Hawke and the way those once-warm eyes have returned to icy shards being thrown at me like daggers.

He's figured it out now...knows *exactly* what I was up to that night, and he's prepared to make me pay for it.

Good luck with that.

I wink at him.

Coen scowls and finally checks his cards, knowing I'm still watching.

But all the time I surveilled him in that game in Atlantic City, not *once* did he do anything that I would consider a tell. He never gave any indication of what cards his hand might hold— even if he's more than willing to show me how he feels about *me*.

Not a twitch of a muscle.

Not a twist of a lip.

Not a shift of weight.

Not a tightening of a hand.

Absolutely *nothing*.

He's a true player, one in complete control of his emotions

—at least sitting at the table. Sitting at that bar, that's a different story. And I've already seen the crack I made in his smooth façade.

It will only be so long before he *breaks.*

A round of bets goes around the table until it reaches me.

I finally look at my cards—a pair of kings. Hearts and clubs. *Not a bad start.*

Hopefully, it bodes well for the upcoming game.

I need the cards to love me today.

After tossing in my chips, I wait as the dealer pulls the flop, offering a sweet smile to anyone glancing my way. Appearing as young and naïve as I can.

They all believe I'm some dumb bimbo who only got into this game because of my breasts and my looks. Let them believe it. The only one here who might have an inkling is Coen Hawke.

And only because he caught me.

All the others were oblivious to my time spent watching and analyzing them over the past several weeks leading into this tourney—which means they aren't as observant as Mr. Hawke.

I have to give him that, at least.

He saw me watching that table in AC.

He *knew* I was up to no good.

And he was right.

I hadn't anticipated him seeking me out at the bar after, but once it happened, there wasn't any reason not to milk it and use it to further my advantage over him.

It clearly worked if his reaction today is any indication.

We make it through five hands—two to me, one to Coen, and one to Giorgio—before I finally catch a tell from the man sitting to Mr. Hawke's left.

Butch, a brash Texan who loves to eat big steaks and talk to anyone and everyone who will listen. I didn't dare get close to him at the tournaments when I watched him, too afraid I would catch his eye and I wouldn't be able to get away without hours of conversation. But I got close enough to witness that when he rubs his forefinger and thumb together under the table where he doesn't think anyone can see it, it means he's already counting his money.

He has an incredible hand.

I survey everyone else around the table, and Coen's gaze surreptitiously darts down to his left. His jaw tenses—the closest thing I've seen to a tell from him. But he isn't looking at his own cards. He caught what his neighbor is doing as easily as I did.

Coen tosses in his bet and waits for Butch to scan the table, as if he's assessing what he wants to do when both Coen and I know he's going to raise with what he's holding.

Butch raises.

The men between us fold.

I call.

The only ones left standing on the hand are Coen, Butch, and me.

Coen casually lays down his cards—four kings, thanks to the help of the community cards.

Smiling at him, I incline my head. "Nice hand."

It's the first thing I've said to him since we sat at the table— the first thing *any* of us have said, save for Butch, who seems not to notice that no one is responding to his comments and questions.

No one is here to make friends or chit-chat except him.

To play at this level, we've all developed our own strategies, and no one's is to get *friendly* with the competition.

What happened between Coen and me at the bar in Atlantic City crossed a line he never would have if he had known who I was and why I was there, and he's fuming over it.

He gives me a little half-grin, victory dancing across his icy blue gaze.

Butch grunts and tosses his cards in—full house, queens and jacks.

That might have been a winning hand in any other round.

But now, it's just Coen and me staring each other down across the felt.

I drag my red-polished nail across the top of my cards, lay them down, and watch the color drain from his face. "A nice hand...but it doesn't beat a royal flush."

Those little hearts all lined up in a row...crushing the hand he was so sure had won.

"Shit..." Coen mutters it loud enough for me to hear, even on this end of the table.

I've broken him.

The stoic man who played with ice in his veins suddenly becomes an iceberg bobbing around, lost in the ocean current, waiting to slam into something to knock it back onto course.

He would never react like that.

Never *has* when I watched him.

He's off balance.

The dealer takes the cards and shuffles as Coen holds my gaze across the table. Tension builds the longer we stare each other down until the hair on my arms stands on end. Energy crackles in the air, and I fight the urge to shiver against the coldness radiating off him.

Butch glances between the two of us, brows rising. "You two know each other?"

I swallow through my suddenly dry throat and shake my head, giving the Texan a soft smile to try to dispel any potential issues that the hatred emanating from Coen toward me might stir up. "No."

The last thing we want is anyone thinking we're together, somehow working the table in tandem. That's the kind of thing that gets you kicked out of tournaments and blacklisted.

Coen crosses his arms over his chest, jaw tense. He knows

what he needs to do, needs to say. He can't admit we've met before, or under what circumstances. "Nope..."

And in reality, we don't.

A short conversation at a hotel bar accusing someone of being a prostitute is hardly *knowing* one another.

But something tells me that when the final cards are dealt in this tournament, when it's finally over, that is going to change.

3

ALLEGRA

The sound of my heels clicking on the expensive marble tile as I make my way toward the elevator gets instantly absorbed by the cacophony surrounding me.

Slot machines.

People chatting and celebrating wildly.

People lamenting their losses.

Including me...

It was close. Came down to just Coen and me. Blue eyes locked with gray. Given the cracks I saw in his armor, I thought it would be easy to read him. Easy to read that final hand. But he's too damn good.

I reach the elevators and press the call button, scanning the casino around me for any signs of someone following me, but the coast is clear. Tapping my foot while I wait, I pull out my phone and shoot off a text.

I LOST.

The three little dots pop up almost immediately.

Before I can read the response, the elevator doors slide open, and I step in, press the button for my floor, and lean back slightly against the wall, letting out a relieved sigh as some of the tension I've been holding all day starts to melt away.

Finally.

These games always exhaust me. Having to be *on*. Having to play that role—the sweet, unassuming girl who has gotten in way over her head. Of course, after enough hands, they realize their mistake. But by then, it's far too late.

Typically, it means they've already lost.

But not tonight.

The blow of losing to Coen makes me want nothing more than to take a long, hot bath in that deep soaker tub waiting in my suite and climb into bed to collapse—

A hand darts out and stops the doors from closing, and my breath catches as Coen walks in, his jaw set hard, spine stiff. Animosity rolls off him in waves, swirling in his gaze, along with something I can very easily recognize—attraction.

Despite it all...

He scans his key card and slams his palm to the button that will take him to the top floor, where the penthouse suite overlooks the Mediterranean.

His icy eyes never leave mine, and I slide my phone into my purse, resting my hands on the bar across the back of the elevator cab.

The doors glide closed, and he stalks closer. Slowly. As if he's a predator and I'm the prey he's afraid will dart if he moves too fast. But even if I wanted to, there isn't anywhere to go.

He pauses a few steps away, slipping his keycard into his back pocket. "I was right."

I raise a brow. "About what?"

For some unknown reason, I actually want to know what he's thinking, what he believes himself to be right about.

Despite the iciness he's throwing out at me, the corners of his lips twitch with amusement. "I *was* your mark."

Hell.

He's got me there.

There isn't any way to deny it. There wasn't any other reason for me to have been there in Atlantic City, watching that game, watching *him*.

And I refuse to feel sorry for doing it. For preparing properly for the match. Grinning, I offer a slight shrug. "Maybe, but what sort of a player would I be if I didn't scope out the competition?"

His gaze rakes over me, from the top of my head down over the low-cut, bodice-hugging black dress that goes to mid-thigh, then across my exposed legs to my peep-toe Louboutins.

"You don't look like any poker player I've ever met." His eyes heat despite the frigid tone of his words. "And I am confident I never saw you before that night in Atlantic City. I would've remembered you..."

I pull my bottom lip under my teeth, and his eyes narrow on the move as I let it release. "I don't know whether I should take that as a compliment or not."

After all, he did think I was a professional at something *other* than cards.

He prowls even closer as the elevator continues to ascend, then rests his right palm flat against the back wall to my side, leaning into me. "Oh, it's *definitely* a compliment."

A little shudder rolls through me at his closeness and words, and I smirk at him, trying to ignore the way his body heat radiates off him and seeps into my skin. How the scent of crisp, clean ocean air seems to cling to him, mingling with the smoky scent of his favored scotch that lingers on his breath.

He was celebrating his win before he came looking for me.

Dipping his head closer, until it brushes my cheek, the same way I did to him before I walked away last week, he releases a little laugh. "I *was* your mark, but you see, you failed."

I swallow thickly. "How's that?"

His lips feather along the shell of my ear, and my legs tremble. "You tried to rattle me, distract me, and it didn't work."

He pulls back slightly to search my face, and all I can do is raise my brows.

"Didn't it? You sure *seem*"—I let *my* gaze rake over him now, from his thick, dark hair, vibrant eyes, sinful lips, and to his crisp white dress shirt under a perfectly tailored suitcoat, down the pants that fall from trim hips, and finally to his expensive Italian loafers—"distracted."

A low growl rumbles in his chest, and with him pressed so close to me, I can feel it in my rib cage.

Coen Hawke is damn near feral, barely restrained.

And it isn't merely anger building up in his blue gaze.

The heat there matches what I saw the other night at the bar when he suspected I was a hooker and was still willing to take me back to his room anyway.

My tongue darts out to wet my lips, and I finally release my grip on the bar behind me and press my hands against his chest to find his heart thundering there.

I turn my head toward his until my lips brush his cheek, but he pulls back.

A muscle in his clenched jaw throbs wildly. "I still *won*."

"Lose the battle"—I grin at him—"win the war."

One of his dark brows rises slowly. "I wouldn't have struck you as a fan of Pyrrhus..."

Hell.

Of all the people in the world, he is the *last* I would expect to recognize where the saying comes from—or to catch the implication that I am far from done with this.

"I do love a good challenge—whether it be reading ancient

military strategy or playing Texas Hold'em with a bunch of over-testosteroned men."

His whole body vibrates with tension.

The man seems to be hanging on by a thread.

Whatever has been boiling up inside of him, threatening to spill over, is about to, and I'd be lying if I said the thought of him unleashing all that on me wasn't exciting and terrifying all at the same time.

It seems I played with fire...

I hold his gaze, not giving in to the instinct to look away or even blink. It isn't just a stare down. It's a *showdown*. No different than what happened at the table.

The elevator cab finally glides to a stop on my floor, and a ding fills the heavy silence between us, the doors gliding open.

I nudge his chest. "This is my stop."

He glances over his shoulder to see the floor, then turns back to me and shakes his head. "No, it isn't."

Fuck.

Heat pools in my core, my belly fluttering at this man's intensity and confidence.

All those triggers I always say I won't let affect me. All those traits I search for so I can *avoid* the men who hold them. Yet, here I am, practically drooling for him and letting him pin me against an elevator wall.

What the hell am I doing?

That brilliant-blue gaze searches mine as the doors close us in once again and we move upward. "Come have a drink with me."

I raise a brow. "A drink?"

He nods, brushing his lips across my cheek, using one hand to cage me in but leaving the other at his side—almost as if he's afraid that if he did place it on the wall and fully confine me, I might fight him.

Which I probably would.

Nobody cages me in, certainly not Coen Hawke.

I beat him at that table—even if I didn't win the final hand —and I'll beat him at whatever game he's playing now. "One drink. That's it."

Another opportunity to get a leg up on my opponent.

Though, maybe that's a poor choice of words because even thinking them is enough to make my pussy throb and visions of *all* the ways my legs could bend around this man flash through my head.

He pulls back and grins, nodding slowly, his eyes drifting from mine down to my lips, my neck, my cleavage, and the shoes again, like he, too, is imagining the ways my legs and these stilettos could wrap around him.

We move up a few more floors, neither of us willing to move or speak.

The ding seems to break whatever trance we're in, and he pushes away from me and snags my hand with his. Rough calluses rub along my palm, the contrast sending little goose-bumps rising all over my skin.

A poker player with the hands of someone who does manual labor...

It struck me the first time we met, when he first touched me, and after playing against him today, I'm even more intrigued by the contradiction that is Coen Hawke.

His voice, low and controlled, laced with his confidence and strength, has taunted me the way his grin has since we met at the bar a week ago. It's the reason I shouldn't be allowing this, but I can't seem to muster up an objection to him pulling me out of the elevator and into his suite that takes up the entire top floor of the hotel.

Massive floor-to-ceiling windows overlook the water and reflect the Monaco city lights.

Bright.

Glittering.

Luminous.

Stunning.

I've seen this view from other buildings, other vantage points over the years, from various homes and hotels in this tiny country, but this is almost as breathtaking as the man whose hand is currently wrapped around my own.

He stalks straight to the bar near the windows and releases my hand to grab a bottle of scotch and quickly pour two fingers. "Are you a scotch drinker?"

I drag my gaze away from the windows long enough to raise a brow at him. "Not really. I prefer bourbon."

A slow smirk tugs at his lips. "You like the sweetness."

"No." I shake my head. "I love the spice and the burn."

Those now-warm again blue eyes darken at my comment, and he reaches for another decanter and pours from that. His fingers graze mine as he slips the glass from his hand to mine. "Oh, I promise you, a good scotch has as good of a burn as any bourbon, and there's something about the rich, smoky, peaty flavor that you'll become addicted to quite quickly."

I take a sip of the bourbon, and the spicy heat dances across my tongue and down my throat as I swallow. "I'll have to take your word on that."

He takes a sip of his own drink, then advances, sliding his free hand around my waist and tugging me up against him—his hard, firm body as solid as a rock, an impenetrable wall, just like the man himself is at the poker table.

Under *most* circumstances.

Today, he was rattled. At least, momentarily. He managed to pull out the win, but I still succeeded in at least putting the tiniest hairline fracture in that wall.

Shaking him was harder than I imagined it would be. Apparently, what happened at the bar wasn't enough to take him off his game.

Impressive and infuriating.

As is the way my body responds to his touch, his closeness, his scent.

He dips his head, his lips hovering barely above mine. "Let me give you a taste so you can see what it is you're missing."

COEN

THIS IS A TERRIBLE IDEA.

I knew it the moment she sat down across that table.

I knew it the second she smiled at me.

I knew it the minute she fucking *winked.*

I knew it when I followed her into the elevator after the game.

I knew it when I closed the distance between us.

I knew it when I allowed myself to cage her in against that wall.

I knew it when my lips brushed her ear, when that intoxicating, light jasmine scent invaded my lungs the same way it did in that bar.

I knew it when I led her in here.

I knew it when I wrapped my arm around her waist and tugged her up against me.

I know it now as my lips hover a mere hairsbreadth from hers, waiting for her response.

Please fucking God, say yes...

Gray eyes, the color of the storms that come in and hit New Orleans, churning up the warm waters and releasing heavy rain on the city, stare me down, unblinking, unwavering, from under thick, heavy, dark lashes.

Even now, she doesn't give an inch.

Almost like she's waiting to see how long my restraint will last.

Seconds tick by, feeling more like an eternity with her sumptuous curves pressed against me, the warmth of her skin permeating my palm, even through the material of her dress, her soft breaths mingling with my own.

Finally, she ghosts her lips over mine. I can't even call it a kiss. More of a tease—something I'm learning this woman is *very* good at. "I could be persuaded to have a little taste."

Fuck.

My cock fully hardens at the sultry dip in her voice and the promise that lies in it, and it pushes into her taut stomach as I slam my mouth to hers fully.

I glide my tongue along the seam of her lips until she finally opens for me, and the sweet, spicy burn of her bourbon meets the smokiness of the scotch I just drank.

She hums her approval, and the sound goes straight to my cock, making it twitch in the confines of my pants. Begging for her to make it again when I'm inside her and can feel what her cunt does when that fucking sound comes out.

I tighten my grip on her waist, digging my fingers into her, and she presses her free hand to my chest, then pulls back, her tongue sliding out over her lips. "You're right. That is good."

Good?

More like staggering...

I watch her casually lift her glass to her bright-red lips and take another sip, her grin visible through the crystal.

She's enjoying toying with me *far* too much.

Fuck, this woman is dangerous.

That night at the bar, I should have walked away.

Even lingering after the game for a drink at the central bar risked someone identifying me and sending word to one of the Hawkes and their many spies. But as soon as I saw her sitting there, that vibrant-green dress called to me like a fucking siren on the sea.

It didn't matter that I thought she was a professional, that bringing her up to my room after I had just won at the tables was the perfect way to end up in a really bad situation.

None of it mattered once I saw her.

Nor does the fact that she played me for a fool, that I let her get under my skin in a way no other player has at that table.

Right now, all I want is her under me, or over me, or in front of me.

However she wants it.

I'll take anything she'll give me.

She eyes me, watching expectantly for me to make another move as she sips at her drink. Her tongue glides along her lips, like she's savoring every last drop of the sweet liquor, when all I can think about is savoring *her*.

"Stay with me tonight."

Her brows rise slowly, as if my request is unexpected, but I don't know how it could be when I'm not exactly hiding the evidence of what I want from her. Nor has she been particularly shy about her intentions with me, either.

Though, it could all be part of the game she's playing.

Given what she's already managed, she's very talented at getting under someone's skin, but even knowing that, I still can't bring myself to regret asking.

Those perfect breasts rise and fall rapidly, barely contained in the confines of her dress. Another carefully planned distraction for all the men at that tournament table—including me. "You know this is a terrible idea."

I nod slowly, watching her otherwise stormy eyes reflect the beautiful lights from the crystal chandelier hanging in the suite. "I know you're a dangerous woman, Allegra. I knew it the moment I saw you in Atlantic City, and you confirmed it when you walked into that tournament today. But the scary thing is, I don't fucking care, at least not for tonight."

She smirks, running a finger down my chest and stopping at my belt. "What about tomorrow?"

My cock aches with her touch so close. My hands itch to have her writhing and wanting the way I am.

"I'm not playing you at the table tomorrow." I trail a fingertip down her bare arm, making her shiver. "I have other games in mind."

A pink blush spreads up her neck and across her cheeks, and she shifts, pressing her stomach against my cock in a way that has me biting back a groan. "Oh, I bet you do, Mr. Hawke."

I grin at the formality. "Coen, please."

Those dark brows of hers rise. "A very interesting name..."

"Is it?"

She nods. "Do you know what it means?"

I snort and take a sip from my drink, wishing she hadn't asked the question. "I do. It was an intentional choice on my parents' part." That familiar agony of knowing what a fucking disappointment I am hits me hard. "It means wise counselor."

"Are you a wise counselor?"

Her question makes me draw back slightly, letting her slip from my hold.

She can't possibly know what she's digging into, what her questions are slowly chipping away at, the pain she's exposing. If I were a more suspicious person, I would say it's almost like she's *looking* for another way in, another weakness to exploit, since her attempt to take me off my game wasn't good enough today. But there isn't any way Allegra could know the sordid Hawke history or how questioning me about it would make me feel like I'm free falling from one of those windows down into the ocean without a damn parachute.

"I don't think anyone in my family would say 'yes' right now, but it was what they wanted from me. What they expected." I snort at the absolute absurdity of how badly things have gone and take a long drink. Releasing a sigh, I shove my free hand through my hair. "At least they're batting 500."

Her soft brow furrows. "I'm sorry. I have no idea what that means."

Allegra's confusion shouldn't be so adorable, but it somehow is, and it's enough to break me from my foul mood and focus on what's in front of me.

I grin at her. "You don't watch much baseball, huh?"

She barks out a laugh and pulls out of my hold, spinning in her tight black dress and sky-high heels. "Do I look like I watch a lot of baseball?"

I examine her over the rim of my glass, taking in every exquisite detail. "No. But then again, I've always been taught not to judge a book by its cover."

Her head tilts, and she gapes at me. "Says the man who thought I was a hooker..."

Ouch.

That one stings a little because I never should have said it, and she's absolutely right to point out my folly.

"I apologized for that..."

She offers a look that makes my heart flip in my chest—some mix of playful coyness and alluring. "Uh-huh. So, what does 'batting 500' mean?"

"It means hitting fifty percent of the pitches thrown to you. That's considered a very good average in baseball, but I meant it in regard to their children."

Her gaze softens, her lips twisting slightly. "I don't... understand."

I snort and take a longer pull from my glass, wishing it were easier to forget all my failures.

This isn't something I should be telling a complete stranger, especially not someone who clearly has had an agenda from day one, but after weeks of running from them—from *it*—I can't seem to stop myself.

It's like some part of me *needs* to talk about it, to unload the baggage I've been carrying around with me, along with my guilt.

"My father's the family attorney, and my older brother, Isaac, is his protégé and has essentially taken over after my father had—"

I clear my throat, struggling to get the picture of him lying in that hospital bed on a ventilator after being shot out of my head.

It takes far longer to clear than I want it to.

That pain and panic clog my throat the same way it did that day the shots rang out at Hawke's Daily Grind.

"He had some medical problems and is kind of being forced to retire—as much as he ever will."

Allegra nods slowly, swirling her drink as she watches me, acutely aware of the shift in the mood. "And you didn't have any interest in that—becoming a lawyer?"

"I didn't have any interest in becoming anything."

Shit.

The answer slips out before I can stop it.

Before I can think better of what I'm saying or what it means.

But the truth should be easy to speak, and that certainly was.

I've never had that drive that burns through Isaac. I've never had the tenacity of Kennedy or the intelligence of Pope. I don't possess the killer instincts of Atlas and Bishop. I don't have the creativity of Jude. And I can't connect with people the way Angelina, Alessandra, and Astrid can.

"From the day I was born, I was the odd man out—the spare."

And nothing has changed.

She frowns slightly. "That's a little harsh, isn't it?"

I wave her off, not wanting to discuss the bitter Hawke family dynamics that have always surrounded me.

No...

I would much rather lose myself in her all night before I head off to the next stop and get back to *that* topic of conversation. "You never answered my question."

Her hips sway in the dress as she advances again. "Which one?"

"I asked you to spend the night."

She clutches her bourbon in her palms. The same hands that held her cards so close to her ample chest—which is exactly what she's doing right now. Just in a different game.

Fuck, she was good...

She doesn't have a tell.

Didn't give anything away while I took one look at her and felt like I was fucking crumbling. Keeping my shit together long enough to win that game took every ounce of self-control I possess. Which means I am *completely* tapped out at this point.

That explains this horrible decision and why I don't care about the consequences of it.

Her lips curve gently into a half-smile, and her eyes dance with the kind of mix of playfulness and intent that makes my blood run hot and my cock ache again. "I'll think about it."

I open my mouth to reply when the elevator dings and the doors start to slide open.

What the fuck?

This is a private suite, only accessible with my room key.

If it were someone from the hotel, they would've called before they came up—

The doors fully open, and I freeze.

Familiar, hard, dark eyes meet mine.

Shit.

They sent in the big guns—literally.

4

COEN

Luca stares me down with so much fire burning in his dark eyes that it's a fucking miracle the entire room doesn't burst into flames around me.

Well, fuck.

They didn't send Dad, or Uncle Savage, or even Isaac. The Hawkes sent Luca fucking Abello. People routinely crumble under the scrutiny of Dad in the courtroom. People fear handling negotiations with Savage. Isaac has proven himself the best mix of both of them. But Luca personifies terror... wrapped in a $10,000 Italian silk suit.

He steps from the elevator in another perfectly tailored one that can't hide the tension in his broad shoulders. Even with his hands relaxed at his sides, his stride casual, I know him well enough to understand it's all an act.

A well-practiced one he perfected over many decades.

One meant to lull unsuspecting targets into a false sense of security before he strikes.

And right now, I am squarely in his sights.

Fuck.

I knew it was only a matter of time until they found me, but I thought I'd have a plan figured out by the time they did. Some way to explain what I did that they could understand.

Right now, I have exactly jack shit...

Plus, Allegra stands only a few feet from me, barely concealed from his view, for only a few more steps into the suite.

Shit. Shit. Shit.

I clear my throat, actually afraid of the approaching man for the first time in my life, despite always knowing who and what he was. "Luca..."

His eyes rake over me and land on the glass in my hand—

"Is everything all right?"

Shiiiiit.

Allegra's sultry voice floats over me, and she steps up to me, putting herself directly in Luca's line of sight—and him in hers. She takes in the man in front of her with wide eyes. "Oh, I... didn't realize you were expecting company."

My grip on the glass tightens. "I *wasn't.*"

Her confused gaze cuts to mine, and I can see her discomfort with the tension permeating the air between Luca and me. It would be impossible to miss it, the way it practically vibrates and becomes its own living thing the longer he stands there.

"Umm...I should go."

I turn fully toward her, giving my back to the type of threat everything in me says I shouldn't. "Don't. He'll be leaving in a minute."

Luca closes the distance between us with three big steps and leans in, dropping his voice so she won't hear from where she stands only a few feet away. "I highly suggest you get your friend out of here before we have what is going to be a very uncomfortable conversation."

Fuck.

A shiver rolls down my spine at what is as close to a threat as I've ever had directed at me from Luca.

For all the knowledge we all grew up with about Luca's history, for all the things we witnessed as we got older, he has always been kind, caring, *loving* with all of us. He's been a member of the Hawke family as much as anyone else who sits at Nana's Sunday table—regardless of what lies in his past.

And he certainly never directed any of the violence he's so capable of at us.

I down the rest of my drink and turn to lock gazes with Allegra again. "We'll pick up where we left off after my friend leaves."

She eyes him suspiciously and shifts in her heels, then slides her half-drunk bourbon into my hand, leaning in to press a kiss to my cheek. "I'll see you around."

Hell.

That sounded a *lot* like a permanent goodbye rather than the "see you later" I had hoped for, but before I can try to persuade her to wait while Luca and I take this conversation elsewhere—or to return to her room where I could meet her later—she offers a tight smile to Luca, then saunters past toward the elevator.

She doesn't even look back; she merely hits the button and disappears into the still-waiting elevator cab.

The moment the doors slide shut, I whirl to face him. "What the *hell* are you doing here?"

Okay, that was dumb.

No one talks to Luca Abello like that and lives to tell about it.

He merely raises dark brows at me, unaffected by my vibrating anger. "Shouldn't I be asking *you* that question?"

Offering an annoyed huff, I storm away from him, back into the suite, and directly to the bar. I down Allegra's remaining bourbon, pour myself another scotch and one for him, then nudge it toward the edge in offering, before I go and lean against the windows overlooking Monaco. "How'd you find me?"

He smirks as he wanders over and lifts the glass, taking a sip of it. "When the ceremony ended and nobody could find you..." —he glares at me in a way that ensures I feel every single bit of the reproach in it—"there was a panic, as you can imagine."

I definitely never intended that.

Though, I should have known it would be the result. Despite my text to everyone when I left that I knew what I was doing and not to look for me. Despite insisting I was going to fix things and begging them to just let me do it...

I still *left*.

I simply disappeared during Cass and Kennedy's reception.

One minute, I was there, standing at the edge of the dance floor, watching Atlas propose to Wren, and the next, I was slipping past security and everyone else while they were distracted and making my escape during the only chance I knew I would ever get.

My texts wouldn't have done anything to quell their fears or anger at my disappearance.

And the fact that I turned off my phone so no one could track me *or* reach me only made things worse in their eyes.

It's been *weeks*, and the Hawkes aren't known for their patience.

Luca swirls his drink and stares down at it almost absently. "We knew you were still in the States for a while because we have a tracker on your passport and would have been alerted if you'd used it."

"I fucking knew it."

He glances up at my muttered comment and offers me a half-smirk. "Good call not using your cell phone or the passport."

I release a heavy sigh and run my hand through my hair. "Until I came here..."

My fucking passport did me in.

Luca nods slowly. "Until you came here..."

He wanders over to a leather chair in the center of the main living room area of the suite and settles into it, casually dropping one ankle over his knee.

"So, what?" I narrow my eyes on him, trying to figure out why we're even having this conversation at all and why he didn't just appear with the muscle he needed to force me into the car that's undoubtedly waiting outside to take us to the airport and one of the Hawke jets waiting to bring me home. "They sent you to drag me back?"

His hard gaze softens for a split second. "They sent me to make sure you were *all right*, Coen. Everybody's fucking worried. What the hell were you thinking? It's been a month and not a fucking word from you. For all we knew, Satriano had already snatched you and taken his pound of flesh or worse."

"I wish..." I mutter before I take another sip and focus out the window.

"Enough of the fucking games, Coen." The snap in his tone forces me to look at him again. "Tell me what you've been up to the last month because all we've been able to piece together after getting in touch with all of our contacts is that you've played in a few tournaments—California, Texas, Atlantic City..." He scowls. "Pretty fucking ballsy heading to my old stomping grounds, by the way."

I smirk. "You may have connections, but so do I."

"My connections received a fucking earful about not alerting me of your presence, believe me."

God only knows what Luca did to them...

The man may have stepped back from his role as the head of the Abello crime family, but that darkness still lingers beneath his polished surface.

Like a coiled cobra, waiting to strike.

Clearing my throat, glancing out at the dark water and vibrant lights. When he doesn't say anything for a while, an awkward, tense silence settling over us, I glance back to find Luca's lips pressed into a firm line.

"I think you need to start with what the fuck happened after the wedding and what all this"—he spreads out his hands —"is supposed to be. Are you hiding from us or from *him*?"

Satriano...

It would make sense to hide from the man I owe so much to, who now has the power and ability to twist my arm and keep me constantly on the edge of panic, wondering what he will ask for. But deep down, I know he isn't the one I've been running from.

Still, I'm not about to admit that to Luca.

I shake my head. "Neither, really."

His gaze goes cold. "That's a fucking lie, and you know it."

A heavy sigh falls from my mouth, and I drop my temple to the cool glass, hating how fucking well he knows me. It takes a moment for me to process what to say, how to explain why I left.

"You're right..." I pause to try to regain enough composure to lose the tremble in my voice. "I didn't want to face any of you. I couldn't after what I did."

"And you thought running off and exposing yourself, where Satriano could hunt you down like a fucking wounded animal, was a good idea?"

I lift my head, allowing my eyes to find his. "No..."

It would be stupid to fight telling him.

Luca can make me talk if he wants to, a hundred different ways. Some I probably can't even fathom. And he'll know I'm holding something back. He'll be able to smell the lie from a mile away.

"Satriano isn't going to be hunting me down because Satriano knows exactly where I am. Just like with the family, I sent him a message. I offered him a deal..."

Luca's face falls and tenses. He drops his other foot to the floor and shifts forward in his seat. "What did you do?"

"What I had to in order to protect Wren and Atlas. What I had to do to protect *all* of you from the fallout of what I did."

He slams his free palm against the armrest. "You fucking idiot. What did you *do*?"

I stare him down, far longer than I thought I had the courage to. Eventually, everyone withers under the stare of Luca Abello, which is precisely why they sent him instead of Dad, Savage, Isaac, Saint, or Gabe—or anyone else, for that matter.

He looks every bit the mob boss right now.

An angry one.

"I told him I'd pay him back for my losses and that I'd do whatever he wanted to work off any debt he believed was owed to him because of what Atlas did in the ring."

Luca winces, then squeezes his eyes closed. He sits back in the chair, releasing a long, hard sigh. "Do you have any idea what you've done?"

I push off the glass and stalk over to his chair, towering over him and feeling big for the first time in my life when he normally has several inches and at least forty pounds of muscle on me. "I made a deal that protects everyone else. It was my mistake. You know what he would have done to Atlas and Wren, and God, their fucking baby... I couldn't risk any of that, nor could I allow him to have that debt to hold over the rest of the family, either."

Luca stares up at me. He drums his fingers on the side of the glass. "Did he respond to your offer?"

"Yes."

And I still remember how badly my hand shook when the reply text came through.

As soon as I read it, I turned off my phone for good, knowing that man would find me if he needed to, even without it.

"What did he say?"

Sweat beads across my brow, the words flashing through my head. "He said, 'You're mine.'"

He clenches his jaws so tightly that a muscle there starts to tic. "You're coming home with me."

"No, I'm not. I've already won back over half of what I owe him. Another tournament or two, and I'll be out of debt."

He shoves up from his chair, getting up in my face. "*Your* debt. But you gave the man a blank fucking check to cash against you once that's done. What do you think he's going to ask of you? What do you think he's going to demand that you do to 'pay off' any perceived debt that Atlas may owe him? Do you know much he told Atlas that fight was worth?"

A shiver rolls through me.

Luca snarls. "*Billions.*"

The emphasis on the *B* is sharp.

As much as the knife I'm sure he has concealed somewhere in his slick suit coat.

As deadly as the gun I know he has there, too.

"I don't care what he asks me to do." I stand my ground. Refusing to break. Refusing to bend to his will. "I'll do it to ensure everyone's safety."

"Let *us* keep you safe."

The emotional tone in his plea tugs at that part of me that *knows* how much he cares, how much they all do, even when I don't deserve it.

"You can't. And you know it."

He throws out a hand sharply, his frustration growing.

"Then let us deal with whatever the fallout is as a family. That's what we do, Coen. No matter what. Hawkes always stick together."

I want to believe that's true.

Want to be able to go home with him.

But even if I could bring myself to get on that plane with him, I couldn't face anyone there.

Not until I've made amends.

Not until I've found some sort of way to keep that monster off their backs.

A monster who lurks around New Orleans, where they're all exposed. "Have *you* heard from Satriano?"

Luca looks away, then downs his drink and sets his empty glass on the side table. He hisses through clenched teeth at the burn. "He's been shockingly quiet since the fight and wedding, which, as you no doubt understand, has left everyone very on edge."

Because no one knew the reason he was quiet—I'd already made my deal.

My mind goes to the people in his immediate crosshairs. "Atlas and Wren?"

Luca runs a hand through his dark hair. "They went to Fiji. They don't get back until the end of next week. Honestly, I may tell them to stay longer. They're probably safer there than they are in New Orleans right now."

"He won't do anything. Not when he has me."

"That's my fucking point." His voice cracks like a whip, filled with violence and a hint of something I never thought I'd hear from this man—fear. "He has you by the balls, Coen. He's going to twist and twist and twist. You have to understand that."

"I do." I knew it the moment I made that offer to him, and I'm ready to face my fate. "It's what I deserve."

ALLEGRA

Minutes tick by slowly.

Each one, my unease and curiosity grow.

I do my best to appear casual, standing just inside the very room we finished the tournament in less than an hour ago, while keeping my eye on the elevator I came down in when Coen's seemingly unexpected "guest" arrived.

The tension between the men. The anger and heat in their gazes. The unspoken words that flowed between them while I stood there. It all screamed that whatever was about to happen between them wasn't anything I wanted to be anywhere near.

And I can't help worrying about leaving Coen with him.

It certainly didn't seem *friendly*.

Not hostile exactly.

But they definitely weren't about to embrace and sing "Kumbaya," either.

I tap my foot, unable to stand completely still as I wait for any sign that one of them survived what went down in Coen's suite.

"Ms. Knight, did you need something?"

I turn back toward Anton and offer him a bright smile, quickly mustering up an excuse for why I'm lingering like a complete creeper stalking someone—which I kind of am at the moment. "I was looking for you, actually..."

Time to turn on the charm.

Shifting slightly in my heels, I position myself where I can keep an eye on the elevator and Anton without him noticing my split attention. I clasp his hands in mine and squeeze gently.

"I wanted to thank you for hosting such a lovely event and for taking such good care of us."

His cheeks pinken at the compliment. "Oh, well, you're

quite welcome, ma'am. I'm glad you enjoyed it, even if you didn't win."

I chuckle lightly and catch the elevator doors gliding open out of the corner of my eye. Leaning in, I kiss each of his cheeks. "Until next time."

Coen's visitor strolls from the elevator, his muscular frame tense beneath his expensive suit.

No bruises.

No split knuckles.

No blood.

No signs of any physical struggle linger on him, but the energy radiating off the man definitely says a battle was waged up in that suite.

Who won?

That question lingers in my head as I fall in behind him, keeping my distance and mingling with the crowd enough that he hopefully won't notice me.

Something tells me that if he does, he isn't the type to be too happy about it.

I increase my pace to get closer but leave at least one person between us in case he turns and spots me. Each strike of my heels against the marble floors makes me wince, but with the buzz of activity around us, he doesn't seem to notice the sharp sound.

Good.

Because he got a good enough look at me upstairs to recognize me, and it's not like I can hide if he happens to turn around.

One hand moves to his suit coat's inner pocket, and I brace myself for what might come out of it. The way he carries himself, it could just as easily be a gun as a phone.

He pulls out the latter and dials someone, bringing the phone to his ear. "He's not coming home."

The words are clipped.

Angry.

And they simultaneously manage to hold so much pain and worry in them that my chest tightens painfully.

He keeps walking, his perfectly tailored suit falling elegantly off his broad, tense shoulders as he makes his way toward the front of the casino. Intelligent and far-too-observant eyes take in everything around him, scanning the casino and the people who mingle around the tables and machines.

A round of cheers erupts at a table to my right, drowning out whatever he says next to the person on the other end of the phone.

Shit.

I try to shift closer, but I'm blocked by a couple hanging on each other and kissing the same way Coen did me upstairs— with the kind of promise that meant I was more than just *considering* his offer to stay the night.

The way his lips moved over mine.

His body aligned so perfectly against me.

That smoky flavor of his scotch invading my mouth, along with one that was *all* Coen Hawke.

My body heats at the memory, a dull ache starting in my core that my strides and movement through the casino don't seem to ease. If anything, the farther I move toward the main entrance and away from the elevator that will take me back to Coen's room, the more it feels like I'm heading in the wrong direction.

The opulent lobby and main doors appear ahead, and I ease my way to the side, keeping myself hidden as I watch Coen's visitor step outside and immediately climb into a waiting limo.

"Never would have thought you had a thing for older men."

I jerk at the sound of Coen's voice so close and whirl to find him standing directly behind me, shoulder leaning against the wall casually, as if he didn't bust me spying on the man who left his suite.

"Shit"—I press my trembling hand over my thundering heart—"you scared me."

He eyes me suspiciously, his gaze moving from me to the place where the limo sat before it pulled away from the curb. "What exactly *were* you doing?"

Spying.

"I'm sorry. I was just a little worried. Things seemed intense with that man when I left you in the room. When I saw him come out, I was curious..."

One dark brow rises slowly. "About what?"

What the hell rattled you so much when I barely could...

"Who he is? What all that was about? He seems very... intimidating."

He snorts and pushes off the wall. "That's precisely why they sent him."

"Who sent him?"

He presses his lips together in a firm line, crossing his arms over his chest as if he needs protection from whoever it is. "My family."

His family sent him?

Even though the limo is long gone, my gaze still trails back to where it sat before it returns to Coen's. "Who is he?"

Coen runs a hand through his thick, dark hair with a sigh. "For all intents and purposes, my uncle. Not by blood, but in every way that matters."

"I see..."

So, I followed his uncle...

I nod slowly, bite my lip, and glance around, looking for any way out of this—an escape route.

Talk about embarrassing.

I was totally busted by Coen.

Twice.

First in Atlantic City and now here...

And my plans to make a clean getaway after the tournament were foiled when he cornered me in that elevator before I could sneak back to the safety of my room and avoid the uncomfortable confrontation I knew was coming.

Though, what happened in that tiny, enclosed space wasn't at *all* how I expected it to go.

He wasn't at *all* what I expected him to *be.*

Rage...I could have handled.

Fury...I could have withstood.

Ire...I could have easily survived and walked away from unscathed.

But whatever *that* was...it wasn't *any* of those things.

There was anger there, lurking beneath his polished surface, vibrating under his tanned skin, but his interest and obvious attraction seemed to override that base need for revenge, or whatever it was he was seeking when he followed me in the first place.

And it overrode *my* common sense.

He didn't force you to go to his suite...

That was my choice.

I could have just as easily said "*no*" to his *drink* offer and let him walk out alone when those doors opened on the top floor. I could have let them close on him and whatever *this* tension is. I could have gone on my way, followed through with the plan I came to Monaco with.

Yet, I chose not to.

And that knowledge somehow makes this moment so much worse, so much more uncomfortable. Because he knows it, too.

I stare into those ocean-water blues, again, remembering how it felt to have his warmth wrapped around me, his hand pressed into my back possessively, his lips on mine, and the promise in his words when he asked me to stay the night.

That damn ache returns to my core.

The need to ease it—

No.

I take a step back, putting some much-needed space between me and the man who threatens to unravel all my well-laid plans with that smirk and the passion burning in his gaze when he looks at me.

With a shaking hand, I pull out my phone and text Buckley, letting him know to bring the car around.

Leaving. Now.

He knows to be ready to go at any moment, so it shouldn't take him long to get here. And he's been with me long enough to recognize the urgency in my text.

I force myself to look up at Coen, who watches me with a furrowed brow, clearly confused by my retreat when, less than an hour ago, I was seriously considering spending the night in his bed. "I...uh...need to get going."

His brows wing up, eyes widening. "What?"

Ignore that surprise and disappointment.

If I concentrate on it, let it affect me, I will end up in a very bad position—like *under* the man in front of me.

He moves toward me as if he intends to pull me into his arms again the same way he did upstairs, but I hold up a hand, stopping his progress immediately. "You're going to leave?"

I motion over my shoulder toward the curb. "I have somewhere to be."

That playful, seductive smirk returns to his lips, and he eases closer. "What happened to considering my offer?"

Despite every reason it shouldn't, a smile pulls at my lips. "I did consider it. Believe me..."

And if we hadn't been interrupted...

Our night would be ending very differently—or not ending at all, given the way he's looking at me now.

"What changed your mind?" He grins. "Am I a shitty kisser?"

I chuckle at that, unable to stop the reaction. Nor am I able to prevent myself from taking the half-step required to close the distance between us. I rest my raised hand over his chest, pushing up on my stilettoed toes to align my mouth over his. "Definitely not that. Quite the opposite. If I stayed tonight, I don't know that I'd be able to walk away."

That confession stings.

Admitting *any* weakness does, especially to a man like Coen Hawke.

He is trained to look for them, to manipulate them and use them to his full advantage—both at the poker table and in life. And he will not hesitate to use mine against me the same way I did him today.

Which means I have to leave with the upper hand any way I can.

I kiss him deeply, sliding my tongue along his, and his arms wrap around my waist, tugging me fully against him. The warm, hard heat of his body presses into me, and a low, rumbled groan vibrates from his chest through my palm still pinned between us there.

Slow and sweet.

This isn't the sexually charged kiss we shared upstairs.

This one is meant to keep him thinking. Keep him wondering. Keep him *wanting* more than just me in his bed.

I pull away breathless, my head foggy and swimming, my body throbbing and pulsing and ready for it to go so much further, but I can't.

Not now, not ever.

He watches me with half-lidded eyes, thick lashes framing that vibrant blue. They beg for me to stay. Plead for it.

Reluctantly, I press another quick peck to his cheek before I change my mind. "I have to go."

I slip out of his hold, and he follows me through the doors and out to the front circular drive as Buckley pulls up to the curb.

Coen's heavy footsteps follow me. "So...this is it?"

His question almost makes my strides falter, but I force myself to keep moving forward. To not look back.

Buckley climbs from the limo and makes his way around to open the door for me. I slide in, and Coen reaches us.

He braces one hand on the roof, the other on the edge of the doorframe, and leans in. "You're just going to walk away?"

A flash of pain dances across his eyes, and for a split second, I reconsider staying. Reconsider what it would mean if I did.

You can't.

I nod. "I have to go."

It doesn't matter that my things are still up in my room— the hotel will ship them to me with one call. And there isn't anything there that I can't live without for a day or two.

But if I spent a day or two with *this* man...it will only mean disaster in the end.

His hand tightens on the edge of the door, and my body remembers what it feels like to have that hand on me, phantom fingers digging into my back, urging me to stay. "When will I see you again?"

I offer a shrug as my only answer.

It's the only one I can give.

He slips back from the limo, disappointment written across his face. Buckley closes the door, and Coen retreats slowly until we finally pull away.

The devastation written across his face hits me far harder than it should.

This was always a game, a way to see if I could get under his skin, and I've proven that I can. I shouldn't care that he seems hurt by my rejection. I shouldn't care that my body is objecting quite strongly to my decision to walk away from him rather than to climb into his bed and onto him.

My hand shakes as I fire off a text.

I WILL SEE YOU SOON.

I slip my phone into my purse before there's any response because I don't want to see it right now.

It will only make things worse.

5

COEN
THREE DAYS LATER

L aughter and music fill Hawke's Daily Grind.

Angelina and Alessandra bustle around, serving coffee and pastries to everyone packed into the space for the reopening. The rest of the Hawkes sit scattered around various tables, playing board games and chatting, voices sometimes getting swallowed by the music coming from the small stage area and the overall vibrancy of the event.

For the first time in a *long* time, my heart feels light. Seeing everyone so happy. So laid back. So carefree. It allows me to— at least momentarily—forget all the threats still looming over us.

Those problems will still exist tomorrow, but today is all about celebrating with everyone I love.

Dad stands out in front of the café near the bistro tables, talking with Isaac and Kennedy, who appear to be in some sort of heated discussion about something. Knowing those two, it could be *any*thing. They love any reason to bicker—the CFO and the attorney going head-to-head to see who wins, the litigator or the ball-buster who takes down anyone who gets in the way of Hawke Enterprises faster than Gabe could with his sniper rifle.

Truth be told, Kennedy wins more than Issac, but even *I* don't have the balls to point that out to him.

A car pulls up to the curb, dragging them away from their conversation.

Shit.

I know the man who gets out—we *all* do.

He's the last person who should be here, and given how angry all three of them look talking to him, they're telling him as much.

My back snaps straight, my entire body instantly going rigid as I watch it unfold in slow motion. Another car appears on the road. Before I can issue a warning, shots ring out, glass shatters, and blood splatters as they crumple to the sidewalk.

"NOOOOOO!"

I jerk awake in my hotel bed, woken by my own scream that still echoes around the room, off all the highly polished surfaces. Goosebumps cover my skin, slick with sweat. My heart thunders against my ribcage, my lungs seizing, refusing to allow me to draw in air.

"Fuck..."

Gasping, I shift fully upright and lean back against the headboard, needing the solid feel of it behind me to help ground me in the *now* as opposed to the past.

I scrub my hands over my face, hoping to wipe away the vestiges of the dream. Even though it comes every night, it still takes me far too long to convince my body and mind that it isn't real.

At least, not *now.*

But it *was* real.

Not that long ago, it was my reality—*our* reality.

Satriano was responsible for almost killing Dad and wounding Isaac and Kennedy. He may have claimed Roselli was the target that day, but we all know the truth—it was a "two birds with one stone" scenario that benefited him either way.

My body won't stop trembling, my hands shaking as I press them to my bare chest, attempting to force my breathing into a more normal pattern.

They're fine.

Everyone is at home.

Safe.

I try to tell myself that each night when the nightmare of a memory comes for me, but it's getting harder and harder to believe it. Especially when I'm not there to *see* it with my own eyes. When I've had my damn phone shut off for almost a month so they wouldn't find me. When I know full well that no one is ever really *safe* as long as a man like Satriano has us in his sights.

Luca's visit the other day proved it's impossible to hide from someone who has the motive and means to locate you. When the Hawkes want to find someone, they will—the same goes for the man I'm now tied to for the foreseeable future.

I reach for my phone on the nightstand with a shaky hand and power it on, suddenly needing to confirm there aren't any messages saying anything is wrong. It's been three days since Luca found me, and anything could have happened in that time.

A flood of messages that were never received or read over the last several weeks all come in at the same time—including one from Isaac sent only a few hours ago.

ISAAC

TURN ON YOUR DAMN PHONE!

He had to know how useless it was to send it, but he did anyway. Just as he had the hundreds of others. I scroll back to

the night of Cass and Kennedy's wedding to when he realized I
had left the reception.

WHERE THE HELL ARE YOU? YOU BETTER
NOT BE DOING SOMETHING STUPID!

Am I?

Leaving seemed like the best option at the time.

The *only* way to protect the Hawkes and endeavor to undo
the damage I did when I placed that bet. But what Luca said
when he tracked me down was right—Satriano *does* have me by
the balls now.

There's no telling what he'll ask me to do. I keep waiting for
him to show up or to contact me some other way—a call to one
of my hotel rooms, a note slipped to me during a game, an
"associate" showing up to give me a message—to make his first
demand beyond me paying back the ten million *plus interest*
that I owe him.

It hasn't come.

It will.

Reckonings always do.

And I have a big one in my future.

Isaac's name flashes across the screen with an incoming
call, almost like he somehow *knew* I had turned my phone
back on. Which he probably *did* since the moment I hit that
"on" button, the family would have been alerted that it was
active.

"Shit..."

By now, everyone has heard what happened with Luca.
That I refused to come back. That I made this deal with Satriano. There isn't any point in attempting to hide where I am
anymore. Not when they can so clearly track my passport and
know I'm in Macau.

It would only take them a few moments to figure out what
hotel, given what's happening here in a few days.

One of the biggest poker tournaments in the world...with the largest purse.

I wouldn't miss it.

I *can't.*

My finger hovers over the "send-to-voicemail" button, but all I can picture is the pained look on Luca's face when I told him I wasn't returning with him. Not to mention the fight I saw behind his eyes and his body language, him trying to tamp down his desire to physically force me to New Orleans.

It absolutely destroyed him to have to leave me in Monaco, to have to *accept* that I wouldn't leave with him.

If he was that upset, I can only imagine how Isaac, Mom, and Dad feel. Doing this to them, leaving without a word, disappearing, was agonizing, but it was the right decision for everyone.

I just hope they can understand that one day.

Maybe tonight, I can do something to help move that needle.

Sucking in a long, deep breath, I swipe the "accept" button. "Hello..."

"Are you fucking out of your mind?"

I wince and climb from the bed in nothing but my boxer briefs, stumbling slightly, still half-asleep and in the lingering grips of the dream. The wall of windows overlooking the vibrant, sparkling city of Macau draws me to it, and I rub the back of my neck with my free hand as I move over to it, loosening the tightness that has formed there when my body went into full-on panic mode during that nightmare.

This late, the entire world is abuzz—stunning, busy, beautiful. Cars whizzing past on the streets below, people bustling along the sidewalks, even people in the hotel pool, despite it being two a.m. here.

All the things I love so much about Macau...the vibrancy and life that explode here are the same reasons New Orleans will always live in my soul. It isn't merely because I've spent my entire life there; there's just something about the city, the people, the *life* that exists only in those streets.

I could have gone home between Monaco and coming here, at least spent a few days in New Orleans and seen everyone, tried to explain, but they never would have let me leave again. They would have found a way to keep me there, keep me locked away for my "protection," when what I'm doing is for *theirs.*

Isaac's frustration and anger are warranted, though, so I can't let his response get to me.

"Hello to you, too, big brother..."

"Luca told us what you said."

I rub at my temples and the headache slowly building between them. "I had no doubt that he would."

His voice dips low, into that "lawyer" tone he takes when he's trying to instill how important something he's saying is. "You can't play chicken with a man like Satriano, Coen."

Gritting my teeth, I force out the reply I don't want to admit. "I know that."

"*Do* you?" He releases a mirthless laugh. "I don't think you do. You know, we would have given you the money to pay him back in an instant."

I tighten my grip on my phone, swallowing my inclination to snap at him for the suggestion. "First of all, he already made it very clear to Atlas and me that no one else could pay off my debt. And even if he had been willing to accept money from the Hawkes, *I* don't want to take anyone's money. I dug this hole; I need to be the one to get out of it."

He releases an annoyed sigh that fills the line with all his irritation. "Fine. Even if I *could* justify you running around the world playing in these tournaments to try to pay back your debt, what you've agreed to after is going to get you killed."

I cringe—both from the sincerity of his concern and the

fact that he's potentially right. Satriano could ask me to do *anything*. And I would be bound to do it, even if it means risking my life.

Still, I can't dwell on that, nor can I agree to it. It would only give Isaac and the others more ammunition to shoot at me regarding why I shouldn't have left.

"You don't know that."

Something slams on his end of the line, probably his fist on his desk. "I do. Have you forgotten who we're dealing with here?"

Of course I haven't.

All I *think* about is Satriano. About what he's done. It even haunts me when I close my eyes and try to forget the world in sleep.

I would much rather embrace the dreams about Allegra that have been interspersed with the less pleasant ones. Dreams of having her in my arms again. Dreams of the way her mouth tasted. Dreams of her saying yes to my invitation and what could have resulted from it.

Those are few and far between, though.

And they're not enough to shake this constant dark cloud that hangs over me.

Sighing, I wander to the bar and pour myself a double bourbon—though I have no desire to consider *why* I chose that instead of the Lagavulin sitting right next to it.

I take a sip as I lean against the couch, examining the opulent suite I've been comped for the tourney. Over the years, I've played so many times here—won and lost so much—that they always offer me the best. Yet tonight, it feels cold and empty, and I get no enjoyment from it like I normally would.

Because you want a specific someone to be here with you.

But even if she were, would it even be safe for her?

Can anyone be safe?

"I had to do *something*, Isaac." My fingers tighten on my

crystal tumbler. "You know he would have come for Atlas, and that would have put him, Wren, and the baby in jeopardy. Atlas did nothing wrong. I did by ever betting against him and putting him in the position for Satriano to ask him to fix the fight. If I hadn't placed that bet against him, Satriano might never have pushed those odds and lost so much. It was *all* because of me. *I* fucked up—"

"You're right, you did. It was fucking stupid, Coen. No one's going to argue with you about that. Did you hurt Atlas by betting against him? Abso-fucking-lutely. Did you bring Satriano down on us—*again?* Sure as shit right, you did." Anger rises in his tone. "But that *doesn't* mean we wanted you to *run,* especially straight to that man. It doesn't mean we don't want you *here.*"

He mutters something under his breath, his exasperation clearly growing.

I can picture him pacing in his office this time of day, having this call with me when he should be focusing on all the other important work he has to do in order to protect Hawke Enterprises on all fronts legally.

Isaac takes a long inhalation that crackles over the line. "Satriano doesn't just want a pound of flesh. He wants *billions* of pounds. What do you think he's going to have you do to work that off—to *ever* satisfy him?"

Anything and everything.

It's an astronomical figure.

The amount he lost when Atlas won that fight. When he did the *right* thing and took back his own life by knocking that fucker out in the ring rather than taking the fall that would have benefited Satriano and the odds his bookmakers had set.

Atlas did everything right.

And I did *everything* wrong.

"I don't know what Satriano will ask of me, Isaac, and I don't care. I'll do it if it means he stays away from Atlas and

Wren, if he leaves the rest of you alone. Luca said he hasn't been in contact with anyone since I left."

Isaac sighs. "No, he hasn't..."

I feel the *but* he doesn't say.

Because he doesn't have to.

We all know there's always an eerie, peaceful calm before a hurricane comes blowing in off the Gulf. And that's exactly what Satriano is—a dark, sinister, swirling maelstrom who brings nothing but pain and leaves catastrophic destruction in his wake.

I can't allow anyone else to be collateral damage.

"That's good. It means I've at least kept him at bay for a while."

"You really think this is going to work? That you're going to be able to appease a mob boss like Satriano, a man who shot at us and who blew up The goddamn Grind?"

I flinch at his words, his screams from that day echoing in my head, along with the flashes of crimson splattered across the bistro tables, chairs, the Grand Opening sign, and the people I love the most. Isaac, Kennedy, and Dad's blood pouring out onto the sidewalk in front of the café. All of us rushing to help to try to save them. Sitting beside their beds in the hospital. Wondering if Dad was ever going to walk out of there alive or if it would be in a coffin.

"Believe me, Isaac, I haven't forgotten. That's why I'm here. I have to—"

Shit.

I don't even know what I want to say.

"I have to fix this somehow, and this is the only way I know to do it."

A silence lingers through the line.

"Come home, Coen. We'll work this out together, I promise. There are ways we can protect Atlas and Wren—"

I wander over to a big, plush leather chair and slowly lower myself into it, dropping my face into my palm and scrubbing it over it. "What about the rest of you? He could come after *any* of us. You know he wanted a Hawke in his pocket, and now he has it. We all know I'm the most expendable one."

"What?" Isaac's voice drops. "Coen, is that really what you think?"

Shit.

I hadn't meant to say it out loud, but now that the words are hanging there between us, it's not like I can snatch them back any more than I can the confession I made to Allegra or my final words on the matter to Luca before he left my suite.

"It's true. I'm the only one who doesn't have a purpose, doesn't play a role in the Hawke world. None of our businesses rely on me. No one does."

This time, Isaac's silence somehow vibrates with anger even from across the world. "Are you out of your motherfucking mind? You truly have lost it if you believe that." He releases a frustrated growl. "*I* need you. Mom and Dad need you. *Everyone* needs you."

"Bullshit!" I shove up out of the chair and stalk back to the bar to refill my drink and immediately down it. "I've been gone for a month, and everything has been chugging along, as it always has. Am I right?"

He snorts. "You couldn't be more wrong. It's a fucking mess. Everyone's running around like chickens with their heads cut off, trying to find you, worrying..."

I flinch. "Mom and Dad?"

Isaac releases a heavy, long sigh that sounds so much like our father that I cringe, squeezing my eyes closed. "They're terrified they're never going to see you again. You can't do this. You can't run and hide, and you certainly can't get further into bed with a man like Satriano. Come home, please."

"I have a tournament in a few days."

"In Macau?"

Shit.

Guess I was right about not needing to hide anymore.

"Yes."

"Fine." He snaps. "Play in your tournament if it'll make you feel better. Pay off the goddamn debt and then get the *fuck* back to New Orleans. Come *home,* and we can deal with the rest."

"I'll think about it..."

"Goddammit, Coen." He sighs. "I knew I should have gone with Luca..."

"You have enough to worry about there without trying to track me around the world, Isaac."

"That's pretty much what everyone else said, but I can't believe he left without bringing you back."

Really, neither can I.

Luca could have forced it.

He could have had men far bigger and stronger than me physically remove me from that hotel room, force me into his car, and drag me onto the private jet.

But he didn't.

Because he *knew* I had to do this.

"I'm an adult, Isaac. I'm not your little kid brother anymore. I can make my own adult decisions."

"Yes, and how has that been working out for you lately?"

I wince and down the rest of my drink. "Love you, too, brother."

Ending the call, I toss my phone onto the small table next to the chair and lean back, letting my head drop to the headrest and my eyes close.

I really fucked up everything.

And Isaac is right.

Satriano is going to come calling.

He's going to figure out what he can use me for, and I'm going to have to pay up. I won't like it. Not one bit.

But I'll do it.

I have to.

ALLEGRA
FOUR DAYS LATER

THERE'S no mistaking the heat of the gaze raking over me.

It sizzles across my skin.

Burns through my core.

Makes me wish I could press my thighs together without anyone noticing me shift in my seat.

He hasn't even fully entered the poker room yet, barely made it to the doorjamb, but I *know* it's him.

No one else has ever raised this kind of response in me simply by *looking* at me. I haven't even met his gaze. I intentionally keep mine focused on the man to my right, whom I've been chatting with casually since I took my seat at the table several minutes ago.

Giorgio was a pleasant-enough opponent in Monaco, and today, he is almost overly friendly, like he realizes he missed some major opportunity then and doesn't want to let it get away now that he has me within his reach.

Perhaps seeing that I am real competition last week has altered his opinion of me.

When I first sat at that table, I didn't have the respect of anyone, but by the time I left—after almost crushing Coen in the final showdown—I had hoped to have gained it.

His flirtation suggests he has less professional reasons for his interest, but the gleam in his eye certainly wasn't there in Monaco. Knowing I can hang with the boys has gotten me a new admirer, one who appreciates a woman who can play a strong game.

But I have zero interest in Giorgio Nikolaou—now or ever.

Only a single man has occupied my thoughts the past week, and it certainly wasn't him.

The one currently being forced to take the sole available seat, immediately to my left, is another story entirely.

Coen...

The heat of his glare sears every fiber of my being as he approaches with sure, unhurried steps—as if he doesn't have a care in the world and doesn't give a shit that I'm here and am directly next to him.

This seating arrangement isn't by chance, and he knows it.

Anyone who has done any research into Coen as a player knows where he likes to sit, which made it very easy for me to make the request to be seated here. Where I have access to him. Where I can use everything in my arsenal to my advantage.

It gives me the high ground in this battle of wills.

He slides into his chair, his immaculate black suit pulling slightly at his shoulders as he leans over slightly toward me, but he doesn't meet my gaze or even look me in the eye. Instead, he grins at the man to my right. "Giorgio, always a pleasure."

Giorgio inclines his head in response, and Coen settles back in his seat, unbuttoning his coat so it hangs loosely over the crisp dark shirt he wears under it. Cuff links with a family crest featuring an *H* with wings glint at his wrists as he casually turns to his left and starts up a conversation with the player to his left—something he typically never does.

So, that's the game we're playing today in addition to poker...

He's angry with me.

Mad that I left him standing on that curb in Monaco.

Annoyed I'm here and didn't tell him I would be when he was so frantic to know when he might see me again.

The man is smart enough to see this for what it is—another tactic to get under his skin.

I knew I'd be at this table in Macau when he asked me that question. I knew he would be sitting at the felt with me. I also understood what letting him know that would have meant—giving him *hope*.

Walking away and leaving him wanting without any idea when he might lay eyes on me again was the stronger play—and I was taught well to always look for the upper hand.

He's off-balance again.

Which means I've already won.

He doesn't acknowledge me at all during the minutes leading up to play, merely watches our game host and dealer as they talk, as if they're discussing the most interesting topics in the world.

The cold shoulder doesn't bother me.

Not when I know what fire blazes inside him right now, what he is struggling to contain. I've seen and felt flickers of it, and even though he's giving off the icy vibes that match the current state of his eyes, he can't undo what's already been done.

He revealed himself to me, parts of himself that *any* opponent would relish having access to because they make the biggest weaknesses, the easiest to exploit during play. And Coen Hawke makes me want to play with him as much as I do the cards being shuffled by the dealer directly in front of me.

Even as the cards are dealt around the table, Coen doesn't glance at me, doesn't acknowledge me. He scans the other players as they check their cards, assessing each of them for a moment or two before moving to the next.

Like me, he's done his homework. He knows how each and every one of them plays, understands any tells they might have, recognizes any weaknesses, but he forgets that I know his now.

And I am not afraid to use it against him.

When the betting gets to me, I finally check my cards and toss in my chips, calling. Coen barely glances at his before calling, too, leaving only five of us in this round.

Many players prefer to be conservative in early hands,

wanting to get a better sense of the table and the cards, waiting for an opportunity to strike against an unsuspecting opponent.

Coen usually plays this way. Conservative. *Smart.* His game is intelligent, built on years of honing his skills. He's won far more than he's lost since he started playing competitively, but he's going to have to get used to things changing in that regard.

Because I've never been one to hang back and watch, waiting for opportunities.

I *make* my own.

The dealer pulls the flop cards, giving us the first real feel for what our hands might be.

Coen doesn't move.

He doesn't breathe.

He is fully in the moment, completely unaffected by the fact that I'm sitting beside him—or at least, he wants me to believe he is.

I may not have spent a great deal of time with Coen, but it was enough to understand how this man lives—with a kind of burning passion that he focuses on the things he loves.

Some assume that's this game.

And Coen certainly does love poker.

But that crack I managed to break in his armor in Monaco taught me something very important—that passion can be redirected, and when it is, he loses some of that cool. The way he followed me out of that casino and to the limo, the way he almost *begged* me to stay, was enough to prove to me that he is far more fragile than even I knew.

Far more vulnerable.

I place my bet, then wait for him to make his move. As he reaches forward to move his chips, I shift slightly closer to him until my leg brushes his.

Coen freezes, his entire body going taut beside me, and I have to fight the grin threatening to pull at my lips.

There we go.

It doesn't take much.

A heated glance.

A tilt of the lips.

A simple touch.

Men unravel so easily, and Coen is no exception to that rule.

After the heated kisses we shared in Monaco and the hopes he held for what would have happened if I had stayed, it will be particularly easy with him.

Barely a challenge.

The next few players to his left place their bets, and the dealer draws the turn card.

Another opportunity to scan the players, to watch for any reactions to what the next-to-last card gave them. To make a decision on how much to wager before the river appears.

Every single person at this table is a true professional with years of experience. If they have a tell, they're good at concealing it. And everyone is doing a very good job today.

At this point, all I have to go on is the cards in my hand and those on the felt.

By the time the next round of bets moves to me, the heat of Coen's thigh permeates my own bare one, even though his dress pants, and he's done nothing to pull away, to put any sort of space between us.

Bad move.

He's playing with fire, and he has to know he's going to get burned.

But maybe that's what he wants.

Maybe he thrives on the pain.

If that's the case, I am more than willing to make him hurt.

He tosses in his chips, calling, as do two more players to his left.

The dealer pulls the river, and I catch Mason Farewell to my far right, flinching slightly as the card appears. Whatever he has, he doesn't like it. Probably a flush or straight that only needed one more card that didn't appear.

Coen remains stoic.

Giving nothing away.

For all I know, he could have a royal flush or a pair of twos.

Time to see if he has a new tell...

I slip my free hand, already resting on my thigh under the table, over to his, which immediately tenses under my palm. Coen's body twitches at the contact, but then he sits absolutely stock-still.

He doesn't look at me, even out of the corner of those shimmering blue eyes.

He doesn't turn.

He doesn't raise the alarm bells with the tournament host or the dealer.

And he won't.

Coen Hawke will *never* publicly announce that anyone has rattled him or that it's possible to get under this seemingly thick skin. Admitting that kind of weakness would be tantamount to opening the floodgates—anyone with any sense would start looking to crack him the same way.

He's the type to suffer in silence.

To try to work through the discomfort and pretend it doesn't affect him when I can feel his flesh trembling and tense under my hand.

Now that all the community cards are on the table, players start dropping like flies, including Giorgio next to me, who tosses his cards face-up onto the table.

I place my bet, raising $5,000, and Coen stares at the cards for a moment, and I give his thigh a squeeze, letting my fingertips dip to the left, brushing against his already semi-hard cock.

A challenge.

One I know he can't refuse.

He leans forward and pushes his chips in, calling.

Everyone else to his left folds, leaving only the two of us.

A showdown that feels awfully familiar. Only unlike in Monaco, this game is only beginning, and we have a long way to go before the final hand will be dealt.

Hours and hours of *this.*

Me toying with him.

Him pretending it isn't happening and doesn't affect him.

It will be a sheer battle of self-control and wits—something that is going to make this game *far* more interesting.

I flip over my cards—a pair of queens to go with the one in the community cards, along with the pair of threes on the felt.

Coen grins, flipping over his pair of kings to go with the king pulled as the river.

He's beaten me.

And despite doing my best to distract him, I never noticed any tell that would have alerted me to the fact that the river gave him a very strong hand.

Impressive.

It just means I'll have to try harder.

I squeeze his thigh, sliding my hand up and in farther, my knuckles grazing his cock. And I have to hand it to the man— he doesn't twitch this time, doesn't move, remains as stoic as ever.

Even as I can feel the tension in his body starting to coil...he manages to maintain.

It's a game of chicken.

Who will give first, Coen Hawke or me?

I know it won't be me.

So, this is going to be fun.

It could be hours before everyone at this table is eliminated, before a winner finally comes out on top. But given the way I can feel his cock rising against his pants, only a few millimeters from my touch, I know I've already won in every way that matters.

6

ALLEGRA

I*'m fucked.*

The moment his eyes met mine across the restaurant, it was certain.

Oh, hell...

I made a huge mistake not leaving immediately after the tournament. As soon as I confirmed my winnings were deposited into my account, I could have made a break for the limo, climbed in, ridden away, and left Coen Hawke in the rearview where he needs to stay.

That would have been the *wise* decision.

That would have been the *smart* thing to do.

That would have been what was *expected* of me.

But my feet didn't take me in that direction.

I couldn't bring myself to just walk away—again.

Some masochistic part of me wanted—*no, needed*—to know what he would do and how he would react after what amounted to six hours of a cock tease with what I was doing with my hand at his thigh.

The icy glint in his eyes as he approaches me now, weaving through the restaurant toward the back booth where I sit, slices through me, giving me all sorts of second thoughts about my decision to stay.

People always talk about self-sabotage, and the way my body reacts the closer he advances, I'm starting to understand what that phrase really means.

I swallow thickly as he finally stops, eyeing the drink in front of me on the otherwise empty table.

He raises a dark brow over those wintry eyes that were so warm when I saw him in his hotel room a week ago but switched so easily to their current state the moment he saw me at the tournament table today. "Mind if I join you?"

I CAN'T EXACTLY DENY him.

Not when I chose to stay. Not when I chose to stay specifically for *this*—to see how what I did affected him. To witness the reaction from a man who prides himself on *never* reacting to anything.

Lifting my drink, I offer him a coy smile, like my fingers weren't just brushing against his hard cock on the table for hours on end. "Of course."

Bad idea.

Every part of me knows it, especially those parts that are tingly and throbbing already.

Coen slides into the booth that can easily seat four people, pushing all the way over next to me, until his thigh brushes mine. The heat radiating from him into my bare leg makes me bite back a groan.

He inclines his head toward the menu sitting on the edge of the table. "Did you order yet?"

I nod, as the waiter returns, having witnessed Coen's arrival.

Coen motions to the menu and my glass. "I'll have whatever she's having—the food and the drink."

Something tells me he isn't going to want a pomegranate martini and roasted lamb...

I glance over at him. "How do you know you're going to like what I ordered?"

He eyes me, those sensual lips of his curling slightly, but that iciness doesn't leave his gaze. "I trust you."

Liar.

The truth is, neither of us should trust the other.

This isn't the world where you make friends.

This is the world where you make enemies.

And while my feelings for the man sitting beside me are certainly becoming more and more complicated, I would never make the mistake of thinking he's a *friend*.

That would be very dangerous.

As would giving in to the attraction I have to the man I should keep at arm's length.

I take a sip of my drink, gulping it down, trying to quell the heat rising in my body, and not merely because of his closeness.

Oh no...

That *look*.

He may be putting on a show right now with the pleasantries, but he is burning mad about what just went down at the table.

The waiter moves away, and Coen takes the opportunity to slide his arm around the back of the booth now that we're alone, allowing it to brush against my exposed shoulders. That scent of ocean air and waves cocoons me as he leans in and dips his head so his lips feather over my ear. "That was quite a show you put on back there."

I grin at him. "Thank you."

He shakes his head, brushing his thumb across his bottom

lip as he examines me with a heated look. "It wasn't meant as a compliment."

I knew that, too.

But this is our game.

Isn't it?

I expected him to come in raging at me. I anticipated fury and hatred. But that isn't what I'm getting. The only thing he's throwing at me is a confusing jumble of mixed signals.

"What do you want, Coen?"

He shifts even closer, until his entire left side presses into mine, his arm wrapping around my shoulders tightly, practically dragging me onto his lap. "Oh, I think you know *exactly* what I want, Allegra..."

I turn my head to fully face him, and though the icy chips still remain in his gaze, something else lies there, that same fire and need that rolled through me when he kissed me in his room. "I thought I made my position on that clear."

He chuckles low, the sound making his body vibrate against mine. His gaze travels over the other diners. "About as clear as mud. You said it would be a bad idea."

I take a sip of my drink, wishing it were stronger to help me manage the truly unhealthy way I'm reacting to his closeness. For hours, I toyed with this man, and I managed to remain *mostly* unaffected by it. But it's taken less than a minute for him to have me trembling and needy with only a look and a few words.

It's a very bad sign for my resolve.

"It would be."

"Why?" He places his right hand on his thigh, and I am keenly aware that's where mine sat for hours, toying with him. "Because this is the game that you play, finding the player likely to win, and then rattling him so you can swoop in and take the prize."

I allow the corner of my mouth to curl slightly. "That's part of it."

"And what's the other?"

The fact that I haven't felt this kind of attraction for anyone in a very long time...

I don't say the words.

I can't.

But the heat crawling up my neck and over my cheeks betrays me.

A slow, satisfied grin crosses Coen's face, and he slides his hand across my knee. Those rough calluses dragging over my smooth skin send a shiver through me, making me inadvertently press into him tighter. "You want to hear what I think?"

Yes.

No.

Fuck.

The fog filling my head seems to grow thicker as he brushes his thumb up and down my skin softly.

"Do I have a choice?"

God...

I hate how breathy and needy that question came out, but I can't even seem to find a way to control my own breathing with that simple, intimate touch of his frying my brain cells.

His warm breath fans my cheek. "I think this has all been one big game to you, only you never intended it to backfire."

"I don't think it backfired at all. I won."

The evidence is sitting in my bank account as we speak.

He nips at my earlobe, making my pussy clench as I squirm. "I wasn't talking about the goddamn card game, Allegra, and you know it. You played with fire, and now you're burning alive."

His hand glides up my thigh, and *dammit*, I shift in my seat. Only instead of closing my legs to the potential intimate touch, escaping the intended intrusion, instead of reaching down and tugging his hand away, I shift them open slightly.

That dull ache in my clit screams for him to keep going even as my head chants what a horrible, horrible mistake this will be.

Coen's voice dips low, taking on a sultry tone that almost makes me come on the spot. "I want you to tell me something, Allegra."

"Wh-what?"

His fingers dig into my thigh, pinning it in place. "How many men have you done this to?"

The first time we met flickers through my head, when he accused me of being a professional. This accusation isn't that far from it, nor is it far from the truth.

I could attempt to lie, but I don't believe Coen Hawke would be satisfied with that. And he deserves the truth, considering what I put him through today.

"More than I should have, and fewer than you think."

Coen pulls his bottom lip between his teeth and nods slowly, watching my face as his hand slides even farther now, playing with the hem of my dress, only inches from where my body craves his touch. He feathers his fingertips there, tickling me and making me squirm. "How many of those men did you take to bed, Allegra?"

I tighten my grip on my martini glass, then bring it up to take another long swallow of my drink, suddenly needing the chilly liquid and the alcoholic courage.

But I don't look away from him.

I can't.

If I do, he'll take advantage of the momentary weakness he will see it as.

"Would it surprise you if I said none?"

His eyes widen. "It would. Because you're very good at this, getting under my skin, distracting me in a way no one else ever has." A little thrill rolls through me at his confession. "But the thing is, Allegra—"

Coen's hand slips farther up now, only an inch from the apex of my thighs.

Half an inch.

Even higher.

The busy casino restaurant around us.

The people laughing and eating.

The waitstaff hustling from table to table.

So many people who could look over and see exactly what he's doing.

But somehow, that only heightens the anticipation, builds the tension.

God, he's going to keep going.

I should stop him.

Stop this.

I should slide out of the opposite side of this booth and walk away, like I did when he caught up with me in Atlantic City and things got *way* too intense.

I should, I should, I should.

Any person in my position would.

Their self-preservation instinct would kick in and send them running. But I'm frozen in place, completely entranced by the man beside me who has a wicked gleam in his eye that terrifies me as much as it thrills me.

I find myself creeping closer to him, leaning into his body, into his touch, opening even farther, wanting the very thing I've been dreaming about since I walked away from him last week. Walked away from what I knew this would be—brutal and toxic but also so fucking good.

He feathers his lips over mine—not a kiss, a tease.

And then his hand finally cups me between my legs.

I try to bite back the groan at the sensation, but it slips out against his mouth, and he issues a low, dark chuckle. That single sound confirms how much trouble I am really in.

"I want to know...what's the endgame here, Allegra? What's your goal? Because I know very much what mine is."

I manage to let out a breathy sigh. "What's that?"

He moves his mouth over to my ear. "I want to see if your cunt tastes as glorious as I think it does. And I want to fuck you until you can't walk out of here. If I had my way, I'd do it all right here on this table."

An embarrassing whimper slips from my mouth, and he adjusts his grip on the most intimate part of me. Cupping me harder. Almost possessively. As if what he holds in that hand now *belongs* to him.

And I have suddenly lost the ability to tell him it doesn't.

"And ultimately, Allegra, I want to bring you to your knees the way you have me."

***

COEN

INSTEAD OF BEING scared or trepidatious, Allegra shudders, her grip on the bench beneath us tightening until her knuckles whiten.

Her thighs close slightly on my hand, but not in an effort to stop me. If anything, she seems desperate to get me to touch her—to do exactly what I just threatened.

She would *let* me eat her out in a Michelin Star restaurant.

She would *let* me bend her over this table and fuck her in front of all these people.

And I would be tempted to do that, if the woman weren't still being difficult.

I press the meaty part of my palm against her clit, rolling it through the thin strip of fabric that covers it, feeling exactly how fucking wet she already is. Her little display at the table today got her all worked up, too. And something about that draws a grin across my face.

"You didn't answer my question, Allegra. What is your endgame?"

Absolutely nothing else is going to happen until that question is answered to my satisfaction.

Because I can't figure this woman out.

Since the moment we met at that bar in Atlantic City, the chemistry between us has been off the charts. And even after realizing what she did in Monaco—knowing she set me up from the get-go—I still couldn't stop myself from wanting her, especially when she very obviously seemed to return my desire. Yet she ran. And she continues to circle around me like a damn vulture, looking for any opportunity to fuck with me—mentally and physically.

The fact that she went *that* far at the table today proves there is no line she won't cross.

But what she doesn't know is that there isn't one I won't cross, either.

As far as I'm concerned, any lines that did exist were obliterated the moment she set her sights on me and decided I was her target. It's open season. Free rein to play dirty.

And one thing the Hawkes know is how to come out on top with someone who believes they have the upper hand.

I swirl my palm again, and she sucks in a sharp breath and swallows thickly, her throat bobbing. Her half-lidded gaze locks with mine. "You mean, besides winning all the tournaments?"

She knows damn well I don't mean the fucking card games.

Pressing against her clit harder, I rock it in a way that makes her gasp. "Yes, beyond that."

"I...well..." Another shift of my hand. "Fuck..." She squeezes her eyes closed. "Wh-what if I said I don't know?"

I still my hand and search her face, and her thick, dark

lashes flutter to reveal her fathomless gray eyes that seem to morph from the color of a cold winter day to the silver when she's turned on. The shimmer now brighter than the stars...

For several seconds, I look for the lie, for proof that she's playing me again or hedging when she doesn't want to admit her intent.

But all I see there is truth.

Maybe for the first time since I met her.

"I believe you."

She seems to relax a little against me, her body releasing the tiniest bit of the tension she's been holding since I first walked into the restaurant.

"And it's okay not to always know what you want, Allegra; at least, that's what my family keeps telling me."

I draw my middle finger up along her damp seam.

Her eyes squeeze closed, those impossibly long lashes spread out across her now-pink cheeks, and she shudders, shifting against me, her left hand tightening on her drink on the table, the right digging into the leather bench seat between our legs. "Coen..."

My name comes out half-whimper, half-plea.

To do what?

Because the way she looks at me, it's as if she's torn between running from me right now or straddling me. I'd prefer the latter, but if she truly wants the former, I'm not the type of man who would try to stop her from leaving.

"Do you want me to stop?"

She gulps and shakes her head, her eyes fluttering open. "No, but I should—God, this is a bad idea..."

There they are again.

Those words.

Bad idea.

I use my finger to pull that wet strip of fabric to the side, then drag the tip along the soaked lips. She holds her breath, her body stilling completely at the contact, as if primed to shatter if I move any more.

My cock strains behind my zipper, aching to be in place of that damn finger now that I finally this woman in my arms and part of me sunk deep in her heat after a week of torture. "Just because something's a bad idea doesn't mean you shouldn't do it."

At least, that's what I keep telling myself.

That's what I told myself when I tried to win back the money I had lost before Atlas ever set foot in that ring and only ended up losing more. That's what I told myself when I placed the bet against Atlas, knowing that if he ever found out, there would be horrific fallout. That's what I told myself when I fled the wedding reception and contacted Satriano to tell him I knew I was at his mercy and that I was willing to do anything to protect the Hawkes, confident he'd take advantage of that.

And she's right.

This isn't merely a bad idea; it's a terrible one.

One that could have long-reaching ramifications when it comes to my play.

Allegra is the only woman, the only person at all, who's ever been able to take me off my game, and this is the most dangerous time for it to be happening.

I can't afford to lose another tournament.

I can't afford any delay in paying back Satriano.

Today was supposed to put me over the top, to get me to the point that I could finally send it to him and be done with at least that part of my debt. I might have learned what he had in store for me instead of constantly wondering what sinister deeds he might demand I do on his behalf.

He won't be happy about any delays, and I'm going to have to face the consequences if he decides to act in the interim.

Whatever they might be.

But with my hand on Allegra's cunt, my finger brushing

along her wet heat, the way her body vibrates and clings to me, I can't seem to say no.

And neither can she.

Red flags fly, completely filling my vision, but they don't stop me from slowly pushing the tip of my finger inside her. She groans, pressing her forehead to mine, her lips falling open.

I chuckle low as I slide into her more and more until I'm fully settled in her slick heat.

Fuck does she feel good...

My cock twitches, begging to be released from its confines, to be allowed to plunge deep and hard into this heaven.

I kiss her temple, her cheek, her lips, as I slowly drag my finger out and thrust it back in, grinding my palm against her clit as I do. "Don't forget where we are, Allegra."

She jerks back, her eyes flying open as she scans the restaurant, apparently just remembering that we're on full display at a very high-end restaurant in a very busy casino in the heart of Macau.

I pull my arm from around her shoulders to grip her chin, watching that silvery gray dance with her arousal. "But you're a poker player...considering what I know you could hide at that table, I'm confident you can keep anyone around us from knowing what I'm doing between your legs."

Her eyes harden to steel at my challenge.

And that's what it is—a *challenge*.

She seems to thrive on them, so knowing I'm watching for her to break, for her to let loose some sound that draws someone's attention, will only make her more determined to keep it contained.

The faster I glide in and out of her, the harder I grind against her slippery, engorged clit, the more intense her stare becomes, those eyes rippling like molten silver.

Her jaw hardens under my grip as she clenches it, struggling to keep from reacting as I increase the pace, but when I slip a second finger inside her, her lips part on a silent gasp. The pink that already covers her cleavage and cheeks darkens, and her thighs clench around me.

I continue to work her up, building her tighter, until her body is so coiled and taut she's dangerously on the edge of cracking. Right there on the precipice. Capable of seeing the end.

And fuck is she beautiful like this.

Wanting.

Needing.

Desperate.

Exactly as I dreamed it would be since the moment I kissed her.

The waiter reappears with my drink and sets it on the table, startling her out of my hold on her face slightly. "Is there anything else I can get for you right away while you wait for your food?"

I shake my head and offer him a smile. "I think we're good."

Allegra attempts some sort of response that comes out more like a moan, but either he doesn't notice or is well-trained enough to ignore it when he knows the type of tip we'll be leaving him for this meal. I keep thrusting into her, even as he examines us with a raised brow, then slips away from the table.

With her this close, my cock threatens to unleash the same way she's about to.

I shift my hand to get my thumb in position on her clit, and she bucks at the change in pressure. My lips to her temple, feeling her entire body vibrating, I curl my fingers deep inside her, into that perfect spot.

Allegra can't fight her gasp, and I chuckle low as I reach for my drink, then take a long, slow sip of the pink martini.

Mmm. Pomegranate.

But I'd much rather be drinking her down.

I'm tempted to drop beneath the table and get my face between her legs, but I have other plans.

Ones I don't intend to deviate from.

Her hips start to roll against my hand, but she somehow keeps the rest of her body still, so that anyone looking won't be able to see what's happening thanks to the long tablecloth.

I return my arm around her shoulders, tugging her against me and nipping at her ear. "Are you going to come for me, Allegra?"

There isn't any way she could last longer.

God knows I can't.

She nods as I swirl my thumb rapidly around her clit. Her pussy starts to clench and tremble.

So fucking close.

I can *taste* it.

I can *smell* her arousal coating my hand.

I *feel* her need for release in her tense body and clenched thighs.

I kiss her gently, letting my lips linger over hers, then pull my arm free again to tilt her chin up until her eyes, half-hooded and soaked in lust, meet mine.

"You've been fucking with me since the first moment we met."

She doesn't try to deny it.

Just holds my gaze as I continue to work her to the brink.

"And I want you to know something, Allegra. Something that everyone eventually learns."

"Wh-what's that?"

A grin spreads across my face as I hold her stare, knowing full well what I'm about to do. "Nobody fucks with the Hawkes."

Her eyes flare as I yank my hand out from between her legs, raise it up to my mouth, and slide the glistening fingers into it. I groan as the flavor of her arousal dances across my tongue.

Rich.

Sweet.

Fucking addictive.

Like I knew it would be.

I adjust my cock to try to conceal the raging erection before I slide out of the booth and walk away from Allegra without looking back.

7

COEN

The familiar sights, sounds, and smells of the Hawkeye Club envelop me the second I walk through the front door. Somehow, after being gone for over a month, it simultaneously feels like I never left and like I've been gone forever.

Thumping bass vibrates through my feet and up my body as the door swings closed behind me, sealing out the sticky New Orleans air and me in with the scent of alcohol and the sweet perfume the dancers wear.

Chantell wraps herself around the pole center stage, draping backward and exposing her breasts to the patrons gathered closely around the front. She flips up and catches my eye, winking in greeting before she continues the routine I know by heart now after seeing it performed so many times.

It's a good crowd tonight—heavy with young tourists and a few older locals.

I scan the bar to check who's working.

Tommy's eyes widen slightly at me.

Guess he wasn't expecting me to come home...

Given how long I've been MIA and that I never told anyone I was coming, it makes sense he's surprised.

But someone knew.

The same way they found me in Monaco and knew I was in Macau.

He points toward the elevator, telling me what I already know.

Everyone is upstairs.

Since the second they were alerted that I boarded that plane in Macau to head back here, they've been waiting for this moment—the showdown I've been avoiding for the past month.

There is no way to dodge it any longer.

I bought myself a minor reprieve when Luca showed up and demanded I return, when I somehow convinced him that I had to stay and continue what I was doing, but it couldn't go on forever.

We all knew I'd have to return.

It just took me a while to accept it.

And as restless as I've always been, unable to commit to one job or one place, somehow coming home, stepping off that plane and smelling the New Orleans air, driving to the club past the same buildings and spots that have been here my entire life, the anxiety I had eased somewhat.

Until I walked in here.

Now that dread has settled back heavily on my shoulders, knowing what's waiting for me.

I don't take the elevator, despite that being much easier. It would also be faster, and I'm not in any rush to get this going. Instead, I slam my hand onto the metal bar across the stairwell door and start climbing.

Tread after tread.

Up and up.

That bass shaking each one under my feet.

It gives me a few extra moments to prepare myself for what I'm about to face, which I desperately need because there's no question it's going to be unpleasant.

The cars lined up outside in our private parking area confirm it. Not only are Uncle Savage, Dad, and Gabe waiting, but Saint is also here.

And God knows who else may have ridden with any of them.

I'm walking into an ambush, but at least I know it and had a very long flight to prepare myself mentally for the showdown. Or at least, to attempt it.

My thoughts kept drifting away from what I should have been focusing on and to the woman I left in that restaurant. And she should be the furthest thing from my thoughts, especially right now.

I make it to the second floor, step into the hallway, and the rumble of familiar voices floats down from Savage's office.

Each step I take draws me closer to facing the consequences of my fuckup in the worst way.

As if having to tell Atlas what I did that night wasn't bad enough...

As if telling them wasn't one of the worst moments of my life...

I went and made it worse.

Rubbing the back of my neck, I approach the open door, feeling more like I am walking the plank for my crime than about to see the people closest to me.

The second I step through the doorframe, all conversation halts, and seven sets of eyes turn to me.

Savage assesses me from where he sits behind his desk, looking every bit the boss and patriarch that he is, while Gabe occupies his usual perch on the edge of the piece of furniture that dominates the room. Dad reclines in the corner of one of the two leather couches with his cane—now necessary due to the damage Satriano did when he shot up the Grind—propped against the armrest. Isaac sits across from him on the matching couch, a hard glare directed squarely at me. Saint leans casually on the far wall near the window, massive arms crossed over his chest with Bishop beside him, offering me an almost apologetic look. And finally, I let my gaze meet Luca's, where he sits in one of the chairs facing the couches, his eyes, dark and hard, locked on me and filled with reproach.

Almost a full house...

Fucking great.

No one says anything, as if they expect me to delve right into this conversation somehow, like I didn't burn down everything and then run away from the results.

What can I say at this point?

Gabe pushes off the desk, heads over to the bar, pours me a scotch, and slips it into my hand with a knowing look, his green eyes flashing with relief, anger, and a bit of sympathy. "You're going to need this."

Hell.

That warning sits heavily in my gut.

I scrub my hand over my face before I take a sip, then force my feet to move and take me to lower myself on the couch next to Dad. The leather creaks slightly under my weight, and I shift, suddenly uncomfortable in the seat I've taken thousands of times over the years.

This place has always been the core of Hawke Enterprises —this office. Where it all started with Uncle Savage and Uncle Gabe. It's the heart of our business, and it has always felt like a home to all of us.

But it doesn't feel particularly welcoming at the moment.

Dad's blue eyes cut to me, and they hold so many warring emotions in them that the drink I just took instantly sours in my stomach. "Glad to see you're alive."

I flinch at the pain in his voice.

The accusation.

The *hurt* that I ran and didn't come to him.

What can I even say that would help, that might help him understand?

Absolutely fucking nothing.

I take another sip, swallowing thickly. "It's good to be alive..."

Savage raises a dark brow, settling deeper into his chair, drumming his fingers on the armrests. "Is it? Because from what I hear, you've been playing Russian roulette."

I snort and shake my head at the implication. "Nope, just poker."

"Fucking hell, Coen." Dad practically snarls at me, turning toward me in his seat. "What were you thinking, disappearing like that? Going to Satriano?"

Wincing, I let my gaze move to the man who first asked me that question.

Luca watches me stoically. He told them every word I said after he left me in Monaco...but hearing it from him is different than hearing it from *me*.

I need to *explain*.

Get them to *understand*.

"I thought I was protecting all of you." I suck in a sharp breath, struggling to keep the emotion out of my voice so they don't think I'm hanging on by a thread when I'm getting closer and closer to that. "I thought I was protecting Atlas and Wren—"

Bishop pushes off the wall and walks around to the edge of the couch, getting closer to me—close enough that I can see her muscles twitching in her arms as she struggles not to grab me and do something she would probably not regret, even though she should. "You know damn well we can protect everyone *here* far better than if you're gallivanting around the fucking world."

She isn't just pissed.

She's *hurt*.

They all are.

And somehow, that's so much worse.

I've always been a massive disappointment. The only one who has never seemed to have any direction in life. Always restless. Always seeking something. And it's never been what they've offered.

What I did was the ultimate slap in the face to the people who've loved me the most through it all.

My ultimate failure.

I swallow my guilt and try to look each and every one of them in the eye—though it's so much harder with Dad, Isaac, and Uncle Savage for some reason. Then I let my gaze drift to Bishop and her father.

Saint hasn't moved. He just stands there, looking like an immovable mountain.

And that's what he's always been.

Our rock.

Our protector and friend.

Which is why what I'm going to say in response to Bishop's statement hurts so much.

"I truly don't mean this to be insensitive or to suggest everyone in this room isn't trying their hardest." This will ruffle the Hawke feathers, and I desperately need some air in my lungs to get it out. I inhale deeply, filling my lungs with the air that smells like the club. "But we keep saying that. You *all* do. Yet...look what has happened. First, Jack got taken from a building that was supposed to be secure. That was supposed to be safe—"

Isaac opens his mouth to object, but I hold up a hand to stop him.

"And I understand there were extenuating circumstances. That she did what she had to in order to protect Vivi, but he shouldn't have gotten that far. He never should have gotten his hands on your daughter, and we all know it."

God, it feels like ages ago...

So much has happened since, only compounding the pain.

Dad presses his lips together in a firm line, as does Uncle Savage, like they're both biting back retorts they know they can't make because it's all true. Luca and Saint keep their hard gazes on me, letting me continue, even though I can see the tension building in both of them. Gabe leans against the desk, hands curled around the edge hard enough to whiten his knuckles.

And I'm only going to make things worse.

"And the Grind went up in flames, thanks to Satriano." My eyes cut to Dad. "Then we almost lost you, Kennedy, and Isaac because of that fucker." I throw up my free hand. "Then Dan Roselli was able to get to the girls and Benjamin...to hurt Atlas and Astrid." I wince, remembering how they looked when they were finally rescued. "We've done everything we can to keep everyone safe, and it hasn't been enough. So, forgive me if I didn't trust in the innate ability of the Hawkes to keep ourselves safe. I think I had reason to be worried..."

That silences everyone.

No one breathes.

No one moves a muscle.

But I can feel Saint's eyes boring into the back of my head.

I turn to look at him—the one in charge of security for the entire Hawke empire—and he glances around at all the men in the room.

The big man finally shifts his massive weight, his jaw hard. "You're right." He runs a hand over his shaved head. "And we've had this conversation before, trust me. There is never any way to one hundred percent guarantee everyone's safety when there are forces outside our control. But going to Satriano isn't the answer."

"Isn't it?" My hand tightens on my glass, and I slug a drink from it, relishing the burn down my throat and stomach. "Pope is stuck stitching up his henchmen to keep him at bay for the 'repayment' he believes he's owed for assisting with the Roselli situation. The man only saved Atlas, Kennedy, and Astrid because he knew it would indebt us to him, and he took *full* advantage of it." I lock gazes with each and every one of them. "It only makes sense for me to do the same. It only makes sense for me to see what I can do to protect us all."

There's nothing different about what I'm doing and what Pope is...

Except they don't believe I can do it.

They don't think I'm capable of handling a man like Satriano.

They don't think I'm capable of handling *myself.*

And I've given them reason to question me.

Uncle Savage finally releases a long, heavy sigh, leaning forward to rest his elbows on the desk. "What has he asked you to do?"

I shake my head and take another sip of my drink. "Nothing yet. I'm still working on the ten million I owe him."

A muscle in Savage's jaw tics. "I'll give you the money."

Fucking hell.

Anger scorches hot through my veins, and I slam my free hand down on the couch beside me and push to my feet. My drink splashes over the edge of my glass, but I don't even care. "And he'll fucking know about that. Don't you *get* it? It's not about the money. It never *has* been. That man wants *more*, and he's going to take it from me."

All the frustration and guilt that have been building for weeks finally boil over. There isn't any containing it now that I've opened the floodgates, and their insistence that what I did was *wrong* is only making me angrier when I wanted to come in here and smooth things over.

"And I'm okay with it because I betrayed Atlas. I betrayed all of you, and I'm not in any position to be doing anything other than begging for all your forgiveness...and doing what I can to make things right."

Dad climbs to his feet with the help of the cane, stepping up into my face, and it's like I'm looking at an older version of myself—if I had actually had half the drive that he seems to have been born with. "Not by sacrificing yourself."

His hand trembles as he reaches out and clasps my forearm.

"Do you think we haven't all made mistakes?" He snorts. "Look at me. Look what happened with Abello and the fallout from it. Everyone got hurt, including my goddamn wife. Yet your mother forgave me. God knows I don't understand how, but she did. So did your Aunt Dani. And we all forgive you, but we won't be able to forgive ourselves if something happens to you."

I clench my jaw, torn between pulling him into an embrace and retreating from the way he's looking at me right now—that mix of love, concern, and empathy. "I'm smarter than you give me credit for, Dad."

His dark brows wing up. "No one here ever said you weren't smart, Coen. You're probably the smartest of any of us—"

I choke on those words and the laugh that they elicit. "Yeah, real fucking brilliant. I walked right into that man's trap."

"No, you didn't." He scowls. "You have a gambling problem, and he took advantage of it. With my history, it's no wonder you were predisposed and probably born with an addictive personality. You can't blame yourself—"

"I do, and I will." I finally tug out of his hold. "And when he asks, I'm going to do whatever he wants me to if it'll ensure everyone's safety."

Savage clenches his fists on the top of his desk. "And until then?"

I shrug. "Until then, I keep playing until I pay it back on my own."

"How much do you still need?"

"Five million. But there's a game in Vegas in two weeks, and I plan on being there to end at least that portion of my debt to the man."

Isaac finally rises to his feet, crossing his arms over his chest, clearly unhappy about what just went down between our father and me. "You lost in Macau?"

My back stiffens at the memory of that game—Allegra's roaming hand and what mine did after—and I clear my throat. "I did."

"To whom?"

An evil temptress...

"No one you know or would want to."

ALLEGRA

MY FAMILY IS in the business.

When Coen told me that, I hadn't imagined *this...*

Good God...

I do a slow, three-sixty spin in the grand lobby of the Hawke Hotel, trying to take in everything around me. But that's nearly impossible.

Even after spending most of my life traveling and countless nights in ritzy, over-the-top luxury hotels, this place has still managed to render me speechless.

And it isn't just the glittering opulence.

It's the unique touches.

Things I can only imagine to be authentic New Orleans flair scattered throughout the design—the golden fleur-de-lis carved at the corner of each door and inlaid in the shiny, Italian marble floors. Bright, festive carnival masks decorating the walls. Magnolias flowing out of massive crystal vases placed on tables and pedestals throughout the massive space...

It somehow feels rich, yet homey. Welcoming, yet clearly offering an experience that will go far beyond what anyone can imagine. And I haven't even made it into the casino yet...

My gaze drifts to the right, toward the entrance to it, where slot machines and tables extend as far as I can see.

Before I can take a single step, a warm, calloused hand curls around my elbow, and a familiar scent wraps around me, invading my startled inhalation.

Crisp ocean waves.

Coen...

"What are you doing here, Allegra?" His deep voice rumbles through me like an earthquake, threatening to knock me off balance in my heels. When I don't answer immediately, his grip tightens and his lips brush my ear. "Well?"

I clear my throat and turn toward him slightly until I can see the warning in his gaze. "I came to play."

It's as honest an answer as I can give the man who will probably *never* trust me.

One of his dark brows rises slowly, and he shifts closer, until his entire body is pressed into the side of mine, his breath fanning my cheek, raising goosebumps along my skin. "Came to play what?" Those callouses drag lightly over my skin as he shifts his grip. "Me? Because we both know that isn't going to happen..."

I shake my head immediately.

Not after what he did to me the other night...

He made it *very* clear that he will *not* be played—despite my best efforts, which came back to bite me.

Hard.

I tried to distract him at that table in Macau, but apparently, all that came from my little game was the awakening of a sleeping giant intent on revenge—which he served *excessively* cold before he walked away.

He left me breathless, trembling, wet, and wanting.

Not a position I often find myself in, nor one I ever want to be in again.

Coen holds my gaze, patrons of the hotel and casino moving around us, eyeing us speculatively. Apparently, the tension between the couple standing so close and glaring at each other in the middle of the lobby is as evident as it is for me as part of the stare down.

What's he going to do?

Walk me out of Hawke Hotel and drop me on the street...

It should be his first inclination and honestly what I expected him to do once he discovered I was here, but I thought I'd have more time to scope out the hotel and casino, to get the lay of the land, and perhaps establish some sort of defensive position before I was captured by the enemy.

That didn't go well.

And the longer this goes on, the two of us unmoving, pressed together with his tight grip on me, the harder it becomes to keep staring into those icy-blue eyes.

It's my turn to raise a brow at him, to force him to act, and the secretive grin he sends my way in response elicits a little shiver of fear and anticipation.

A security guard in a black suit approaches, with his gaze zeroed in on Coen's hand on my arm. "Is there a problem, sir?"

Coen finally drags his focus away from me to smile at him. "I'll take care of Ms. Knight personally."

The man gives him a little nod of acknowledgment. "Yes, sir."

As soon as he moves away from us, I turn my head toward Coen. "You're going to take care of me, how? Throw me out on my ass?"

He starts to lead me away from the lobby and casino, his firm grip on my arm directing me toward a bank of elevators and preventing me from holding my ground unless I want to be dragged across the Italian marble. "I should, shouldn't I?"

Probably.

If I were in his position, I likely would.

Yet, this elevator clearly doesn't lead outside to the streets of New Orleans.

The doors glide open the moment he hits the call button. We step in, his hand still coiled around my arm, ensuring I'm not going to bolt. My heart thunders against my ribs; the thought of being confined in an elevator with Coen Hawke again is enough to make my legs shake.

Coen maneuvers us to one side, then swipes a keycard across a reader and hits the button labeled *PH*. But before I can be sealed in with him and my fate, two other couples enter, which means that whatever Coen wants to say or do is going to have to wait until we don't have an audience.

Because something tells me whatever it is wouldn't play well with Hawke Hotel customers.

And here, Coen has to maintain some level of professional decorum.

This is the shining jewel in his family's empire, and he wouldn't do anything to tarnish it simply to get his revenge against me.

Would he?

Coen offers the others a smile as they each scan their keycards and press the buttons for their floors.

The elevator doors close.

Tension permeates the air.

Everyone seems to notice, glancing toward us a few times, even though we haven't done or said anything to draw their attention.

We rise three floors, each number ticking by slowly. It stops, and one of the couples disembarks, leaving us facing the other.

I give them a tentative smile, and they shift awkwardly, their gazes dipping to Coen's hold on me.

Coen's hand tightens as if in response.

I turn my head slightly so I can whisper to him. "Where are you taking me?"

"Somewhere private where we can have a *conversation*."

Why do I think that word doesn't mean to me what it does to him?

I raise a brow at him. "Isn't that what we're doing now?"

He smirks, dark humor dancing across his cold gaze. "This isn't the type of conversation I'm talking about..."

Well, that's ominous.

The other couple finally exits on their floor, and the elevator continues up until we reach our destination without another word from either of us.

It dings, the doors opening to reveal a small entryway and a single door labeled *PENTHOUSE*.

"You have a thing for penthouses, huh?"

He scowls and leads me toward the solitary entrance. "I happen to know it's unoccupied at the moment."

Coen swipes his key and pushes open the door, directing me inside, but it's impossible to concentrate on what the room looks like when he still has his hand on me.

Those callouses brush my skin. The heat of his fingers seeps into me. And I can't help the way the memory of them moving inside me rushes to the forefront of my mind.

He marches me into the main living space—two floors tall, with bright Louisiana sunlight pouring in from the windows and a crystal chandelier hanging in the center. A rounded staircase curves up the far wall, leading up to what I have to assume is the main bedroom, but I don't have time to examine it any further.

Coen loosens his hold on me, allowing me to slip free and turn to face him fully.

One of his dark brows rises over the vibrant blue. "What are you doing, Allegra? Because I'm sick of the games. You know you're not welcome to play here."

I set down my purse on an end table next to a low, white leather couch. "Who says I came for the tables?"

His pupils dilate, his throat working on a thick swallow. "Apparently, my warning didn't take."

"Oh"—I approach him cautiously as one would a wounded, untrusting animal, nodding slowly—"it definitely took. My legs shook all night."

And I had to slide my own hand between them to ease the ache when I got back into my room—though I refuse to admit that weakness to him.

I stop just in front of him, only a few feet separating us, offering a coy smile as the memory of our *game* in Macau surfaces, blazing hot. "What about you?"

"What about me?"

Inching closer, I allow my gaze to dip to his crotch. "Don't think I didn't notice the way you adjusted your cock before you slid out of that booth, Coen. I wasn't the only one affected by your little game."

"*My* game?" His brows rise incredulously. "What about *yours*? You've been playing one with me from the minute we met."

There isn't any point in denying it.

"I was, but can you blame me?" I smirk. "Don't *you* research *your* opponents?"

Coen crosses his arms over his chest, the motion pulling at the crisp white dress shirt he wears. "Of course, I do."

I spread my hands to point out the opulence of the suite and the life he clearly lives. "You just pay your minions to bring you the information, right?"

He scowls at me because I've hit the nail right on the head. His family is precisely the type to have a massive security force and people who specifically do their digging and dirty work. All he has to do is request information on anyone he knows will be at those tables he sits at, and his people will bring him anything they can find.

"Well"—I reach out and run a finger down his chest, his hard pecs tightening under my touch—"not all of us have the benefit of a staff to do our bidding. I don't own a hotel…"

"Neither do I."

I lean in. "Your family does. It's semantics. Anything you want is within reach…"

In retrospect, that might have been the wrong thing to say while I had any part of my body touching this man. I hadn't meant the words to sound like an invitation, but it's exactly how they came out.

His brow rises slowly, heat flickering in his gaze that goes far beyond that of the anger that's permeated it so heavily. "Is that so?"

The way the question rolls off his tongue, he might as well be on his knees with it buried between my legs.

This would be the time to retreat.

To back away a few steps…

To put space between him and me before things go horribly awry…

But things already *have* gone awry.

They have since the minute he sat next to me at that bar in Atlantic City.

So, I don't retreat.

I nod.

He considers me for a moment, his hand coming up to wrap around my wrist where my finger is still pressed to his chest. "It could be…if I actually trusted you."

Good God, I have completely lost control at this point.

"Do you have to trust me to fuck me?"

His eyes flare, and he steps into my finger until my hand is fully flattened against his chest, and I can feel his heart beating a rapid tattoo under it. "Is that what you want, Allegra, for me to hate-fuck you?"

I grin at him. "Do you hate me?"

He snorts. "You cost me the win in Macau."

"You cost *yourself* the win."

His lips part to offer an argument.

"Coen...don't blame me because you lost control, because I played the better game..."

And played him.

It may have been dirty tactics. It may have gone well beyond the bounds of what any player would consider appropriate. But he was still the one who let it affect him. It still broke his epic control.

"You may have beaten me at poker that night, Allegra, but I think I *won*."

Raising a brow, I tilt my head slightly, examining him. "How's that?"

That mouth that has promised so many sinful things curls into a smooth grin. "You're *here*, aren't you?"

Shit.

And he knows why.

Because my legs still wobble slightly at the memory of his hand between them. I still get wet at the thought of his fingers moving over my clit. My body vibrates, even now, like it did that night, ready and waiting for him to finish the job.

He shifts closer, our bodies now fully aligned, our hands pinned between us, his still wrapped around my wrist. "I must have done something right. I figured I'd never see you again, or at least, not until the next big tournament."

"Vegas?"

That scowl of his returns. "I should have known...but what I don't understand is why the sudden interest?"

"What do you mean?"

He searches my gaze as if he'll find the answer there. "I've never seen you on the circuit before. Now, you're everywhere."

I raise a shoulder and let it fall. "I didn't need it as badly before."

"Need what?"

Isn't that the ultimate question?

What do I need...

What does anyone...

Leaning in, I ghost my lips over his. "The wins."

"But you do now?"

I nod.

He slides his free hand through my hair, grasping my head and holding me steady, preventing me from pulling away, exerting his dominance and letting me know I'm not going to pull one over on him again. "You're not going to win with me."

I shift my body to his and feel his cock harden along my stomach. "The evidence would suggest otherwise."

"If what you need is a good, hard fuck, I'm more than willing to comply, Allegra. But what I won't do is continue whatever this fucking game is between us. I need that win in Vegas. So, I'll make you a deal."

"What kind of deal?"

"This." He rolls his hips against mine, and I have to stifle a groan at the rush of need that simple motion sends through me. "In exchange for your word that you won't play."

I raise a brow. "Because you know I can beat you?"

"Because I don't want any distractions, and somehow, I've let you become one. A beautiful, beautiful distraction."

I consider his offer for a moment. Consider walking away from this so I can still play. But with his body pressed to mine, his hot breath fanning over my face, the desire and hatred burning in his eyes, we're so close to combusting that I don't know if it's possible to stop it at this point.

"Okay, Mr. Hawke, I agree to your terms."

He grins, but the way it splits his face sends a shiver down my spine. "Good, because I would much rather slide into you than take my cock in my hand like I had to in Macau..."

8

ALLEGRA

I'*m in trouble.*

That devious glint in his eyes is all I need to see to know it before his mouth brushes over mine and he steals the little yelp that slips from my lips as he tugs me even more firmly against him.

He devours me, his tongue sweeping along mine, lips moving like they're trying to pull the breath straight from my lungs. Like he's trying to memorize them in case he never gets this chance again.

Thorough.

Aggressive.

Possessive.

And so fucking intoxicating.

I could so easily get drunk off this man. Off the way he kisses me. The way he holds me. The way every stroke of his tongue feels like it has a direct line straight to my clit.

My body hums to life when he does this, and I wrap my arms around his neck, holding him to me. All the power and intensity that vibrates under his skin finally leaks out and soaks me in his passion, promising so much more.

Promising to drown me in it the same way his eyes do.

I failed so badly when it came to Coen Hawke.

The game I played with him was too dangerous. Too personal. Too intense. Too *everything.*

And I definitely lost.

Because actually *liking* Coen and wanting *this* was never part of any plan I had concocted in my head.

I pride myself on always being ready before I face down an opponent, but I was *not* prepared for this one.

He outplayed me.

Masterfully.

He turned the tables, became the invader instead of the defender.

Coen got that upper hand I cling to so tightly.

He groans as he explores my mouth, nips and sucks at my lower lip, and crushes his cock against my stomach, backing me up until something hard hits my ass.

Strong hands release my hair, and he slides them down to my thighs and lifts me easily. I catch a glimpse of the long, low bar he's settled me on the edge of when I drag my mouth from his to get a much-needed gasp of air.

My shoulders press against the wall behind me, and Coen invades my space, issuing a low growl that vibrates through me as his hand roams up my inner thigh. "I got a little taste of you the other night, Allegra."

I shiver at the memory of his fingers moving inside me and the way he licked them clean before sauntering away as if he didn't just leave me with the biggest case of blue clit in history.

"But I have to tell you..." He kisses across my cheek, grazing his lips down the column of my neck to my collarbone and sinking his teeth in there. I jerk at the sharp bite of pain and shift against his hard cock aligned so perfectly to my core. "It wasn't enough. Not even an appetizer, really. You see, I'm a hungry man, and when I get hungry, I devour delicious things until there's nothing left of them."

Fuck, why did that sound like a promise and a threat all rolled into one?

Probably because it is both.

Because this man is certainly capable of destroying me in very real and delicious ways.

He pulls back.

Those eyes that seem to alternate between flinty iciness and welcoming warmth now blaze with an inferno of need that threatens to consume me while he's barely even touched my body.

He nudges my knees wider with his hands, his calloused palms grazing my bare inner thighs, and my body starts trembling.

Fear, anticipation?

Revenge can be sweet, but not when you're on the receiving end of it. And Coen Hawke definitely has plans for me that involve vengeance. It flashes in his eyes. Vibrates in the way he trails those fingertips across my skin. Lives in everything he intends to do to me.

Those hands find the hem of my dress and slowly glide it up, lifting my ass slightly to force it up to my hips.

I bite my lip, trying to stop myself from whimpering, struggling to stop myself from begging for him to move faster, for him to touch me, for him to just fucking do something, instead, he watches me from under hooded lids, then slowly sinks to his knees in front of me.

He sucks in a sharp breath when he sees my bare pussy. "You do play a dangerous game, Allegra."

I let out a heavy breath. "Why do you say that?"

Coen leans in, warm breath floating across my already damp skin, making me shiver. "Because you came to me fully exposed. Why?" He raises a brow, eyes flicking up to meet mine. "Did you hope you'd find me? Is that why you came to the hotel? To do *this*?"

His question hangs in the still air.

If I don't answer, I know he won't keep going.

I hold my breath as his fingers skate up closer to my aching core. "No, I was...curious..."

A slow, lecherous grin curls his lips. "About what? The family business or me? Because I'll tell you something, Allegra. If you think you're getting any information that might help you take this casino for even a single fucking cent, you're wrong."

His thumb grazes along my slit, spreading the embarrassing arousal up and over my clit with one slick swipe.

Fuck.

I wrap my hands around the end of the bar, searching for any sort of purchase as my hips buck at the contact. "Maybe I was just curious about you."

He pauses with his thumb pressed against that tiny throbbing bud at the apex of my thighs.

I lock my gaze with his, prepared to throw down the gauntlet. "Maybe I was curious if you could actually deliver on what you promised in that restaurant booth."

His pupils dilate, the lust in them only deepening. "You wanted me to slide under that table and bury my face between these luscious thighs, didn't you?"

I bite my bottom lip and nod, and he issues a low rumbling approval.

"You wanted me to bend you over that table and fuck you in front of all those people? You would've let me..."

I don't bother denying it.

There's just something about Coen Hawke. Something dangerous. Something wild. Something restless and unsteady. Like he can't be put into a cage, and anyone who tries is only going to end up getting torn apart by his resistance.

"Probably, but then they never would've invited me back to play, would they?"

He chuckles low and resumes slowly brushing his thumb up and down my slit in a way that has my hips bowing up. His left forearm comes up across my pelvis, holding me down. "I don't know what to think about that, Allegra." He tilts his head sideways, examining me. His eyes intent on where his finger plays so relentlessly with me. "And I don't know what I should do with you. Punish you for what you did to me?"

I shake my head. "No."

The grin he gives me doesn't offer me any hope. "Or reward you?"

"For what?"

He slides his thumb inside me, and I gasp at the sensation. "For actually finding a way to distract me and being the first one ever to do it."

Shiiiiiiiiit.

Again, that sounds more like something that would warrant a threat, not a promise of the type of pleasure his touch does.

He withdraws his thumb, and I whimper only to have him drop his head between my spread thighs and lick me from the base of my cunt all the way up over my clit in one long, slow glide that has me bucking against his hold.

Fuck.

My grip on the counter borders on painful, and I drop my head back to the wall behind me.

Bottles and glasses on the bar rattle.

Coen doesn't seem to care.

He groans his approval. "Fuck, do you taste good..."

I bet he does, too...

My mouth suddenly waters, wondering what his cock would taste like. About the flavor of his cum coating my tongue and sliding down my throat...

He laps at me again, probing as deep inside me as he can, fucking me with it the way I wish he would with his cock.

"Sweet." Lick. "Delicious." Lick. "Mysterious." Lick. "Dangerous." Another slow glide that makes me want to beg. "Fucking exquisite." His eyes flick up to meet mine. "So many reasons this shouldn't be happening..."

I gasp and nod.

"But you still want it, don't you, Allegra? You came all the way to New Orleans to find me for *this*."

He glides his tongue across my cunt, sipping and drinking down my arousal, laving and sucking at my flesh, but not giving me what I really need.

Him.

I need *him.*

I need him inside me.

I need him filling me.

I need him pummeling me.

I need it hard and rough.

I need him to unleash all that pent-up aggression toward me and direct it into utterly destroying me for any other man.

But I grit my teeth, refusing to beg this man, even as my entire body pulses and coils and wants to buck against what he's doing.

The man is committing slow, sensual torture.

I knew I was in trouble the moment I made the decision to come here to seek out Coen Hawke, but I had no fucking idea it would be this much.

COEN

THERE ARE SO many things I could do to Allegra...

So many ways I could make her pay for her little game and the way she played me so perfectly.

I could master my revenge the same way she did her manipulation.

But with my face buried between her legs and the sweet taste of her cunt coating my tongue, all I can think about is how incredible it would sound to hear her come. How staggering it would feel to have this pussy tightening around my cock as I pound into her. How those nails of hers biting into my neck and my back as I ride her would only make me drive into her harder.

And that's exactly what she wants.

She wants me to unravel.

If I give her that, she wins again.

That isn't happening...

Getting the upper hand with a woman like Allegra doesn't happen often, if at all. Most men will never experience it. Yet, I somehow managed it that night in Macau. I had enough strength to walk away from her.

I don't have that now, but it doesn't mean I'll make this *easy* on the woman who has haunted my dreams for weeks now.

When her face appears in them, it's to taunt me with those soft brushes of her hand against my cock, to work me up into a frenzy when she has no intention of doing anything about it.

It's better than the alternative nightmare that still follows me, but it's a harsh reminder that she can't be trusted.

No matter how sincere she might have sounded when she claimed this wasn't part of her game.

I can't give her what she wants now.

To do it would concede far too much to someone who has already taken more than she should have.

I force myself to slow, to dip my tongue into her and lick every square inch of her tight, peachy skin.

Her cunt.

Her glistening thighs.

Kissing my way down to her knee and then up the other side, only to repeat the move on the other leg.

Until she's shaking so badly that the entire bar rattles, reminding me of what's right next to us.

Grinning, I reach out and grab the bottle of bourbon.

Her eyes flutter open to watch as I pop the top off the decanter and take a swig.

"I can see why you like bourbon, Allegra. So sweet..."

I pour it across her slick core.

She yelps slightly at the contact, but before she can say anything else, I bury my face there, licking and sucking and consuming every sweet drop of the drink—and her.

A lethally addictive combination.

"Oh, fuck!"

She gasps, one hand shifting from the edge of the bar into my hair and tugging at the strands as she angles my head and grinds her hips against my face.

I groan my approval—at both the combined flavor of the booze and Allegra and the aggressive desperation it's elicited in her.

My cock, painfully hard and incessantly aching, presses along the zipper of my pants. "Fucking hell, Allegra. I could so easily get addicted to you."

She tosses her head from side to side, eyes clenched closed, body taut and quaking under my ministrations. "Coen, I need..."

"You need to come?"

With a groan, she nods, her hips moving as much as I'll allow with my forearm braced against her, holding her down and at my mercy.

"What if I don't want to let you come?"

Her eyes flash open to meet mine, panic seeping into the gray, making them almost black. "You wouldn't. Not again."

I offer her a slow grin, dragging my hand up her inner thigh as I rise to my feet, slipping two fingers easily into her drenched core as hers fall away from my hair. She groans at the intrusion, clenching around them, and my cock twitches, begging to be there to feel those walls constricting around it. I curl my fingers inside, finding that perfect soft spot, and she bucks against my hand, trying to grind her clit to my palm the way I toyed with her in Macau.

But I shift my grip, preventing her from doing just that.

"Would I, Allegra?"

She nods, breathless and panting. "Yes."

"Why do you think that?"

"Because," she gasps, "because I fucked with you."

"And how many times did you fuck with me, Allegra?"

She whimpers, clenching around my fingers as I probe and drag them across that hyper-sensitive spot over and over again, refusing to touch her clit and give her what she really needs. "T-t-twice. I did it twice."

I lean in, ghosting my lips across hers, capturing another little mewl as I allow my thumb to just barely graze her most sensitive spot. "So, it would only be fair for me to stop right now. Wouldn't it? For me to leave you here, shaking and wet and needy like I did the other night?"

Her thick, dark lashes rise slowly until her half-hooded gaze meets mine. "It would." She slides her hand into my hair again and tugs. "But you won't do that."

So sure of herself.

I raise a brow. "Why not?"

She pushes herself up away from the wall until her mouth hits mine in a bruising kiss that has me almost coming on the spot. Her other hand leaves the edge of the counter, and she grasps my cock pinned between us. "Because you want this as much as I do. And if we don't fuck today, then every time we sit at the table with each other, it's going to be like this. Neither of us able to concentrate. Both of us playing a different game instead of concentrating on the one on the felt."

Fuck, she's right.

She's so fucking right.

It's only been a few weeks since I first saw her, and ever since, I haven't been able to get this woman out of my head.

This kind of obsession kills my ability to think straight. Crushes that part of me that has been trained to remain impassive. It was all gone the moment I met her.

I crash my mouth to hers again, and she releases my hair to fumble with my pants, finally freeing my aching cock. It springs out, and she tears her mouth from mine to look down at it, her gaze widening.

"Jesus…"

Chuckling, I press my thumb into her clit, and she groans, her eyes closing, forehead dropping against mine. "He has nothing to do with what's happening right now, Allegra. Now, tell me you want my cock…"

She whimpers, reluctant to do it.

Already, I've put her in the submissive position, somewhere she is not used to being. Making her say it is asking too much. But I need it all the same.

"Tell. Me."

I push harder.

She drags her head back, locking her gaze with mine. "I want all of you, Coen Hawke."

Fucking Christ…

She grasps my cock and strokes it in one long motion, her thumb brushing over the pre-cum leaking from the head, making my finger move across her clit in response.

A little strangled sound slips from her lips as she guides my cock straight to her core. The blistering heat and wetness engulf the tip, making me grit my teeth, my body tensing against the desire to drive straight into her.

"You think I'm going to fuck you without a condom?"

Her gaze holds mine. "I don't play *those* games. I'm on birth control, and I've been tested."

"Me, too."

Thank fuck.

Because I want to feel all of her...

The rippling of her cunt as she comes with nothing between us.

No barriers, no games, just this.

And that's all the convincing I need to shove into her in one long, hard thrust.

It rocks her back onto the bar, and one of the tumblers falls off the edge and shatters on the floor. Glass shards scatter across the marble, pieces sliding under the furniture, but I don't care.

I know exactly how much those cost us to put in this penthouse, but it's a small price to pay for the feeling of her hot, wet core clenching around me.

"Fuck..."

It comes out more growl than word, and I bury my face against her neck, dragging my hips back to plunge into her again.

One of her hands finds my nape, the other tightening around the counter to try to keep herself steady as I pound into her.

Each thrust drives her back until she's pressed to the wall.

I grasp her thighs and spread them wider, dragging her forward to the edge so I can grind into her, against her clit, giving her the friction she needs while I get deeper and deeper inside her, bottoming out with each thrust.

Her nails bite into my neck.

Glass rattles as another crystal tumbler inches toward the edge with each slam of my hips. Her hand snaps out and pushes it back, and I chuckle against her damp skin, kissing my way to that spot on her collarbone I sank my teeth into earlier.

I lave my tongue across the indentations, and her pussy clenches in response, rippling, her hips driving to meet mine.

Allegra enjoys a little pain with her pleasure.

That will certainly keep things interesting.

Her entire body is primed.

Tensing more and more.

Her grip becoming more demanding.

She's preparing for what's coming.

Bracing herself for the onslaught.

I pull my head back and take her mouth again, needing that taste, wanting to devour all of her, and she lets me. And with each drive of my hips, it feels like winning a little battle in this war she started that night in Atlantic City, but also, somehow, losing a little bit of myself to a woman I know I shouldn't.

"Coen—"

My name comes out like a prayer offered to a god she doesn't fully trust to answer it.

And if I had more strength, I might stop this now and walk away.

But I have lost that ability when it comes to her.

I shift her position again, dragging one leg up over my shoulder so I can plunge down into her at a different angle.

She gasps, her eyes rolling back as her head drops. "Fuck. Yes, right there."

A few more hard strokes are all it takes before she explodes, her nails scoring my skin, her cry echoing off the expensive marble and glass in the penthouse.

Her pussy squeezes my cock like a vise and draws out my own release. My balls tighten up, and I grit my teeth, trying to hold off, but I can't. I come in hot spurts inside her, burying myself to the hilt, wishing desperately that I'd had the strength to walk away from her, like I should have.

9

ALLEGRA

C oen's cock twitches in me.

His chest heaves against mine.

Our heavy breaths mingle as we both come down slowly from the high of our releases, trying to get our bearings and regain control of our faculties.

What the hell just happened?

My body buzzes with energy, tingling everywhere, every nerve ending flaring and sparking and making me twitch. He slides my leg down from his shoulder and his hand around my back to support me as I start to sag even more, losing my ability to stay remotely upright.

His lips flutter along my temple. "That was far better than you deserve after what you did to me." He nips at my ear, and I shiver, clenching around him and drawing a low groan from deep in his ribcage. "But I think we should do it again."

I can't fight the grin that pulls at my lips or squeezing him again as his cock already starts to re-harden. "It depends on what game you want to play this time—"

An electronic clicking sound drags his attention from me and toward the door before it pushes open.

The stunning umber-skinned woman who stands on the other side of it narrows her dark eyes on our compromised position. She tilts her head slightly, the long braids twisted high at the top of her head in a bun, moving with her.

Her gaze darts to the shattered glass on the floor beside the bar, and Coen moves to block her full view of me, but I can still see most of her if I lean to the side.

"Jesus Christ, Bishop. Knock much?"

She scowls and leans against the doorjamb, keeping it open to the small foyer and elevator. "Everyone was worried when you vanished"—she raises a black brow—"for obvious reasons."

I try to peek around Coen to get a better view of her, but he shifts again, completely blocking my view of her or hers of me.

"Soooo..."—she drawls the word, intentionally dragging it out with a note of annoyance and maybe humor in it—"I checked where your keycard was last used." One hand spreads wide enough for me to see it from around Coen's protective shield. "The penthouse. You know this isn't your own private fuck palace, don't you?"

He grits his teeth, a muscle in his jaw flexing as his hands tighten around me, clutching me closer. "Get the fuck out."

"We're supposed to meet Savage, Ken, and Cass in the lobby in ten minutes. Or have you completely forgotten?"

He mutters, "shit" under his breath.

Oh, he definitely did.

Though I can't blame him for being distracted. I certainly was from my original mission in coming here as soon as he touched me down in the lobby.

I glance up at him as he finally allows his gaze to return to mine, an apology written in it. "I'll meet you down there."

Bishop huffs. "If you're not down in five minutes, I'm coming back for you."

She lets the door close behind her and, as soon as it clicks, Coen sags, releasing a long, heavy sigh.

"Shit. I am so sorry about that…"

He's apologizing to me? After everything I've done to him?

I'm not entirely sure what changed or how we went from hate-fucking to him protecting me from embarrassment and now apologizing for something that wasn't his fault in the least.

That woman seemed equally appalled and amused at our situation in a way that only makes sense if she's close with Coen.

"Who was she?"

He pulls back, giving me an almost annoyed look. "For all intents and purposes, my babysitter while I'm home."

I raise a brow at him. "You need a babysitter?"

Maybe that was the wrong thing to ask, if the look he tosses at me is any indication.

He shifts his hips away, his cock slipping from inside me with a groan from him and a wince from me at the sudden loss. "It's a long fucking story I don't have time to tell right now, nor would I even if I did." Taking a step back, he shoves his hand through his hair, mussing up the locks that are already in disarray from my hands. He tucks his wet cock into his pants, zips them, and rebuckles his belt. "Stay right there."

Where the hell else am I going to go when I'm sprawled across the bar with his cum filling me, my body still a quivering mess…

Although, I suppose there are worse places to be.

Though, maybe not ones as embarrassing as being caught literally pants down and legs spread with a dick buried in you by a total stranger.

Coen stalks over to the sink at the far end of the bar, wets a hand towel, and brings it over to me, sliding right between my legs where he just was and pressing it to my core.

It makes me shiver, despite the warmth of the water.

"Believe me, I would much rather be cleaning you up and getting you dirty again in the shower right now." Sincerity laces his words. "But I can't miss this meeting."

I swallow thickly and nod as he gently cleans me in a way I wouldn't have expected from a man who seemed so intent on doing damage only a short time ago.

When he pulls his hand away, his eyes lock with mine, and he bends down, kissing me long and slow. His tongue glides along the seam of my lips until I open for him and allow it to tangle with my own. One of those throaty groans of his curls through him, and when he tugs his mouth from mine, there is regret in his gaze, along with that glimmer of something dark and dangerous.

"I have to say, the thought of you walking around the rest of the day with my cum dripping out of you is pretty much the highlight of my existence up until now."

Hell.

That shouldn't be hot.

Right?

I shiver and shift off the bar, my dress falling back into place, and he's so close, it doesn't take more than a millisecond before our entire bodies are pressed together again. "What makes you think I won't leave here immediately and go shower?"

He raises a brow, then reaches up and grips my chin, tilting my face to his, that intensity returning. "Because you want it there as much as I do."

Fuck.

It.

Shouldn't.

Be.

So.

Hot.

This growly possessiveness he is displaying today would normally be such a huge turnoff for me. I despise men who try to dominate and act like they control the world and everything in it, including me. But somehow, with Coen, it's different.

It just is.

And my pussy, still damp with his cum, clenches, wishing he were back inside it.

He glances at his watch. "I have to go."

I swallow. "Me too."

Really.

I hadn't intended to stay.

I hadn't intended *any* of this to happen.

Not really.

Maybe deep down I had *hoped* it might, but I never believed it was actually possible, given everything that went down between us.

I move to step around him and make my way toward the door. He tosses the wet rag onto the counter and follows after me, catching my hand to tug me back as I reach for the handle. "You're not leaving New Orleans, are you?"

God.

There's so much hope in his voice that I'll say no. That I'll tell him I'm staying.

I bite my lip as I stare up at him and melt under the plea in his eyes. "I thought you'd want me gone."

A war rages in those fathomless blue depths—that anger and hatred he harbored for me because of my betrayal mixing with the lust we both just felt.

Still feel.

It's a lethal combination.

One we felt combust around us and shatter us into a zillion pieces.

He shakes his head. "I'm not sure, but I know I'm not done with you yet."

How this man can say things like that and simultaneously sound threatening and promising is a mystery for the ages. One I would very much like to solve, given the chance. "I'm not leaving yet, if you want me to stay."

His brow rises. "I do."

That shouldn't warm my heart.

Shouldn't make it flutter so crazily like this, but somehow it does.

Just like with everything having to do with Coen Hawke, it's a contradiction in everything that should and shouldn't be.

The last thing I should be doing is spending any more time than necessary in New Orleans. I didn't even book a hotel when I made the split-second decision to come.

"I have to head to my meeting. Where are you going to stay? Let me get you a room."

I shake my head. "I don't think it would be a good idea for me to stay here."

His brow furrows. "Why not?"

Turning away from him, I tug on the handle, and it pops open. I motion to the lock. "Because my guess is your key card opens every door in this place."

A slow, lewd grin spreads across his face. "Why do you make that sound like a bad thing?"

I step out into the hall, tugging him with me. "Because I understand you, Coen Hawke. And I don't trust you one bit."

"*You* don't trust *me*?"

His brows pop up as I push the button on the elevator and lean against the wall, facing him. I release his hand and push my disheveled hair from my face. "Why should I?"

He leans in, bracing his hand above my head. "Because, as I said, I was far too kind to you in there, kinder than you deserve... That should earn me some trust."

If that was him being kind...

I shiver, and the elevator dings.

He steps back to allow me to turn and move into it, then immediately cages me in again, pushing me against the wall with his hard, lean body, pinning me to it.

Without tearing his gaze from mine, he reaches out and presses the button for the lobby, then kisses along my jaw in a way that has my legs trembling, even as I can feel the cum still left inside me slowly starting to seep out.

I clench my thighs together.

"So, you're not going to tell me where you're going to stay?"

I shake my head.

"And how will I get in touch with you?"

He won't.

He pulls his head back, that question so similar to the one he asked me in Monaco.

I smile at him, offering him hope I didn't then. "I'll find you again, Mr. Hawke."

We whoosh down, staring at each other until the elevator dings and the doors slide open.

Someone clears their throat, and Coen glances over at the four people waiting outside the cab.

One, the woman from upstairs. Another, a stunning blonde with vibrant-blue eyes that tell me she must be a Hawke, in sky-high designer heels and a stunning pencil skirt and blouse that screams "I'm in charge." A drop-dead gorgeous man with sandy-blond hair and a keen gaze. And another who is the spitting image of Coen, which means it must be his father or maybe his uncle.

Definitely family.

That one raises dark brows. "Aren't you going to introduce us?"

Coen mutters a curse under his breath, takes my hand, and pulls me from the elevator to where they wait. "Allegra, this is my uncle, Savage, my cousin, Kennedy, and her husband, Cass, and you've already met Bishop."

Bishop smirks at me, crossing her arms over her chest, making the insane muscles in her arms bulge slightly.

This woman is vicious.

It certainly explains why she wasn't at all worried about going right at Coen upstairs.

I clear my throat. "Nice to meet all of you. I have to get going."

Before the evidence of what we just did appears on my lower thighs.

I glance up at Coen. "I'll call you."

He nods as I start to slip away, not even bothering to ask me how I will get his number. By now, he must know I have my ways, too.

"Don't run off so soon..." Savage's words freeze me in my tracks, and I turn back to them. He offers me a smile that lies somewhere between friendly and concerned. "Any friend of Coen's is a friend of ours." He tosses his nephew a look. "Why don't you join us for Sunday family dinner tomorrow?"

Coen's eyes widen, and he shakes his head. "I don't think that's—"

Kennedy grins, her red lips tilting in a devious way that makes me sure I was one hundred percent right in my initial impression of her. "Oh, I think that's exactly what needs to happen."

COEN

EVEN SIX HOURS LATER, my body still vibrates with a strange mixture of pleasure and exhaustion. Muscles twitching. Hands and cock tingling, remembering what it felt like to have Allegra in my arms, to be buried inside her. Her taste still fills my mouth and coats my tongue, her scent invading every breath I take.

On top of my encounter with the woman I thought I'd never see again, the tedious hours spent with Savage, Cass, and Kennedy—along with my new shadow, Bishop—going over the heightened security measures at the hotel as well as additional plans for the new building across the street that will open soon, I've been on my feet for almost sixteen hours and every fiber of my being is feeling it.

I unlock my condo door and step inside, relieved to finally have Bishop off my back, at least for the night, now that I'm locked away tight in the building guarded in the lobby on a floor accessible with a code only the Hawkes know.

Leaning against the door, I release a long, heavy breath and let my eyes drift closed.

What a long fucking day.

All I want to do is take a hot shower, maybe relive my encounter with Allegra as I rub one out, then climb into bed and never get out.

Though, it would be a lot better if I had her with me.

Christ.

I scrub my hands over my face and push off the door.

Images flit through my head.

Fantasies that likely can never be reality.

I can't even imagine what we'd be like in a bed together like that, with all night laid out in front of us and *zero* interruptions from pesky family members.

Combustible.

That's what we would be, and I know it.

What happened in the penthouse was only a spark, ready to ignite something much bigger, something neither of us is ready for or would likely survive.

"You look tired, Coen..."

The slightly accented voice slips through the darkness of the living room, freezing me instantly. Goosebumps rise on my skin as dread coils around my spine and tightens until I can barely move, even if I wanted to.

I don't have to be able to see in the darkness to know who it is.

Not when I would know that voice anywhere.

Any of the Hawkes would.

That's the sound of danger.

I take a second to try to regain my composure before advancing farther into the condo until the dim moonlight trailing in from the patio windows offers enough light to see the man sitting in the leather armchair near the fireplace.

He offers me a tight smile.

"Damon"—I incline my head toward him—"to what do I owe the pleasure of this visit?"

He chuckles, low and deep, the sound lacking all humor and full of sinister intent. "Oh, I think you know very well what I'm here to discuss: your debt."

I force myself to turn my back on the man, even though every instinct in me screams never to do it, but I have to show I'm not afraid of him. Even if my legs are trembling and my hands shaking as I make my way to the bar. "Drink?"

"Whatever you're having."

Too bad I can't slip some cyanide into it.

That would sure solve a lot of problems, even if it created another one by setting his crew on us in retaliation.

I pour myself a bourbon and one for him, then make my way over and offer it with an extended hand. He looks up at me, leaning back casually in the chair, and I scan the darkness of the room.

No sign of any of his guards.

Even now, with all he has done, he trusts me enough to

know that I won't try anything with him. If I did, I know what his men would do to the rest of the family.

Besides, however he got in here undetected, it would have likely been impossible with those goons who don't know the meaning of the word discreet.

Satriano motions to the couch facing him. "Take a seat, Coen. Relax."

I snort as I lower myself into the plush leather.

He kicks one ankle up onto his knee and takes a sip of his drink. "Where do we stand on repayment?"

I take a gulp of mine, keeping my gaze locked on the most dangerous man I've ever known. "I should have all of it next weekend."

His silver brows rise. "That quick?"

I nod.

"And what about the *other* repayment?"

My shoulders tense, and I look down at my glass, swirling my drink, trying to forget how the taste of bourbon in my mouth reminds me of Allegra. "You haven't given me any indication of what you would like me to do in that regard."

"No ideas?" He gives me a grin before taking another sip. "And here I thought you were intelligent, Coen."

I lean back and watch him carefully, trying to assess what it is he wants from me. "There are so many things you could ask for, so many things I can offer. How am I supposed to know which one you want?"

He nods slowly. "I guess that's fair. And I wouldn't want there to be any confusion between us." His foot drops to the floor, and he leans forward slightly. "I'll make this very clear. I've left your family alone, allowed Atlas and Wren to run off to Bali for the last month—"

I cringe—he knew exactly where they were.

That shouldn't be a surprise.

"Allowed them to bask on the beach and pretend like every-thing was fine, but it's far from it, Coen, not with the amount of money both you and he cost me. I never would have set those odds if you hadn't confirmed how bad off he was before the fight. I never would have lost that kind of money if it hadn't been for your bet. Yes, Atlas is ultimately the one who betrayed me by failing to throw the fight, but it also lands squarely on your shoulders."

I clench my jaw and my hand around the glass.

He doesn't need to remind me.

I'm acutely aware of where I stand.

"Damon, stop toying with me and tell me what the fuck it is you want."

He issues another low chuckle and rises from his chair to pace over to the windows. "That's one thing I've always appreci-ated about you Hawkes. You're very direct. You don't beat around the bush. That's a quality I look for in partners."

"We'll never partner with you." I practically growl. "I think that point has been made abundantly clear."

"Has it?" He raises a brow and takes a sip. "Your cousin still cares for my men at the clinic."

"Because you made him." I try to keep the anger from my voice, but it still makes it tremble. "You forced him by threat-ening the rest of us and by insisting we *owed* you for your involvement with the Daniele Roselli situation."

He would have let Atlas and Astrid bleed out on that filthy warehouse floor if he didn't think he could get something by saving them—and that's precisely what he did. He got himself a skilled emergency room doctor, not to mention a surgeon, if it really came down to it and he needs to call in Mom.

"I could have left them to die... Would that have been preferable?"

I can't even respond to that without lashing out in a way that will only dig my grave deeper.

One thing I have to do is watch what I say to this man.

Not give away anything.

"Look, Damon, I know where I stand. I'm *yours*. And if any of us move on you, you have enough power and enough men to ensure that the rest of us pay for it."

He offers a slow grin that seems to flash in the streaming moonlight. "I'm glad you understand that. But as I've mentioned, I've developed a bit of a fondness for you Hawkes. I would hate to have to do any of the unsavory things I've somehow become known for." His shoulders rise and fall. "As long as everyone continues to cooperate, there won't be any need for it."

I grit my teeth. "Tell me what the fuck you want me to do."

Just get it over with.

He scowls. "We can be civil, can't we?"

"This from the man who shot up the Grind, almost killed my father, my brother, and my cousin—"

"And the man who saved Atlas, Kennedy, and Astrid's lives. Let's not forget that."

Fuck.

As if he'd ever let us...

I down the rest of my drink.

"I'll tell you what, Coen. Once you repay the ten million"— he grins—"plus interest, which is what? Another million and a half by now?" I cringe and nod. "Then we'll set to work on the remainder of your debt."

A chill slides through me again, despite the heat and spice of the bourbon in my gut.

"We'll start simple. I've managed to acquire ownership of half a dozen casinos along the Gulf Coast..."

My back stiffens as I watch him.

He what?

The man must know that makes him our biggest competitor with our plans for expansion. We've already purchased lots in six major cities between here and Corpus

Christi. Things are already in motion, dates set, millions and millions laid out to help build the chain we started with Hawke Hotel.

He relaxes slightly. "I would like them to become the preeminent places to host tournaments such as the ones you've been playing in."

"Poker?"

"Poker, baccarat, anything else we can come up with."

What's he getting at?

"How do I play a role?"

Hard eyes meet mine. "You'll play whatever role I want you to. To start, I'll use you as a plant in various tournaments, along with others, to help control the play."

"You're going to rig the tournaments?"

He grins, taking a sip before issuing a chuckle. "The odds are always against you in a casino. Didn't your family ever teach you that?"

"You don't think you'll be caught?"

"My own brother tried to kill me." He shrugs. "If he couldn't catch me, no one can."

And that's exactly what I fear.

For all the Hawkes have tried, the man appears to be untouchable. He somehow survived a car bomb, managed to stay hidden for decades while building a lucrative criminal empire, and swooped in to establish control over Roselli's territory so quickly it would make a person's head spin.

"You want me to play for you?" I raise a brow, skeptical that it could be this easy. "That's it?"

"For now...until I think of *other* ways to use you."

If that isn't ominous, I don't know what the fuck is, and I suddenly wish I still had a full drink.

Because I can already see where this is going—what he will ask me to do.

What he will *make* me do.

Hawke Hotel can't stand as his biggest competitor.

If this first location is as successful as we anticipate it being, there will be ten more locations scattered along the coast within five years—a rapid expansion plan. And Satriano doesn't want a competitor.

Either we partner with him, or he eliminates us.

Plain and simple.

10

COEN

The moment Allegra steps from the sleek, black Town Car onto the sidewalk in front of Nana's house, it's abundantly clear this is an even worse idea than I initially thought it was when Savage suggested it and Kennedy insisted.

Coupled with the lingering unease brought on by Satriano's surprise visit last night, the little shudder of anticipation that rolls through me at her approach isn't a good one.

I am so fucked...

In the long list of *bad ideas* where Allegra and I are concerned, this tops it.

I never should have allowed this to happen.

Never should have put her in the position to be the night's entertainment at the Hawke table.

And that's exactly what she'll be—on display—and it will be open season to pepper her with thousands of inappropriate and invasive questions.

But there wasn't any way to say no. Not after both what Bishop saw in the penthouse and Savage witnessed in the elevator. Once he extended that invitation and Kennedy threw her excitement at the idea on top, if Allegra hadn't come, it would have raised even *more* uncomfortable questions.

They would have wondered why I was hiding her—and that is *not* a story I intend to reveal to *any* of the Hawkes.

It's bad enough I crumbled so completely under her wiles, but to admit that to the family when I'm already skating on such thin ice would have been too much for even me to bear.

Be her buffer.

It's the least I can do, knowing what she'll face the moment she sets foot inside.

I lean against the front door jamb, tracking her journey up the walkway in a pale-green dress that offsets her eyes and another pair of patent leather Louboutins that make her toned legs seem a mile long.

A slow smile spreads across her lips as she approaches and steps up to me, stopping just out of my reach. "Hi."

"Hi..." I let my gaze sweep over her now that she's closer, from her luscious, wavy dark locks floating down over her shoulders to her tasteful cleavage and peachy skin that makes my mouth water to explore it. "I didn't think you'd come."

She raises a brow, tilting her head slightly. "Why not?"

I snort and glance back at the carnival that is Nana's house on a Sunday evening. "I had hoped you had some self-preservation instinct."

Those pink lips of hers twitch into a smirk. "I think we already established that I don't."

Neither do I.

If I did, I wouldn't have flirted with her at the bar in Atlantic City. I wouldn't have confronted her in that elevator in Monaco and brought her up to my room. And I sure as hell never would have laid a hand on her in Macau, let alone fucked her the way I did yesterday.

So, at least we're in the same boat.

I can't help but grin at her.

This lightness in my chest shouldn't exist simply by seeing this woman again. My hands shouldn't itch to touch her and hold her again. Fucking her was meant to get this out of my system, to avenge what she had done to me somehow so we could move past the tension and I could get back to winning without interruption.

Instead, I find myself craving more of her.

I tug her up against me and give her a long, slow kiss, savoring the feel of her body aligned with mine again. The warmth of her in my arms. The taste of her on my tongue again.

"Will you two knock it off and get inside?"

Pope's annoyance cuts through the fog Allegra has created in my brain, and I glance back at him. He raises a brow from where he stands a few feet behind me, holding Benjamin in his arms. A smirk pulls at his lips, and he inclines his head toward Allegra. "Welcome to the shitshow."

Hell.

I pull her inside and close the door behind us. "He's not wrong. I meant to warn you before you accepted my uncle's invitation, but we didn't get a chance to speak alone before you left the hotel."

And I would have told her if she had called like she promised. But all I got was a text from an unknown number asking for the time and address for dinner—and I couldn't very well explain any of this to her in a message. I don't even think I could explain a Hawke family dinner verbally to anyone in any other way than Pope just described it.

"It *is* kind of a shitshow..."

She laughs softly, examining the small foyer of Nana's house. "How come?"

Leaning in, I rest my hand on her lower back. "Because the entire family is expected to be here on Sundays."

"What do you mean by 'the entire family?'"

"I mean *everyone*." I lock gazes with hers, trying to convey an apology for what will hit us in a few seconds. "All thirty of us, if you include Nana."

"Shit." She chuckles lightly, but it's full of nervous tension. "That's...a lot of Hawkes."

"It sure is. And believe me, even *we* get overwhelmed. So, whenever you're ready to bail, just say the word, and I'll try to come up with some excuse for leaving early that won't get me into too much trouble."

She smiles at me, a bit of that unease melting away from her body. "I'll be okay. I know how to handle myself."

"I have no doubt that you do."

This woman has already proven her ability to stand her ground and hold her own at a table with some of the best players in the world—multiple times.

She bested *me*.

She can certainly handle herself with the Hawkes.

Hopefully...

We make our way in and past the living room where most of the family gathers—chatting, playing with the babies, or arguing over board games laid out on the floor. Every single set of eyes follows us as we pass, but I don't pause long enough for anyone to lay into her.

There will be plenty of time for that once we get to the table.

I usher her straight to the kitchen, knowing if I don't, Nana's going to lose it. The old woman has already spent the half hour I've been here trying to milk any information she can get from me about Allegra, and since I know very little, I haven't had much to offer her. Which only seems to intrigue Nana more.

Popping my head into the busiest room in the house on Sundays, I quickly scan the usual suspects. "Nana?"

The matriarch of the Hawkes peeks over her shoulder from

her spot at the stove. Aunt Storm checks us out from where she slices bread at the counter to Nana's left, as does Aunt Skye, who appears to be working on the tiramisu for dessert in the far corner.

Their gazes barely touch me, sweeping over Allegra with a keen interest that makes me wonder how anyone survives these dinners.

Nana turns toward us and wipes her hands on a kitchen towel. "Is this her?"

I roll my eyes. "No, it's a random woman I found on the street." Laughing at the annoyed look Nana throws at me, I urge Allegra forward. "Yes, Nana, this is Allegra. Allegra, this is my grandmother and my aunts, Storm and Skye."

Before Allegra can even say hello to them, Nana steps over and pulls the unsuspecting woman into a hug that has her stiffening. "It's so nice to meet you. I'm so glad you could come." She pulls back, motioning toward the dining room with the hand still clutching the towel. "You can take a seat. We're almost ready." Returning to whatever she's handling on the stove, she calls over her shoulder, "Tell everyone."

Allegra leans into me, dropping her voice low. "Do you all sit at *one* table?"

I snort as I lead her to the dining room, waving everyone in from the living room directly across from us. Those who are elsewhere in the house or outside will have to fend for themselves because I am not about to leave Allegra alone for one second for these vultures to start picking at her. "We do now..."

Her eyes widen as she takes in the massive custom-made table that seats up to thirty. "Wow. I don't think I've ever seen a table this big...or a room that could hold it, except in a restaurant, of course."

I snort, remembering how small and tight this room was when I was growing up. How uncomfortable family meals became as more and more kids joined the Hawke ranks. "We had to put an addition on Nana's house and also take the space from the kitchen where the breakfast nook once was. And this table was custom-built for her and the space."

Allegra examines the polished wood, running a finger over its surface. "That doesn't surprise me—it's absolutely beautiful and doesn't look like anything you could ever buy at a furniture store."

"It fits everyone—for now. But as soon as Benjamin and Giovanni are old enough to require their own chairs and more great-grandchildren start appearing, we might have to figure out a kids' table in the living room or something."

A wispy look clouds her gray eyes, almost as if she's on the verge of tears, but before I can ask her if she's okay, everyone starts filing in. And I go on high alert, readying myself to defend the woman at my side.

I stand behind my seat and pull out the one next to me for Allegra.

She slides into it as I do mine. "Who normally sits here?"

"My brother."

Her soft brow furrows. "Will he be mad that I took his spot?"

He has a lot of things to be mad at me about, but offering Allegra his usual chair isn't one of them.

Isaac enters the room, Jack trailing after, leaning down to whisper something to Viviana. Giovanni must already be asleep in one of the bedrooms or the Pack 'N Play in the living room.

They take in the seating arrangement, and Isaac smirks, giving me a knowing look as they settle one chair over from their typical spots.

I rest my hand on top of Allegra's and squeeze it gently. "It's fine. We switch up seats a lot, depending on who is here or who might bring a...friend." Though that word seems all wrong for

Allegra. "Trust me. Everyone is getting a kick out of you being here. That won't be what stirs the pot."

"What do you mean?"

Well, shit.

I opened the door to that one.

Should have kept my mouth fucking shut...

Tugging my hand away, I shift in my seat and pull my napkin from the holder beside my plate to set it on my lap. "I've never brought anyone to Sunday dinner before."

She raises her brows. "Never?"

I shake my head, somehow still holding her gaze, even though she must be able to see how uncomfortable that admission made me.

It may seem innocuous, but it means more than she can possibly imagine.

Or maybe she can, given the shock on her face.

I finally tear my gaze from hers, scanning the table as Uncle Savage pours a glass of wine from one of the waiting bottles at the foot of the table and passes it down our side.

It finally reaches me, and all eyes seem to follow my movement as I pour a glass for Allegra and then for myself. "You're going to need this..."

And many more.

With so many ears listening, I don't say that part out loud, just scan over everyone at the table, trying to preemptively determine who poses the most danger to the woman at my side.

The only open chairs tonight are Atlas and Wren's, since they still aren't back from Bali after deciding to extend their stay, and Luca's, but he steps into the dining room last, probably coming in from the backyard where he likes to enjoy his pre-dinner drink.

His eyes immediately land on Allegra.

That steely, dark gaze of his sweeps over her the same way it did in the hotel room in Monaco.

Assessing her.

Seeking out her weaknesses and intentions.

Anger immediately heats my blood, that protective instinct kicking in when Allegra certainly doesn't need my protection. That doesn't stop me from sliding my hand down onto her bare knee in support.

Goosebumps pebble on her skin at my touch—or maybe it's fear, given the man who is staring her down.

I lean in, letting my breath ruffle her hair. "Don't let anyone at this table intimidate you."

She turns her head toward mine, so our lips are a mere hairsbreadth from each other's. So close it's indecent. Especially in front of everyone watching us like hawks. "Nothing intimidates me."

Hell...

I believe her.

Even when I had my hand between her legs in a very public place and was *milliseconds* from getting her off, she held her ground and maintained her composure.

Mostly.

Still, the Hawkes circling promise to be far worse—especially the man taking the seat across from us. He continues to watch Ajustllegra as Nana, Storm, and Skye enter with the food and start placing the serving dishes around the table.

The grub arriving is the only thing that distracts everyone from their assessments of Allegra and briefly redirects their attention as they all start grabbing for serving spoons, baskets of bread, and bowls of salad.

All except Kennedy, who grins from her end of the table near her parents. "I am thrilled you could join us, Allegra. There are so many questions to ask—"

I toss her a warning look she should know well after all these years. "Kennedy, play nice..."

Cass snorts as he places a serving of lasagna onto Kennedy's plate, then Charlotte's, and finally his own. "You forget who you're talking to."

Kennedy elbows him enough to make him flinch, but he grins at his new wife.

His arm slides across the back of her chair. "I love you to death, *cherie*. But one thing you are not is *nice*."

She scowls, but the annoyance doesn't quite reach her eyes. Rather than argue with him about something she knows is true, she digs into her food, shoving a bite into her mouth and chewing a little too violently.

At least temporarily, I've managed to intervene and cut off the start of the inquisition, but it's still coming. Once everyone settles in and has a few bites of food and sips of wine, the questions will start rolling in.

A momentary reprieve...

I accept the passed food, piling my own plate high and offering each item to Allegra, then drape my arm around the back of Allegra's chair and lean in. "I'll give you the quick rundown of everyone. It may help you understand some of the dynamics you'll see tonight, but if you don't remember them all, it's fine."

Her eyes drift over everyone digging into their food. "There's no way..."

Smirking, I start at the head of the table. "Obviously, Nana's in the place of honor. To her left is Skye and her partner Gabe, then their daughter Astrid." She gives us a smile as if she heard her name. "Her twin brother, Atlas, and his fiancée, Wren, aren't here." I sweep over the two empty chairs, my gut tightening. "Next, my Uncle Landon and Aunt Storm and their daughters, Angelina and Alessandra, the blonde one in between them is Jude, Angelina's boyfriend, and Allie's best friend. Next to Al is her boyfriend, Pope. They have a son named Benjamin, who you saw Pope holding when we arrived."

She nods, following my fast non-introductions.

"Then Byron and Luca, Jude's adoptive parents."

When her gaze finally lands on him, she tenses. "Why is he looking at me like that?"

I brush a light kiss to her cheek. "Don't worry about it. Luca looks at everyone like that."

Ignoring his stare as I continue the quick intros and everyone else eats, I move past him. "At the foot of the table is Savage, then his wife, Dani, they're Kennedy's parents. Then Kennedy, the CFO of Hawke Enterprises, her husband, Cass Whitaker, and their daughter, Charlotte. Isaac, his wife, Giacomina, who everyone just calls Jack, and their daughter Viviana. They have a baby boy named Giovanni, who is sleeping somewhere in the house. Then on your other side are Bishop, and her and Pope's parents, Caroline and Saint." Mom gives me a small smile from the end of the table. "And then my parents, Stone and Nora."

"Wow."

She reaches out and grabs her wine, taking a long sip. "You're right, I do need this."

I chuckle and cut into my lasagna. "Things are just getting started."

ALLEGRA

Despite Coen's assurances not to worry about the dark and stormy Luca, a shudder rolls through me under the scrutiny of the man sitting on the other side of the table. Even with several feet of solid wood between us, it doesn't feel completely safe to be in his sights.

I knew when I saw him in Monaco that something was up with him.

He seemed to see right through me, even for the few

seconds we were in the same room together. The way his gaze goes so far beneath the surface and tries to dredge up those things I keep locked away makes me shiver, despite the warmth in the room.

The last thing I want is more scrutiny.

Too much digging is going to resurrect things better left buried.

I reach out and take another sip of my wine to try to calm myself.

Coen was right. I did need this.

The sharp tannins and rich flavor fill my mouth and immediately help settle me slightly, and my hand barely trembles as I place the glass back on the table above my plate that Coen filled with delicious-looking dishes.

Better to concentrate on the food than what one of his uncles may or may not think of me.

As everyone starts eating, chatter fills the room, the focus no longer *completely* on me, though I catch various quick glances in my direction. Especially from Coen's mother, near the end of the table to my left, who seems to be deliberately trying to give me some space rather than bombard me with questions.

With so many people talking, it's impossible to follow the conversations, even as I try to eavesdrop the best I can as I dig into my dinner. The delicious flavors of home-cooked Italian food dance across my stomach, and I issue a little moan at how damn good it is.

Coen's hand slides to my knee again and squeezes, and when I glance at his face, he's barely able to contain a smirk before shoving a bite into his own mouth.

I watch him chew, and his tongue darts out across his lips.

Hell.

Was it really only yesterday that his mouth was devouring me?

If I keep staring at him like I want to eat *him* during dinner, things are going to get a lot more awkward—fast.

As I start to look away, a set of matching blue eyes meets mine from just beyond Coen's side of the table.

Isaac...

The spitting image of the man beside me.

Even if I didn't know they were brothers, it would be obvious. The same strong, chiseled jaw. The same broad shoulders and muscles that make their dress shirts pull with each movement. The same mouth that seems to whisper things even when they aren't saying anything.

He takes a sip of his wine, watching me, and motions between Coen and me. "So, how did you two meet?"

Coen almost chokes on the bite of food in his mouth and pounds against his chest, then grabs his water and drinks, clearing his throat as he glances toward me.

And so, the questions start...

I load up my fork with another bite of baked ziti that might be the best I've ever tasted, anxious to eat rather than spend the evening responding to the inquisitive Hawkes. "I'm a poker player."

A hush settles over the table, all the other conversations dying with my words as if I confessed to murder rather than being a card player.

Shit.

Was I not supposed to say that?

I whip my head toward Coen, trying to figure out why they reacted that way.

Crap.

His clenched jaw tics.

He is *not* happy, and he tenses, almost as if he's waiting for something to explode around us.

Jack leans forward slightly, bracing her forearms on the

table so she can see me better around him. "Did you two meet playing?"

Coen continues to hold my gaze, waiting for my response, but he doesn't do or say anything to stop me or give me any indication I should lie about it. He remains tense, but either he can't or won't intervene in this line of questioning.

I nod. "Yep."

Before anyone can respond, I shovel my food into my mouth. If I'm eating, I can't answer questions and get myself into more trouble, which I very well might have, given how uneasy Coen looks as he returns to eating.

Kennedy grins, her shrewd gaze narrowing on both of us, seeing *far* too much for a woman at the other end of the table from us. "Did you *beat* him?"

Damn.

She is observant.

Or she's just a really good guesser.

I can't fight the pull of the corner of my lips, even though something tells me that I shouldn't be gloating around these people. "I'm batting 500."

Coen's head whips back toward me, his eyes flashing at the use of the analogy he taught me—which seems completely appropriate, given the circumstances.

We've faced each other twice on the felt, and we've each come away victorious once.

But seeing the darkness drifting across his eyes and his quick glance toward his parents and then Isaac, the food I just ate starts to feel more like a rock sitting in my stomach.

It never occurred to me *not* to say that.

That it would be a reminder of what he told me about his family.

I've definitely said the wrong thing.

Savage watches the conversation unfold, chewing slowly

until he finally swallows. "You must be pretty good if you beat *him*..."

I offer a nonchalant shrug, taking a bite of my food, even though I've suddenly lost my appetite, and hoping we'll move on from the interrogation before it takes a turn down a path I am not willing to explore.

Dani offers a kind smile. "Who taught you how to play?"

My shoulders tense, and I force a return half-smile at Savage and his wife. "Just a family friend. It was fun when I was little, and it turns out I'm pretty good at it."

Coen snorts next to me. "Pretty good?" He raises a brow and waggles it playfully, some of the humor returning. "She's a shark."

Luca leans back in his chair, casually swirling his wine, never taking his eyes off me. "Yet you're swimming with her."

Oh, hell...

Coen's hand tightens on his fork hard enough to whiten his knuckles and glares across the table at him.

His "uncle" seems completely unaffected by the look of sheer ire in Coen's eyes. Luca takes a sip of his wine and pointedly raises a dark brow. "Should you be doing that when there's already blood in the water?"

All that food in my stomach now churns at the tension rippling across the table between the two men. Though it seems like *I* should be the one who is glaring at him, based on the fact that the accusation was an attack on *me*.

Coen grits his teeth. "Should you be butting into something that isn't any of your fucking business?"

"Whoa." Nana's eyes shoot between them from her spot at the head of the table. "Language. Play nice..."

Her repetition of Coen's warning to Kennedy draws chuckles from almost everyone around the table—except the man next to me.

His hand slides down across my knee again and squeezes, giving me as much reassurance as he can.

Though it isn't much.

Not when I can still *see* and feel the hostility rolling off Luca like a hurricane coming in off the ocean.

I'm used to having people underestimate me and second-guess my motives. In Coen's case, it's warranted, but his family doesn't know that. They *shouldn't*—unless they're the most perceptive people on the planet. Which I guess they might be, given the looks I'm receiving from several of them.

The one Coen introduced as Angelina smiles at me, waving a hand dismissively toward Luca. "Don't worry about him. Sometimes he forgets he's not the one in charge anymore."

Jude chokes on whatever he's chewing and glances her direction, then quickly darts his gaze toward his father. Byron snickers at the insult tossed at his husband, then takes a drink of his wine, the whole family gawking at Angelina.

She doesn't even seem to notice, glancing up at me between bites. "So, where are you from?"

I push the food around on my plate a little bit. "All over, kind of."

Her little sister, Alessandra, raises a brow. "Army brat?"

I shake my head. "No. My mom was just a bit of a free spirit. We lived mostly on the West Coast, though—California, Oregon, Colorado for a bit."

And that's more than enough about me...

There are thirty people sitting around this table. Which means there *must* be more to talk about besides me.

"What about you?" I scan the table up and down both sides. "Have you all always lived here?"

There are so many of them.

Each of their gazes filled with so many stories when they meet mine.

Gabe digs into his plate, watching me out of the corner of

his eye. "Most of us were born and raised here, except for Landon, Saint, Jack, Vivi, Byron, and Luca." He motions vaguely toward them. "They are our transplants."

I nod and take a bite of the lasagna that's good enough to bring tears. Warm and comforting. It tastes like home. "Thank you again for the invitation. This is all delicious. I haven't had a good home-cooked meal in a long time."

The older woman offers me a kind smile that brightens her eyes. "Your mother doesn't cook for you anymore?"

I still with my fork halfway to my mouth, then swallow through the lump clogging my throat. "She passed away quite a while ago. And she was the only family I had left, so..."

Shrugging, I try to brush off the painful memories threatening to make the *happy* tears that formed only moments ago fall and give away far too much of a past I don't want to relive.

Maybe if I act like none of it really matters, they'll let it go.

Coen's hand tightens on my knee, and Nana gives me a soft smile.

"Well"—she spreads her hands wide—"the Hawkes are very good at taking strays under our wings, aren't we?"

Everyone raises their glasses in a silent toast, then takes a sip of whatever is in front of them.

There are so many people. So many faces. It's hard to know what to say and to whom—or if I should keep my mouth shut and eat until I need to be rolled out of here in a wheelbarrow.

Coen's parents sit to my left, and I catch them watching me as everyone keeps eating during a few moments of relative silence broken only by clanking silverware, groans of approval, and more wine being poured.

Neither has said a *word.*

Not a greeting.

Not even a smile in my direction.

They've both just *watched.*

From Stone, the cold, hard look is chilling. Nora's is warm, though, and she gives me a tight smile, her gaze immediately darting to her youngest son.

Her worry has nothing to do with me.

It's all about *him*.

That makes me feel a little better about them basically ignoring me since we sat down, but the silence is too good to last.

The man Coen described as a ruthless interrogator and cunning lawyer leans forward slightly, resting his forearms on the table. And I'm staring at what Coen will look like in thirty years. "So, where do you call home when you're not out trying to beat my son at the tables?"

I bristle at his question and the barb attached to it, clearing my throat. "I have a place in New York."

He nods slowly, and Luca's dark brows rise at my confession.

I can already see the wheels turning in his head, like he plans to use that offered information somehow.

Coen's mom offers me a kind smile now that her husband has broken the ice. "It was nice of you to come visit him. Have you been to New Orleans before?"

I shake my head. "Never. It was a bit of a spur-of-the-moment trip, actually."

Definitely not planned.

Nor was any of what has happened since I got off that plane.

"Do you plan on staying long?"

Coen turns to me, waiting for me to answer with an anxious energy radiating from him, despite his best efforts to appear impassive.

I meet his gaze and see the hope filling it.

Shit.

"I...uh...haven't decided yet." I take a drink of my wine again, my cheeks heating under the assessment of almost everyone, save for Vivi and Charlotte, who have vacated their seats and run off giggling to the living room. "I do have other obligations."

That hope falters from his eyes, and instantly, regret that I'm going to have to leave—and soon—sits heavy on my chest.

But I can't stay.

It would be bad for both of us.

Him especially.

The last thing Coen needs is a complication like me, and I am definitely becoming one.

We return to eating in mostly silence, various side conversations popping up about things I can't quite follow.

These people all know each other so well. They easily fall into discussions of everyday basic life. Laughing at inside jokes. The couples around the table casually kiss each other or touch, unconcerned that anyone could see.

There's so much love here.

So much *acceptance.*

My throat closes as tears sting my eyes again.

Kennedy's red lips twist in annoyance at something Cass says, and she looks at her father. "Cass and I were just discussing the timeline for the second tower. I think we can get it opened within three months. Do you agree?"

Leaning back in his chair, Cass gives his wife a dubious look, then glances at his father-in-law. "I think it's going to be closer to five."

Savage reclines slightly, drawing his hand across his stubbled jaw. "That all depends on a lot of factors that are out of our control. But now that Coen's back"—his gaze cuts to him— "that should help move things along. We can have him there daily to help monitor and expedite."

Cass nods. "It would be a big help."

Bishop snorts and takes a sip of her drink. "Which means I'll be there."

Saint glances at his daughter. "I can put someone else on him, if you'd rather not be."

The woman who walked in on Coen with his cock buried deep inside me smiles at both of us. "Oh, no. I find protecting Coen quite interesting."

I can't help the little laugh that slips out, and everyone's focus returns to me.

Coen's heated gaze meets mine, and he smirks in a way that promises that no matter what happens at this table the rest of the night, he's going to make it up to me—or make me pay for it —after.

11

ALLEGRA

Coen is on me the second the door to his condo closes behind us, pinning me to the hard wood and slamming his mouth to mine, stealing my breath and trying to take my soul straight from my body.

I groan as he presses into me, his already hard cock pinned between us, grinding against my stomach. Frantic hands bury themselves in my hair, angling my head to give him the access and angle he desires as I cling to his shirt, holding on for dear life as he destroys me with one damn kiss.

It goes on forever.

A thorough exploration. A claiming. A release of something he's been holding on to all night and couldn't contain one moment longer.

And I fall right into it.

Allow myself to drift into that place where all that exists is him and his lips moving over mine.

When he finally tears his mouth away and presses his forehead to mine, he pants heavily, squeezing his eyes closed as if he's searching for some sort of control he's lost along the way tonight.

It takes me a few moments to locate my own. "What was that for?"

He lifts his head, his warm, welcoming eyes meeting mine. "I didn't think you'd come back with me after that."

I shouldn't, but I laugh, releasing my hold on his shirt and spearing my fingers through his thick, dark hair. "You're surprised I survived the inquisition?"

My question makes him chuckle darkly, and he kisses me again, near the corner of my mouth. "That wasn't even bad. You should see them when they really get ramped up. It's like being flayed alive."

A tiny shiver courses through me with the knowledge that he's likely not kidding or exaggerating what that group is capable of. Tonight proved they're more than willing to pepper a complete stranger with invasive and personal questions relentlessly for hours on end.

Even after dinner finished and the table had been cleared, every time I turned around, I found another Hawke there, waiting for me with at least a dozen lines of inquiry ready to throw at me.

I dodged and weaved like a true prize fighter, only answering when necessary and doing my best to divert the attention or involve myself in another discussion or activity that might save me from the worst of it.

And through it all, I learned another very valuable thing about the Hawkes.

I *like* them.

They're good people who are sarcastic, and funny, and who rib each other and push buttons *because* they care. *Because* they love every single person at that house tonight. They care about what happens to them, even if they occasionally irritate nerves and draw ire.

None of it is permanent.

Except the love.

Except that warm feeling of acceptance that seemed to permeate the air there.

That same warmth seeps into me now, staring into Coen's eyes, as if I'm swimming in those Caribbean waters with the summer sun beating down on me.

Coen's hand slips up my dress between my legs, easily finding my slick core. "No panties again..."

I groan at his feather-light touch, the calluses grazing over my skin—a tease more than anything. "I'm nothing if not predictable."

He chuckles low. "You are *anything* but predictable, Allegra Knight."

It almost seems like a compliment.

I gaze up at him, at the need and desire in his eyes, my heart flip-flopping with the urge to either save myself and run or throw myself at this man before I can take that first step. "What are we doing, Coen?"

His gaze darkens from a warm, tropical blue to darker, stormy waters. The kind people get swallowed by and are never seen or heard from again. And that's the way it always feels when I'm like *this* with him—like being swallowed by a storm of passion. "What do you mean?"

What do *I mean?*

It would be so much easier if I actually knew, but the question came out before I had a chance to consider what I was actually asking and why.

Does it matter?

If this is merely lust we have to get out of our systems, then there's nothing wrong with enjoying it while we have the opportunity. If it's something more...

That is where the danger lies.

I press my hands to his chest, his heart beating steadily under them. "I mean *this*. What are we doing?"

"Well..."—he kisses his way over to my ear, warm breath fluttering my hair before he tucks it back—"I know what I *want* to do."

The promise lacing his words makes me press my thighs together against the dull throb centering there, but all I manage to do is pin his hand and earn a throaty growl from him.

And I'm suddenly *very* interested in what Coen has in mind, even if that wasn't what I was asking, and he knows it as well as I do.

"What's that?"

Coen nips at my bottom lip, then pulls it between his teeth before letting it go. "I told you earlier that I took it far too easy on you. Now that we have my place and no interruptions, I think it's time I paid you back."

My pussy clenches, desperately wanting it while that little shiver of fear courses through me, making me question everything I thought I knew about sanity.

"What about you, Allegra? What are *you* doing?"

He raises a brow, waiting for my response, and it takes longer than it should for me to come up with one because staring into his eyes, pressed against the door, it's hard for me to remember why I came back here with him in the first place—other than to feel his touch again, his warmth, his fiery passion all directed at me.

And I know just the way to stoke it further.

"I was thinking..." I trail my fingers down his chest, stopping at his six-pack. "It was time for payback for what you did to me in that restaurant booth."

There are so many ways I could torture this man. So many tricks I could use to leave him breathless and begging the way I was that night...

But the grin he gives me before he presses his lips to mine

and reaches down and grasps my thighs, lifting me easily to wrap them around his waist, tells me that he won't go down without a *fight*.

He carries me through his dark condo, down a hallway, and into what must be his bedroom.

His scent permeates the air.

Masculine.

Crisp.

Like warm ocean waves on a sunny day.

And despite the dark shadow that often seems to hover over him, that's precisely what Coen is—bright and warm. If I didn't know better, I would almost think I'm safe with this man, but we both know there's too much history between us now, too much unsaid and too many lies told to ever really believe that.

It won't stop either of us, though.

Not tonight.

He stalks over to the bed, each step causing his cock to grind in exactly the right spot. I push against him, tightening my thighs, needing the friction, wanting more, and he groans as he lays me down on the comforter and settles on top of me, aligning his strong, hard body over mine.

His lips find my jaw, then my neck as he slides the tiny straps of my dress down my shoulders and exposes my breasts. My nipples pucker, hard as a rock, both from the chilly air in his room and the desperate need for him to touch me, to do something other than get me worked up.

He growls a low approval at the sight of them, then dips his head and takes one in his mouth, lightly grazing his teeth along the turgid peak.

"Fuck!"

My hips buck up against his, grinding, seeking, my body ablaze already after his lingering touches during dinner. Those reassurances he gave me while his family questioned me like it was a job interview.

Each brush of his hand. Every squeeze of his palm. All the lingering glances and half-smiles all proved how protective he can be—even of someone who hasn't given him any reason to be.

If anything, he should be protecting himself from *me*.

From what I am capable of.

But tonight seems more like it will be about what *he* is capable of now that he's gotten me where he wants me.

Our first time together was so frantic. Filled with a burning hatred on his part and a desperate need *not* to break on mine. Tainted by all the things left unsaid and the resentment he felt for me. Lust inextricably entwined with the desire to *win* something that would never be satisfying.

He never explored me.

Never got to know what I like.

What my body responds to.

But I've suddenly realized giving him that opportunity right now might be a bad idea, given his crystal-clear intent.

Pleasure bordering on pain.

Sensual torture.

His hand slips up between my legs and finds my core, easily sinking two fingers into my slick heat. I buck and clench around him, and he holds me steady, clamping his thumb down across my clit, preventing me from moving as he licks and sucks and flicks his tongue across the peak of my breast.

I writhe under him, his body keeping me prone. His mouth swirling and lifting me higher and higher. Each draw on my nipple feels like a direct line to my most sensitive spot. It throbs and aches, and I squirm harder against his tight hold.

He lifts his head. "Sensitive, aren't we?"

It isn't really a question.

More of an observation of a weakness that he will absolutely use against me.

I press my lips together firmly, biting back a strangled moan of frustration that wants to slip out, *refusing* to admit that he's right, that he's discovered my Achilles' heel. But it doesn't do any good because he sees the truth in my gaze and offers a lecherous grin as he drops his head to the other side, giving it the same treatment.

He sucks on it hard, drawing the entire nipple into his mouth, then bites, his tongue quickly spreading over the sharp sting, and my pussy clenches around his fingers.

Not.

Enough.

I try to shift my hips, desperate for some friction, but he refuses to let me move, keeping me pinned.

He wanted to torture me?

Well, he's doing it.

The man has no idea how easily I could come from this, but I think he's starting to understand, given how soaked and slick his hand is where it's buried between my thighs.

He slowly burrows his fingers into me as far as they'll go and withdraws them, dragging them along the inside of my cunt on the retreat. I groan low and deep, my hands clutching at his comforter to try to find *any* purchase.

Any fucking *relief.*

"Could I make you come just by doing this?" He flicks his tongue across my nipple again, then grazes his teeth over the other. "You're soaked, Allegra." He thrusts in and out of me, the sound of my embarrassingly wet arousal filling the otherwise silent room. "I think I could."

He drops lower, kissing his way across my abdomen as he drags my dress down over my hips.

His tongue dips into my belly button, and I buck like a wild horse desperate to free itself from the bridle. He pulls his hand free of my legs long enough to pull my only clothing off and tosses it on the floor. Leaving me fully naked. Exposed to him with nowhere to hide.

Coen settles back over me, still fully clothed, and very obviously enjoying his little game with me, evidenced by the way he lifts his glistening fingers to his mouth and licks them greedily. His hand returns to offering torturous ministrations, moving inside me, curling and thrusting but never *quite* where I need it, while my nipples ache for more of the treatment they just received.

"I can't let you come that easily, Allegra. What fun would that be?"

I groan, arching into him. "Sounds fun to me..."

The low chuckle that rumbles through him doesn't give me any hope of it happening fast.

Coen is going to make this hard.

And God knows he has it in him not to allow it at all because he wants to demonstrate that he is the one in control after I've proven I can take it away from him with a smile, a glance, a touch.

He slips back onto his knees, pulling his fingers free from inside me—

I push up onto my elbows. "No, don't—"

A sly grin plays on his lips, and he shifts off the end of the bed and slowly starts to unbutton his white dress shirt.

Each one that pops free exposes more lightly tanned flesh...

Hard, broad chest...

Immaculately sculpted abdominal muscles...

Fuck, he's beautiful.

That body was *earned.*

The callouses on his hands that so surprised me the first time the rough skin dragged against mine told me he was so much more than he first appeared.

Not just a pretty rich boy.

He has *worked.*

Hard.

This billionaire heir does the things that need to be done, regardless of what they are.

And it has done him *good.*

He shucks off his shirt, letting it fall to the floor with my dress, then reaches for his fly, popping the button and undoing the zipper on his dress pants before he slips out of them, allowing his cock to spring free.

God...

This man has been inside me.

Moving.

Grinding.

Touching.

Fucking me into oblivion.

It's barely been twenty-four hours, yet all I want is more of him.

All of him.

He steps up to the edge of the bed and easily grasps my hips and flips me onto my stomach in a move that demonstrates just how fucking strong he is.

Fuck.

I've never particularly enjoyed being manhandled during sex, but there's something about Coen Hawke and the way he controls everything, allows me to just be and forget all the reasons life has made this such a terrible idea.

He leans over me, pressing his hot cock between my ass cheeks, nipping at my shoulder. Lips drag over the spot. Then he pulls my hair over to one side, tilting my face back to look at him. "You know what game I want to play, Allegra. This is your last chance to concede."

I suck in a sharp breath, trying to fill my lungs before I know he's going to do things to me that won't allow me to anymore. "I already told you. I love to play, and I thrive on challenge."

"Oh, Allegra, that is the wrong fucking thing to say to a man like me."

COEN

ALLEGRA LOOKS LIKE A STUNNING, heavenly gift spread out before me. An angelic offering from God. Her skin practically glows against my dark comforter in the moonlight shining through the window. Like a beacon drawing me to her.

A moth to a flame.

Though, maybe the Devil sent her.

A wicked, beautiful temptress sent to test my resolve after I've already committed so many horrible sins. A final trial before the fate of my soul is sealed for eternity.

So many mistakes.

So many sins built on stupidity, greed, and hubris.

I've accepted that I have to pay the price for them.

But none compare to what I want to do to Allegra. The sins I want to engage in with her.

So many ways I want to take her and make her beg.

So many ways to make her scream my name...

So.

So.

Many.

But I have to be patient. Choose my words and my actions carefully. And patience is very hard for a man like me.

Rushing into things without fully thinking them through is what got me in my position with Satriano in the first place. It's what made me keep playing while I was losing. Taking chances I *never* would have otherwise. It's what made me believe one bet could cure it all and allowed me to disregard the potential ramifications because I *believed* I couldn't lose.

And Allegra might well be another in a long line of bad choices resulting from rash decisions.

I knew she was dangerous the moment I saw her at that bar, but it didn't stop me then. It didn't matter that I thought she was a professional. I would have taken her back to my suite and fucked her senseless anyway.

Even confirmation of what she's capable of hasn't been enough to keep me away.

Nothing could right now.

Not now that I know what she tastes like.

Not now that I've had her incredible cunt wrapped around my cock.

Not now that I've seen her come alive with my family and really be *her* instead of the version of herself she thinks she has to be at the poker table.

Tonight, I saw her be shy.

Sweet.

Generous with her time and affection when it came to Viviana and Charlotte wanting to monopolize her.

She was everything I didn't know was there but had the smallest hope might exist beneath the façade.

And tonight, she's *all* mine.

I drag her hips back and up so her ass is in the air, a beautiful offering, her glistening pussy right there for the taking. My palm curves around each cheek, her smooth skin so soft and flawless. Dropping to my knees, I bury my face between her legs, feasting on her wet cunt, her arousal coating my tongue and filling my mouth as I lick it from her quivering thighs and lips.

"Fuuuck..."

She jerks against my face, and I wrap my arm around her thighs, tugging her back, keeping her there.

Immobilized.

At my mercy.

My cock aches the longer I eat her sweet pussy, and I reach down and grab it with my free hand, stroking the length several times. Twisting my wrist. Tugging sharply. Brushing my fingers over the slick pre-cum on the head. Until I can't take it anymore...

I have to be inside her.

I have to take her.

Waiting any longer wouldn't just be torture for her.

It's driving me to the brink of madness.

I release my grip on her, push to my feet, and drag my cock through her wetness, coating the head thoroughly before I slam into her. Driving her forward and down onto her forearms. Rocking her completely off her knees.

She gasps, taking *all* of me from this angle, her ass cheeks bouncing with the thrust.

So.

Fucking.

Deep.

I bottom out inside her, driven all the way to the hilt.

A low growl of appreciation rumbles through me, and Allegra's cunt squeezes along my length in response. I grasp her hips, fingers biting into the flesh, and draw back until only the head of my cock remains inside her.

Her pussy clenches, trying to draw me in, and I don't have the ability to stop my hips from rocking forward, from plunging into her again.

"Oh, God..." Her strangled cry echoes through my room with every thrust and retreat. "Oh, fuuuuck, Coen!"

It's the single most beautiful sound I've ever heard.

I roll my hips, dragging the head of my cock along that spot deep inside her. She twitches, clasping and unclasping, gripping, desperate to keep me in each time I withdraw.

Her hands twist in the comforter, and she buries her face in it, her cries muffled but the sound of skin slapping against skin fills the room.

But it isn't enough.

Not yet.

I pull my cock free.

Allegra whimpers, pushing up to look over her shoulder at me. "Why'd you—"

I drag my thumb through her drenched core, then slip it up around her most forbidden place. She jerks at the contact, and as I thrust my cock back into her waiting cunt, I slowly slide my thumb into her tight, puckered hole.

A muffled groan falls from her parted lips, and she drops back down, pressing her forehead into the comforter, squeezing in both places enough to force me to grit my teeth and dig deep to find every ounce of self-control I have left so I don't come immediately.

Somehow, I knew what she needed.

What she wanted, even if she couldn't voice it.

I rock my thumb in and out of her in time with my cock.

Slow and lazy.

Not at all the way I want to take her.

But if that's what she wants—hard and rough—that's not what I'm going to give her.

Not this time.

I want her close to the edge for so long that she's begging for it, frantic, completely losing herself for something that only *I* can give her.

And apparently, I was right about what she wants.

Because the more I fuck her in long, slow, deep thrusts, the deeper I shove my thumb, the harder her body trembles. Her pussy ripples. Her face buried in the comforter muffles her muttered curses, but the way she clenches the fabric and my cock tells me everything her words can't.

She finally turns her head to the side so I can hear her. "Motherfucking Goddamn prick!"

I grin at her insult and the fact that she doesn't know how much it turns me on to know I've brought her to the point that those words are falling from her mouth.

Leaning forward, I press my free hand down next to her face to support my weight and kiss her cheek. "If you want me to be a prick, sweetheart, this isn't anything. I can certainly honor that request."

She whimpers as I still inside her, buried deep, holding her immobile on my cock and hand.

"If I wanted to, I could do this for *hours*, leaving you hanging, wanting, desperate. And completely at my mercy."

To prove my point, I drag my thumb out, then push it all the way into her asshole again, and she groans, tightening around it the same way she does my aching length.

Like a fucking vise.

I brush the hair from the side of her face and lick her ear. "You like that, Allegra, my finger in your ass?"

Another whimper and an almost imperceptible nod.

"I thought so." I pull my hips back slowly so she can feel every inch of my cock, then plunge into her again deep. "And that's very good because I'm going to fuck your ass."

She freezes, her body going rigid, her eyes fluttering open to meet mine.

"Have you ever had anyone in here before?" I thrust my thumb in and out of her, and she shakes her head, that low rumble of approval rushing through me again. "Good."

I'll be your first and your last.

I don't say those words, but they somehow echo in my head all the same.

They feel right.

No.

Fuck no.

You cannot fall for this woman, Coen.

She's toxic and came to me with an agenda from day one. Plus, it would be stupid and selfish to expose her to the kind of danger I'm smack dab in the middle of with Satriano. But Christ, does she feel good wrapped around me, clenching my cock, her body so responsive and primed.

"Do you want it, Allegra?" I plunge into her again in both places to drive home my point. "Do you want my cock up your ass?"

The mewl that falls from her lips as she nods sounds less human and more animal, and an addictive rush goes through me at knowing she does. And that only makes me want to withhold it from her more.

I slip my thumb out, and she groans and looks over her shoulder at me as I continue to thrust into her cunt slowly, then stand fully and drag her hips back and up, spreading her knees even wider to change the angle and redouble my efforts.

Gasps fall from her parted lips.

Her body trembles so hard it shakes the bed as much as my thrusts do.

My fingers dig into her hips.

And I can't keep pretending this isn't torture for me, too.

I unleash.

Fucking her *hard.*

Long.

Sharp.

Punishing strokes.

A rhythm that won't allow me to last much longer.

The slap of our skin and bodies coming together echoes violently around the room.

She gasps and cries out, clutching the comforter, and the way she begs for release might as well be fucking kerosene being thrown on the fire that's been raging since the moment our eyes met at that bar.

I reach around and find her clit, clenching it between my thumb and forefinger and twisting it as I continue to drive into her, unable to keep the game up any longer.

Allegra told me what she wants.

But I'm not going to give it to her tonight.

I have to keep something from her, hold something back to protect myself.

That's becoming harder and harder.

After seeing her at the Hawke table, surrounded by the entire family, everyone I love and care about, everyone I'm doing all this for, it felt almost right to have her there.

Like she belonged.

Just like she belongs *here*. In my condo. In my bed. In my arms. Locked together in the most intimate way imaginable, with nothing between us except the lies I still feel like she's telling me—or at least the things she's holding back.

I *know* she isn't being one hundred percent honest with me. It's obvious since I was taught to sniff out a liar from a mile away at a very young age by the man who excels at it in the courtroom, but even knowing that, I can't bring myself to walk away.

And that's fucking terrifying.

I can't fall for a woman like Allegra, who's walking sex and danger and lies and ulterior motives.

They ooze out of her the same way my cum does from my cock as I bury myself to the hilt and her pussy clenches and drags out my orgasm. I collapse on top of her and roll to the side, dragging her with me, keeping myself embedded deep inside her.

It takes several moments before I can process thoughts again after that. The little rapid-fire shocks of pleasure still making my body twitch and my brain foggy.

But one thing screams at me with crystal clarity.

Something I should have demanded before we made it this far.

Before I brought her to Nana's.

Before I introduced her to the entire family.

Before I allowed myself to give a damn about her.

Kissing the back of her sweat-dampened neck, I brush my lips against her ear. "You want my cock again...anywhere..."—I glide my palm over her ass cheek—"then I'm going to need you to come clean about everything. Do you understand?"

I can't do this if I can't trust her.

She nods but doesn't say anything before her body sags even more and she drifts off to sleep.

12

COEN

Well played.

The two words scrawled across the king of hearts stare back at me.

Taunting me.

Making everything that happened last night, all that I shared with Allegra into a trivial joke—just another fucking game to her.

I flip the card between my fingers, gritting my jaw so hard that it actually hurts, my brain stuck in a constant loop of feeling like a fucking idiot since the moment I found the card sitting on the nightstand when I woke this morning—to an empty bed where Allegra should have been.

All I found were cold sheets and this even colder note.

It's not that I really expected her to stay long...

But I hadn't anticipated her not even saying goodbye.

She just...vanished.

Into thin air.

As if she were merely a figment of my imagination.

The only proof I have that any of it happened was the taste of her on my tongue and the smell of us on my sheets. And this damn *note*.

Whatever the fuck it's supposed to be...

A goodbye.

A fuck you.

A threat.

I slide the card into my back pocket before making my way up the stairs to Mom and Dad's porch. Bright flowers spill out of the planters, and Mom's swing sways lightly in the morning breeze.

Peaceful.

Home.

The old Victorian house Dad meticulously renovated will always be that, no matter how long I've lived on my own. No matter how far away I travel, chasing a game or seeking an escape. No matter how restless I may get staying here for too long, this place is where I'll return.

Always.

I punch the access code into the electronic lock and push the door open. "Mom? Dad?"

Stepping in, I pause and wait for any signs that they're still here.

Dad is supposed to be "retiring" and limiting his time at the office, but we all know that isn't really happening, much to Mom's chagrin. And she shows absolutely no signs of even *considering* leaving her job at the hospital, so this is about the time of morning they start taking off.

I hope I caught him...

This isn't a conversation I want to have in front of Isaac at the office.

Mom pokes her head out from the kitchen at the back of

the house. "Coen, what are you doing here?"

I close the door behind me and approach as she sets down her coffee mug on the counter. "I need to talk to Dad."

Her eyes narrow, the green flashing with immediate concern. Is everything okay?"

No, not at all.

Nothing has been okay for a very long time.

And I don't even have the guts to go to Uncle Savage and Gabe and tell them about my unexpected visit from Satriano.

I'll let Dad do the dirty work.

He can relay all the relevant information from the shakedown. After all, he's the only one who could ever really understand how I got into a position like this. He can't judge me—much—considering what he did for Abello all those years ago.

At least, that's my hope.

A sliver of understanding.

I certainly won't get it anywhere else.

Every day I've been back, it has been like walking on eggshells around everyone, with them all watching me with that *look* in their eyes, as if they expect me to break at any point.

Or they're waiting for the other shoe to fall.

Mom squeezes me tightly, then pulls back, searching my face, clasping my cheeks between her palms—fully in *doctor mom* mode now. That look is all too familiar. The one she wears when she knows there's something wrong and she's desperate to fix it with a hug, a long talk, or medication, if necessary.

Her intelligent eyes look for any signs of illness or injury. "Baby, you're worrying me."

I force a tight smile. "I'm okay, really. It's been good being back, working at the hotel..."

It isn't a complete lie.

I actually enjoy it there far more than I have any of the other Hawke establishments I've spent time in over the years, slinging drinks, helping wait tables, managing other employees at the various businesses.

Maybe it's because it's a casino; somehow, it feels more like home after how much time I've basically lived in them. Maybe it's knowing how important the success of Hawke Hotel is to everyone. Or maybe it's because what I do there—help put out fires and manage the property—feels like something I'm actually *good* at.

Mom doesn't appear convinced, though.

Squeezing her wrists, I pull her hands down. "Really."

She lets out a long sigh as footsteps sound on the stairs, interrupting whatever medical rundown she would have probably given me otherwise.

Every muscle in my body tenses, waiting, and I turn to see Dad making his way down slowly. Left hand braced on the banister. Right on the cane he now needs, since one of Satriano's bullets tore through his hip and damaged the nerves in his leg.

His gaze lands on me and narrows immediately. "Is everything okay?"

Because I would never just be here to say hello to him and Mom...

If I'm here, it means I've fucked up again. He doesn't *say* that, but he doesn't have to. The look he's giving me—and the one Mom did the moment I walked in the door—is enough to convey it loud and clear.

Mom sighs, squeezing my arm before stepping away to the counter and grabbing her coffee again. "He says it is but that he needs to talk to you about something."

Dad finally reaches the bottom step and makes his way into the kitchen, glancing back at me. "Coffee?"

I shake my head. "No thanks. I'm going to stop by the Grind before I head to the hotel."

He sets to work making it while Mom downs whatever is left in her mug, sets it in the sink, and gathers her purse from the stool at the counter. "Well, I was just on my way to the hospital, but if you need me to stay—"

"No, Mom. I appreciate the concern, but—"

She holds up a hand. "Don't you tell me it is unwarranted or that I'm overreacting. You disappeared for a *month*, Coen. Not even a damn phone call to tell us you were all right and not dead at the bottom of the ocean or being tortured in Satriano's dungeon somewhere. Don't *ever* do something like that to me again."

There it is.

One of those *things* people haven't been saying but that I can see in their eyes. Hearing her finally voice it makes my chest tighten—the guilt threatening to suffocate me.

Of all the people I left behind when I disappeared from the wedding, Mom was the hardest for me.

And apparently it was for her, too.

I'm surprised it's taken her this long to finally unleash on me.

Nora Hawke doesn't get angry often, but when she does, no one wants to be on the receiving end of it. But staring at her tear-soaked eyes now, I can see that she isn't angry.

She's devastated that I did it and terrified I'll do it again.

With good reason.

We all understand this is *far* from over.

"I won't, Mom..."

My reassurance seems hollow when I don't *really* know what Satriano will demand from me, but it's the best I can offer her at this point.

Some of the pain melts away from her face, and she kisses my cheek and heads over to Dad. He tugs her into his arms, pulling her fully against him, then dips his head and whispers something into her ear that I can't hear. It has her cheeks pinkening before she kisses him gently.

"I'll see you later." She winks. "And I'll hold you to that."

I look away from them, focusing on the patterned tile rather than their affectionate display.

At least it improved her mood.

She slips out the back door to head to the carriage house where her car is parked, and I lower myself onto one of the stools while Dad stands across from me with his own mug, resting his cane against the marble countertop.

He takes a sip, eyeing me over the rim. "So, what did you need to talk to me about?"

I sigh, scrubbing my hand over my face.

Is it too early to drink?

The man in front of me would tear me a new asshole for even joking about that, given his sordid history, but this would be easier with some liquid courage.

It was hard enough being at dinner last night and not saying anything, not letting them know that Satriano had finally made an appearance—and his first demand. I couldn't do it before Allegra arrived. If I had, the entire night would have been focused on *that*, and I don't need her dragged into my mess.

But there isn't any running from it anymore.

I have to tell him.

"Satriano came to see me."

His entire body stiffens, his hand tightening its grip on the mug. "When?"

Clearing my throat, I avert my gaze rather than see the inevitable reaction. "Saturday night."

"And you're just telling me now?"

I glance up at him and see the smoldering mix of concern and anger in his blue eyes. "I didn't want to ruin Sunday dinner, especially with Allegra there. She doesn't need to get pulled into this bullshit."

Apparently, I didn't need to worry about it, since she intended on leaving without warning the entire time.

He presses his lips together in a firm line, a muscle in his jaw ticcing wildly as he stares me down. "What did he say?"

Not a lot.

And that's what has been bothering me since the moment he walked out of my place.

I rub my neck, staring out the window that overlooks the garden in the back where Isaac and I spent most of our childhood. "Well, he wants his money..."

"And then?"

Releasing a little sigh, I turn back to Dad. "And then, he wants me to help him stack games at his casinos."

Dad's brow furrows deeply. "*His* casinos?"

I nod slowly. "Apparently, he's been buying them up along the Gulf Coast."

And he *knew* I would tell the rest of the Hawkes about this development.

It wasn't by *chance* that the man appeared when he did. I've been home for over a week, and he chose that *moment* to come to my place for a reason. Just like he chose now to let it be known what he's been up to—becoming our biggest competitor.

"Shit." Dad scrubs his hand over his cheek. "How did we not know about this?"

"How does he get away with any of this without us knowing what's going on?"

"I guess it shouldn't be a surprise." Dad leans his hip against the counter, relaxing slightly, but really, I know he's taking the weight off his bad leg. "After all, this shit with him all started with him trying to partner with Cass when he was Falco Enterprises to open the hotel casino across from us. It makes sense he wouldn't completely abandon that business plan. It's a surefire way to fuck with us. And there is a lot of money in it..."

"And a lot of ways to rig the system in his favor on the casino floor."

Dad's eyes meet mine, and he nods.

The more I think about it, the more obvious this move becomes. And the dumber I feel for not having seen it coming. "There's a reason the mob went to Vegas and dug their heels in. And apparently, Damon thinks that bringing me in to play and stack the tables is going to help his bottom line."

"Well"—Dad sighs—"I suppose there are worse things he could ask you to do…"

That's exactly what worries me.

Satriano won't battle us for supremacy in this hotel and casino war. He will just eliminate us any way he can—and now he has an inside man.

"It's too easy, Dad."

He nods, his salt-and-pepper hair shifting with the movement as he sets his mug in front of him on the counter. "I know, son."

"This is only the beginning."

Without any way of anticipating what his end game might be.

We've never been able to, when it comes to Satriano. He appeared from the literal grave after Isaac killed Leonardo and slowly worked his way into our lives while observing us undetected. Then he struck—hard and fast—and caused irreparable damage in his bid to take over New Orleans from Roselli.

Each blow hurt the Hawkes more and more.

Dad is living proof of the damage he caused.

Yet, the man continues to string us along. To play us in some sinister chess game where we can't see the board or strategize our next moves.

"You haven't told anyone else about meeting with him?"

I shake my head. "I didn't know how to. I can't—" Emotion lodges in my throat, and I try to swallow past it. "I can't keep apologizing when nothing's getting better. Things are only getting worse…"

My hands start to shake, all the frustration and guilt and need to destroy the man who now has me in a chokehold finally boiling over.

"Fuck!"

I grab Dad's mug and chuck it across the kitchen.

It shatters against the tile, ceramic and coffee splattering across the pristine floor, the same way it feels like I've been splintered since the moment I made the biggest mistake of my life.

Dad barely flinches.

He casually glances at the damage. "I understand how you're feeling, son. I've been there. How do you think I felt when I discovered what *I* had done? What those actions had wrought?"

Tears burn in my eyes, ones I've been holding in for months, refusing to let fall because it felt like caving, like surrendering. "What the fuck do I do? I can't tell him no, and God only knows what he'll ask of me next."

Dad offers me a grim look. "You know we'll figure something out. We always do. I'll talk to everyone today. We'll come up with a plan now that we know about his hotels. We'll dig. We'll find his weakness and a way to take him out."

That reassurance should make me feel better, but somehow it doesn't.

Mostly because no plan ever seems to be enough to counteract whatever Satriano is planning.

And something tells me it goes far beyond what he's already asked of me.

ALLEGRA

THE LOCK on the hotel room door beeps as I swipe my card across it. I push open the door and step in, letting it close behind me with a heavy *click* that seems to echo through the still, silent, impersonal space.

There's nothing homey or friendly about it. Not at all like the warmth I felt in that penthouse at the Hawke Hotel.

This place is sterile.

Feels empty, despite being fully furnished with high-quality finishes and pricy accessories.

Still, I breathe a heavy sigh of relief at making it inside this door safely.

Thank God, I didn't stay at the Hawke Hotel.

Coen would've come after me.

I know that without a shadow of a doubt.

At least this way, I have a chance of getting out of here without having to see him again. Without having to look into those infinite blue eyes and find all that passion that filled them last night, along with something far different than the hatred I found there when I arrived only two days ago.

Less than forty-eight hours since I touched down in NOLA.

Things changed.

We went too hard, too fast.

Like a runaway train, we barreled down an unknown track, completely unaware of where it led or what might await us at the end—and it turns out it was heartache.

For both of us.

Because I heard his words last night as I fell asleep.

His demand that I come clean and tell him everything.

As if it's that easy.

I step farther into the suite, tossing my purse onto one of the chairs before I make my way into the bedroom and straight to the bathroom, kicking the door closed behind me and cranking on the water in the shower as hot as it'll go.

It still won't be able to match the scalding heat of that man.

Dammit.

The moment I left the Hawke Hotel on Saturday, I should have headed straight to the airport and flown back to New York. I should have ignored the pull to Coen. Declined the invitation to dinner from his family. Locked away my own desire to see him again and to learn more about him.

He was just supposed to be a mark.

But somehow, Coen Hawke has marked *me*.

He's permanently seared himself into my skin, and I don't know if it will ever be possible to shake him or this feeling.

I have to try.

And there's only one way to do that—I have to put as much distance between us as possible and keep it that way.

The plane should be ready and waiting on the tarmac within an hour. With the car service already waiting for me outside after bringing me back here from Coen's this morning, it won't take long for me to flee New Orleans and put Coen Hawke squarely where he belongs—locked away in the mistakes of my past.

Steam starts to flood the bathroom, and I slip out of my dress, letting it fall to the floor so I can step under the hot spray.

I need to wash that man off me.

His touch...

His scent...

It's already hard enough to think clearly without it clinging to me.

The thought of you walking around the rest of the day with my cum dripping out of you is pretty much the highlight of my existence up until now...

His words from the other night haunt me as if he were standing in the shower with me right now, saying them in my ear as he pumps inside me with purpose.

I reach between my legs and feel the evidence of last night, still slick inside me. Proof that it was real. That *he* was real. That the pleasure and connection were very, very *real.*

Maybe the only real thing in my life anymore when so much of it is acting and playing games.

"Fuck..."

Hot tears pool in my eyes, and I drop my forehead against the tile, letting the spray beat down on my shoulders and back. My limbs quiver with the memory of his touch, of his cock slamming into me, of the way his mouth moved over every inch of my body and centered right between my legs where my hand is now.

Dammit.

The throb.

The ache.

The need still lingers there.

Even after a night like that, I still want *more.*

Despite my best efforts not to give in to the need, my fingers roll across my clit of their own accord, knowing exactly what I crave.

A tiny moan slips from my lips, and I remember how it felt to have his hand there, those calloused fingertips, that wicked tongue...

All those sinful parts of him.

Coen Hawke is absolutely nothing like I thought he would be. How a man can be so intense, so brutal in so many ways, yet also bring so much pleasure is one giant mind fuck that I am not prepared to try to sort through. Nor do I have the time.

Need to leave.

But at this moment, another need overpowers that self-preservation instinct. I brush my fingers across my clit, my hips bucking at the sensation and memory of what he so expertly did there.

Rough.

Harsh.

So.

Fucking.

Good.

I slip two fingers inside me, rubbing my thumb over my clit as I thrust into myself, groaning at the feel of my already swollen flesh after an entire night under him, and over him, and in front of him. A glorious night of coming more times than I could even count...

My orgasm comes quickly, barreling through me, leaving me shaking and gasping under the waterfall.

I pull my trembling hand away, stepping back fully into the water and turning my face up to it.

It does nothing to wash away the memories that I feel are likely going to cling to me for far longer than I would like them to.

Leave.

The Hawkes are the type to go to great lengths to keep me here if they want me to remain in New Orleans. Coen could easily find me, using his connections and resources at the various hotels in town. Even though I'm here under a fake name, I don't have any doubt he could track me down—given enough time.

And I need to be gone before he does.

I quickly shampoo and condition my hair, then scrub my body of the remnants of the man who will not be so easily forgotten from my dreams.

Don't.

The more I think about it, about *him*, the harder it's going to be to get on that plane. Already, the thought makes me almost queasy. I turn off the water, climb out of the shower, and towel off, wrapping myself in a big, fluffy hotel robe before tugging open the door and stepping out into the bedroom and the much cooler air.

Goosebumps immediately cover my skin, and I glance at the clock on the nightstand that seems to taunt me.

Each passing minute is one Coen could show up at my door.

I dig through my still-packed weekender bag and pull on a thong, a pair of leggings, and a loose T-shirt, then throw everything from the bathroom counter into my luggage.

It isn't much, and it doesn't take me long to be fully packed and ready to go.

Always be prepared to make a quick exit.

It was one of those life lessons that always seemed so strange as a child, but I finally understand its importance.

I step out into the living room portion of my suite to grab my purse and go meet the car outside, but I freeze at the familiar eyes staring at me from the chair across the space.

Icy.

Cold.

He leans back casually, but given the posture and what I know about the man, it's anything *but* casual. This is an ambush, a very intentional one.

All I can do is stand here like a deer stuck in the headlights, watching them race closer while there's nothing I can do to stop them or leap out of the way. "W-what are you doing here?"

One brow rises slowly. "I could ask you the same thing."

Shit.

"I...thought you were out of town..."

The corners of his lips twitch, but it isn't with amusement. It's *annoyance.* I would recognize *that* look anywhere. "Is that why you came? Because you thought I wouldn't know?"

"No—"

He doesn't give me any time to object or explain further. "*Sit.*"

My spine snaps to attention at the command in the single word, and I tighten my hand on the strap of my bag, desperate to cling to literally anything solid right now when it feels like everything is spinning out of control.

There isn't any way to escape what's about to happen.

Too much has already been set in motion.

Things I can't take back.

I was so terrified about Coen finding me, about him confronting me about last night and why I ran this morning.

But I was worried about the wrong person...

Slowly, I lower myself into one of the chairs facing him, and his gaze rakes over me, assessing and finding me wanting.

My unexpected visitor releases a long, low sigh, his eyes scanning over me. "I'm disappointed, Allegra. You were supposed to get close to him, watch him, make sure he wasn't going to fuck me over. What you absolutely weren't supposed to do was fuck *him*."

13

FOUR DAYS LATER

COEN

Frank Sinatra croons through the speakers while just outside the window to the left of my table, lights dance and water shoots from the Bellagio fountain in a choreographed dance intended to captivate.

I stare at the show but barely see it, taking a sip of my pre-dinner drink. A huge part of me wishes I could delight in the spectacle the way the tourists lined up along the front of the fountain do.

They *ooh* and *ahh*. Take photos and videos. Some dance on the filthy Las Vegas Boulevard sidewalk. Others just gape at the display, stunned by its grandeur and beauty.

There was a time when I was the same.

When I could *enjoy* moments like this.

Sitting in a beautiful restaurant with a good drink in one of the most exciting cities in the world, watching a show made of nothing but water, lights, and music, that has become one of the major tourist spots in a town filled with them.

Not tonight.

Maybe not any night ever again.

My dark mood has followed me since Monday morning when I woke up to an empty bed and then had to go have that very uncomfortable conversation with Dad. As I had hoped, he did the "dirty work" and explained to the rest of the family precisely what went down when Satriano met with me, what he asked me to do, and the interesting information I learned about his new businesses.

But my mood didn't get any better as the week progressed, compounded by the various "mini emergencies" that seemed to pop up around the hotel and casino.

Keys that wouldn't work.

Malfunctioning machines.

Drunk patrons.

They're just growing pains.

We've been open for less than six weeks.

There are bound to be complications and minor problems here and there. That's true of any business, especially one that caters to tourists in a city like New Orleans. But now it's become *my* job to ensure they're resolved.

Since the moment I returned home, I was thrust into this role at the hotel, which I hadn't expected to be waiting for me when I got back. It's important—work Savage or Gabe or even Cass should be handling. But they have enough on their plates, and somehow, they handed it to me like it was always intended to be that way.

Executive General Manager.

I'm not even sure *what* that title means, but at least staying busy kept me from having too much free time to dwell on how Allegra disappeared or the gaping hole it seemed to leave in my heart when it shouldn't have mattered.

She's not the type of girl who stays.

I knew that the first time I met her.

But I let one incredible night together somehow convince

my better judgment to take a hike and allow my soul to desire hers in a way that is truly unhealthy.

Evidenced by my current inability to even watch the show outside with any hint of joy.

Bishop observes me from her seat across the table from me. "Are you going to be like this the whole trip?"

Fingering my glass, I scowl at her. "You didn't have to come with me."

She raises a brow. "To Vegas or to dinner?"

"Either."

She snorts and swirls her fruity drink before she takes a sip and tosses her long braids over her bare shoulder, exposed in the silvery thin-strapped dress that hugs her toned body. "Yeah, right. Like anyone, including me, was going to let you leave town again without an escort."

Tonight, she doesn't look like she's working as my body-guard. She's ready to go out on the town, even though she knows full well I never do the night before a tournament.

A nice dinner.

Perhaps a few drinks.

Then to bed early so I'm prepared for what will meet me at the table.

I pull my glass to my lips and take a long drink. "You mean a fucking *babysitter*."

She grins. "Same thing, isn't it?" Leaning back slightly in her chair, she tips her drink toward me. "And maybe if you hadn't run last time, you wouldn't need one."

Smartass.

I scowl at her and return to watching the water show. At least *it* can't talk back and point out very accurate facts that I don't want to be reminded of. Like that Satriano got to me so easily less than a week ago when I should have been untouch-able—something Gabe, Saint, and Bishop have been looking into almost non-stop since.

"Did you or your dad ever figure out how Satriano got into my building?"

It's a low blow, a dig at her ability to actually *do* this job, and she knows it. But Bishop doesn't ruffle easily—if at all.

She lets it roll off her back. "No...which is why we changed the code for the elevator in your building and your condo. The best guess from the tech guy, as of when I talked to Dad earlier today, was that Satriano somehow hacked the digital system, got in through the back door, and used a skeleton code to get up."

That's comforting.

I'm about to tell her as much when Bishop issues a low whistle. "Well, I'll be damned..."

The surprise in Bishop's voice draws my attention from the window and toward her, but she isn't looking at me.

She's watching the front of the restaurant, and I follow her gaze.

My heart stops for a second, then begins to beat rapidly as Allegra approaches, weaving her way through the tables and around waitresses and waiters, the slit in her slinky red dress revealing her entire leg with each step.

Good God...

I down the rest of my drink and motion to our waiter for another one as she reaches us, but she doesn't look at me.

She focuses on Bishop, offering her a genuine smile—or at least I think it is. It's almost impossible to tell if *anything* is genuine with this woman. "Bishop, it's nice to see you again."

Bishop raises her brows slowly at Allegra, then glances over at me. She may not have any idea what really happened between us earlier this week, but given my foul mood before we came—and now—she must have a pretty good guess. "Is it?"

"I didn't mean to interrupt." Allegra finally allows her gaze to slide to mine. "But I figured you'd be here the night before the tournament, and I hoped we could talk."

It's my turn to raise a brow at her. "Talk?"

There are so many things I would love to say to this woman, that I *would* have if she hadn't disappeared from my arms, my bed, my condo, my fucking city like a damn thief in the night.

Even with my people trying to locate her, they didn't have any luck.

She wanted to vanish into thin air and did a damn good job of it.

And she clearly didn't give a single fuck how it affected me.

Yet she wants to talk...

Allegra pleads with her eyes the same way she did when she was under me, begging for me to give her release less than a week ago. I eventually caved to her then—gave in to my most base need to see *hers* met, despite my desire to make it last and ensure she understood what it's like to be on the receiving end of the Hawke ire.

I gave in to *her*.

Everything in me screams not to do it again.

Not to let her in.

Not to give her even a single inch.

Because she's the type of woman who will take that inch and turn it into a mile—maybe more.

But I've never been particularly good at listening to my better judgment.

It's what got me in this mess in the first place.

I turn my gaze to Bishop. "Would you mind finishing your drink at the bar...where you can keep an eye on me?"

God knows she isn't going to *leave* the restaurant. She's my permanent shadow for as long as this Satriano business continues, which doesn't seem to have an end in sight.

Bishop scowls but pushes to her feet, adjusting her dress. "Fine, but as soon as my food arrives, I'm coming back."

Allegra offers her a knowing grin. "Fair enough. I wouldn't want to miss it, if I were you, either."

Offering me one last long look of warning, Bishop stalks away in her heels, a strange mix of power, muscle, and grace that only she can pull off. She slides onto an empty stool at the end of the bar, only a few yards from us, but far enough away and separated by enough tables that she won't be able to hear our conversation.

Something tells me I won't want her to.

Allegra slowly lowers herself into the chair across from me, her gaze reserved, the usual energy she exudes dimmed by something I can't quite place.

Regret?

Does she actually feel bad *about how she just left me?*

That would be hoping for too much, and I learned long ago that having any sort of dreams only means having them squashed under life's proverbial foot. This woman certainly already did that with one of her stilettoes.

"How did you know I'd be here?"

She offers a half-smile. "At dinner at your grandmother's, you said Lago was your favorite restaurant in Las Vegas when Pope was talking about taking Alessandra there." Her slender shoulders rise and fall, making the low-cut *V* of her dress shift to expose even more of her absolutely perfect breasts. "I figured you wouldn't miss the opportunity to come here the night before the tournament."

So, she was paying attention...

And to something so small.

I don't know if I should be happy about that or annoyed.

"You disappeared on me..."

She absently plays with the napkin Bishop tossed on the table, staring out as the fountain show winds down. "I know." Her bottom lip disappears under her teeth, and she finally meets my gaze again. "I wanted to apologize for that."

"Why'd you run?"

Her eyes soften, but there's something else underneath it.

It looks an awful lot like fear.

"You know why…"

I lean forward slightly across the table. "Do I? I think you're going to have to remind me because all I know is that I went to bed with my arm wrapped around you and my dick still buried inside your cunt, but when I woke up, the sheets were cold, and you had left that note like a goddamn calling card from an assassin."

She winces, and I immediately regret how that came out, but not the words because they're all true.

That note was the ultimate *fuck you* to me.

A slap in the face after what we shared that night.

I introduced her to the entire family. She played board games with Vivi and Charlotte after dinner and melted into the fabric of our Sunday night so easily that it almost seemed as if she were meant to be there all along. Then what we shared at my place after…

And she just *left*.

She releases a long sigh as the waiter slides my drink onto the table and takes the empty glass from me. "Anything for you, miss?"

Allegra shakes her head. "No. I'm good. Thank you."

He moves away from the table, and I shift back slightly, almost afraid to get close to her again. Even this slab of wood between us doesn't seem like enough to stop me from doing something stupid, like lunging across it and smashing my mouth against hers.

"Look, Coen, I know you think this is all a game—"

My spine snaps straight at her words, her attempt to shift the perception of what went down, and I snort, shaking my head. "Isn't it? You sought me out in Atlantic City. You played me like a fucking fiddle. Then again, in Monaco and Macau. Then you show up in New Orleans acting like…" I search for the right way to explain how it felt to see her at Hawke Hotel, for what happened in that penthouse. "I don't know. Like maybe something had changed, and I thought it did that night." Shoving my hand through my hair, I shake my head, looking away from her and out over the now still lagoon that will be filled with another show in only half an hour. "Maybe it was naïve to believe that someone like you isn't *always* playing a game."

"You were playing one, too."

Her soft accusation makes me grit my jaw, and I turn back to face her.

"You're not wrong, Allegra. I was. *Was* being the operative word. That changed for me because I thought it had for you. Especially after dinner with my family..."

She averts her gaze—unable to or unwilling to look at me.

Or maybe because she fears what her eyes will reveal.

I asked her to be honest with me.

Told her I needed that.

And she let me take her in that bed over and over again that night. Knowing damn well what I expected in return when we woke in the morning. And rather than give it to me, she *ran*.

"All I want is to be able to trust you, Allegra. And if you can't give me that, then..."

I let my words trail off because I don't really want to say them. Even the thought of actually saying it feels like acid crawling up my throat.

She fiddles with the napkin again, considering my words. "It's complicated, Coen."

Leaning forward, I drop my voice and lower my head until she's forced to meet my gaze. "No, it isn't. Either you're with me because you want to fuck with my head at the table or you're with me because you want to fuck me...and maybe more. Those are the only two options."

She releases a heavy sigh, a pink blush rising across her cheeks. "You know it's the latter."

I raise a brow at her. "Is it? Because you're here in Las Vegas when one of the biggest poker tournaments in the world is being held at the Venetian. One you knew I was playing in and that you promised you wouldn't. So, did you come here to talk to me, or did you come here to play?"

Her shoulders tense.

It's all the answer I need.

"That's what I thought." I huff back into my chair again and take a long sip of my drink. "You know damn well the two of us should not be at a table together, Allegra. It isn't fair."

That silvery-gray gaze cuts to mine again. "Life isn't fair, Coen. That's something I learned a very long time ago."

"Believe me, I'm well the fuck aware of that fact. But you *deliberately* going out of your way to mess with me, to rattle me, to throw me off my game..." I tighten my fist on my drink, remembering the *threat* in Satriano's gaze when he sat across from me in my condo and laid down his expectations. "You have no idea what you're putting at risk."

I need to win to pay him back.

I need to win to keep him from looking *elsewhere* for someone to assume the debt he believes both Atlas and I owe him.

"Then explain it to me, Coen."

"I can't. But know it's about more than winning a fucking card game for me."

Her dark brows rise, surprise lighting her face. "What could possibly be worth more than five million to you?"

"You met all of them on Sunday night."

ALLEGRA

COEN'S WORDS twist like a knife in my gut as the faces of all the Hawkes flit through my head like a movie. Replaying every minute I spent with them all on Sunday—a night that reminded me of what a family really is.

And made me realize that not having one had caused more damage than I cared to admit.

His mother, who sought me out after dinner and apologized for the interrogation, saying she would love to grab coffee one-on-one and get to know me better.

Those little girls who begged me to play Trouble with them while everyone else enjoyed their dessert and sat around chatting.

The babies who eventually woke and wanted attention, each of them cuter than any human being has a right to be.

All the cousins who chatted with me like I was always a member of the family, explaining inside jokes and telling me stories about each other that I have no doubt someone in that house didn't want told.

Even the less-than-welcoming members of the Hawke family, like Luca, Saint, and Gabe, who all watched me suspiciously, were never outright hostile. Given how I met Coen, I couldn't exactly blame them for getting that vibe and questioning my motives.

But through all of it—every conversation, every joke, every playful rib, even the minor arguments that broke out—I could feel how much they *cared.*

Not just about Coen but about every other person at the table.

Guilt and jealousy eat away at me like acid, burning me from the inside out the longer I sit here with him. He waits for me to respond to his statement, but I'm not sure how.

It shut me down *fast.*

The winnings from this tournament *aren't* what is most

important to Coen Hawke, and I should have known that the moment I walked in Nana's door—if not before that.

I manage to swallow that lump in my throat and nod slowly. "I see..."

Coen fingers his glass, allowing that smooth, polished, practiced façade to fall back into place. "So, tell me, Allegra, what do *you* care about?" His gaze shifts to mine, filled not with anger but pity. "Besides stabbing me in the back?"

I flinch at his words because they're not far from the truth.

He leans forward again. The blue of his eyes sparkling from the candle in the center of the table. "I looked into you, you know. After Monaco. We have a lot of connections, people who can find out anything about anyone..."

Stilling my desire to shift restlessly, I raise a brow. "And?"

"And your mother passed away when you were twelve."

Despite my best effort to remain unaffected, I flinch again. "Yes. I already told you that at dinner."

The corner of his lips tips up slightly. "You offered some very broad brushstrokes of your life, but you definitely held things back. Where did you go after that?"

I swallow thickly, then reach forward and take his drink, my fingers brushing over his, the contact lighting my whole body with that same fire I've been trying to forget. His eyes follow my hand as I drag it across the table toward me and then raise it to my lips and take a long sip from it.

The spicy, warm bourbon washes over my palate, and I swallow and raise a brow at him. "Bourbon?"

That same heat I just felt burns across his eyes like fire on water. "I've suddenly developed a taste for it."

My pussy clenches at the memory of him pouring it on me and licking it off. The sweet burn and slow glide of his greedy tongue seeking out every last drop.

Fuck.

I press my thighs together, thankful the table conceals the

move from the man who can so easily turn my body molten with a few words and a look.

"Where'd you go, Allegra? Because you don't seem to have anything that you care about. No ethics or morals. No people in your life. My sources say you popped up at a few boarding schools in the States and Europe, but then you've kind of been living as a nomad, occasionally going back to your place in New York, but mostly moving from hotel to hotel. I assume chasing games."

He watches me and waits for a response that I don't offer.

There isn't much I *can* say.

"That about sums it up, doesn't it?" His jaw hardens, his hands tensing on the table. "Are you even capable of caring about anyone else, Allegra? Is that the problem?"

The accusation raises my hackles. "Don't pretend you care about me, Coen."

He jerks forward so fast that I recoil slightly. That flame burning through his eyes has become a raging inferno that looks ready to consume anything in its path.

"You think I don't care about you?"

The need to defend myself against the pain in his voice gets the better of me. "I think you want revenge for what I did to you...and it would be warranted—"

"Goddamn it, Allegra." He releases an annoyed sigh, spreading his palms flat on the table. "Of course, I do. *Did.* But if you think that hasn't changed..."

He sits back with a huff, his chest rising and falling rapidly.

His eyes hold a wildness and slightly unhinged look that make him apppear downright feral.

I have never seen him this worked up before—at least, not when his head or cock wasn't buried between my legs.

"What has you so on edge, Coen? And don't say it's just about me because it's not."

A muscle in his clenched jaw tics as he watches me. "There

are things going on that I can't tell you. And honestly, staying the fuck away from you right now would probably be in *your* best interest as well as my own. It would probably be safer for you."

"Safer?"

"The Hawkes have enemies. Powerful ones. We always will."

Which would explain why Coen has never brought another woman to Nana's for Sunday dinner. Why he never *truly* opens up to me about anything important.

He's afraid.

If he lets someone in, that exposes them to whatever perceived danger he thinks is bad enough to keep everyone locked out from what really makes him who he is.

"So, that means you'll be alone the rest of your life?"

His lips press into a firm line. "*Everyone* at that table who you met has suffered for being a Hawke...or being with one."

The mental gymnastics it takes to follow his logic makes my head start to pound. "So, you're trying to protect me now even when you're angry and making demands of me?"

"Maybe."

"What if I don't need protecting from you, Coen?" I shrug. "The only thing I seem to need protection from is myself."

"Why is that?"

I take another sip of his drink, staring at the amber liquid. "Because I've been making bad decisions."

"Like? Come *clean*, Allegra."

The way the word comes out almost a growl reminds me of the way his voice wavered and dipped as he fucked me within an ounce of sanity.

And I find I can't lie to him.

"Like thinking I could mess with you...and it wouldn't mess with me, too."

The corners of his lips twitch into an almost grin at the admission. "Finally, some honesty."

"I was honest with you the other night. About everything…"

Need soaks his gaze, matching the throb in my core. We didn't say much. We didn't need to. Our bodies. Our touches. They spoke volumes.

"Everything we shared was real, Coen."

The anger…

The need…

The heat…

The passion…

He fucked me raw, and I would let him do it again and again if he asked because, somehow, I've come to actually *like* Coen Hawke.

Something I never could have anticipated.

And if I had known it was even a possibility, I would have run the other direction as fast as my heels could carry me.

"And what do you want, Allegra? Tell me right here, right now, or this is *over*."

I force myself to meet his gaze, even though what I'm about to say is going to be hard for me. Nearly impossible. There's only one thing I've ever wanted. One thing that has always seemed to elude me. "I want to be in control of my own life."

Those dark brows of his furrow. "You're not?"

The truth threatens to spill out like a tidal wave.

But it can't.

At least, not all of it.

"I haven't been for a long time. I've been spiraling, feeling like other people are constantly pulling the strings and leading me in the wrong direction."

Taking me places, forcing me to do things I don't want to in the name of loyalty.

"Did I do that, Allegra?"

A smile pulls at my lips. "That remains to be seen. But it certainly wasn't the direction I thought I'd go. We could be *very* bad for each other, Coen."

"Or *very* good."

His response comes so quickly, without any thought. And I want to believe that it's true, that there's more to this attraction than just sexual, the heat of being opponents across the felt and lovers in the dark, but I don't know if I can.

Trust.

That word has never meant much to me.

It couldn't when it was so hard to find it after Mom died.

And I don't know if I can trust Coen Hawke.

His family seems quite adept at lying, at putting on a façade. His father is a big-shot trial lawyer, and so is his brother. And given what Coen has told me and what I've observed, I have no doubt that Coen is capable of everything they are.

All the tricks that help them convince juries in a courtroom and get the upper hand against opponents anywhere else.

Yet staring across the table at him, I have a hard time believing he's lying now. Not when the sincerity in his gaze radiates and the hope there matches my own.

The waiter appears with two plates, sets one down in front of him and one in my spot.

Before I even have a chance to say anything else, Bishop appears. "I told you I'd be back when the food came."

Coen and I hold each other's gaze across the table for a few seconds, long enough to make sitting here in Bishop's seat with her standing beside us awkward.

There's more to say.

So much more.

I slowly push the chair back and smile at Bishop. "Enjoy your dinner."

She offers me a sympathetic look as she takes her seat, pulling her napkin into her lap.

Before I can walk away, Coen climbs to his feet and closes the few steps to me. The warm, spicy bourbon on his breath and that crisp, masculine scent that seems to cling to him settle over me.

I inhale greedily, in case it's the last time I get the opportunity.

He dips his head to my cheek, feathering his lips over my ear, and tugs me against him, slipping a key card into my hand. "Venetian—Presidential Suite."

I shiver at the invitation and promise in his words and close my grip around the card, terrified he might realize his mistake and take it back.

His hand tightens around mine, and he brushes his thumb across my fingers, raising goosebumps across my skin. "I would very much like for you to be there when I get done with dinner." He pulls back until his gaze meets mine. "We'll finish this conversation. No games this time."

If only it were that easy.

I nod and slip from his hold, forcing myself to walk away from them and not look back because if I do, one of them might see the tears streaming down my face now.

14

COEN

I never thought a dinner at my favorite restaurant could be agonizing, but every minute that passed, every bite I took, every word of small talk Bishop tried to make, the more I stopped craving the delicious food I was eating, and instead wished for it to be over, so it could be *now*. So I could be standing here, in the threshold of my suite, staring at Allegra.

She sits on the couch, waiting for me, just like I knew she would be.

Or at least, *hoped.*

There was always a chance she would run again.

Maybe that's why my knee kept bouncing and my hand kept tapping on the tabletop. Maybe that's why my heart felt like it was trapped in a vise the entire time I sat there with Bishop.

Because I wasn't one hundred percent sure she *would* be here.

And now that I've finally laid eyes on her, I couldn't drag them away even if I tried.

Christ, she's beautiful.

Her dark hair cascading forward over her shoulders, settling above her breasts, making my fingers itch to bury themselves in those tresses. Her red lips that beg to be kissed and devoured. And those stormy-gray eyes searching mine as she slowly climbs to her feet.

I let the door close behind me, not even realizing I've been standing here with my hand on the knob for an embarrassingly long time.

Allegra twists her hands nervously in front of her as she moves away from the couch. "How was your dinner?"

Her typically strong, steady voice wavers slightly, making that vise tighten around my chest again.

I approach her slowly, not wanting to crowd her, considering how jittery she seems to be tonight.

Allegra has never been like this with me before. She's never openly displayed this kind of weakness—signs of her humanity that prove she isn't a cold, heartless machine going through the motions.

It's always been a show for her, a need to demonstrate that she's stronger, smarter, but she's never really been in control.

She said it herself earlier.

And right now, she definitely seems to be out of sorts—shaken by the conversation we started at that table but never got the chance to finish.

"It was good. But do you really want to talk about my dinner?"

Biting her bottom lip, she shakes her head. "I guess not..."

She's nervous.

I probably should be, too.

Allegra's showing up certainly wasn't even a remote possibility in my head when I left to come to Vegas. All I've felt for her since I woke up Monday morning to an empty bed and that note has been a vibrating rage. The fact that she hunted me down at Lago and is standing in front of me right now should scream *trap* after everything she's done.

So, I should be nervous...

I should be very cautious with her and determine her true intent rather than act on the intense physical pull that tries to draw me right to her.

"I told you we would finish our conversation."

Allegra nods slowly. "Yes..."

"So, let's do that." I cross my arms over my chest, holding my ground and keeping enough space between us that I won't be tempted to touch her and short-circuit my brain. "Unless you're afraid to?"

She shudders slightly, squeezing her eyes closed. "I'm fucking terrified, Coen..."

Her confession almost makes me close the distance between us.

Only absolute willpower keeps my feet rooted in place.

"The truth can be a scary thing...and I told you back in New Orleans that I wanted you to come clean, that I wanted you to be honest with me. You ran. So, this is your opportunity, right here, right now, to tell me what you really want, Allegra. You said you weren't in control of your own life. You said you felt like you've been spiraling. This is your opportunity to stop that."

She releases a long, heavy breath, pushing her thick, dark hair back from her face. "I don't know how to stop the spiraling. I don't think it's as easy as you seem to believe it to be." That uncertainty in her gaze threatens to split my chest wide open. "But one thing I'm absolutely sure of is that I wouldn't have come to Las Vegas. I wouldn't have *needed* to if I didn't want *you*, if I didn't want *this*, despite all the complications and reasons I shouldn't."

It's as close to opening up to me as she's ever come.

And I can see how uncomfortable she is with the vulnerability she's showing me right now.

Allegra just laid all her cards on the table.

It's the final showdown.

And she's waiting to see what I will play.

I slowly close the few steps between us, staring down into her swirling gray eyes, a hurricane of uncertainty that threatens to swallow her whole if she can't find a safe haven in the storm. Tilting her face up to mine, I brush my thumb across her bottom lip. "You can have me, Allegra, and I'll help you stop the spiral."

That's a promise I shouldn't be making, no matter how much I want to be able to fulfill it.

Not when Satriano looms over me and can make me do his bidding with a single word or snap of his fingers, and it will inevitably be something far worse than fixing games at his casinos.

It will be things that would put Allegra in the kind of danger the Hawkes have been running from for what feels like forever.

Protecting her means pushing her away.

But I can't when I can see how much she needs something strong to cling to, a place to set anchor and weather whatever maelstrom is swirling around her.

She *needs* the spiraling to stop, and I can't bring myself to walk away from her when she's like this. Especially not when my entire being screams that I can be her savior. That somehow helping her will redeem me from all the mistakes I've made.

Allegra sags against me as if my words have released some sort of tension in her that has held her upright this entire time. Her hands curl around the lapels of my jacket, and I wrap my arms around her, tugging her fully to me, accepting her weight and that of whatever has brought her to this point.

I brush my lips over hers gently, holding her tightly, letting her cling to me for as long as she needs to.

It took a lot for her to be here, for her to show up, for her to admit any of this to me, especially after the way we left things, the way *she* left things.

A woman doesn't like having her pride hurt, but she sacrificed it to come here and make this confession. To supplicate herself at my feet and beg for forgiveness.

And I'm going to reward her for it.

I deepen the kiss, cupping her face between my palms, holding her steady as I attempt to convey everything that's so hard to say. Both because I don't know how to but also because I fear, if I ever manage it, it might send her running again.

She sucks in a sharp breath as my mouth moves over hers, demanding and insistent.

All the things that seem to bring that flame that burns inside her back to life.

She presses into me tighter, as if she can't get close enough.

I kiss her with everything I have in me, with all the frustration, confusion, and aggression that's built up over the last several days since she disappeared—pouring it all into the kiss.

Into her.

The wanting.

The needing.

The desperation I've felt since she left me.

And now that there aren't any more games, now that she's finally letting me see those other sides of her, I want it all.

Her sassiness.

Her strength.

Her humor.

Her struggles.

Her fears.

I lift her easily, and she loops her arms around my neck, her thighs squeezing my hips as I walk us back toward the bedroom, where I plan to spend the entire night lost in this woman.

But I can't wait.

I need her *now*.

Stopping halfway down the hallway, I pin her to the wall, my cock pressed between her legs, aligned precisely so that every twitch and roll of her hips brushes it across her clit. "I sure as hell hope you've stuck to your no-panties rule."

She chuckles against my lips, tunneling her fingers through my hair and jerking my head back slightly. "You think I would come to you like this with any sort of barrier?"

Hell.

The many layers of meaning in those words wrap around me, as much a declaration of honesty and affection as I might ever get from this woman.

It's enough to make that razor-thin thread of control I'm still clinging to snap, and I slam my mouth to hers again, grinding my hips in a way that has her breath falling from her mouth on a startled gasp.

I slide one hand between us and find the hem of her dress, lifting it so I can drag my fingers along her slick core. "You're always so wet and ready for me."

She releases a little laugh—the sound is the most light and carefree thing I've heard from this woman since I met her. "It's almost embarrassing what a slut I am for you..."

"Fuckin hell, Allegra..."

Her words awaken something primitive in me, the need to mark and claim and conquer, unlike anything I've ever experienced before.

I keep her pinned to the wall with my chest as I pull my hand from her cunt and reach between us to free my cock. Every second it takes me fumbling with my goddamn belt and zipper feels like an eternity, but when I finally manage to get my pants down, I don't hesitate for even a second.

Eyes locked with her half-lidded, lust-soaked gaze, I plunge into her hard and deep, easily gliding in her drenched core as it expands to accept me.

"Fuck!"

Her head falls to the wall, her nails scoring my neck. She contracts around me, squeezing so tightly it's almost painful to hold back my desire to come instantly, and I unleash a low growl that fills the hallway.

"You have no idea what you fucking do to me, woman." I draw my hips back and slam into her again. "No. Fucking. Idea."

"I think I do..." She moans on another thrust, then locks her gaze with mine. "Because you do the same to me."

Bloody hell...

Every retreat and advance, I claim her in a way I haven't been able to before, because this woman owns *me*. She did from the minute I saw her at that fucking bar; I just never really wanted to admit it.

It doesn't matter what she's done in her past, only that she's committed her future to me, to this, to us, to seeing where this leads, and as her pussy contracts around my cock, as she clamps down on me, with each drag of my hips, I know I won't be able to walk away, and neither will she.

It's too intense.

Too uncontrollable.

All we can do is ride it out and see where it takes us.

I kiss her hard, angling her head where I want it, digging one hand into her hip, the other at the back of her neck, clutching and holding her tightly. My hips pound her into the wall.

The art hanging on it shakes violently, rattling like it's about to come off.

But I don't give a fuck if it does.

I want to break every last wall this woman has up.

And that starts tonight.

Right fucking now.

ALLEGRA

WHAT I JUST SAID TO Coen was either very right or very wrong, given the way he turns almost animalistic. Slamming into me, burying himself deep, like he can't get close enough, like he's trying to cement himself there permanently.

Each time he retreats, the head of his cock drags along that perfect spot, and lights flash across my closed lids. But then he's right back, filling me, grinding his pelvis to mine to rub against my clit.

God, this position...

All his raw power on display as he keeps me pinned and maintains complete control over me—mind, body, and soul.

I cling to his neck, digging my nails into his tight flesh, the corded muscles rippling under my hands while his mouth moves over mine in another mind-bending kiss that momentarily short-circuits my brain.

Then we're moving.

He pulls me from the wall, hands at my back, supporting my weight as he walks us over to the bed with his cock still embedded deep inside me. All while he kisses me wildly, as if it's his only way to get oxygen.

The sheer intensity of Coen like this threatens to overwhelm all my senses, and I can already see he's barely begun.

His eyes gleam as he leans forward and lowers me to the mattress. Only, instead of coming with me, he pulls back and steps away, his cock slipping out.

No...

I whimper and reach for him, but he tugs off his suit coat,

tossing it behind him without taking his eyes off me. He toes off his shoes, removes his pants and socks, and then gets to work on the buttons of his shirt.

His hot gaze roams from my face to my spread legs, my dress still hiked up around my waist.

"By the time this shirt is off, you better be naked…"

Still clouded by the force of his passion, it takes a second for me to process his words.

But he doesn't have to tell me twice.

I pull my dress up and over my head, tossing it off the side of the bed as he comes to stand at the edge of it between my legs. He bends down and caresses my cheek almost reverently, calloused fingertips skimming over soft skin.

He stops with his lips a mere hairsbreadth from mine. "I hope you're ready for this, Allegra. I hope you're ready for all of me."

It sounds like a warning.

Maybe one I should heed.

A shiver rolls through me at the drop in his voice, and he kisses me as if he's trying to quell the reaction. But I'm not afraid, not of Coen.

No matter what he might be thinking. No matter what might be going on in that head of his. No matter how feral he may be, balancing on the edge of control, this man would never hurt me.

I reach between us and wrap my hand around his cock, still slick with my arousal, and he groans against my mouth, thrusting into my tight grip.

"God, I love when you touch me, Allegra."

The feeling is very mutual.

Whether it be his hands, his mouth, or his cock, Coen Hawke has mastered my body and has no problem using that knowledge to destroy me in the best ways.

Turnabout is fair play…

I twist my hand around his cock, basking in the way his entire body trembles with my touch. "Then fuck my mouth."

Coen tenses, his hard muscles twitching slightly as he pulls back and stares at me. He brushes his fingers across my lips, slipping his thumb into my mouth. I suck on it and swirl my tongue around it, earning me a low groan.

"Believe me, sweetheart, I would love to fuck this pretty little mouth and to come down your throat. But I had something *else* in mind for tonight."

He pulls his thumb free of my lips, and it clicks what he's saying.

I finally understand the warning he just gave me.

Oh, God...

What he did to me the other night flashes through my head. Where that very same thumb went and what he asked me that night. My response...

Everything clenches in response to the memory.

He pulls back enough that I'm forced to release my grip on his cock and smacks the side of my thigh, his eyes dancing with the kind of wicked intent that matches the grin pulling at his lips. "Roll over."

And like the love-sick, obsessed woman I apparently am, I comply without question, getting onto my knees and elbows.

I look back at where he stands at the edge of the bed, cock in his hand, ready to do unspeakable things to me, to sin in the kind of way only a man like Coen Hawke can.

He steps forward until his hot skin brushes mine, then reaches around me with his free hand and wraps his forearm around my breasts, his warm lips skating across the back of my neck. His cock slips through my arousal, practically dripping from me at this point, then up over my ass, making me tense. "Do you still want me here, Allegra?"

Fuck.

I do.

I never thought I would want any man to go there, but I want him to take me.

I want *him* to be the one who finally does it.

I want to give him that, to give him me, for us to share the experience, for him to take me *completely*.

Trying to prepare myself mentally for what's coming, I nod.

He releases my breasts to lift my chin up until my eyes meet his. "I need to hear you say it."

God...

Coen needs the confirmation.

He needs to ensure I am one hundred percent on board with this, even though I already told him I wanted it the other night. Even though I'm naked and slick and quivering in his arms. He still wouldn't even consider it if I said no.

This man...

Where the hell has he been my entire life?

I hold his gaze, unable to look away due to his grip on my chin. "Y-yes."

One of his dark brows rises. "Yes, what?"

Oh, God, he's going to make me say the words...

All the years of playing the game, of having to remain strong and unbreakable, of being forced to maintain an impenetrable veneer, battle against what my body tells me it wants.

And it wants *that*.

Even when my brain is telling me that it's giving him too much when I should be keeping my cards close to my chest.

Too much power.

Too much control.

Too much. Too much. Too much.

But as hard as my mind may be working to convince me otherwise, I know it isn't too much.

Not with him.

With him, it's *right*.

"Yes..." It comes out barely above a whisper. If his face

weren't so close to mine, he might not even hear me. "I want you to fuck my ass."

Those blue eyes of his flare, the pupils dilating until they're almost completely consumed with black. Then those luscious lips curl up into a grin that completely changes his face, like I've just given him the greatest gift he's ever received in his life. "Good girl. I promise I won't hurt you."

"I-I trust you..."

Those words seem to be what he's been waiting for because he drops a quick kiss to my lips, releases my chin, and then stands.

The loss of his body heat instantly makes me shiver, but he runs his hand from my clit up and back, spreading my slick arousal around my asshole before coating his cock by rubbing it along my seam.

Fuck.

I bite my lip, gripping the comforter as my body tenses in anticipation of what's coming.

His hand slips around my front, those talented fingers gently rolling across my clit. I buck at the contact, little sparks of pleasure coursing through me, and I finally release the groan I've been holding back.

He chuckles low, his other finger circling my wet asshole before slowly easing in a fraction of an inch. I clench around it, and he keeps rolling his fingers over my clit, his hard cock nestled between my legs, getting coated in my arousal that flows like Niagara fucking Falls.

That finger slips all the way into me easily.

"Good girl. One more."

He moves his finger back and forth inside me.

Fuck...that feels so good.

Combined with the way he's working my clit, I'm so close to coming already. My entire body is one massive, trembling, sloppy mess, and we haven't even gotten to the main attraction.

Coen leans forward, his chest pressing to my back again. "You're not going to come. You're going to wait."

I've never been one to believe that a woman can come on command. It certainly isn't anything I've ever experienced in my lifetime, but the orgasm starting to build suddenly ebbs a little. Still there, on the periphery, but not knocking at the door, ready to burst out of it anymore.

Hell.

A few words from him and my body responds so easily.

Like it knows who it should be listening to.

I whimper and nod my agreement now that he's proven he *can* apparently control me with his words as much as he does his hands, mouth, and cock, and he slowly works a second finger into me.

Gasping at the intrusion, my breath catches, and I hold it, clamping down.

"Relax, Allegra. Breathe."

I try to do as he asks.

Relax my body.

Allow him to do his magic.

The fingers of his left hand continue to move over my clit while the ones on his right slowly work into me fully and spread me open. He drags the head of his cock across my dripping core one more time with a swirl of his hips before slowly withdrawing his fingers and easing the head inside my ass.

"Oh, fuuuuck!" I gasp at how thick he is, how full I already feel with only that tiny bit of him inside me, dropping my forehead to the mattress, burying my face in the plush comforter to muffle my strangled mix of a groan and a scream. "Fuck... Coen..."

"You're okay, Allegra. You're doing so well."

His encouragement, coupled with his fingers moving rapidly over my clit, quickly melt away that momentary panic that hit.

My body shakes.

Heat boils deep and low in my core, and I instinctively clench where his cock would normally be—and where it currently is.

He issues a low, rumbling groan. "You're going to come for me now. It will help you relax."

Coen adjusts his hand at my core and twists my clit between his fingers, and like a fucking stick of dynamite...I *explode*.

Fuck. Fuck. Fuuuuuck.

Pleasure courses through me, my pussy clenching, body convulsing, ass tightening around the head of his cock. He keeps moving his fingers over my clit.

Keeps working me through the orgasm as he slowly pushes his cock deeper into me.

Until it feels like he's completely consumed me.

Until it feels like he fucking owns me.

My orgasm finally ebbs, my limbs heavy and wobbling, and I drop down onto my forearms, resting my chest against the mattress, unable to hold myself up any longer.

Coen's arm wrapped round my waist keeps at least that half up, and he slips his hand from my clit, down to my pussy, and slides two fingers in, fucking me there as he slowly eases his cock back, then pushes it in a fraction farther than he had been.

"Christ, you're so fucking tight, Allegra. Feels fucking good..."

I can't help the inclination to squeeze around him in response, to tighten, but his thrusts in both places, the slow, steady rhythm he sets that allows him to push deeper with each drive of his hips, quickly relaxes me into an almost trance.

My mind slips into a hazy fog of pleasure I didn't know existed.

I want to float in it forever.

"That's it." He grinds his palm against my hyper-sensitive clit as he keeps fingering me. "God, you're so good at taking my cock in your beautiful cunt and your stunning ass. I wish you could see what you look like right now with my cock shoved up it."

Fucking HELL.

He can't *say* things like that to me.

It isn't *fair.*

It isn't *right* for a man to be this...

Just *this.*

I whimper, wishing I could see myself through his eyes, wishing I could see all the things he does that somehow allowed him to forgive me for everything I've done—or at least, the things he knows about.

He keeps pushing into me slowly, ensuring he won't hurt me as he works up another orgasm so quickly after the first.

This one feels different, though.

Almost like my body is starting to unravel, ready to come apart at the seams...

My limbs feel disconnected, like I'm floating on some magical cloud of ecstasy controlled by the man fucking me so beautifully.

"Are you going to come again, Allegra?"

God, he's so observant.

He can already tell I'm on the precipice.

That it's so close I can almost reach out and grab it.

I nod. "Y-yes..."

"You're going to come with me this time."

God, yes.

That.

That is what I want.

What I *need.*

To feel his release riding mine.

I nod, desperately trying to hold it back when it threatens to tear me apart at the simple swipe of his fingers.

He keeps pumping into me, the head of his cock dragging against spots I didn't even know existed.

I squeeze around his fingers in my cunt and around him *there* and glance back to find his neck muscles strained, his jaw clenched, his eyes focused on the spot where he's buried inside me.

"Now, Allegra."

And as soon as my pussy starts rippling, when the first seam starts to tear, he pushes in all the way and roars, the sound echoing through the room, along with my strangled cry as I completely and utterly shatter.

15

ALLEGRA

L ying here, half draped over Coen in the dark, leg tucked between his, ear resting directly over his bare chest, the steady thumping of his heart beneath my ear lulls me into a sense of calm I haven't felt, maybe ever.

My body thrums, still aching deliciously from his touch, his attention, from the multiple times he made me come again after our long, hot shower where he basically had to bathe me like a child because my body was too wrung out to function.

It was sweet.

Attentive.

And also, somehow, one of the most intimate things I've ever experienced.

Which is saying a lot, considering what this man has done to me.

He slowly runs his fingers down my spine, simultaneously making me shiver and want to crawl closer to him—which is impossible at this point.

Just like it would be impossible to extricate myself from his arms if I tried. He holds me possessively, burying his face into my hair, letting his lips linger on my forehead, touching me and kissing me any chance he gets.

Almost like he's afraid I'll disappear if he stops.

But I won't run again.

Not if I can help it...

Not after this man has given me *everything* in one single night and left me awed by his strength, his determination, his focus, his relentless drive to ensure my pleasure, and given me everything I needed when I was nearly at my breaking point.

It all demonstrated to me that Coen Hawke is exactly who I thought he was.

Maybe not at the beginning.

I definitely misjudged a lot about him when I met him in Atlantic City.

But once I got to know him, after I saw him with his family and really understood who he was at his core, I knew he was a *good* man with a *good* heart and wicked intelligence.

Which makes the way he sometimes talks about himself all the more confusing and painful...

"Can I ask you something?"

My question breaks the comfortable silence that's finally settled over us after the frenzy, and he shifts slightly under me, tipping his head down to meet my gaze.

"Of course." His brow furrows. "But why does it sound like I should be worried?"

I grin, ghosting my lips across his strong pecs and feeling him twitch beneath me. "The first time we met—"

"The bar?"

"No." I shake my head. "I mean the first time we talked in your room in Monaco..."

Trepidation darkens his eyes. He has no idea where I'm going with this, and maybe I don't, either.

"Yeah?"

Maybe I shouldn't bring it up.

It could potentially unsettle this detente we have seemed to have found, the momentary peace before all the troubles of the world beyond this room manage to creep into our psyches.

But searching his face, I know I have to.

I can't let what he said go, not when it's clear he really believed those words when he said them to me back then and probably still does.

"You said something that's kind of stuck in my head."

This entire week, after meeting the Hawkes and spending time with them. After seeing how they all interact. It's been impossible to forget his words. They've played on a loop along with the pain in his voice when he said them.

Coen tugs on a lock of my hair, twirling it around his finger. "What's that?"

I swallow thickly, pushing myself up onto one elbow so I can see his face better, judge his reaction.

Even in the dark, it's impossible not to see how handsome he is, how in the moment he is, relaxed and dare I say, even happy. Those glittering blue eyes focus on me with all his attention he's already given me all night.

No one who is this attentive, this caring, this loving with someone he has every right to despise should ever think the kind of things he said.

"You told me you were the spare, that you did nothing with your life while your brother was everything your parents and the rest of your family hoped he would become."

His eyes darken, gaze narrowing on me slightly. "I guess I did say that."

I chew on my lip, contemplating how to phrase this.

Maybe it isn't my place to say anything—it probably isn't.

After all, despite the *many* ways we came together intimately tonight, we barely know each other. And what we do know has been based on less than completely honest situations. A relationship—or whatever this is—built on very unstable ground.

He reaches up and brushes the hair back from my cheek, tucking it behind my ear. The feather-light ghosting of his calloused fingertips draws goosebumps across my bare skin, wanting to feel that touch everywhere again, aching for it as much as I am for answers.

"Well, I guess it stuck with me, especially because that certainly isn't the impression I got at dinner."

His body tenses under me. "It's complicated." A long, slow breath slips from between his lips. "And it isn't anything I particularly want to get into right now. It would ruin the mood."

I grin at him and lean in to kiss him gently, letting my lips linger longer than really necessary. Maybe as an apology for the fact that I don't intend to let it go so easily. "I don't think anything could ruin my mood right now."

He chuckles low, dragging me fully across his naked body, his semi-hard cock pressed between us, and almost instantly coming to full attention again. I groan as he kisses me long and deep, but I force myself to pull back, not to immediately give in to the desire to just slide down onto him right now and take him.

I push up and straddle his hips, keeping his cock pinned under my pussy, laying my hands across his chest as I stare down at him. "Your family loves you. And God, there are a lot of them..."

He grins at that, despite the trepidation coloring his gaze.

"I didn't get the impression anyone is disappointed in you. In fact, it seems like you're pretty invaluable to them, and there is no denying how much they all love you."

Nothing I said was particularly radical, but Coen's jaw still hardens as he looks at me.

"They wanted me to become my father, both Isaac and me.

Imagine having two loaded guns willing to walk into any courtroom, any meeting, any situation, and defend what the family
has built without any reservation."

"That's what your dad and Isaac do?"

He nods. "But it never felt right to me, sitting in that courtroom with Dad. I was just..." His shoulders lift and sag, but
given the topic of conversation, I know the shrug is anything
but nonchalant. "I was restless, always have been, doing any
one thing, staying in any one place too long, it just"—he shakes
his head and runs a hand through his hair—"isn't for me.
That's part of why I play in so many tournaments. I love New
Orleans, but I need to not be there all the time. It will always be
home. I'll always go back to it, to them, but I like to travel. I like
seeing the world."

"You like *winning*."

A slow grin spreads across his lips, and he slides his hands
to my hips, gripping them tightly. "I do, and I get very frustrated
when little temptresses like you try to distract me from it—and
succeed."

I return his grin. "Still, I don't think they're disappointed in
you. They just want you to be happy. It seems like that's all they
want from anyone around that table, and maybe they don't
think that you are..."

Something darkens his gaze, fear or regret. Maybe a bit of
both. "I've given them reason to believe that."

I raise a brow. "How so?"

He scrubs a hand over his cheek, breaking eye contact in a
way that makes my heart clench. "I made a few really, really
bad decisions last year. Managed to lose a lot of money at the
tables."

"Really?"

He nods. "A lot."

"I...wouldn't have expected that. You're a very controlled
player."

"Normally, I am, but I was out of sorts. There was a lot happening at home with the family, and I let things spin out of control. And then, to try to fix things, I did something even worse."

My chest tightens at the pain in his voice, so much so that it actually hurts to take a breath. I lean forward and brush my thumb across his lips, silencing him. "It couldn't have been that bad. You don't have it in you."

He snorts. "It was that bad." His jaw hardens as he debates how much to reveal. The struggle between wanting to end this topic of conversation or revealing something so *real* to me that he likely really needs to with someone dances across his gaze. "I betrayed Atlas and the rest of my family."

"He's the cousin who wasn't at dinner? The boxer? I've seen a few of his fights on television." I give him a half-grin. "That title fight was something else."

His hand tightens on my hip, the other sliding to my opposing thigh. "It sure was. And it's the reason I said what I did that first night we met, the reason I know they're disappointed, the reason I know I can never make it up to them."

"I don't believe that. You can forgive just about *anything* when it's someone you *love*."

COEN

ALLEGRA SAYS the words so emphatically that it's evident she knows from personal experience and isn't merely waxing poetic or trying to boost me up when she thinks I need some sort of reassurance.

I tunnel my hand through her hair, dragging her down until our faces are so close I could move a fraction of a centimeter and kiss her, but I don't. "I appreciate the pep talk."

She grins. "That isn't what this is, Coen. I just want to understand you better, understand the Hawkes..."

"Why?"

Searching her gaze, I try to find her angle. What game she might be playing, even though we promised that part of our relationship was over. But the only thing looking back at me is sincerity. The kind that makes the last several hours we spent together feel even more meaningful.

She shrugs. "Because now that the game is over, maybe I don't want a rematch. The next dinner could be less awkward... and I might actually stand a chance if I understood that family dynamic."

"Before...when you said anything can be forgiven when it's someone you love. You sounded like you were talking from personal experience."

Allegra tries to hide it, but she tenses slightly like she didn't want me to pick up on that and now regrets saying it.

"Your mom passed away when you were young..."

She pulls back out of my hold, running her hands through her insanely disheveled hair. "She did."

"Where'd you go after that?"

It hasn't escaped me that she avoided the question—twice —at the table.

Whatever happened after her mother died, it isn't anything she wants to discuss with me.

Which only makes me want to know more.

Losing a parent like that must be devastating. After Dad was shot, for those weeks when we weren't sure if he was going to recover or what he would be like if he ever did, it felt like I had already lost him. And that was agony.

If he were actually gone, if we had to close him into the Hawke family crypt with Grandfather and Aunt Star, I might not have been able to survive it.

Yet Allegra did...and at such a young age. It had to have shaped her. Helped turn her into the woman she is today.

She averts her gaze, picking at some imaginary loose thread on the expensive sheets we now lie in. "I was mostly in boarding schools, bouncing around the U.S. and sometimes Europe."

I slide my hands to her hips, squeezing tightly. "Which I already know."

And I make it very clear with the look I give her that I'm not going to accept her telling me the same information and avoiding the ultimate question again.

Her lips curve into a sad smile. "You know...I envy what you have. A big family that loves you. Who all support each other. Who will always be there for one another, no matter what."

The tears I thought I caught in her eyes at Sunday dinner suddenly make a lot more sense now, hearing how gut-wrenching those words were for her to speak.

My heart aches for the pain in her, for that little girl left alone in the world. "You never had that?"

She shakes her head. "My mom and I were close, best friends. But once she was gone..."

Her breath hitches, and I pull her to me, dragging her down across my body and allowing her to bury her face against my neck. A warm drop hits my skin, and I tighten my hold on her, pressing my lips to the top of her head.

I cling to her for several minutes, allowing her to cry, to release whatever emotions she's had bottled up for so long.

Skimming my fingers along her spine, I think about her description of the family.

"You're not wrong about the Hawkes, about us always being there and supporting each other..." I release a sigh, wishing I could go back and change it all. "That's why what I did is so bad. It was the opposite of the very thing that makes us a family. I bet against Atlas in the title fight."

She pulls back slightly, with red-rimmed, teary eyes meeting mine from below a furrowed brow. "Why?"

A question I've asked myself too many damn times to count.

"Because I was in the hole. Because I was spiraling. Because he was, too, after he got shot a few months earlier. He was recovering, and I knew him well enough to understand that it wasn't going well. He was struggling. *Hard.*"

I let my mind drift back to all those training sessions that were too painful to watch. Seeing Atlas struggle with *anything* in that gym just felt *wrong*. Everything about his injury and recovery felt like some bad dream none of us could wake up from, and it only seemed to be getting worse as I kept losing more and more money.

"I didn't think there was any way he'd be ready for that fight, that he'd stand a chance. I thought it was a surefire way to make back everything I had lost. I bet against one of my best friends, my cousin, my family, and Hawkes don't do that. We always bet *on* each other."

She feathers her fingers across my cheek, then cups it in her warm, soft palm. "You made a mistake. We all do."

"This mistake has the type of consequences I may not be able to recover from, that *we* may not be able to."

"Everyone seemed fine at dinner." She laughs, the sound washing away some of the sadness in her eyes. "The only tension was the way everybody kept grilling me."

I chuckle. "God, that wasn't even bad. You should see them when they *really* get fired up. I think they were holding back slightly because they didn't want to scare you off."

"Have they done that before? Scared people off?"

"Oh, hell yes. But like I said, you're the only woman I've ever brought to Sunday dinner. And given all the issues going on, they probably didn't want to do anything that might send me running again."

"You would run? But I thought you were like basically in

charge of the hotel and are helping with the second tower across the street?"

She really was paying attention at dinner.

"I am...and I actually like it. I didn't think I would, to be honest. Nothing else has ever really seemed to click. Maybe it's because I spend so much time in hotels and casinos, but it feels more like home, like where I'm supposed to be, than any other job I've ever had in the family business."

Her hand slides around my side, and she squeezes gently. "See? Not so restless after all."

I chuckle low. "I wish that were true. But I'm here, aren't I? Chasing another tournament win."

Allegra doesn't need to know *why* it's so much more than that, why it's so important. The less she knows about the Satriano situation, the better. I can keep her insulated from it—from him. I can keep her safe.

She kisses me gently, letting her lips linger on mine. "That doesn't mean you have to *keep* doing this."

I tighten my grip on her, and she lies back down, settling her face into the crook of my neck, comfortably tucked in like she belongs here.

And God, I wish what she said were true...

For the first time in my life, I might actually *want* to stay. I might actually *want* to take a role in the Hawke empire for longer than a few days, weeks, or months.

And it might not be possible.

I try to hide my reaction to her words, how easily she says it when I know I can never stop, that I will have to keep doing it as long as Satriano demands it.

I'll have to play for him, win tournaments for him, rig them any way he sees fit, for as long as he asks me to.

Just like Pope, I'll be stuck in this strange relationship with the man who could easily destroy all of us.

And he's going to make me do that, too.

Deep down, I know where this *thing* with him is heading.

He's going to make me betray the Hawkes.

He's going to make me fuck it all up all over again.

I trail my fingers down her back, feeling her relax more and more into me until she finally falls asleep, her even breaths floating across my skin, her hand pressed over my heart.

It's the kind of vulnerability that's so hard for her, but she's doing it so easily with me.

She's already revealed so much of herself to me tonight.

But she still hasn't answered that question about where she went after her mom died...

Wherever it was, whatever happened there, it scares her enough that she doesn't want to confide in me about it. Either she's still running from those memories or still living through them, and it's almost like she doesn't want to get me involved the same way I don't want her anywhere near the mess I'm currently embroiled in.

And that scares me almost as much as Satriano does.

16

ALLEGRA

The rustle of bedsheets and the slight creaking of the bed from the other room float out to me in the living room area of the suite before Coen's voice.

"Allegra?"

I hear it—the *panic* in the way he says my name, mixed with the last remnants of sleep, that makes him sound even rougher and more gravelly than usual.

He thinks I left him again.

I probably should have.

It would have been easier if I had simply disappeared, if he believed I didn't care. If he thought I was a cold-hearted bitch who played him to win a tournament, then only used him for some mind-blowing sex before I went on my merry way, it might have been easier for him to accept than the truth.

But that isn't an option.

Not anymore.

Not after last night.

Not after lying awake for hours, watching him sleep, feeling that steady rise and fall of his chest as he slipped into dreams that made him fitful and sent him reaching for me again.

Not when I know *why* he can't sleep soundly.

I swallow the emotion threatening to choke me, intending to call out to him and let him know I'm still here, but he appears in the archway leading back to the bedroom before I can.

Deliciously disheveled.

Dark hair askew.

Hard muscles on display.

Boxer briefs, that he must have tugged on when he climbed out of bed, hug his package perfectly.

God, he really is a beautiful man.

Inside and out.

And he is who he is because of the Hawkes, because of the love and support they gave him. Because of the role models he had in his life who taught him how to be a truly good person.

That makes all this so much harder.

He runs a hand over his cheek, now covered with dark stubble. "There you are..."

The relief in his voice simultaneously lifts my heart and shatters it at the same time.

Fuck.

I offer him a tight smile as I fight through the sob that threatens to slip out at the mere sight of him. "Here I am."

He wanders out into the living room, narrowing his eyes on me. "What are you doing sitting out here?" Bending, he feathers a kiss across my lips, grinning against them. "Waking up would've been a lot better if you'd still been in bed...for *both* of us."

The promise in his words makes me shiver. Because he can absolutely deliver on it. Spending *any* time like that with Coen is...fucking magical. The kind of thing you only read about in romance novels.

But just like that fiction—this isn't real.

None of it can last.

Not with the biggest lie of all still filling the space between us.

I force a smile and nod, but he immediately seems to catch my mood, his brow furrowing.

He cradles my face in his palms, examining me carefully. "What's wrong?"

Fucking EVERYTHING.

I want to scream it at him. I want to scream into the void that feels like it's been enveloping me for weeks. But it's been far longer than that, if I'm truly being honest with myself. This spiral has gone on for so long that I don't even know which way is up anymore.

"There's something I need to tell you..."

His brow furrows, and he steps back, letting his palms fall away from my face to take the seat beside me. He quickly pulls my hand into his and squeezes it. "Okay?"

God, I don't want to do this.

If there were any other way, *any*thing I could do to save him from this pain, I would do it. Even if it cost me everything, I would do it without thought in a heartbeat.

"You said no more games." I glance over at him and watch his shoulders stiffen. "I should have told you this from the beginning, but I didn't know you then. I shouldn't have let it get this far—"

His face pales. "Let *what* get this far?"

A single tear slips from my eye, despite me trying desperately to keep them at bay, and I tug my hand free from his, unable to bear his touch when I'm about to confess my sins. "None of this was supposed to happen."

His jaw clenches, his body starting to tremble. "None of *what*?"

I spread out my hands. "This. You. *Us*. I wasn't supposed to..."

The words won't come out.

But they don't have to for Coen to sense he isn't going to like what I'm about to say.

A low growl slips from his chest, so different from the ones full of sexual promise he's offered me over the last twelve hours. "Whatever it is, Allegra, just fucking tell me already."

Rip off the Band-Aid.

"I wasn't just in Atlantic City to scope out my potential opponents. I was there for you...specifically."

He rests his forearms on his knees, leaning forward. "I kind of figured that. None of the other players from Monaco were in Atlantic City for that game."

I shake my head, swiping away another tear. "No, you don't understand. I was there for you because I *had* to be."

Coen swallows thickly, his Adam's apple bobbing.

A sob threatens to climb up my throat. "I was sent to watch you."

He remains deathly still—unnaturally so. "By whom?"

I meet his suddenly icy, hard gaze. "By someone powerful enough to make me do it."

His hands tighten into fists, and he shoves up to his feet. "Fucking Satriano."

Somehow, hearing *him* say his name instead of having to utter it myself makes it a little easier to breathe.

It shouldn't, though.

That name is going to be what undoes *all* of this.

"I'm so sorry... I never meant to—"

Coen whirls to face me, his entire body locked up tight with barely contained rage, fists at his sides. "What the *fuck* does he have on you?"

It takes a moment for me to process what he's asking. "What?"

"What. Does. He. *Have*. On. You?"

That would make me do this...

That is what he's asking.

He's trying to figure out what sort of blackmail material he's holding over me and how I became so entangled with a man like Damiano Satriano.

"It isn't that simple."

A single step draws him close enough that I can see him trembling. "He sent you to spy on me."

I nod.

"To get close to me?"

I nod again. "He wanted me to make sure you weren't going to fuck him over. He wanted me to ensure that you were still capable of playing for him, that you were as good as everyone always thought you were, given your recent losses—"

"And he wanted you to be a weakness that he could exploit, if he needed to."

The way he says it rips my chest open, and I climb to my feet, moving toward him to try to stem the flow of agony that seems to be rushing from him, but he backs away.

"What the fuck?" He scrubs his hands over his face. "This can't be happening..."

"Coen, I'm sorry."

I reach for him, but he bats away my hand, flinching at my attempt to touch him; when only hours ago, we were wrapped up together in bed as close as two people can be.

"Satriano needs control—"

"And he didn't think threatening my entire fucking family was enough of a way to control me? He had to send in his whore?"

I flinch at the word, but he isn't wrong in that assessment.

From where he's standing, that's exactly how it looks.

It doesn't matter that it isn't true. It doesn't matter that I was explicitly told *not* to get too close. It doesn't matter that I really fell for him or that I wish I could take it all back.

Tears stream unbidden down my cheeks, and my chest heaves as I struggle to fill my lungs through the sobs. "It wasn't supposed to be like this. I wasn't supposed to...I wasn't supposed to actually like you."

"Oh, fuck you, Allegra." He points a shaky finger at me. "You've played me from the start, and you're still playing me now with these fake tears."

"No." I shake my head, wrapping my arms around myself. "I just couldn't lie to you anymore. Do you have any idea what he'll do if he finds out that I told you?"

He steps into my space now, looming over me, anger flashing in his gaze. "You're going to tell me everything he said to you about me, everything he asked you to do, every word he's ever uttered to you about my family."

I nod, desperate to offer him *anything* that might prove to him that he's wrong about what this is between us. "He said you were important, but that he didn't know if he could trust you, that he didn't know if you still had it in you to play like he needs you to. And he didn't know if you would run and hide or stay and fight."

His hand moves to the base of his head, and he rubs his neck, pacing. "Fuck."

"So, he wanted me to get close, to give you a reason to keep coming back to the table and, in turn, repaying him and proving you could still hack it."

He gapes at me. "But you *beat* me."

A little half-smile curls my lips, despite the utter despair enveloping me. "I wasn't supposed to, and he was pretty fucking pissed about it. He didn't realize I had gotten under your skin that much, that I had that much control over you."

His jaw clenches at my choice of words.

"I did that because I was already attracted to you, and *I*

wanted the upper hand, to see if I could rattle you. I did it because I wanted it. Not because Satriano asked me to."

He stalks away, shoving his hands through his hair and tugging on it. "And when you let me fuck you in the penthouse, what was that? Assuring your win at any future event by *completely* getting in my head so that you can pay back whatever debt you owe him faster, too?"

"I can never pay back the debt I owe Satriano."

My words hang in the air between us, as thick and heavy as his rage.

His shoulders square, as if he's preparing for battle. "Get the fuck out."

"Coen, no, I'm sorry. I never meant—"

He growls again. This time, a warning. "Get the *fuck* out of my room."

I shiver, hating the change in his tone, the shift from lover to whatever the hell this is.

This is the Coen he thinks his family wanted.

The one they expected to walk into a courtroom and tear people apart, limb from limb.

I knew what was coming, that there was no way I'd escape any of this unscathed, but it hits me harder than I care to admit how much I actually give a shit about him, about all this, about what I've done to him.

"Please let me explain—"

"You've explained enough, and I don't want to hear any more of your bullshit excuses and lies. None of this was real, and you knew it from the beginning." A mirthless laugh slips from his lips, and he shakes his head. "You're a very good actress, Allegra. I'll hand it to you. Last night, I almost believed..." He trails off, his hands fisting at his sides. "You have three fucking minutes to get dressed and get out of here. And I never want to see you again. Do you understand me?"

I nod as the tears soak my vision, making the man who gave

me the best night of my life—more than once—nothing more than a blur.

"I *am* sorry."

Slipping past him back into the bedroom, I fight through the trembling that threatens to make my legs collapse. I strip away the hotel robe I wrapped myself in this morning and drag my dress off the floor, where we tossed it in our haste last night.

My hands shake so violently trying to pull it on that I can barely do it.

I don't even bother with my heels. I snatch them up and throw my purse over my shoulder.

It's everything I came with—except my heart, which will remain here with Coen, even if it is shattered and he doesn't want it.

I take one last longing look at the bed we shared, remembering every touch, every kiss, every thrust, and the way he completed me so fully, remembering what I destroyed.

COEN

THE USUAL LIGHTS, sounds, and excitement of the casino floor feel like being bombarded with rapid gunfire today. Shot after shot slamming into me violently. Tearing through me. I squeeze my eyes closed against the assault on my senses, my footsteps faltering slightly.

Bishop's hand closes around my elbow. "Are you all right?"

I glance over at her next to me. "Fine, just...tired."

Emotionally fucking wrung out.

Destroyed.

Lost.

Something I can't even put into words.

She waggles her eyebrows, releasing her grip on me as we

keep moving through the Venetian toward the high-stakes poker room. "I figured you were up late last night with Allegra, but I've never known you to do anything that would put you so off your game on a day like this."

I clench my jaw to keep from lashing out at her when this has nothing to do with Bishop and her friendly observation. She doesn't know Allegra betrayed me in the worst way possible, that it was all a fucking sham set up by the man who seems intent on ruining my life and that of the rest of the Hawkes along with it.

Bishop is just being herself—nosy with no filter. And since she has had to play my shadow since I returned to New Orleans, I already feel bad enough. She certainly doesn't need me snapping at her for something that is completely not her fault.

Just keep walking.

If I don't put one foot in front of the other and *force* myself to move toward that tournament...I'll end up back in that bed.

Drowning in her jasmine scent.

In the scent of us *together.*

And I might never get out.

Going catatonic isn't an option today—unfortunately.

I weave around a gaggle of women with matching shirts indicating they're on a bachelorette trip and beeline toward the room I'm expected at in only a handful of minutes.

Bishop's gaze stays on me the entire time instead of worrying about our surroundings, which is supposed to be her job. "Did something happen?"

I chance glancing over at her again as we keep moving. "Why?"

"You seem unusually grumpy this morning for somebody who undoubtedly spent the night buried inside a woman he seems rather obsessed with."

Fucking hell.

Wincing, I scrub my hand over my cheek. "Was I that obvious?"

The one damn time in my life I become obsessed with a woman and she ends up being a plant. A scammer. Just another one of Satriano's minions who is working off her debt to the man who also owns me.

What are the fucking chances?

Maybe it's karma for what I did to Atlas. People always say payback is a bitch, and it definitely feels like someone is paying me back for something with this entire thing.

Bishop snorts. "We all saw the way you looked at her at dinner. That girl got under your skin...and fast."

"Don't fucking remind me."

Her brows wing up. "So, something did happen."

I sigh, pausing for a moment to let a stumbling couple, who look like they've been up all night doing exactly what Allegra and I were, pass. "You could say that..."

But I'm not about to tell her what Allegra confessed.

It's too embarrassing.

It's still too raw.

The betrayal.

The pain.

How the fuck did I fall for that?

For her?

How did I not see it coming?

How did I not know?

My chest tightens the same way it has every time I thought about that woman and what she did to me since she walked out of the presidential suite more than an hour ago.

All through my shower...scrubbing my skin until it's red and sore to try to get rid of her scent and the feel of her all over me.

Changing multiple times...trying to find clothes that her

smell doesn't cling to, even though she never even touched them.

I couldn't help glancing at the bed, remembering what it felt like to have her in my arms. Hearing the echo of her gasps as she came on my cock. Feeling the flutter of her lips along mine.

It was all an act.

A fucking game she *swore* she wasn't playing.

So were her tears this morning.

And the last thing I want to do is reveal that—yet again—I let a snake into our lives.

I'd much rather wallow in my own self-pity and stupidity, but Bishop needs to know. They all do...eventually. It's not something I can keep quiet about.

Which means, no matter how painful it might be, I have to tell Bishop and everyone else.

"She's working for fucking Satriano."

Bishop's steps falter, and she grabs my arm, halting my progress and pulling me off the main walkway and to a quieter area near the wall. "What?" She stares at me, waiting, and when I don't answer fast enough, she digs her fingers into my skin. "Coen, explain!"

I suck in a long breath, trying to steady my heart that doesn't seem to want to cooperate. "She fucking played me, Bish. From the first fucking minute I saw her, she was working an angle."

"What do you mean?"

"She was working for Satriano the whole time. Getting close to me, watching me, ensuring I would play. Ensuring I wasn't going to bolt and disappear, ensuring I wasn't going to fuck him over."

Her lips open and close a few times, her shock evident, as is the concern in her gaze. "Oh, my God, Coen—"

I jerk out of her hold. "I don't need your fucking sympathy right now. I have a tournament to win."

She narrows her eyes on me. "And what about her?"

I move back into the flow of people wandering the casino floor, stalking toward the door of the tournament room, wanting to get this started and over with as quickly as possible. Needing to so that I can get home and try to figure out some way to forget any of this ever happened and that she ever existed.

"I don't know what I'm supposed to do about her. I told her to stay the fuck away from me. If she gets within a hundred fucking yards of the room today"—I pause and motion to the casino—"you get her the fuck out."

"Of course." Bishop squares her shoulders, putting on her game face. And I'm not looking at my cousin anymore. I'm staring at the badass Saint trained her to be. "That's why I'm here, to protect you. I'm sorry that I didn't realize I needed to from her. I really thought you two were—"

I freeze and whirl to face her. "You thought we were what?"

She offers a half shrug. "The real deal. I don't know. I mean, it was obviously a sexual thing to start, but I saw the way she looked at you at dinner and when she showed up last night, wanting to talk to you...it seemed like it mattered. Like you mattered."

Which somehow makes it all worse.

"Yeah, well, it turns out she's a really fucking good actress and that's it."

Really. Fucking. Good.

"I'm sorry, Coen. Have you told—"

"No!" I cut her off a little too harshly. "And I'm not going to —at least not right away."

Her brow furrows. "Why not?"

"It doesn't matter. She's out of my life now. Out of the picture. She won't be back to cause any more trouble."

"Are you sure?"

"She wouldn't dare try. And it's irrelevant if she does. Satriano just lost his spy. *I* finally hurt *him*." For the first time since I woke alone this morning, I feel my lips start to curl up into a smile. "I finally got the upper hand."

"How so?"

"He doesn't have any way to monitor what I'm doing anymore and can't be used against me as any sort of leverage if I don't do what he wants. And that means I took back a little bit of control from that bastard."

She gives me a sympathetic look. "If that's the way you want to look at it."

It's the only way I can.

If I don't, it will follow me into the room.

We finally reach it, and I make my way over toward the table I've been assigned to for the first round, which will begin in just a few minutes.

Glancing at Bishop, I sigh. "If I don't think about it like that, there's no way that I can play today. And if I can't do that, he'll come after all of you."

She presses her lips together in a firm line, her dark eyes narrowing on me. "Are you sure you're up for this today? After everything that happened?"

"I don't have a fucking choice, Bishop."

The casino host, Devin, steps up and shakes my hand. "Welcome, Mr. Hawke. We have your seat right here."

He ushers me into one, asking if I need anything to eat or drink before we get underway, and I glance back at Bishop, who stands behind me, eyes vigilant, darting across everyone in the room, and to the door, watching for any threats, that now include Allegra.

None of this was supposed to happen.

I wasn't supposed to actually like you.

Her hollow excuses and empty apologies echo in my head. Taunting me the same way her breathy gasps and moans do.

Fuck.

I scrub my hands over my face and lean my elbows on the table. Sheer exhaustion overtakes me, and for the first time in my adult life, I *don't* feel prepared at all for this game.

All those rules Dad laid out for me.

All the things he taught me about how to win.

They all mean nothing when my head and heart are filled with Allegra's bullshit and too many questions to ever sort through.

Butch settles into his seat at the far end of the table, adjusting his cowboy hat to tilt it toward me. "You look like shit."

Of course he would be here.

"Gee, thanks."

The Texan smirks. "This have anything to do with your lady friend?"

My back stiffens. "What?"

He winks at me. "Saw you two having a cozy dinner last night, but she isn't on the player's list today…"

"No, she isn't."

And if she knows what's good for her, she'll never show her face at any tournament I'm at again.

His eyebrows waggle. "Trouble in paradise?"

There never was a fucking paradise.

Just Hell.

Only, I never realized I was in it until it was too late.

17

COEN

The only thing in the world that might have even a remote possibility of hurting as much as what Allegra did to me with her confession is getting punched by Atlas.

Which is why, as soon as I landed back in New Orleans and discovered he and Wren had come home over the weekend while I was in Vegas, this had to be my first stop.

Not home to my condo to wallow. Not to Mom and Dad's house to tell them what happened. Not to the club to drown myself at the bar after revealing my defeat to Uncle Savage and Gabe and the rest of them.

Here.

I climb out of the SUV and stare at the gym, watching Atlas move around the ring through the massive storefront windows. Even shadowboxing, he's incredible. He moves with such precision. Such speed and power.

How did I ever doubt him?

That familiar guilt tears at my stomach again, and I let my gaze drift to the left, to Wren's Pilates studio.

She bustles around inside with several of her clients, getting ready to start a class, with a bright smile on her face.

Apparently, their vacation did them both some good.

After the fight and the wedding, not knowing what Satriano might do, they had to leave to feel safe, but now that I have my deal with him, have taken the debt fully onto my back, hopefully they can concentrate on being happy and getting ready for their baby instead of constantly looking over their shoulders.

Bishop joins me on the curb, and the movement draws Wren's gaze out to the street.

Her eyes meet mine, and her entire body stiffens for a second before a forced smile spreads across her lips. Then she returns to what she was doing, as if I'm not even here.

I can't say I blame her.

It's well deserved.

And so will be whatever the man in the ring decides I am due.

Bishop gives me a knowing look. "You sure you want to do this right now?"

Haven't you been beaten up enough?

That's what she's *really* asking without actually saying it.

And frankly, I do already feel like I've gone eight rounds with the likes of Atlas after what Allegra did to me. But I owe it to Atlas to face him and what I did like a man instead of hiding and licking my wounds until I'm ready to get beaten down again.

Might as well take it all at once.

"Yep..."

I tug open the gym door and step inside with Bishop right on my heels.

Astrid and Isaac stand on one side of the ring, watching Atlas train, but all eyes turn to me the moment the door closes behind us.

Isaac raises a brow. "You're back."

I nod, shoving a hand through my hair. "Just landed half an hour ago."

Astrid's gaze travels over my athletic shorts and T-shirt—certainly not my typical attire, even when traveling. "And you came straight here...dressed like *that*?"

The wheels are already turning behind her eyes, and Atlas spits out his mouthguard and moves to the ropes, leaning against them. "Why is that?"

There's no point beating around the bush.

No excuse I can offer.

No apology deep enough to even begin to heal the wound I created.

Atlas and I haven't spoken since the night before the fight when I confessed to him what I had done, the position I had put him in. When I revealed how little faith I had in him.

I couldn't bring myself to face him after he refused to throw the fight and ended up walking away with the belt—and a major enemy in Satriano. I couldn't bring myself to look him in the eye at the wedding, either.

Not knowing I was the reason he had to take Wren and disappear from New Orleans, or he would be risking their lives.

But I *have* to meet his gaze now.

And I can still see the anger simmering underneath the icy blue, the same way it did that night I came clean.

I hold out my hands, palms up in surrender. "I'm here because there's absolutely nothing you can do to me in that ring that I don't deserve."

His eyes widen.

Isaac guffaws, uncrossing his arms from his chest to hold up a hand. "You are *not* getting in the ring with Atlas today."

I scowl at him, already tugging off my shirt. "I don't need your protection."

Bishop snorts from where she leans against the wall behind me. I look over my shoulder and scowl at her, but she has the audacity to just grin at me.

Maybe I should invite her for a match, too.

Next to Atlas, Bishop is the most lethal in the ring, and she would certainly be a challenge.

But right now, my annoyance with her is overpowered by my need to make it up to Atlas somehow.

He scans my face, searching for something. Hesitation maybe. Fear. The *normal* things someone would feel when offering themselves up as a human punching bag for the light-heavyweight champion of the world. "You really want to do this?"

Astrid's gaze snaps to her brother. "No, you *can't.*"

Atlas steps back from the ropes, bouncing on his feet. "If it'll make you feel better for me to kick your ass, I'm more than willing."

He pops his mouth guard back in, motioning for me to come to him.

That man is *going to kick my ass.*

Anyone with any sense of self-preservation would run in the other direction, but I toss my T-shirt onto the bench that runs along the ring, toe off my shoes, remove my socks, and slide in under the ropes.

The familiar scents of the gym and feel of the mat under my feet help me focus on what I need to do to not *die* today.

Isaac grabs the ropes, face twisted in concern. "Are you fucking nuts? You haven't trained in months, and Atlas has every reason not to have any control when it comes to you."

I roll my shoulders and shake out my arms, bouncing on my feet and trying to warm myself up. Bishop appears with tape, gloves, and headgear and climbs in with me to help me put them on, since Isaac clearly won't. She gives him a look that tells me she's thinking the same thing, but Bishop also knows what Allegra did, so she understands she's not going to be able to talk me out of anything.

Not when I need a good beating to distract me from the emotional pain threatening to tear me apart.

Astrid leans into the ring from the other side, murmuring something to Atlas that I can't quite hear, but he waves her off, dismissing whatever she said with a determined set of his broad, strong shoulders.

My eyes drift to the massive scar across the left one—the very reason I bet against him in the first place.

That bullet should have ended his career.

Instead, he walked away from the devastation with a fiancée, a baby on the way, and the belt.

Was the pain worth it for all that?

Right now, I think I'd give anything not to feel this way. I'd take a bullet. I'll take a fucking beating...

Bishop wraps my hands and finishes securing my gloves, looking up at me with intense, dark eyes. "I couldn't find your mouth guard in your locker."

I shrug off the concern. "It's been a while. I don't know what happened to it."

Her lips curl. "Well, don't lose your teeth, pretty boy."

She attaches my headgear, then smacks me on the temple and climbs out to watch with Isaac and Astrid—neither looks particularly happy about what's about to go down.

If Jimmy were here, this would never be happening, and if Wren were aware of what was going on here, she would be flying over in a second to stop it before it started.

But there isn't anyone to stop it now.

I face Atlas.

People always called him a rebel.

They said he didn't quite fit into the Hawke family or the perfectly coiffed, manicured picture we present to the world. He never lived up to what was expected of him. In that way, we've very much been the outsiders our whole lives. But at least they *had* expectations for him. With me, I've always just floated by, drifted restlessly, like a lost puppy searching for a place to settle.

And look where that's gotten me.

Look where it's gotten all of us.

Atlas motions for me to come at him.

The anger in his gaze hasn't abated. If anything, having me in here and within reach of his powerful right hook seems to have only made him more determined.

He takes the first swing, and I manage to duck out of the way to avoid being knocked unconscious two seconds into the sparring match.

We've always done this for fun and to help him train.

But this is neither.

Both of us entered this ring with an agenda, and he seems intent on his, throwing a right hook that glances off my shoulder. I take the opportunity to make a jab that glances off his rib cage.

He raises his brow. "I thought I was supposed to be the one kicking your ass."

His words are garbled slightly by his mouthguard, but the humor in them and the surprise that I actually touched him remind me of who we were before everything went to shit.

I grin at him.

God, I've missed this.

The banter.

The comaraderie.

The challenge.

The love that underlies it all.

But I can't even enjoy it.

Not when I know what I did to him.

His next swing is so fast I don't even see it coming and lands on my temple. My head snaps to the side, and despite the head protection, my vision goes dark, my ears ring, and I stumble sideways.

The world sways, and I sag against the ropes, trying to clear the buzzing and fogginess encroaching on the edges of my brain.

"Careful, Atlas..."

Through the ringing, Isaac's warning echoes through my head.

I don't want him to be careful.

This is what I deserve, an ass beating to end all ass beatings.

And despite it all, even with as angry as he might be, I know Atlas and trust him. He will never use his full force against anyone who isn't at his level—which means none of us. He may want to hurt me, but he won't *hurt* me.

Atlas bounces on his feet. "Come on, Coen." He mumbles the words around his mouth guard, then gives up and spits it out. "Let's go. It's just you and me now."

But it isn't.

It's not just the two of us in the ring.

It's *all* of us.

Atlas is every one of the Hawkes I betrayed, everyone I lied to, who I'm still lying to since I haven't told anyone but Bishop about the truth Allegra laid out for me.

Guilt claws at my chest as I push off the ropes and advance on him with renewed purpose.

He wants me to put up a fight, so I'll at least *try*.

I throw out a combination, hoping to sneak one past his guard, but he's too good, anticipating every move and easily blocking, only to land a blow to my shoulder and chest.

The pain renews my purpose—give him what he needs.

Pushing through it, I swing, dancing around him and looking for any opening. I somehow manage to land one to his shoulder, but in the process, I expose myself to a right uppercut that lands squarely in my rib cage.

Fuck.

Pain explodes.

All the air rushes from my lungs.

My vision goes completely black.

I double over, crumpling to my knees.

"Enough!"

Astrid's voice cuts through the cloud of agony. Forcing my eyes open, I see her climb into the ring and put herself between me and her brother. She pushes on his sweat-slicked chest, his breaths heaving in and out of him as he glares at me.

"Atlas! Stop!"

He stares down at me. "If my new championship belt isn't enough, maybe that proved to you that I'm not the fucking pussy you thought I was."

I gasp for breath, struggling to get to my feet again, and swaying unsteadily. Isaac slides into the ring and wraps his arm around my waist, helping me stand.

Wincing at the icy-hot, shooting pain through my ribs, I shake my head. "You know...it...wasn't...like that."

Atlas' eyes meet mine. "It was. You dug yourself into a hole, and you thought my weakness was your way out of it."

That much is true.

But it isn't that I doubted how good he is. It's that I saw how much damage that bullet had done to him, how he wasn't fully recovering. His struggles tore all of us apart, but in the end, it was too tempting a proposition. An easy way to get back to even.

Atlas rolls his shoulders and finally releases a long, heavy breath, as if he's resigning himself to something. "But it's over now..."

"What is?"

"This." He motions between us with his gloved hands. "I forgive you."

"What?"

I couldn't have heard him right...

He pushes Astrid out of the way slightly and steps up to me. "What you did was really shitty. Beyond shitty, but at the end of the day, we're family and we always will be. No matter what kind of things we do to each other. You bet against me, and I broke your ribs. So, we're even."

With that, he saunters to the edge of the ring, then slides under the ropes and stalks back toward the locker room.

I sag into Isaac's hold.

He shakes his head, helping me toward ropes. "You're such a fucking idiot, kid."

Isaac isn't wrong.

"I am."

And I didn't learn my lesson.

I let Allegra walk right into my life and betray me. I didn't learn anything about making rash decisions with my heart instead of my head. But I won't make that mistake again.

ALLEGRA
THREE DAYS LATER

I WOULD HAVE THOUGHT, after weeks of traveling, going from country to country, tournament to tournament, that finally being home at my place in New York would be a relief.

Comforting.

Relaxing even.

But in the last couple of days, since I came back from Vegas, none of those things have been true.

Nothing has felt right.

Not my bed.

Not my clothes.

Not my life.

If I can even call this living.

It's as though I'm wandering around in a thick, dark fog, with no sense of direction, unable to find anything solid to cling to or orient myself with. And it's all because of Coen.

This wasn't supposed to happen.

When I said those words to him, I meant them.

I never intended to fall for him.

Never intended to care about what Satriano was doing to him, about how he was twisting a knife in the Hawkes' backs and forcing Coen to be a pawn.

It was just par for the course.

The same things Satriano has done for as long as I've known him.

None of it mattered until I actually met the man with the Caribbean-blue eyes, warm smile, and wicked mouth. Now he's gone—for good.

And it feels as if a part of me has been ripped away, like those seams Coen tore apart and then expertly mended with his touch, his kiss, his affection, are all unraveling again.

Even venturing out for my favorite bagel and coffee hasn't done much to improve my mood. Yesterday, I couldn't even take a bite. But at least I made it out of the condo.

Today, I haven't even gotten out of bed, and it's almost noon.

Bone-deep exhaustion has kept me under the covers, head buried beneath a pillow, blocking out the sounds of the vibrant city just outside the windows that let in the offending light.

It's the only place I can feel anything even remotely resembling peace because I certainly can't find it when I try to sleep.

All that comes when I close my eyes are memories that only bring pain.

After spending the night in his arms, in his care, being worshiped and consumed by that man, I don't think I'll ever be able to sleep again.

That realization, the anger of knowing this agony will *never* get better, finally forces me to shove off the covers and slip out of the sheets that I wish smelled like him, like us.

It would be torture, but it would be *something* to cling to.

Anything.

I don't have anywhere to go. Nowhere to be. Nothing to do except let my anger and despair build as I wander around the condo, aimlessly moving from one room to the other, staring at all the luxurious things that decorate it...

And hating all of it.

I walk over to the stunning handmade Murano glass sculpture shaped like jasmine—my favorite flower. It likely cost a small fortune, and when I first received it, the gift took my breath away and made me feel special and loved. It made me feel *seen*.

Now, all I see is the ugliness it represents.

It's evidence of the spiraling of my life that I've been trying to stop.

I knock it off the pedestal it sits on.

It falls to the polished tile floor and shatters, but I don't even flinch at the sound or the shards of green and white glass that scatter across the room.

I relish it because it matches the way I feel.

Shattered.

Splintered.

Torn apart.

Destroyed.

That look on Coen's face when he realized I continued to lie to him, even though I promised no more games, was enough to break me.

He had every reason to believe nothing had changed over time. Every reason to question my motives and feelings and not to believe a single thing I said to him. But it was too hard to tell him, knowing what it would do to him and to us.

It was selfish to keep the truth hidden so I could have more of him.

But I knew it wouldn't last forever, it couldn't, and now I have to deal with the fallout, no matter how painful it might be.

I aimlessly walk over to my television, the only companion I've had for days, and yank it off the wall. The massive 100-inch screen crashes onto the floor, cracking with a noise that echoes through the loft space and helps cement the reality that he's gone in my heart.

You don't have anyone to blame but yourself...

I move over to the bar, ready to either drown myself in alcohol so I won't feel the agony anymore or toss the crystal decanters of expensive booze so I can get that moment of satisfaction from watching them shatter.

But the condo door clicks open behind me before I can grab one.

Shit.

Only one other person has the key, and it's the last person in the world I want to see right now.

"What happened here, *bambina*?"

The nickname he always used with me when I was a child floats over me. And where it once brought comfort, like a familiar, loving caress that soothed my tears through scuffed knees and other childish problems, now it only feels like salt being poured on an open wound.

I turn to face him.

As the door closes behind him, he raises a white eyebrow at me. "Redecorating?"

I've spent days on the edge of a full-on breakdown, and today, I'm trembling, right at the precipice, but I refuse to cry in front of him. I won't let him see how much all of this has affected me.

He doesn't understand weakness.

He doesn't appreciate the intricacies of caring about someone the way I do Coen.

He wouldn't be able to wrap his head around my anguish, and he certainly won't offer me a shoulder to cry on even if he somehow did.

I square my shoulders and make my way into the kitchen, giving him my back. "I'm going to make an espresso. Would you like one?"

His low chuckle follows me, and he settles on one of the stools at the counter. "That's a silly question, *bambina*. I never turn down an espresso."

I know.

And I hope that it will take his focus off what he just walked in on.

But something tells me his arrival wasn't random.

He knows I've been home for days, that I didn't stay in Vegas as planned to play in the tournament. His men have probably been watching the condo, letting him know when I have ventured out and that I basically haven't, except for those few vain attempts.

He hasn't called, hasn't appeared until now.

I keep my back to him as I make the drinks, the sound of the machine firing up filling the awkward silence between us, until I have the two tiny espresso cups. The rich smell of espresso brewing hits my nose, and my stomach rumbles, reminding me that I have barely eaten in days and desperately crave caffeine, too.

He remains at the counter, watching me as I drop a cube of sugar into mine, then turn back toward him and set his in front of him.

"*Grazie.*"

I take a sip, knowing better than to look away from him while I do. This man uses any chance he has to assess people, to find their weak spots and learn how to exploit them.

It's what he's good at.

Far too good.

I learned from the best, which is why it's so much harder to keep him from seeing the things I want to keep hidden from him.

"I'm worried about you, Allegra."

Resting my hip against the counter, I try to remain casual, even though he just saw the evidence of my meltdown. "How come?"

He very judiciously doesn't mention the broken television or the pieces of glass glittering all across the floor. "Because you haven't been yourself lately..."

How could I be?

I bristle at his comment, the ease with which he dismisses the reason I might be upset with him and the entire situation. Shifting uneasily on my bare feet, I lock gazes with him to ensure he understands I'm not messing around. "I'm done with Coen Hawke."

His silvery brows rise as he takes a sip of his drink and assesses me over the rim. "Are you?"

"My effectiveness has reached its end."

He spins his cup in his hands, staring down into it. "I believe I'm the one who should make that determination. Not you."

Under any other circumstances, with any other mark, it would be his call, but he has no idea what went down between Coen and me. He can't possibly comprehend how impossible it would be to get within ten feet of Coen again. "He's done with me."

He tenses. "What happened?"

I know that look.

I've seen it a thousand times in my nearly thirty years on this planet, and I know what comes after it. The reason he developed the reputation that always precedes him.

He doesn't like failure, and what I have done is fail.

Spectacularly.

I could lie to him. I could tell him things just didn't work out, but he would see through that, see through me. The same way he always does everyone else.

"He knows the truth."

He freezes, his hand curling around the espresso cup. "And how did that happen?"

His sharp gaze watches me carefully to ensure I won't try to bullshit him. He wants the truth; he needs it to advance his plans.

I can't lie to him.

I won't ever be able to.

"I told him the truth."

He slowly raises his cup to his mouth and sips his espresso before setting it on the counter and leaning back slightly. "Why'd you do that?"

It's posed as a simple question, but it's one that doesn't have a simple answer, nor is he as casual about it as he's trying to make himself appear. Anger simmers beneath the surface of his olive skin. Anger I've seen directed at so many people over the years but never at me until this moment.

My legs tremble, and I try to steady myself against the counter before I make this admission. "Because I care about him."

He stills, his back stiffening.

"You do what you have to, but I'm done fucking with Coen Hawke."

What's left of my heart can't handle seeing him again or being asked to push him and play him any further.

"Perhaps you shouldn't have gotten personally involved..."

I slam my mug onto the counter, my frustration boiling over as the tears I've been fighting start to burn in my eyes. "I don't know what you want from me."

He rests his arms on the counter, leaning toward me, ensuring I meet his gaze. "Your help in securing my empire. And you know exactly why I'm doing all this."

"It's fucking secure!" I spread my hand out absently. "Look at the way you play everyone like they're puppets. You already have him by the balls. He doesn't want anything to happen to the rest of the Hawkes. He'll do whatever you ask. You don't *need* me involved."

He raises a brow. "Are you sure about that?"

"Yes."

Coen will do anything to protect the Hawkes, and that includes selling his soul to this man across the counter from me.

Settling back again, he shakes his head. "I never expected this from you, *bambina*. I thought I could trust you."

"You can. I just can't be involved with anything having to do with the Hawkes."

He issues a low humming sound, as if he's considering my words and downs the rest of his espresso. His eyes stay locked on me as he climbs to his feet, rebuttoning his suit coat. "What am I to do with you now, Allegra? If I can't rely on you to be my ally, does that make you my enemy?"

I shake my head. "Of course not. But I just can't. I can't mess with him anymore. Find another way to keep an eye on him. If you really need another weakness, it can't be me. I won't ever see Coen Hawke again."

He raises another silver brow. "Able to predict the future now?" A slow grin spreads across his face. "That's an incredible talent to have, Allegra. I hope it serves you well."

"I'm not your enemy..." It comes out sounding far too much like a plea for my liking, but I had to reinforce those words. "You have Coen for whatever you need him for. Please don't push me on this anymore. Please."

I hate asking him for anything, even more so to actually have to beg for it.

But I don't have any other choice right now.

We both know what he's capable of and how dangerous he is when he wants to be. The Hawkes are still squarely in his sights, and that means there's always a chance Coen's going to get hurt even more than I've already hurt him.

I can't be part of making things worse.

I'm barely surviving Coen as it is.

18

TWO WEEKS LATER

COEN

I watch the casino floor on the hundreds of monitors covering the entire wall in front of us. All the happy players as they win and the not-so-happy ones when they lose.

Nothing out of the ordinary.

Nothing I don't see every single day when I come to work.

Still, the hairs on the back of my neck stand on end, my knee bouncing incessantly, a nervous energy I can't shake coursing through me. "I don't like this. Something feels off."

Gabe turns his head toward me, raising a sandy-blond brow from where he stands beside me with his arms crossed over his chest, examining the monitors with his well-trained eye. "How so?"

It *looks* like a normal day.

There hasn't been a single issue since I arrived three hours ago.

And we've spent weeks planning for today.

But it isn't normal.

Pretending that it is will only cause us to let down our guards when we need to be on full alert to avoid imminent disaster.

It's the biggest day for Hawke Hotel since the grand opening, one that will help establish our position as one of the premier locations to stay and play.

I keep scanning, keep searching for that *one* thing that would warrant this feeling I've had in the pit of my stomach all morning. "I don't know. Just a feeling."

Gabe nods slowly, narrowing his eyes as if he might be able to ascertain what has me rattled simply by looking at me himself. "Well, as a Ranger, I learned to trust my gut because it was very seldom wrong."

"That isn't very reassuring."

He offers a shrug. "It wasn't supposed to be."

That's one thing I've always greatly appreciated about Uncle Gabe. The man doesn't beat around the bush about anything. He doesn't pull punches. He will tell it exactly like it is, even if it leaves others uncomfortable.

But his warning to trust my gut sits heavy in it.

Something is wrong.

I'm not seeing it yet, but it's there.

I let my gaze drop to the screen showing the high-stakes poker room where we're about to host our first tournament, one we arranged to bring in some of the biggest players in the world. "I just don't believe that Satriano isn't going to make some sort of move soon. And today would be the perfect day to do it."

He's been radio silent in the weeks since Vegas, but we all learned a long time ago that just because we don't hear from him doesn't mean he's not up to something behind the scenes that's going to get all of us into a position we don't want to be in.

Especially me, since I'm his new toy.

And he's already proven how much he loves to fuck with me.

Gabe follows my line of sight to that particular screen. "I agree with that logic, but we've got everyone watching for anything even remotely suspicious. Saint and Bishop are out on the floor on top of our regular security and the extras we brought in. If he's dumb enough to do something today, we'll stop him."

I grind my teeth together, wishing I could so easily believe in the infallibility of our careful planning. "I hope you're right."

My voice doesn't hold any confidence because I have none.

Not after Allegra's confession.

It has rattled me more than I care to admit or even acknowledge to myself. And for the almost two weeks since Vegas, I haven't been able to stop thinking about what else I missed when I was so blinded by her.

Did I say something I shouldn't have to her about our operations?

Did I reveal something about the family that could put us in more danger?

I can't help thinking it's a distinct possibility that I did.

Because I didn't just let down my guard with Allegra, I completely obliterated it.

And it never even crossed my mind that she might have been a plant, that I was supposed to fall for her for that very reason.

Maybe it has just put me on edge.

"Maybe I'm overreacting..."

Gabe glances at me. "I don't think you're overreacting, Coen. I don't think anyone can overreact when it comes to Satriano."

If I had been more cautious, nothing ever would have happened with Allegra. I would have recognized that it was about more than a card game for her, more than just about winning. She was working a *job* for the man I hate most in this world.

And I fucking missed it.

I absently rub at my still-sore ribs, almost wishing the pain was still fresh, a reminder to always keep my wits, to pay attention to everyone's motives, to remember that anyone can stab you in the back.

Especially with a man like Satriano pulling the strings.

"You really can't just take that fucker out?"

Gabe snorts and smacks me on the shoulder. "Believe me, if that were an option, we would've done it a long time ago. But you know if we tried it, his entire organization would come for us. He already has things in place. If something were to happen to him, it could make things even worse."

"Worse than this, being at his beck and call?"

It's almost like he's being intentionally absent. Building to something. The way things get eerily still before a major storm slams the coast.

"We'll be ready. Don't worry."

"Ready for what?" Savage comes up behind us.

I was so engrossed in my conversation with Gabe and watching the screens for any signs of trouble that I didn't even hear him enter the monitoring room.

Gabe sighs. "Anything Satriano might try."

Savage nods and scans the monitors as my phone buzzes in my pocket.

I slide it out and tense at "unknown" flashing across the screen. "Just a second. I need to take this."

And not in front of them.

For weeks, I've dreaded every text, every phone call. I've dreaded stepping into my own damn condo, afraid that man will be waiting for me again, despite insistence from the entire security team that it is locked down tight. But right now, I'm more worried it might be *her* on the other end of the line.

Satriano...I can handle.

My complicated feelings for Allegra are another matter entirely.

Gabe and Savage start talking, pointing to something on one of the screens, ignoring me as I step out into the hall and force myself to accept the call.

"Hello?"

"Coen..." Just the sound of his voice is enough to make my skin crawl. "I hope you're well."

Only because if I weren't, I wouldn't be of any use to him anymore.

I'm not at all surprised he's calling today. It justifies this unease. "What do you want?"

"The time has come, Coen."

My blood runs cold. "For what?"

"For you to do me another favor."

Shit.

Even though I anticipated it, knew it was coming and that I wouldn't like it, it doesn't mean I'm ready for it. Every fiber of my being wants to rebel, wants to tell the man to fuck right off and do his own dirty work.

But then my mind drifts to Atlas and Wren, to the rest of the family, and I can't bring myself to say those words.

"What do you want me to do?"

I can almost *hear* his satisfied grin.

"I have someone who's going to come and play in your tournament today."

My body tenses immediately.

Allegra?

The ache in my ribs intensifies as my heart gallops and my breathing stalls. "Who?"

For a few seconds, I don't think he's going to answer, almost like he's dragging it out intentionally, torturing me with the fact that it might be her.

Does he know her cover is blown? Does he know she came clean?

"The man's name is Alan. And you are going to ensure he wins."

And there it is.

What I knew was coming.

His first step in weaseling his way into Hawke Hotel, either to take it over or to take it down completely. "You want me to rig the game?"

"I hear the purse is quite large, almost four million. You can't expect me to walk away from that when I have an inside man."

Anger heats my blood as I pace farther away from the surveillance room's sliding glass doors. "You can't expect *me* to be able to rig a tournament with an hour's notice in your favor, either, nor can you expect me to do it in a casino my goddamn family owns."

"For now."

"Excuse me?"

"They own it *for now*. Any number of things could happen in the future that could take that establishment out of your hands."

It isn't even a veiled threat.

It's a statement of intent.

"That's your ultimate goal, isn't it? To take the hotel from us."

"Believe me, Coen, partnering with you and having the resources and strength of Hawke Enterprises and the family behind me would be far more beneficial, not to mention easier. But you've repeatedly told me, as have your uncles, your father, and your quite-animated brother, that it would happen over their dead bodies, which doesn't leave me much choice, does it?"

Fuck.

I scrub my hand over my face and glance up and down the hall to ensure no one's within earshot. From here, I can still see Savage and Gabe talking with one of the security personnel, likely going over the last-minute plans for the tournament before the players start arriving in the room.

"Go to the front desk and pick up the package that was left there for you. It contains a marked deck."

"You can't be serious. You don't think anyone will notice?"

"They won't. My player knows what to look for. No one else will notice the discrepancies on the backs of the cards."

"You haven't met my fucking family."

He chuckles low. "This is what you agreed to, Coen. I don't want you to have to suffer the consequences of trying to deny me. So, let's not argue about this."

Shit.

I don't have any choice, and he knows it. "Fine. I'll see what I can do."

"That isn't good enough. Make it happen."

He doesn't say "or else" before he ends the call, but he might as well have.

Fuck. Fuck. Fuck.

The man knows exactly what he's doing, wedging his foot in by asking me to do something like this when he really wants more. Next, he'll ask me to start skimming, and eventually, he'll figure out a way to take over the hotel entirely.

This isn't good.

This is really, really fucking bad.

I slip back into the monitoring room, and Gabe and Savage both glance over at me as I approach them.

Savage immediately notices my shift in mood. "Everything all right?"

For the briefest split second, I consider not telling them about the call, but they're too observant, too smart, far too fucking intelligent not to notice if I swap out the fucking deck. "We need to have a talk, privately."

I scan the security personnel seated at the various consoles and incline my head toward the hallway.

They know what I'm about to say, or at least suspect it, without me even uttering the words.

Gabe issues a low curse. "Does this have to do with our friend?"

I grit my jaw and nod. "And I was right about today. He's made a demand of me that I'm not sure I can ignore."

"Sir?" One of the security personnel turns back toward us and motions me over. "You gave us this photo, asked us to keep an eye out for her." He flashes me the picture of Allegra we handed out to everyone, and my blood runs cold again. He points to the screen and taps the main casino floor. "She just walked in."

Fuck.

I turn from the counter and stalk toward the doors, Gabe and Savage on my heels. "We're going to have to talk as we go. We don't have much time."

Gabe steps through the sliding doors first, then looks back at me. "Before what?"

"Before it all goes to shit."

ALLEGRA

Maybe this was a bad idea.

The moment I made the decision to get on that plane and come to New Orleans, I started second-guessing my sanity. It only got worse on the ride here. And now that I stand in the middle of the Hawke Hotel casino, the nagging feeling that this is going to backfire—badly—is suddenly even stronger.

I scan the casino, searching for that familiar mop of thick, dark hair that I spent so many hours running my fingers through and tugging on while he was fucking me or had his head buried between my legs.

They itch to do that even now. My body refusing to accept what my brain already knows—that he's gone forever—no matter how badly I may want to make things right.

Today is one step toward that, though I don't expect it to make a dent in what I owe Coen Hawke. At least, I know I'm finally doing the *right* thing. For the first time in a long time, I feel good about that.

I meander slowly down the main walkway of the casino, looking for Coen, but I also know that he'll be looking for me.

Without a shadow of a doubt, they have me on a list and have alerted everyone to be on the lookout for me today—of all days.

It's only a matter of time before he or someone else spots me and tries to throw me out on my ass.

If he had done that all those weeks ago when I came, things would have been so different. I wouldn't have ever had Coen Hawke, known what absolute pleasure feels like, but I wouldn't have broken his heart and my own in the process.

I've been both living for and haunted by those moments of happiness he showed me, but I'd give them all up to go back and prevent this tidal wave of pain from crashing down on him.

He doesn't deserve any of it.

A door opens along one of the walls to my left, a bank of slot machines separating me from it.

Coen steps out, his uncles, Gabe and Savage, with him, and his hard, flinty eyes find mine almost immediately.

He was definitely looking for me.

And this was definitely a mistake.

He made it very clear he doesn't want to see me again, that if I tried, there would be consequences to pay. I'll pay them, starting with the way my heart seizes in my chest just seeing him.

The hatred that simmers in his gaze brings tears to mine.

I knew what to expect after seeing it that morning in Vegas, but the past two weeks have apparently diminished it somehow in my mind.

This is going to hurt.

Coen stalks toward me through the crowd, jaw set hard, shoulders tense, perfectly tailored suit moving over that hard, muscled body I know so well.

I stand in place, waiting for him.

Showing him I'm not afraid and I'm not going to run.

I can't.

Not until I tell him what I came here to do.

When he finally stops a few feet from me, the tension and animosity filling the space between us overpowers the din of the casino and makes everything else disappear.

No loud machines.

No louder gamblers.

It's only the two of us.

"I told you I never wanted to see you again, Allegra. What the fuck are you doing here?"

Gabe and Savage stop on either side of him, waiting to hear my response.

Either they know exactly what happened between Coen and me, or at least they think they do. But even *he* doesn't truly understand it or how complicated things got.

He couldn't when he wouldn't let me fully explain.

"I came to warn you about what Satriano is going to do."

He raises a dark brow and glances between his uncles. "Why would you do that?"

I swallow thickly and step closer. "Can we go somewhere more private?"

If anyone overhears this, it could be very bad for the Hawkes and this place.

He shakes his head. "If you think I'm going to be in a room alone with you, Allegra, you're fucking nuts."

Shit, I guess we're doing this here, and with an audience.

Gabe and Savage keep keen eyes on the people moving around us, ensuring no one is paying attention to our conversation.

I guess there's nothing left to do but give Coen the warning I came here to relay. "He is going to ask you—"

Coen holds up a hand. "He already has."

Shit.

As soon as I knew what Satriano was planning, my first inclination was to call and warn Coen. But I knew he wouldn't take my calls. None of the Hawkes would. And even if I managed to leave a message, as soon as he heard my voice, he would have deleted it.

This could only come from me in person.

But maybe I'm too late.

"And what did you tell him?" I glance at the two men on either side of him, who don't seem surprised by the conversation, so he really must have told them everything. "Did you agree?"

"I didn't have much of a choice, did I?"

"Don't do it."

I step forward and wrap my hand around his wrist. That same crackle of electricity that seems to pass between us every time we touch jolts through me, and he flinches as if he felt it, too.

His eyes slowly lower to my hand. "I don't think you have any say in this, Allegra."

I plead with him with my eyes the best that I can. "There

are things you don't know, that you don't understand. I can *help*."

His brows fly up. "*You* help *us*?"

He barks out a laugh that gets swallowed by the noise around us. Gabe and Savage keep scanning to ensure no one's overhearing, but people are too busy drinking, playing, and enjoying themselves.

"Let me play."

His mouth gapes. "What?"

All eyes are back on me.

"Let me play in the tournament." I tighten my grip on him, trying to emphasize my point. "I know how he operates. I know the deck. I can beat the man he sent."

Coen glares at me, unmoved by my offer. "I'm surprised he didn't send you in the first place."

"I told him I wouldn't do it."

One dark brow rises. "Yet, you're here."

"Hell, I'm not here for him, Coen. You really don't understand that, do you?"

A flicker of something passes through his eyes.

Disbelief.

Hope.

I'm not sure which.

Savage moves closer to us. "So, you want to play against the man sent here by Satriano to win this tournament? I am not seeing how that would be any different. He still wins either way and has gotten us to compromise our casino."

I swallow the bile rising in my throat at what I'm about to say, what I'm about to do, and what it could cost me. "No, he won't win because I'm done working for him."

As soon as I say the words, I know it's the right thing to do.

I've been agonizing about it for weeks, going over every single moment I spent both with Coen and his family. And I realized one very important thing—I can't do it.

I can't watch a man like Satriano destroy these people.

Not if there's anything I can do to protect them.

They're not bad.

They're loving. They're ambitious. They're brutal at times. They're many things, but they're not bad people, and his hatred of them, whether warranted or not, shouldn't result in the type of things he's been planning for them.

"This is just the first step in a massive plan, Coen. You can't let him take it."

His eyes narrow. "That's almost exactly what I said to Gabe earlier."

Gabe gives me a tight nod.

Coen looks at him and then at Savage.

The man who sits at the head of Hawke Enterprises, who runs a multi-billion-dollar empire, offers his nephew a nod. "Your decision. You know her and him better than anyone else does."

"And how fucked up is that?" He tugs out of my grip and stares me down. "I want to make one thing very fucking clear, Allegra. If you do this, if this happens, if we let you play, it has nothing to do with *us*." He motions between us. "I don't care if you win or lose. As soon as you're done, you fucking leave, and I never want to see your face again."

I wince.

"This is about my family, our business, not about this sham of a relationship or whatever the fuck it was supposed to be that you created, got it?"

I clench my teeth to force myself to bite back the argument I want to make. The objection to how he classified what happened between us. Because it's all wrong. He has it *all* so, so unbearably wrong.

But this isn't the time or place to argue about it.

He's made how he feels very clear, and nothing I can say is

going to change his mind, certainly not in the next hour—tops —that we have before the first cards are dealt.

All I can do is nod my understanding, even if I didn't agree with a single word he said.

He scowls, then shoves a hand through his hair. "Let's set this plan in motion if we're going to do this."

"Please, Coen, trust me. I realize how hollow those words must sound right now, but please."

His shoulders finally give slightly, and he steps closer until his chest brushes mine. That familiar warmth instantly permeates my skin.

And damn, do I miss him.

The feel of his hard, strong body against me. His scent wrapping around me and invading every breath I take.

My body aches for him.

I want it all back, but I know I've lost him.

I've blown my chance of ever being with Coen Hawke in the way I truly want to, free of ulterior motives and lies, but I can at least do this for him. I can give him a potential way out.

"Fine"—his voice rumbles low—"but if you betray me again, there will be a price to pay that you aren't going to like."

I have no doubt that he'll follow through on that, and it won't be the same kind of torture and attention he paid to me in bed. "I understand."

He glances at his uncles. "We'll let her play."

"We don't have much time." I glance at my watch to confirm. "I'll walk you through the deck."

He gives me a sharp nod, then grabs my elbow and starts to lead me off the casino floor toward the hotel lobby, no doubt to grab the deck Satriano would have had to send for them to use.

His lips brush the back of my ear as we walk. Those callouses skate over my skin, and my steps falter. "Do you remember what I told you that night in that booth in Macau?"

How could I possibly ever forget?

He said a lot of things that night, but there's only one he could possibly be referring to.

I nod. "Nobody fucks with the Hawkes."

"Remember that today. Anytime you say anything. Every move you make at that table. Hell, every fucking *thought* you have, you remember that."

A shiver runs down my spine, and for the first time since I met him, I actually fear Coen Hawke and what he might be capable of.

19

ALLEGRA

I've sat across the table from a lot of dangerous men.

Men with power.

Men who were willing to do anything to get what they wanted.

But after hours of play, the most dangerous one sits across from me now.

Alan LeBlanc may not have known who I was when I sat down, but he sure as hell knows now.

The way he is watching me, assessing me, he's figured out that I know how to read the cards the same way he does. Which means now that we've reached the final hand—the one that will determine who wins the entire tournament—we're on a level playing field.

Not something any of the other people who have already been eliminated could say.

One by one, they dropped out, melting away from the table with their tails tucked between their legs, likely heading straight for the bar to lick their wounds.

We got lucky that no one noticed or suspected what was going on.

But Alan and I are both smart enough to know how to play and not draw attention to the fact that we're walking away with it.

And I am *so* close to doing just that.

Despite knowing I shouldn't, I lift my eyes from my cards and seek Coen's where he stands against the wall in the far corner of the high-stakes poker room.

Watching.

Waiting.

Brooding.

He's barely moved since the tournament started, other than to speak with a few employees who approached and whispered something to him. And I've done my best to ignore the man, to keep my focus on the game so that Alan doesn't use any lapse in concentration to do something that could lose this for me.

That could lose it for the Hawkes.

Coen doesn't even acknowledge when my eyes meet his. He continues to stare with that icy-cold gaze, his jaw clenched, body rigid and unyielding.

He doesn't like this one bit. If he had it his way, I would have been tossed out onto the street. He didn't want to accept my help. And he sure as fuck doesn't believe me. He doesn't trust that this is real, that I truly am willing to betray Satriano for him and the rest of the Hawkes.

There's only one way to prove it to him.

I have to win.

And then, I have to do what he asked and walk away from him forever.

I shove the rest of my chips into the center of the felt. "All in."

Alan raises a brow, then his lips twitch into a little feral grin, and he does the same, nudging his stack forward. He gives me a coy grin. "Are you sure you don't want to just chop it?"

Hell no...

The offer to split the pot rather than have this final showdown would be enticing to a lot of players, but I see it for what it is—his attempt to save face rather than potentially lose.

And I won't give Satriano even a partial win.

I smile at Alan sweetly. "I think I'll pass."

He shrugs and sits back in his chair. "Your fucking funeral."

His words stiffen my spine.

He doesn't mean it as just a colloquial saying.

He means it potentially literally because he knows I'm betraying Satriano.

Because he knows what will be waiting for me if this money doesn't go to him—or even if it does.

Satriano will know I came and played.

He will understand I made my choice...and that it wasn't him.

Which means he will come for me.

He always does.

I flip over my cards and watch Alan's humor fade quickly. His eyes drift across the community cards, then up to meet mine. The flicker of anger is all I need to know to confirm I won.

Alan stands and reaches across the table, extending his hand. "Well played."

I accept it, and he tightens his grip so much that it hurts.

He leans closer; the only one who might be able to hear us is the dealer. "You better be prepared for what's coming for you."

Before I came here, I thought I was. I believed I had mentally prepared myself for the fallout that would come from this choice, but now a vise seems to constrict around my chest, threatening to suffocate me.

What have I done?

Alan releases my hand and slinks off to try to figure out a way to save himself because he's going to have to face Satriano, too, with the fact that he lost—to *me*.

I release a shuddering breath and turn away from the table to find Savage approaching. His intense stare reminds me of my promise—to get lost fast once this was done. And there isn't any time to waste because if I don't get out of here fast, I won't stand a chance of getting out of New Orleans safely and hidden somewhere before Satriano tracks me down.

Even if I can get away, it will only be a matter of time before he's at my doorstep...

I twist back to the table and snag a card, then fumble in my purse until I find a pen, quickly scribbling a message on it.

By the time I'm finished, Savage is waiting, with his brow furrowed as I hand it to him. "Deposit the money wherever you choose. And give this to Coen."

"Wait, Allegra—"

But I don't.

I can't.

Just like I can't let the tears pooling in my eyes fall.

I *won*.

I did what I came here to do.

They should be happy tears, but they aren't. They're filled with frustration, longing, fear, and so many other emotions that I can't pinpoint them all.

I move past Savage, ducking out with the flow of the crowd, fleeing the room while avoiding eye contact with Coen or anyone else.

This time, I won't make the same mistake.

I won't linger.

I have to get out of here and out of New Orleans quickly.

It's my only chance.

If I stop, even for a minute, to try to talk to Coen, to try to convince him that everything he thinks is wrong, I would only be wasting precious time I don't have.

And it wouldn't change anything between us.

I practically run down the casino aisles, weaving around people who are stumbling around with Mardi Gras beads and drinks in their hands, until I make it to the main entrance, where I had the limo company ensure the driver would be waiting for me—no matter how long it took.

My gaze darts across the street to the second Hawke Hotel tower going up, almost fully completed.

It would have been nice to see it...

But I can never come back here for so many reasons.

Not just to the Hawke Hotel, either. I can never return to New Orleans.

That thought finally makes the tears begin to flow, and the driver comes out and holds the door open for me.

I slide into the back seat, the door closes, sealing me inside with my own misery.

It was the right thing to do.

No matter how many times I remind myself of that fact, it doesn't make the twisting in my gut any better. It doesn't solve the problem I've created for myself by saving *him*.

I helped the Hawkes in a way only I could have.

If they had openly defied his order to fix the game in favor of Alan, there would have been catastrophic repercussions. But they've done nothing wrong, and that's the true beauty of my plan.

Coen did exactly as asked—he put the stacked deck into the dealer's hands.

That should have been the end of it.

That should have *ensured* Satriano's plant won the tournament and firmly held the Hawkes in a stranglehold.

I was the factor he never counted on...

But he should have.

That man never should have underestimated me.

The driver raises a brow in the rearview. "Where to, miss?"

"Airport, as fast as you can."

He nods and glances at his side-view mirror before he starts to pull out from under the massive awning and onto the drizzly, damp New Orleans street. But my door flies open before he can pull away from the curb more than a foot or two.

I jerk away from the open door, prepared to face the wrath of the man I betrayed.

But the one who slides in and settles next to me in the back seat isn't the one I thought would be following me.

It isn't Alan or any of Satriano's other planted men.

It's the *other* one I betrayed.

Coen stares at me, those unbelievably blue eyes of his somehow a mix between flinty ice and warm Caribbean blue.

The driver either hasn't noticed that Coen joined me or doesn't care, and he pulls off into traffic. I press the button to raise the partition, unsure what Coen might say that I might not want him overhearing.

Once it's fully up, I turn to Coen. "What are you doing?"

"What does it look like I'm doing?" He holds my gaze, giving nothing away about his intent. "You ran again."

I set my purse down on the seat next to me, my body already heating under his assessing gaze that I can't quite figure out. Angry? Shocked? Thrilled? "I have every reason to run, Coen. He'll come after me now."

Coen's hard jaw tics as he looks at me. "You knew exactly what you were doing, the danger you were putting yourself in."

I nod, and he flips the card I handed Savage up so my message is visible.

I'm sorry. It was all real.

"And this?" He flicks it with his finger. "Was this just another move in the game?"

Even now. Even after what I just did for him. He still doesn't believe me. He doesn't understand how important he is to me.

Tears stream down my cheeks now, and "No. I can't keep living like this."

"Like what?"

"A life that isn't mine." I bite back a sob, choking on the reality that I haven't really lived my own life for so long that I forgot how to and what it felt like to really be *free*. "That doesn't make me happy."

Coen lowers the card to his lap, his hand still clutching it tightly. "What *does* make you happy, Allegra? Because I thought we already established you don't seem to care about anyone or anything."

Those words slice at my already-bleeding wounds, tearing me open even more, shredding me so painfully that I actually release a frustrated cry. "I care about *you*! God"—I release a little mirthless laugh—"and for some reason, I care about your big, crazy family. I don't want to see you all hurt."

He works his jaw. "A little late for that, isn't it?"

It definitely is.

I could spend ten lifetimes trying to make up for what I did to him, and another ten thousand trying to make amends for what Satriano has done to them—and continues to.

But I still don't think it would be enough.

Not for the Hawkes.

Not for Coen.

"I know today can't make up for everything that happened, for everything that I've done, but I have so much to tell you. So much more that needs to be said..."

If he'd only listen...

He reaches out and wraps his fingers around my jaw, holding my gaze steady on his. "I only need to know one thing from you right now, Allegra."

The intensity of the way he searches my eyes makes my heart stall for a second. "What's that?"

"Are you done playing games?"

A long, slow breath slips from my lips on a sob, and I nod, swiping at the tears that cloud my vision.

And Coen kisses me before I even realize his intent.

COEN

I NEVER INTENDED to go after Allegra.

I never intended to climb into this car with her.

And I certainly never meant to kiss her.

Not after everything she's done.

The way she lied to me and manipulated me isn't something that can be so easily forgotten and maybe not ever forgiven.

It's all I could think about all day as I watched her play.

Card after card.

Hand after hand.

She played an *incredible* game.

Calm.

Cool.

Professional.

She did it *all,* knowing that as soon as the final hand was dealt, she was fucked either way.

Whether she won or lost, Satriano would know what she had done—and that's worse than him potentially losing the money. It was a statement to him that she was taking her life back, and Satriano isn't the type to let anyone just walk away.

But she did it *anyway.*

That was the first hint that maybe she hasn't been *completely* full of shit.

A glimmer of hope that at least a fraction of what we shared might have been real.

The longer I watched her play, the more it began to feel like maybe I had made a mistake in not listening to her, in not letting her explain more that day in Vegas.

And when Savage handed me this card and said she left, I read the words and felt like my chest was being ripped open, like I was being flayed alive by her and her words.

Because *good God*, I want to believe them.

Racing through the casino, all I could think was that it *could* be real.

Lunging for the door before the limo pulled away, I prayed for it to be unlocked so I could get my answer before she left for good.

And now, despite every reason she can't be trusted, with my mouth on hers, that little moan slipping from her lips, I can't deny the fact that I *do*, even if I shouldn't.

I trust her.

She came here today and *proved* that whatever happened to bring us together, it wasn't all an act.

What we shared that night in Vegas was *real*, as real as anything I've ever experienced in my life, and if I ignored that because I got hung up on my own pain and embarrassment and anger, I don't know that I would ever be able to forgive myself.

So, I have to forgive her.

The same way Atlas did me for something equally awful that I did without any excuse except my own selfishness and idiocy.

And so, I release it.

I let it go.

All the resentment and anger and loathing I felt since she revealed the truth in Vegas. I replace it with the all-consuming *need* I have for this woman.

The limo moves onto the main street, and I angle Allegra's

face, trying to reach the places she would never let me before, that I could never get to with the barrier of lies between us.

And she opens for me so sweetly, gliding her tongue along mine, gasping and clutching at the front of my suit.

I let the card fall to the seat so I can drag her up and over me until she straddles my hips across the seat. She whimpers slightly, settling her core along my hard cock, and her heat sears me even through my pants. The fabric already starting to dampen.

"No fucking panties again, huh?"

She grins against my lips, wrapping her hands around my neck and gripping me as tightly as I do her hips. "I'm not in the habit of wearing them anymore..."

I tunnel my fingers into her hair and tug her head back, holding her away from me for a moment, locking gazes with her. "Why? Because you were hoping a moment like this might present itself?"

Her gaze softens.

The intense haze of lust fades, replaced by a sincerity that stops my heart.

She shakes her head. "I never thought a moment like this would be possible. I never believed for a second that you could forgive me for everything I did."

I know that feeling all too well.

For so long, I didn't think it was possible for Atlas to ever forgive me. The fact that he has is still sometimes difficult for me to grasp, even after two weeks of Sunday dinners, sweaty gym training sessions, and dozens of conversations that somehow fell back into feeling completely natural without any of the tension I thought would never go away.

So, what Allegra is saying rings true in my heart.

She didn't think we would ever be in this position again. It was so out of the realm of possibility that she wouldn't have even considered it when she came back to New Orleans, especially after what I said to her the last time we saw each other.

Yet, here she is, teary-eyed, panty-less, wet and ready, and she still doesn't seem to grasp what I'm trying to tell her.

I cradle her face in my palms, brushing away the tears from her cheeks with my thumbs. "I forgive you, Allegra. Because I have to. Because if I don't, it will eat me alive the same way the entire situation has been for the past several weeks."

"I've been so fucking miserable."

Her confession swells my chest. "Me too."

Another tear slips from the corner of her eye and trickles down her cheek, and I brush it away with my thumb and drag that across her lips. Her tongue darts out across its pad, and my cock twitches.

This woman is everything I've ever wanted.

Beautiful.

Smart.

Sexy as hell.

And *brave*.

So fucking brave to have come here and taken this stand for us—and for herself.

She presses her forehead to mine, releasing a long sigh, heavy with all the emotions we're barely managing to contain. "I've missed you, Coen."

Her whispered confession wipes away any self-control I had left, and I slide my free hand up under the hem of her dress to find her slick core.

"Fuck, I've missed you, too." I slip a finger along her slit and kiss her. "I've missed the taste of your mouth." Another kiss. "Your cunt." Another. "How you feel on my fingers and my cock..."

She whimpers and grinds down against my hand.

"I've missed those little noises you make when you're frustrated and want to come."

Almost as if on cue, one slips from her mouth, and I catch it in another kiss that quickly turns frantic.

Nails score my neck.

Her hips roll against me.

My fingers slip easily inside her. "And you're ready for me, aren't you?"

She nods, groaning, her hands tightening on me, those nails biting into my skin harder. "So fucking ready..."

Her hands leave my neck and reach between us to my belt, freeing my cock and sliding the material away to give herself room.

The limo turns left, and we slide slightly on the leather seat, both of us laughing as I pull my hand away from her core and she settles herself against the head of my cock.

I lift my fingers to my lips and lick them clean as she slowly engulfs me, sinking down inch by inch, her scalding, wet heat enough to make my balls seize up and want to release immediately.

Fuck.

She drops her forehead to mine, her breath ragged when she finally settles down on me. I move one hand to her hip, keeping the other tunneled in her thick, dark hair. She tries to move, tries to shift up, but I keep her down, completely still on my cock.

Her head slowly lifts, and her eyes search mine.

"I forgive you, Allegra, but it doesn't mean I don't feel that I'm entitled to some revenge."

Those stormy-gray eyes flare, and I can't fight the grin pulling at my lips, bracing my feet and shoving up into her an extra quarter of an inch I couldn't before.

She gasps, her eyes rolling up as her head drops back.

I kiss up her neck and across her jaw until I get to her ear. "But I don't have the willpower to do it now..."

"Oh, thank God."

There will be plenty of time for *those* games.

The ones *both* of us enjoy.

But not now.

I release my hold on her hip, allowing her to rise until only the head of my cock stays inside of her, then sink back down so slowly that the glide feels endless. "Oh, fuck..."

She rolls her hips and squeezes her cunt around me, her groan filling the space as we barrel down the street, neither of us caring about the destination or when we might get there.

It's all irrelevant at this point.

This woman is only going one place—back home with *me*.

I hold her against me, clinging to her, relishing the feel of having her in my arms again. It's only been two weeks, but it might as well have been two decades since I last tasted her, since I last felt this completeness.

It's so wrong to want someone this much, especially when you know they're bad for you, when you know how toxic they can be, when you know they're willing to lie, steal, and cheat for someone as dangerous as Satriano.

But I do believe her, and I've forgiven her for everything that came before today.

This is our fresh start.

Our chance to really come together with nothing between us. No more lies. No more half-truths. No more games.

And as she rides me, grinding down with each upward thrust of my hips, it feels like I'm finally home. Like all these years spent wandering were all for *this*.

The restlessness settles in my soul, bound to this woman who needs me as desperately as I need her. Like an anchor mooring me in a storm, she's become the one thing that finally feels right and like it's *mine*.

Allegra cups my face and angles my head, kissing me with a wild abandon, like she can't get enough, like she's been starving since we were last together and I'm the only one who can satisfy her hunger.

And I let her take and take.

She moves frantically now, gliding up and down on me, squeezing with each retreat and clamping as she bottoms out.

My balls draw up tight.

That low tingle starting at the base of my spine.

"Fuck, Allegra." I tug on her hair, tilting her head away from me so I can bite down on her collarbone in that same fucking spot I wanted to mark her the first time we were together.

She twitches on my cock, her whole body fluttering as she comes. Tensing, her back arches, her pussy rippling and clenching around me as her orgasm slams into her.

The drag and pull of her pussy walls finally unleashes my release, and I groan, burying my face against her damp skin as I come deep inside her.

And it simultaneously feels like finally letting go and finally finding the one thing I've been looking for my entire life.

Allegra collapses, her entire weight settled against my chest, my cock still embedding inside her. Every warm flutter of her breath along my skin makes me twitch and cling to her even tighter.

The car moves through the streets. Stopping at lights. Making turns.

It goes on for so long with us just holding each other that I almost forget we are going *somewhere*.

Her lips feather against my neck. "There's something else I need to tell you."

Instantly, that moment of post-orgasmic bliss vanishes. That tentative tone in her voice, the hint of fear, is enough to make my hand at her hip tighten in warning. "What?"

She pulls her head back, her lids still at half-mast and glazed over, but they sharpen quickly to a stormy uncertainty. "You asked me once what Satriano had on me."

"Yeah?"

But this isn't at all the time or place to have this discussion.

We'll have to come up with a plan to deal with Satriano and the fallout of what went down today. I just don't want to do it right now.

"You don't have to get into it right now, Allegra. We have time."

She shakes her head, fear filling her gaze again. "No, we don't. It's what I was trying to tell you in Vegas, what you never let me explain. Satriano doesn't have anything on me. But that doesn't mean I don't owe him."

"I don't understand. Why the fuck would you owe a man like Satriano anything if he isn't holding some sort of debt?"

Nothing she's saying is making any sense, and the longer it takes her to respond, the more she trembles, and the more terrified I become of what she's about to say next.

Her lip quivers, and the tears form in her eyes again. "I know what he's planning, what he wants from you and your family. I know everything."

"Why would he confide in you, Allegra? Why do you owe him *anything*?"

She swallows thickly, steeling herself for whatever she's about to say and the response she seems to be anticipating from me. "He confided in me because he trusts me. And I owe him because he's my father."

20

ALLEGRA

Even safely curled up on Coen's couch, wrapped in his soft sweatpants and T-shirt, after a long, hot shower, I can't stop shaking. My entire body trembles violently, and I pull my feet up onto the leather and wrap my arms around my knees, trying to control it.

Coen slides his hand onto my thigh, trying to give me some strength and encouragement for what I'm about to do.

What I have to do.

It's time to come clean about *everything—finally.*

And I have to do it with an audience...

Savage, Gabe, Stone, and Luca all sit around Coen's living room, each watching me and waiting for me to start with my formal confession.

As soon as I told Coen the truth in the limo, I broke down so completely that I couldn't get another word out, and he seemed to realize that trying to question me would have been fruitless at that point.

It felt like I sobbed the whole way here and during the

shower Coen insisted I take while he was right there, holding me through the continued tears and panic.

Instead of running from my truth, this time, he seems intent on listening—and ensured the people who needed to know most would be here to hear it all, too.

Coen squeezes my leg. "I want you to tell them exactly what you told me..."

I glance over at him, and he offers me an encouraging smile that warms his eyes.

This entire time, I thought telling him the truth, finally putting it all out there, would be the end of things, but instead, it feels like the beginning of something bigger, something stronger, something truly powerful.

I release a heavy sigh, then look at the Hawke men waiting not so patiently across from us.

All they know is that Coen called and said they need to come over right away.

They're in for a real surprise...

And not a good one.

I shift uncomfortably under the scrutiny. "Well"—I swallow through my suddenly dry throat—"Damiano Satriano is my father."

You could hear a pin drop.

It's so silent that I might have thought they hadn't heard me, save for the tensing of Gabe's jaw, the dark flash across Luca's gaze, and the look Savage and Stone exchange.

I don't know what I expected.

Gasps?

Recoiling?

Not this...silence.

It sends another shiver through me, and Coen brushes his lips against my temple.

"Keep going. Tell us everything."

Everything.

Where do I even start?

At the beginning.

"He's my biological father, but I didn't even meet him until I was twelve..."

Coen brushes his thumb over my thigh gently, the soft material shifting under his light caress. "When your mom died?"

I nod, and all those painful memories rush back.

That police officer coming to the school to tell me there'd been a car accident...

Telling me she was gone...

Realizing I was completely alone in the world...

"I didn't even know he existed. Mom had never really told me anything about my father, and I honestly never asked. We were a team. Best friends." I shrug, tears pooling in my eyes. "I never felt like I was missing anything by not knowing who he was or having a relationship with him. The state was prepared to put me into foster care when this man just...showed up."

Savage leans forward slightly, listening intently. "Where were you living at the time?"

"Near Olympia, Washington."

He bobs his head slowly, as if he's processing the information. "Remote?"

I nod. "I didn't realize until much later that the places my mom was choosing were very deliberate."

Gabe leans back in his chair, crossing an ankle over his knee. "She was hiding from him..."

It seems so obvious now, looking back on it as an adult with all the information.

Constantly moving.

Homeschooling.

Living in remote areas with tiny populations.

Keeping to ourselves as much as possible.

She was protecting me.

"I didn't know that when I met him. He wasn't the man you all know with me."

Coen and the rest of the Hawkes give me skeptical looks, and I can't really blame them.

"He appeared at the social worker's office and squatted in front of me with so much kindness in his eyes, so much affection, that I instantly felt at ease with him. And he told me he was my father." I release a little mirthless laugh. "I thought he must be lying. But then he pulled out a picture of him and my mom from years earlier, and he explained that they had met when she was backpacking through Europe and had been together. He said he had been searching for her for years…"

Gabe narrows his eyes on me. "Was any of that true?"

"I don't know." I shake my head. "I mean, I saw photos of them together that prove they did meet when my mom was in Europe and were together for at least a couple of months, given the dates on the pictures. I don't think she realized who or what he was at that point. He was already in hiding. Everyone believed his brother had killed him. He was living under a different name." I shrug. "He was just a handsome, charming Italian man she met and fell in love with before she decided it was time to pack up and move on."

Stone's gaze flicks from me to Coen, then back to me. "Did she know she was pregnant when she left?"

That's what I've been asking myself for years.

Why did she leave him?

"I think she must have. He always described her leaving as very *abrupt* and without warning. There one day and gone the next."

I wince at my description and turn my eyes to the man seated beside me.

That's what I did to him.

We spent a wonderful night together, and I just *left*.

I can't imagine what that felt like for Coen.

He squeezes my leg again, as if he can read my thoughts and is telling me it's okay, even when it never really will be.

Luca, who has remained silent thus far, meets my gaze as I force myself to continue.

"I think she found out who he was and hid the pregnancy from him intentionally. It's the only thing that explains her rapid departure and the way we lived once I was born. She had to have known..."

Stone spins the head of his cane in his hand. "So, what happened when your father came for you?"

"They let him take me, so whatever evidence he provided was sufficient for the courts, though if it hadn't been, I don't think that would've stopped him. He packed me up on a private jet and flew me to a remote villa in the Alps." I huff out a laugh, remembering the sheer awe I felt walking onto that plane and then riding in a fancy car up to a massive house filled with beautiful, extravagant things. "I realized he lived a very different lifestyle than the one Mom and I had. He told me his real name once we were there, not the one he used when he picked me up. And he told me why he was hiding—or at least, a very sanitized version. He explained why it was so important to never tell anyone who or where he was. It wasn't until I was sixteen or seventeen that I realized what he was..."

Even now, when I'm furious with him and terrified of what he'll do when he gets a hold of me, I can't bring myself to call him what he is—a mobster. A killer. A violent man capable of horrific things.

Luca nods slowly, running a hand across his stubbled jaw. "Because you'd been away at boarding schools?"

I nod, surprised he said anything given his silence thus far. "He did it for my safety, I think, because he worried having me with him would be a way to get to him. He didn't hide my name either because there was no reason to. I had no connection to him. As far as anyone was concerned, he was dead, and I was just some random girl."

Coen pulls his hand off my thigh and tugs my arms from around my legs so he can twine his fingers with mine.

I stare at our connected hands.

How tightly he clutches mine.

It's still hard to understand how this happened when only this morning, it seemed impossible, but Coen Hawke is back to being my rock, and he's still trying to stop my spiral even when I'm telling them things that should make them all despise me even more.

He squeezes my hand. "So, what happened when you were sixteen?"

A shudder rolls through me, goosebumps pebbling on my arms as I clench my eyes closed against the vision that flashes before them.

It's the last thing I want to relive.

But they have to know *everything* if I have any hope of a future with Coen—and right now, that's all I want.

I breathe through the nausea roiling my stomach and hold Coen's gaze. "I saw him shoot someone point blank, and he didn't even flinch."

"Jesus Christ..." Coen tugs me closer to him, then easily scoops me into his arms to settle me in his lap, apparently not giving a shit that his father and uncles are sitting here with us.

I bury my face against his neck, absorbing his strength and breathing in that scent I've become so addicted to.

"I'm so sorry you had to see that."

"Did he know you saw him?" Luca's cool, calm voice draws my head back, and I meet his questioning gaze.

"Not then, but eventually, he did because I was a really shitty actress and I wasn't very good at concealing how uncomfortable I was around him and his men."

Coen rubs his hand up and down my back. "So, what did he do?"

"He told me everything about his brother, about the way he grew up and how awful their father was. He told me that no matter what I may have seen him do, he would never hurt me. And he never has." I meet each and every one of their gazes to ensure they're paying attention. "That's something I need all of you to know." My heart clenches tightly as I struggle to say the words when they sound so hollow to these people. "He was a good dad to me. He took care of me. He loved me. He did all the things with me that dads do with their kids. I didn't really understand how different everything was until much later. He kept me insulated. I never saw that violent side with my own eyes again, but I knew it was there. And the older I got, the more I began to pick up bits and pieces of conversations, information left out on desks and counters..."

It was how I began to understand how *vast* his "business" really was.

And I got a taste of what running an empire required.

Hard lines being drawn.

Rules in place.

Consequences for stepping out of line or failing.

It became almost normal for me after so many years surrounded by it.

Gabe's lips twitch slightly as he looks between Coen and me. "Who taught you how to play poker?"

I can't stop my grin at his question. "My dad's head bodyguard. He was quite the shark."

Coen squeezes me and kisses my neck. "So are you."

Is that a compliment?

My eyes naturally drift to Luca, who made the comment about swimming with sharks when there was already blood in the water at dinner. But instead of finding that same hard, dark glare he gave me that night, now he looks almost pleased.

Like his distrust was vindicated.

I give him a tight smile.

He nods toward me. "And how did you end up playing against Coen?"

My gut immediately tightens painfully, and I must flinch because Coen tightens his grip on me and feathers his lips over my ear.

"It's okay. We need to know everything..."

His reassurance helps me try to figure out where to start.

"Well, after I graduated from college without really any idea what I wanted to do, I was kind of drifting. Traveling and partying with people who weren't really my friends, just leeches who took advantage of the fact that I had a basically unlimited cash flow thanks to Dad and my skills at the tables. It was Dad's idea that I come work for him."

Savage clenches his jaw. "Did you want to?"

As a father to a daughter only a handful of years older than me, I can imagine how this looks.

And it isn't good.

"I know what you all think, but he never asked me to do anything but play cards and distract other players. Occasionally chat them up to get information."

Coen tenses slightly under me, and I know he's wondering what I might have told Dad about anything he revealed to me.

The fact that he has to even wonder that makes acid crawl up my throat.

So does the fact that all the men in this room—including the one whose lap I sit on, wrapped in his strong arms—believe I was also *sleeping* with at least some of them.

I shift in Coen's hold so I can face him fully because what I'm about to say is for *him,* not for the other Hawkes. Taking his face in my hands, I brush a thumb across his jaw, rough with stubble I would love to feel abrading my thighs. "I never slept with *anyone* connected to my father's business dealings or requests. Ever."

Until I met you.

There isn't any need to tack on that confession. I can see in Coen's warm blue eyes that he understands that this has been different from day one.

COEN

FOR THE FIRST time since we met, I look into Allegra's eyes and can honestly say I know with one hundred percent certainty that there's nothing else she's holding back.

What happened between us had nothing to do with her father.

It had everything to do with this pull neither of us can seem to escape.

We hold each other's gazes for what feels like an eternity, and it must be because, eventually, Savage clears his throat.

Allegra reluctantly drags her eyes from mine, and Savage inclines his head toward me.

"And how did *this* start?"

This.

I knew we would get to this point eventually, where she would have to explain how and why her father sent her to me, and it isn't anything I haven't already told them after Vegas. But that conversation was cut short, and tonight it seems like Allegra has a lot more to say.

Through the lens of knowing Satriano is her father, it makes everything that's happened appear in a new light— nothing hidden in the shadows.

Allegra resettles against me, and I can feel the tension vibrating through her body.

She's already done so well.

Opened up completely and held nothing back.

I twine my fingers with hers to offer the only support I can right now.

She's silent for a moment, like she has to think about it. "He has talked about the Hawkes for a long time, since his brother's death. And when Coen's debt came to him, he knew he could use him as leverage."

It's impossible not to cringe hearing myself referred to like that.

Leverage.

That's all I am to Satriano.

A way to strong-arm our business and further build his empire.

Allegra presses her hand to my chest, directly over my heart, as if she can sense that I so desperately need it at the moment. "He needed to be sure Coen could and would still play and couldn't be easily taken off his game."

At that, I slide my hand around and cup her ass. "I failed at that..."

She grins. "Yeah, you did. But you played well, and you paid it all back."

The humor fades instantly at the reminder. "Not all of it."

Savage nods his agreement. "I appreciate your honesty and what you did for us today, Allegra, but Coen is right. Your father is still going to come for the debt he believes must be repaid, and now, he's also going to come for you."

For some reason, hearing Savage say the thing we already know somehow makes it ten times worse—like *speaking* those words will ensure they come true. As if they wouldn't have if we had all pretended it wasn't going to happen.

I wrap my arms around Allegra protectively, tugging her against my chest and kissing her softly, trying to stop the uncontrollable trembling that seems to have returned with Savage's warning.

Her light jasmine scent swallows me as I lose myself in the kiss, in the feel of her in my arms.

It's still hard to wrap my head around the fact that she's here with me, that the bridge I thought had been burned between us has somehow found a way to mend itself.

And it's all because she had the strength to take a stand against her father.

Confessing all of this must be beyond difficult, revealing her painful family history to people who despise one of the most important people in her life. But she's done it with an open heart.

By the time she finally pulls away from the kiss, Savage, Gabe, Dad, and Luca are all looking anywhere but at us and the display of affection that may have slightly crossed the line between inappropriate and full-on mouth fucking.

Allegra leans into me but turns her head to face Savage. "He will come for me, but I want to make something clear—my father would *never* hurt me. Not physically. No matter how angry he might be." The truth resonates in her strong words, and I know she firmly believes what she's saying, even if we can't. "Now, will he lock me up in some ivory tower somewhere with a dozen guards to ensure I can't leave and get into any other trouble, to ensure that he can control what I do with my life? That's another story and well within the realm of what he might attempt."

Gabe shakes his head. "We won't let that happen."

Dad nods his agreement. "Absolutely fucking not."

Allegra looks at each of them, playing with the hem of my T-shirt to keep her nervous trembling at a minimum. "You can't make me that promise."

Savage nods. "Yes, we can. You're helping us, which means

we will protect you. But we need as much information about him and his plans as you can give us."

Because everything has been an uphill battle where Satriano is concerned.

From the day "Damon" first appeared, the lives of the Hawkes have been like hamsters running on a wheel, trying to get one step ahead of him. And we have always failed.

Even the tiniest thing Allegra could offer might make all the difference.

I press a kiss to her temple. "Please, anything you can tell us. You never know what might be important, what might turn the tide."

She trembles in my arms, and I tug her against my chest, giving her a minute to compose herself again. I lock eyes with Dad, Savage, Gabe, and finally Luca, holding his extra-long to get my point across.

They need to give her time.

If they push her too hard, I'll end this right here and now.

No one pushes back.

They all understand what she's going through, how she's being torn in two, being asked to *further* betray her father—who she so clearly loves—for us.

She's already proven that she's a better person than her genes would suggest. Maybe that's her mother's influence from before Satriano got his hands on her. Or maybe that's just Allegra.

A complicated woman who has kept me on my toes and will continue to for as long as I have her.

The word *forever* flashes through my head, but I quickly push it away.

This isn't the time to think about crazy things like that.

Allegra pulls away from me, tears stain her cheeks, and I swipe them away and kiss her forehead.

She sniffles and then wipes her hand under her nose. "I know what he wants."

Everyone in the room tenses, including me.

It was the one thing we've been waiting for, to determine his ultimate goal. After all this time, all the moves, all the threats, the man and his motivations are still as much of a mystery as they were the first time we ever met him.

Savage raises a brow. "I think we would all be very interested in hearing it."

She releases a heavy sigh, filled with her frustration, her reservation, her pain. "You guys think all he cares about is money and power. And I can understand why you believe that. Those are two of his favorite things." Her lips curl into a half-smile that doesn't quite reach her eyes. "But ultimately, I don't think that's what matters most to him."

I rub my hand up and down her back gently. "Then what does?"

Her gaze meets mine. "This." She spreads her hands out. "Family. Having people you can count on, who have your back."

Everyone stares at her, including me, and when it's clear we're not following, she throws her hands up.

"Look at how he was raised. His father was a fucking monster, and he turned Leonardo and my father into mini versions of himself. Leonardo tried to kill his own brother to take control. If my father hadn't been smart enough to actually fake his death, Leonardo would have tried again after his first failure. My dad never had the kind of unconditional love and support that you guys give each other. He's never had *this*."

The gears start turning in my head, and I finally start to see where she's going with this. "Until he had you…"

"Exactly." She nods. "He's a different person with me. I can see…"

She trails off, and I can see the battle waging in the swirling gray of her eyes, not wanting to say what she really feels.

"It's okay, Allegra." I tighten my grip on her. "Just tell us."

Her bottom lip disappears under her teeth, and she considers for a second before finally nodding. "I can see who he would have been if he hadn't been raised like that, if he'd had a normal childhood with *normal* role models and morals taught to him. I can see that there's good in him."

Luca lets out a low, dark chuckle. "It's very sweet that you think that, but I promise you, that man's soul was born pitch black and lacking."

She glares at him. "Why is it you think you know him so well?"

"Because I *was* him." He sits in his chair, looking like the king, when in this room, that honor belongs to Savage. Even after all these years, even after giving up his title and his role, there's no shaking that aura that permeates the air around Luca Abello. "My father had an empire like yours does, and he had a family, but in the end, all he cared about was the money and the power. We were easily discarded. And I had it, too—that wealth and power. It's intoxicating. Addictive. It's a high you can't get anywhere else—"

She shakes her head. "That's not my father. That's not him."

Luca presses his lips into a thin line.

Allegra shifts on my lap to fully face Luca. "My father is doing this because he thinks he's creating something for *me*. Because *I* am the most important thing to him. And if you gave him the chance, I think he would embrace the Hawkes the same way..."

Savage, Gabe, and Dad all recoil slightly while Luca smirks.

Of course, it sounds nuts to them.

This man has been a thorn in our side for years, and he isn't going away.

All of our previous conversations with Satriano—all the threats, the promises, the vague statements—come back in a wild rush that threatens to drown me as I sort through them.

Bits and pieces take shape.

Starting to form an idea.

"He has asked us to partner with him several times…"

Dad gapes at me. "You can't be seriously saying we consider it."

I hold up a hand. "Just let me think."

Because even I know how unhinged this all sounds.

But there's a thread of something there that my mind keeps wanting to latch onto.

"He's had countless opportunities to finish what he started when he attacked the Grind. He could have taken us all out on the day of the groundbreaking. He could have let Atlas, Astrid, and Kennedy die at the hands of Dan Roselli. I'm sure his goons could have hunted each of us down individually at any point and taken us all out—"

Gabe snorts. "I would have liked to see him try."

"He didn't for a reason, just like we never went after him for a reason. Because it's mutually assured destruction. If he touched any of us, we'd go after him. If we went after him, his people would come after the rest of us. It's a vicious fucking cycle we're stuck in."

Savage considers me for a moment, tapping his fingers on the arm of his chair. "So, what? Are you suggesting we play his fucking game, that we pretend to be friends so he feels like he has a big, happy fucking family?"

The icy words slice through me. "I don't know what I'm suggesting. All I'm saying is that what Allegra's noted makes sense. He hasn't acted because it isn't what he really wants. He's giving us the opportunity to make a different decision, to partner with him, to find a way to coexist peacefully—"

"You can't coexist with a man like him." The warning from Luca draws everyone's attention back to him. "You can all try, but I'm telling you, we'll pay for it in the end."

21

THREE DAYS LATER

COEN

Allegra's knee bounces wildly under the table, and I reach across it and place my hand on top of hers next to her uneaten beignet and the napkin she's shredded while we've sat here waiting.

"Don't be so nervous. Remember, treat this like any other game. Stay calm and cool. Hold your cards close to your chest."

Her gaze cuts to me—the first time she's actually looked at me in the ten minutes since we arrived. Instead of enjoying her breakfast, she's been constantly scanning the street and sidewalk around us at Café du Monde, on high alert.

And she's become a bundle of nervous energy that needs to diffuse quickly.

Those pretty lips of hers twist at me, analogizing meeting her dad to a poker game—but it seemed a good way to describe it, and I thought it might be enough to drag her from what could be a spiral of nerves. "Was this really the best place to tell him to meet us?"

Her brow furrows as she looks at the throngs of tourists

surrounding us, occupying every table and wandering on the sidewalk.

I lift her hand to my lips and kiss her knuckles gently. "Absolutely. All *this* is exactly why we chose Café du Monde."

Her eyes widen slightly before she returns to watching everyone suspiciously, as if any one of them might be a spy for the opposition, the way she was for her father. "Why?"

"Because it's always packed with tourists, and your dad is far too intelligent to do something stupid in such a public place."

At least, that's the theory we're working under today.

And it hasn't failed us in the past when we've had to meet with Satriano and wanted to protect ourselves from an ambush.

Public places.

Busy times.

Lots and lots of witnesses.

Allegra considers me for a moment, then releases a heavy breath and nods. "You're probably right."

"Besides…"—I kiss her fingers again, earning a little shiver from her—"I haven't gotten to take you to do any of the touristy things in town."

A smile plays at the corner of her lips. "No, you haven't."

In the few days since the tournament, since our talk with the rest of the Hawkes and her full confession, we've barely left my condo. Not because I'm afraid of what Satriano will do— more because I can't get enough of this woman and don't want to let her out of my arms or my bed.

Her scent permeates every surface of my condo, her presence there becoming so familiar and easy that I can barely remember a time when she wasn't with me.

I suck one of her fingers into my mouth and her eyes widen, her cheeks pinkening.

"Wh-what are you doing?"

"Getting some of the powdered sugar off."

Allegra glances at her beignet. "I haven't even eaten it yet."

I grin at her. "But you *touched* it. Or is this sweetness from you fingering your cunt? You naughty girl..."

She laughs, and I finally get to see her relax slightly—precisely my intent. If she goes into this so nervously, she could make a mistake. And father or not, she needs a clear head to deal with a man like Satriano.

"It'll be okay, Allegra." I squeeze her hand. "You know we have to do this. If we don't..."

I trail off, unwilling to take the next logical step in that thought.

She says he won't hurt her, and I believe her because I know Dad could never hurt me. Savage could never hurt Kennedy. None of the Hawkes could ever hurt their children, no matter what might come between us. And for some reason, Satriano strikes me as a man who lives by the same principle, despite everything *else* he seems to have no qualms about doing.

And after talking more with Allegra the last few days about growing up with him as a father, it sounds like what she said that night is true. He really was a pretty normal dad. Taking her to ballet lessons. Horse riding. Ski trips and summers at the beach.

All the things a normal dad would do—when she wasn't off at boarding school.

Constantly moving from place to place, country to country to different schools and houses doesn't sound like the easiest way to grow up, but it turned Allegra into who she is today, and I could never be anything but thankful for that.

Her back suddenly stiffens, her gaze zeroing in on something behind me, and I glance over my shoulder as a black Town Car pulls to a stop at the curb.

I clench her hand tightly. "Just remember the plan."

She gives me a tight nod, then sucks in a long, deep breath, squaring her shoulders to physically prepare herself for the showdown with her father that's about to come.

It had to happen.

We couldn't just sit around and wait for him to try to take her, for him to force her away. Because if he had taken her and locked her away somewhere the way she described it, and I couldn't get to her...

I would burn the whole fucking world down to find her.

So, I'm not about to let that happen. Not if there's any chance of resolving this peacefully.

It seems like an impossibility with a man like Satriano, but I have to try.

The alternative isn't anything I'm willing to consider.

I quickly scan around us, checking to ensure everyone's in place.

Bishop sits at a table in the corner of the outdoor patio, newspaper up and sunglasses covering her dark eyes, but I can feel their focus on us like a fucking laser similar to the one Gabe has on his sniper rifle from the roof of the building across the street—just in case. Saint leans against the wall of the main building near the window, pretending to wait for an order, his huge presence unmissable.

We didn't dare bring any more than that for fear that Satriano wouldn't make an appearance if we had a large show of force. Of course, he knows we wouldn't come alone, but there isn't any point in setting things off on a bad foot before we've even begun.

Two of his men climb out of the car after him and fall in line behind him.

Satriano approaches our table with a sly grin curling his lips. "*Bambina...*" He bends down and kisses Allegra on each cheek affectionately, then slides into the chair directly across from me and next to her. "Thank you so much for the invitation to join you this morning."

I snort. "Is that what you thought it was?"

His smile falters. "Are we back to being rude, Mr. Hawke?"

"You tell me."

I raise a brow, and Allegra slides her hand under the table and squeezes my knee, reminding me of the plan, which definitely isn't to antagonize him.

Damon glances at the uneaten beignet and the cup of chicory coffee Allegra hasn't touched, either. "Not hungry this morning?"

She shakes her head. "I suddenly lost my appetite."

"Well, I do hope it comes back." He reaches forward and tears off a piece of the beignet, popping it into his mouth and licking off the powdered sugar from his fingers. "Because as much as this place can be a tourist trap, they really are *divinamente squisito.*"

"We didn't come here to talk to you about pastries."

He chuckles. "I didn't think you did. I assume you wish to discuss Saturday's game." Allegra swallows so loudly I can hear it, and Damon's gaze moves to his daughter. "Am I to assume it was some sort of statement?"

"I would think that was pretty fucking clear."

His gaze cuts to mine, hard and sharp. "Oh, it was, and I'm not very happy about the fact that you failed to live up to your end of the bargain."

"Hey"—I hold up a hand—"that's bullshit and you know it. I did exactly what you asked. It's not my fault a better player came around."

Those typically hard eyes soften with pride as they move to Allegra. "Yes, Allegra certainly is that. Spectacular, isn't she?"

"She is."

And I definitely haven't told her that enough.

Something I will remedy as soon as we get back to my place.

Damon focuses on his daughter again, reaching over to rest

his hand on her other one atop the table. "Am I to assume this means you're done working for the family?"

She presses her lips together, and a war rages in her eyes, a battle between the love of a daughter and the morals of a woman who wants to draw a line in the sand she won't cross. "I was done before Saturday, *Papà*, and you know it."

He shakes his head, *tsking,* and lifts her hand to look at it. "You know, I missed your whole childhood. Missed seeing those tiny baby hands and holding you in my arms. By the time I got to you, your mother had already sunk in deep."

"Don't talk about my mother like that."

The confident defiance in her tone snaps his gaze up to hers. "She stole you from me. Prevented me from knowing my daughter for twelve years of her life."

"She was trying to protect me from you..."

He raises a brow. "Do you need protecting from me, *bambina*? What have I ever done that hasn't been in your best interest? That hasn't been completely for you, Allegra? Since the moment I picked you up in that shithole you were living in, I've done nothing except what I thought was best for you."

It's exactly the argument I expected him to make, justifying his sinister actions with this idea that it's all for Allegra's benefit —to ensure her safety and to leave her wealthier than she can probably even imagine.

"I don't want it, *Papà*."

His jaw hardens, and he tightens his grip on her hand.

She jerks it out from under him. "You're right. I'm done working for you."

His gaze lifts to me, fiery and determined. "So...you've made your choice then?"

Allegra doesn't hesitate. "I have."

He nods slowly. "Well, I do hope you're happy with it because it will be a final one."

I slam my hand against the table. "Don't you fucking threaten her."

His eyes widen. "That wasn't a threat, Mr. Hawke. Just a statement of fact. She's decided to cut ties with me. That's fine. She's an adult and is well within her rights to do so. But if it's really what she wants, then she needs to understand the ramifications." He turns his gaze on her. "Your condo in New York— gone. The places in Denver, London, Paris, Madrid, Monaco, Morocco, all the other countries you've spent so much time in —gone. Your access to my private jet, your access to your bank accounts—all of it gone. If you are going to partner with the people who won't partner with me, then you've made your decision."

He pushes away from the table, but before he steps away, he turns back to me. "Unless you've reconsidered?"

I think back to the conversation we had the night Allegra came clean and have continued to have over the last few days about whether partnering with Satriano might be the way to end all of this.

But so far, no one's been on board, and I can't say that I fully am, either.

Is making a deal with the Devil better than trying to defeat him?

"No."

Damon spreads out his hands with a tight smile, but his eyes remain cold, detached. A dangerous look from a man like him. He may have come knowing what Allegra did, but deep down, he thought he stood a chance of convincing her to come back to him. "As I assumed."

He bends down and kisses her on each cheek again, which seems to startle her back in her seat. "Goodbye, Allegra. *Tutto ciò che ho sempre fatto è stato amarti.*"

ALLEGRA

ALL I'VE EVER DONE IS love you.

His parting words won't seem to stop repeating in my head.

He never says anything without thinking precisely about how it will affect the listener. And they definitely hit their mark with me. He knew exactly what he was saying and how it would affect me long after he walked away from that table.

For so long after I went to live with him, I had a hard time believing he could love me.

How, when he didn't even know me?

Yet, time and again, he proved to me that I was the most important thing in his life. He demonstrated that all he wanted was what was best for me, which is precisely why he used those words today, to try to get under my skin, to try to get me to cave and come back to him.

And I hate to admit that for a split second, it almost worked.

I almost ran after him to throw my arms around him and tell him I love him, but it wouldn't have done any good because where I really wanted to be is where I am right now, in Coen's arms, cocooned in his strength with his heart beating under my ear and his arms wrapped around me tightly.

He shifts slightly, burying his face in my hair. "Are you awake?"

I nod.

"What's wrong?"

His voice, still gravelly with sleep, rolls through me, and it doesn't take much to ignite my need for him, even though we've already spent hours wrapped up in each other.

I shake my head. "Nothing. Nothing's wrong. I'm just..."

"Overthinking things again?"

Should I love or hate that he knows me so well already?

I nod, trying to bury my face against his neck, trying to hide how embarrassed I am for still feeling this way about a man who did so many horrible things to Coen and his family.

Coen slides his hand under my chin, tilts my face up, and silences all the noise in my head with a single kiss.

Too bad it only lasts a brief moment before he pulls away, brushing a stray hair away from my face.

He gives me a sad smile. "It's hard to turn it off, isn't it?"

"What?"

"When you love somebody...it's hard to turn it off, even if you want to."

The depth and sincerity of his words can only come from someone who has suffered it himself.

My chest aches. "Why do you sound like you're speaking from personal experience?"

He narrows his gaze, his hand sliding back to cup my nape. "Do you really have to ask me that?"

Energy crackles between us, something far more powerful than the mere sexual attraction we've always seemed to have in spades. His thumb brushes reverently across my cheek, and he tilts his head slightly, like he's waiting for me to process what he's said.

Wait...

"You don't mean..."

I try to pull back, but he keeps me exactly where he wants me with his firm grip, forcing me to continue to look into his eyes.

"I *do* mean it, Allegra."

"But... Coen, it's been less than two months." I release a mirthless laugh. "And for most of that time, you hated me."

"No." He drags me up over him easily. "I didn't hate you. I hated *myself* for wanting you so much when I knew I shouldn't."

His confession rattles me as much as mine must have him. Maybe more. Because it doesn't make any sense. It can't.

"You don't love me, Coen. You don't even know me."

He takes my face in his palms. "I know enough. You sacrificed yourself for my family when you had every reason not to. You could have stayed at home, pretended none of it was happening because it didn't affect you. You could have maintained your relationship with your father, but you didn't. You chose what was right even though it cost you something huge. That tells me *all* I need to know."

Tears pool in my eyes, a combination reaction to his words and the emotional upheaval that happened today.

My bottom lip trembles as I try to hold in the sob threatening to come out. Before it can, Coen kisses me. Softly this time. Unrushed. Filled with more than just sexual attraction.

He pulls back only enough to press his forehead to mine. "I promise that things are going to get better, that they're going to be okay."

And then his lips are back on mine with another torturously reverent kiss.

But it doesn't take long for it to grow more heated, for my body to ache for him, even though he just took me a few hours ago.

His hands slide down to my ass and squeeze, using his leverage to adjust my position so my pussy glides along his cock pinned between us. "I hate seeing you cry..."

I laugh through the tears. "I hate crying. God..." I swipe at them. "I'm such an emotional mess. I swear, I'm not normally like this."

A grin tugs at his lips. "I know you're not. And while you may think there's no possible way that I know you, I *do*."

"From those reports you had your people dig up on me?"

He smirks, playfully swatting my ass. "Partially, but I've watched every move you've made since we first met, Allegra. Not only at the poker table."

His lips trail down my neck.

"I've memorized the way you walk. The way you drink. The way you laugh and smile." That wicked mouth reaches my chest, and he slowly tugs one nipple into his mouth, making me instantly clench *everywhere.* "And I've memorized your body..."

He moves to the other breast, letting his warm breath drift over it, making the already hard peak ache. "And I have memorized what you like..."

Those talented hands squeeze my ass and then he slides one over, slipping his fingers so close where only *he* has been that it makes me grind down on him in anticipation.

A low chuckle shakes his chest. "And what you *love.*" His other hand slides around and slips easily along my drenched core. "And I've learned what I love most about you."

Torturing me?

Because that's what this feels like.

A prolonged demonstration of pure domination with fleeting touches.

"Wh-what's that?"

He drags me up farther, until I'm seated just above his cock. "How good you taste after I've come inside you."

Oh, my fucking God.

He did *not* just say that.

This man's filthy words are my kryptonite.

I'm powerless to deny what I want when he urges me to say it, and when he does *this*—tells me exactly what *he* wants in such an open and sensual way—I have no choice but to admit that he completely owns me.

My pussy clenches at the fire in his eyes.

Like he's literally *burning* for me.

Good God.

Strong hands tighten on my hips, and he smacks my ass. "Climb up here and sit on my face."

"What?"

"Grab the fucking headboard and sit on my face." He digs his fingers into my skin. "I'm going to make sure that any tears you have for the rest of the night are only because you can't handle another orgasm. Do you understand?"

Fuck yes, I do.

And it sounds like a much better alternative to being stuck in my own head.

I slowly follow his command, shuffling up on my knees over him until I'm straddling his shoulders, my pussy centered directly above his face.

He grins up at me as he glides his fingers through the wetness coating me that we both know full well isn't just my arousal. His cum still fills me since we both passed out and never made it to the shower earlier.

Those talented fingers play there, slipping through the moisture, drifting it across my clit, dipping into me only briefly, before he pulls them away.

Coen brings them to his mouth and licks, issuing a primitive, appreciative groan. "There it is."

Christ.

My breath catches at the gleam in his eyes.

The feral look of an animal about to devour its prey.

He holds my gaze for a moment, almost like he's dragging out my anticipation on purpose, before he finally lifts his head and he's on me.

His mouth latches onto my core.

"Oh, fuck!" I grip the headboard as my body seizes, my hips bucking and rolling against his face. "Fuck. Fuck. Fuck!"

He thrusts his tongue inside me as deep as he can, like he's trying to clean me out with it, and good God, he might be able to.

So fucking good.

They say lawyers are supposed to have silver tongues, but

this non-lawyer who never wanted to be one sure as fuck has a golden one.

Every flick across my clit. Every lick along my slit. Every thrust of his tongue inside me. They wind me tighter and tighter.

My hips move of their own accord, grinding against his face, chasing the release of everything that's been pent up inside me, refusing to be let out any other way.

All my nerve endings spark. My limbs shake. That heat stares low in my belly.

"Fuck, Coen…"

He drags his face away from my flesh. "We can do that next, I promise."

I laugh, struggling to keep my eyes open against the sensual assault happening between my legs.

He slides two fingers into me, curling and finding that spot he knows drives me absolutely *wild*. Those calloused fingertips drag over it in a slow, come-hither motion as he sucks my clit into his mouth.

I gasp, the start of my orgasm already there on the periphery.

Little lights starting to flicker, warning of the oncoming lightning storm.

"When you come, Allegra, look at me."

It's impossible to process his words when my brain is already fried, concentrating on the feeling of his hand and mouth rather than his words. "W-what?"

"Open your eyes and look at me."

I manage to follow his command and stare down at the man who has changed my life so fucking quickly. In a matter of weeks, I went from being miserable, stuck tied to my life because I'm a Satriano. Even if I don't bear the name, I bear the burden of what my father expected of me.

But now that I'm free of it, of *him,* it feels like I'm finally free of everything that has held me back.

I reach down and grip his hair with one hand, tugging on it sharply in the way that I know always makes him give me that low growl that borders on savage.

His chest vibrates with it, the vibration running up through my legs.

As I stare down at him, he keeps moving his fingers inside me, then flicks his tongue over my clit, never looking away.

I struggle to keep my breathing even as he redoubles his efforts, alternating between long glides, sharp strikes, and grazing teeth.

"Eyes. Fucking. Open."

Every time he pulls his mouth away to issue another command, I whimper.

But then he's right back there, giving me *exactly* what I need.

He suctions his mouth around my clit, and it hits me so hard that I'm blindsided by it.

My eyes stay locked with his for only a second before my whole world goes bright white, my hips grinding down against his face wildly. He issues a groan of approval, devouring me, licking and sucking until I finally collapse onto the headboard.

His arms snake up around me, and he starts to help me slide back down, but my stomach hits something wet.

I force my eyes open and look at him. "Did you...come?"

He grins and slowly glides his tongue along my lips, allowing me to taste the flavor of our releases together—and now I know exactly what he's talking about because it's intoxicating. "I sure as fuck did. Eating your cunt has to be my favorite thing in the world, and knowing I had been inside you, that you were still filled with me..." He kisses me lightly, keeping his lips against mine as he continues. "It's something so..." He shakes his head. "I don't even know how to explain it—"

"You don't have to."

A second passes before he pulls his head back, and as soon as his gaze locks with mine, I know I'm right about what he's feeling and what he's trying to say.

"Knowing you're mine, all of you, it changes everything."

His gaze softens. "Exactly."

Renewed tears, these *happy*, the kind I don't mind, start to fall. "I've always felt a little adrift. Constantly moving with my mom. Then being sent to different schools in different countries. Moving from house to house, so we didn't stay in one place for too long. All of it gave me this sense of—"

"Restlessness?"

I grin at him. "Yes, but since I've been here with you, I've felt grounded."

He tunnels his hands in my hair, bringing my mouth to his, stopping just short of kissing me senseless again. "Me, too. Suddenly, I'm not so restless anymore. I'm just...home."

EPILOGUE
ALMOST THREE MONTHS LATER

ALLEGRA

"Wow, I guess Kennedy was right." I stare up in awe at the second Hawke Hotel tower across the street from the original building. One week short of the three-month mark from the day of the infamous Sunday dinner when the argument took place, and they're almost ready to open. "She called the three-month opening date."

Coen stands next to me, hands tucked into his pockets, giving me a half grin. "Don't tell her that. The last thing Kennedy needs is her ego stroked more."

Bishop glances over her shoulder. "Shit."

"What don't I need?"

Kennedy rushes the last few steps across the street in her high heels with Cass right behind her and joins Coen, me, and Bishop in front of the building, watching the lighting company put the finishing touches on the signage.

Her sharp gaze zeroes in on it, our half-overheard comment apparently forgotten. "You know, if that hadn't been on back order, we could have opened a week ago."

Cass wraps his arm around her from behind and tugs her against him, pressing a kiss to her cheek. "You still won, *cherie*. One week wouldn't have mattered either way."

She huffs. "But I would've felt better about it having won by more."

I roll my eyes and turn to Coen. "Seems everyone in your family has that competitive gene."

"You just figuring that out now?" He grins and pulls me to him, pressing a kiss to my forehead. "I would have thought you had us pegged as sore losers from the start."

"Ugg." Bishop watches with an annoyed twist to her lips. "God, look at you guys, all sappy and hanging on each other."

I look over Coen's shoulder at her, giving her a knowing grin. "You know you'll be the same way when you finally find someone who can put up with you."

Her mouth falls open in mock offense. "Ouch. Hey, Coen, have I ever told you I really like this one?"

He squeezes me. "I do, too. Should I keep her?"

Bishop pretends to consider it, running her thumb across her chin. "Maybe. We'll have to see how things pan out..."

It's all said in jest, but immediately, that vise that always seems to live around my chest starts to tighten, and I pull out of Coen's hold to walk back toward the car.

"Hey, where are you going?" He chases after me and grabs me by the wrist, halting my retreat. "Why are you running off?"

"I told you. I'm doing the one o'clock class with Wren."

"Right..." He rubs his neck and glances back at Bishop, then at me. "Let me just—"

Bishop throws up her hands. "I'll go with her as long as you're going straight back to the hotel and will have someone on you."

He scowls, annoyed that we continue to need fucking babysitters. But the truth is, the longer Dad goes without contacting me, without making any sort of move directly against the Hawkes, the more it starts to feel like he's building to something bigger, something far worse than anything he would've planned prior to me defecting.

So, continued twenty-four-hour bodyguards for everyone, heightened security at the clubs, restaurants, and hotel...

A massive expense.

A massive inconvenience.

A bigger danger.

And it's all my fault.

My gut churns, and I press my hand against it to prevent myself from gagging, like I found myself doing several times over the last few days.

Coen's gaze immediately drops to follow the movement. "Are you okay?"

I swallow the bile rising in my throat and nod. "Yeah, just...I don't know. Why hasn't he called?"

"I don't know." Coen glances back at Kennedy and Cass, who seem to be in a heated discussion with one of the members of the crew about something on the sign. "I thought by now, he surely would've asked me to play in one of his tournaments."

Me too.

We've managed to track down at least two of the casinos in his control, and they've both hosted games since we last met with him, yet he never contacted Coen—or me.

None of it makes sense.

He was so thrilled to have Coen by the balls, to be able to control a Hawke so thoroughly. Yet, he hasn't used that advantage.

He presses his lips together and shakes his head. "He probably hasn't called because he doesn't trust me anymore. Not after what happened."

It feels like we have the same conversation every couple of weeks.

We go days and days pretending like it's normal to have Bishop, Saint, or one of the other armed guards following us around day after day, from the moment we step out of our condo until the moment we step back inside it.

But it isn't.

It's far from it.

"Should I call him?"

"What?" He closes the distance between us, gently pinning me back against the car. "Why would you even suggest anything like that?"

I sigh.

"Do you *miss* him?"

The accusation in his question makes me flinch.

He grips my chin and lifts my face, so I'm forced to meet his eyes. "Do you?"

I can't lie to Coen.

I promised I never would again, and I haven't, not since that night I came clean. "I do, a little bit. I know you don't understand it because you don't know him the same way I do. He's not the same man to you, but he's still my father. If yours just disappeared out of your life, how would you feel?"

As soon as I say the words, I wish I could take them back.

That darkness that always seems to haunt him whenever his father's injuries come up crosses his eyes again.

"I'm sorry, Coen. I didn't mean—"

He sighs. "I know you didn't."

My father was responsible for what happened to his.

At the time it occurred, I didn't know about the shooting at the Grind. I didn't know anything except that the Hawkes were a family Dad wanted to take down because of what happened to his brother, because he wanted control of all of New Orleans and they seemed to be standing in the way, with too much leverage, too much power.

But now I know them.

All thirty-plus.

Even the little one on the way, growing in Wren's belly, who has already started to kick every time I do a class and talk to her, almost like he recognizes my voice already.

These people have become my family as much as Dad ever was, but it doesn't mean I can just forget him or the way I feel about him.

"Don't apologize for loving your father, Allegra." He releases his grip on me to run his hand through his hair and glance back at Bishop, who's trying to break up the argument. "Don't call him, please. Let sleeping dogs lie, all right? He'll come up for air eventually. Gabe, Saint, and Luca have put everything they have into monitoring all the sources who are looking for him across the Gulf Coast. But he's not in town. He's not here. So, we should count our blessings."

"Until we run out of them."

"We won't."

I press my hands to his chest. "I really wish you would stop making those types of promises to me."

He grins. "I thought you *liked* my promises."

"Oh, *those* kind, I definitely do." I push up onto my toes to kiss him. "And you can make me one when we get home, but I have to run to my class." I pull my head back from his. "Bishop?"

She turns toward her name and sees me wave her over. After issuing a final chastisement to Kennedy and Cass, she then jogs to where we wait. "You ready to go?"

I nod, and Coen steps back reluctantly, letting me open the car door and slide inside.

Bishop takes the passenger seat and then rolls down her window to yell out at him, "Hey, Coen?"

He turns back. "What?"

"Seriously, straight to the hotel with Kennedy and Cass until somebody is on you."

"Yeah, yeah, yeah…"

He waves a dismissive hand, but I know he's not going to fight the order.

None of us will.

Not until things are resolved, which is starting to feel more and more like it might be never.

Bishop rolls up her window, and I start the car and pull away from the curb.

She eyes me as we head toward the gym and Pilates studio. "Are you okay today? You seem a little off."

I nod. "I am. Just have a lot on my mind."

"Your dad?"

It isn't a hard guess to make, considering Satriano is at the forefront of *every* Hawke mind and has been for months. The more time passes, the harder it becomes to forget his veiled threats or all the plans he had that I know he won't just abandon.

I glance over at Bishop and nod before returning my attention to the street. "I just feel so guilty, I guess, for completely cutting him out."

"Sometimes you have to cut away the cancer, if you want the healthy cells to survive, right?"

"Are you comparing my father to a cancer?"

She shrugs. "Isn't that what he is to you? You thought he was totally benign, right? And to *you*, he was. But to the rest of us, he has grown like an out-of-control tumor that one day will snuff us out."

Not an analogy I've ever considered.

But it makes more sense than I'd ever really like to admit.

"Jesus, I guess he is…"

"You would tell us, right? If he contacted you?"

The light turns red in front of us, and I slam on the brakes and turn to her. "Of course I would. Why would you even ask me that?"

She holds up her hands defensively. "Because it's my job to protect the Hawkes, and that includes you now."

For that split second, I thought she was accusing me of something. That the trust and friendship I believed we had built over the last several months was all an act so she could keep an eye on me the same way I did Coen.

But there's no deception in her words.

Only stark, sincere affection and commitment to her job.

It's the kind of no-strings-attached love that I only get when I'm with the Hawkes, that they offered me so freely while Dad's love felt like a noose threatening to tighten.

That love from Coen and the rest of the family is what has kept me going when there were days I wanted to crawl into bed and never get out. When I wanted to go to a dark place, they kept me in the light.

But it leaves me wondering what Dad has to keep him sustained, to force him not to give in to the darkest parts of him now that he doesn't have my love—and what he might be capable of now that he's lost it and me.

COEN

TOMMY SLIDES my scotch across the bar to me, and I take the glass and thank him before I raise it to my lips and down a sip.

Allegra elbows me playfully. "Scotch tonight? What happened to bourbon?"

I grin at her. "I thought we should save that for when we get home."

Her eyes widen, her pupils dilating with her instant arousal because she knows exactly what my favorite thing to do with her favorite drink is. I lean in closer to her at the bar at the Hawkeye Club, even though with the sound of the music and people talking, no one would be able to hear me anyway.

I dip my head close to her ear. "Though...we don't have to wait until we get home. Gabe isn't here. So, his office should be open upstairs." I glide my hand up her inner thigh. "He has a couch and a desk..."

She squeezes her legs closed, trapping me and preventing me from advancing. Her eyes dance with amusement and promise. "I don't particularly want one of your aunts, uncles, cousins, or employees walking in on us fucking tonight, Coen."

"Who said anything about fucking?"

Scowling, she bats my hand away.

I chuckle as the first chords of "Kashmir" start up, and my humor instantly fades.

Bishop gapes from her seat on the other side of Allegra, turning toward the stage with wide eyes. "Did you know about this?"

I shake my head and motion for Tommy to come over.

Before he can get away from mixing drinks, Isaac steps through the door and makes his way over to the bar, settling on the stool on my other side. His brow immediately furrows. "Is that 'Kashmir?'"

I nod.

He gapes, turning toward the still-empty stage. "What the fuck?"

"I know, right? I was just about to ask Tommy."

Tommy finally finishes whatever he was working on and hustles over to us. "What's up, guys?"

Isaac points absently toward the pole. "I want to know who's about to walk onto that stage to our mom's song."

Tommy's eyes widen slightly. "Oh, shit. I didn't know..."

He wouldn't.

He wasn't even *alive* when Mom was on stage, nor were we. But still, it's like a retired jersey; you don't just give that song to a new dancer, especially not when the OG is married to the club owner's brother.

I smell a Hawkeye Club scandal...

A cute redhead finally emerges from backstage, swaying her hips to the beat of the song, the sultry low bass thumping through the club, setting the mood for an intense, slow, sensual dance.

Isaac sighs, then turns his back to her and looks over at me. "I heard you were with Cass and Kennedy earlier."

I snort and nod. "Yeah. They got into it again."

"Not shocked."

"You think they've made up by now?"

He snorts. "I'm sure they have."

"Where's Jack?"

"She didn't want to come tonight. Said she was tired and not feeling well."

I glance over at Allegra, who's watching the new dancer intently, completely unbothered by the fact that the song has sentimental meaning to us. "I'm sorry Jack isn't feeling well. Did she go see Mom or Pope?"

Isaac shakes his head. "Nah. If she isn't feeling better by tomorrow, I'll have Mom come take a look at her, though. It's probably nothing, just overly tired."

"Has Gio been sleeping well?"

He snorts and accepts the beer Tommy brings him, tilting the bottle in thanks before he takes a swig of it. "Not really, but Vivi is old enough to go in and try to comfort him if he wakes up crying. Most nights, by the time we get in there, he's already back asleep."

"She's a good big sister."

Pride brightens his gaze, and he grins. "The best." He leans around me, suddenly looking much more serious. "Hey, Allegra?"

She gets pulled from her viewing and turns to him. "What's up?"

"I wanted to ask you something."

Something about the tone of his voice sets me on edge, and I protectively wrap an arm around her as she leans across me so she can hear him over the music.

"Yeah?"

"Well, I got a call at the office a little while ago about somebody named Michael McDonald. Does that ring a bell?"

I feel her immediately stiffen, and her eyes go to that dark, steely gray they always do when she's afraid.

"Why?"

Isaac catches on immediately. "One of our contacts said his name popped up on an international flight, and apparently, he's on a list of known associates of your father. We're monitoring any sort of movement for obvious reasons, especially with the opening of the second tower in a week."

Suddenly, Allegra's not the only one nervous.

I keep my arm wrapped around her, hoping she can't feel how tense I've suddenly gotten. "Who is he?"

She swallows thickly. "Um, a guy who used to work for my dad."

"How long ago?"

Shrugging, she chews on her bottom lip. "A couple of years, I guess?"

"What do you mean by 'used to?'"

"Well, I haven't heard anyone mention him in probably a year and a half. I assumed he either moved on or..."

She doesn't finish the sentence.

But we both get the picture.

If he did anything to disappoint or piss off Satriano, he's probably sleeping with the fishes right now.

Isaac drums his fingers on his beer bottle. "How well did you know him?"

She shakes her head. "I never even met the guy. But I heard enough to know that you don't want to cross him."

A strange silence hangs between us for a moment, the tones of the familiar song and the hoots and hollers of the patrons filling the void.

Isaac finally clears his throat. "Well, he's here."

The smoky scotch I just drank threatens to make a reappearance. "What do you mean?"

"The flight he got on, the end destination was New Orleans, and it landed several hours ago."

"Shit." I shove my hands through my hair, looking from him to Allegra. "But Satriano isn't in town anymore."

Isaac shakes his head. "Not as far as we know."

Allegra nods her agreement. "I haven't heard from him, not since we met with him months ago."

That ultimately doesn't mean *anything*.

"He always likes to make a grand entrance, though, and appear at the most inopportune times for us. We have an opening. You know what happened at the groundbreaking."

Isaac curses under his breath and downs half his beer. "Yeah, and then at the hotel opening, he tried to have Atlas throw the fucking fight, which would have crushed the high of the event. What do you think he's going to do now that we've got the ability to double our income at the hotel starting next week with a second tower?"

Allegra's face suddenly loses all color, and she presses her hand over her stomach again. "Oh, God…"

I rub her back. "Are you okay?"

She nods, but the paleness of her skin and her unfocused gaze suggest otherwise. "I'm going to go to the bathroom. I'll be back."

"Are you sure you're all right?"

But she doesn't offer an answer, just slides off her stool and rushes toward the bathrooms along the far wall.

Isaac watches her with concern. "She didn't look all right."

I slide off my stool. "No, she didn't. I'm going to go check on her."

She didn't feel well earlier today, either.

But she said she was fine and still went to Wren's class. Bishop would have told someone if she noticed an issue there or after. And if Allegra hadn't been up to it, she never would have agreed to meet me here tonight for a drink after I finished up at the hotel.

I hustle after her and push my way into the women's bathroom, not giving a shit who else might be in here.

The door to the handicapped stall stands ajar, and I can see Allegra's feet sticking out as she kneels in front of the toilet retching. The sound fills the air, and I wince, worry instantly consuming me as I rush through the bathroom to her.

"Babe? Are you okay?"

She gasps, trying to catch her breath, and I drop to my knees beside her and grab her hair, helping her hold it back. "I don't know. My stomach's just been off..."

"I'm calling my mom. You and Jack are both not feeling well at the same time."

She glances over at me, breathing heavily, trying to swallow before she retches again.

"Your dad would never—"

"Poison us?" She shakes her head, then seems to regret it as another wave of heaving rocks her body. Coughing through it, she gasps. "God, no. He wouldn't..."

I wish I could be as sure.

"Well, something's going on..."

I pull out my phone from my pocket and use voice commands to initiate a call to Mom. Pope will be next. Both Allegra and Jack are sick, and we just discovered one of Satriano's "associates" is in town.

A sense of absolute dread settles over me as I wait for her to answer.

BISHOP

THE NEW REDHEAD at center stage isn't bad.

She could have a decent career here, if she hadn't been stupid enough to dance to Nora's song.

Doc isn't going to be happy about this...

I chuckle to myself, picturing the fallout that will result from her discovering what happened.

And she *will* find out.

My guess is that at least three people have called or texted her or Stone about it already.

But maybe I should, too, just in case...

I reach into my pocket to grab my phone when the women's bathroom door flies open, and Coen stalks out with Allegra cradled in his arms.

Oh, shit.

Rushing to the other side of the club, I meet him on his way to the front door. "Is she okay?"

He shakes his head. "She's sick, and apparently, Jack is, too."

"Shit. That can't be random, right?"

His jaw hardens as we reach the bar. "I don't know." He nudges Isaac with his arm. "Mom and Pope are going to meet us at the clinic. Go get Jack—now."

The panic in his gaze sets Isaac in motion. He launches off his stool, already bringing his phone to his ear as he heads toward the door.

I follow Coen closely, unable to tear my gaze from how pale and clammy Allegra looks. "I'm coming with you."

"No, stay here. If something is going on, where would the

most likely place be for him to hit? Either the hotel or here. Call your dad and tell him what's happening—and keep your eyes *open*."

"I always do."

He finally reaches the door, and I pull it open for him and watch Isaac rush to help get Allegra in the car.

Fuck. Fuck. Fuck.

Not good.

This is not good.

I pull out my phone to call Dad, and movement at the end of the bar catches my eye.

A blond guy sitting at the other end from where Allegra, Coen, and Isaac had been slowly pushes his stool away from the bar and rises to his feet. With his back to me, all I see is the sandy mop of hair and black leather motorcycle jacket.

He reaches into his back jeans pocket, pulls out his wallet, and tosses cash onto the bar before he slowly saunters toward the exit.

There's something about the way he carries himself.

The set of his shoulders.

His sure steps.

Whoever he is, he's trouble.

I HOPE you enjoyed *Restless Hawke.* Delve further into the Hawke Family world and find out what happens next in the battle with Satriano in Bishop's story *Renegade Hawke!*

Get your copy: books2read.com/RenegadeHawke

To stay up to date on news, sales, and releases from Gwyn, join her newsletter here: www.gwynmcnamee.com/newsletter

ACKNOWLEDGMENTS

Every time I write a book, I realize what an incredible team I have. Without Renee, Patricia, Stephie, and Caoimhe, I couldn't do it. Thank you for loving my worlds and words and for helping me make them great!

ABOUT THE AUTHOR

Gwyn McNamee is an attorney, writer, wife, and mother (to one human baby and two fur babies). Originally from the Midwest, Gwyn relocated to her husband's home town of Las Vegas in 2015 and is enjoying her respite from the cold and snow. Gwyn has been writing down her crazy stories and ideas for years and finally decided to share them with the world. She loves to write stories with a bit of suspense and action mingled with romance and heat.

When she isn't either writing or voraciously devouring any books she can get her hands on, Gwyn is busy adding to her tattoo collection, golfing, and stirring up trouble with her perfect mix of sweetness and sarcasm (usually while wearing heels).

Gwyn loves to hear from her readers. Here is where you can find her:

Website: http://www.gwynmcnamee.com/

Shop: http://www.gwynmcnameeshop.com/

Facebook:https://www.facebook.com/AuthorGwynMcNamee/

FB Reader Group: https://www.facebook.com/groups/1667380963540655/

Newsletter: www.gwynmcnamee.com/newsletter

Instagram: https://www.instagram.com/gwynmcnamee

Bookbub: https://www.bookbub.com/authors/gwynmcnamee

Tiktok: https://www.tiktok.com/@authorgwynmcnamee

OTHER WORKS BY GWYN MCNAMEE

Billionaires of New Orleans:

The Hawke Family Series

Savage Collision (The Hawke Family - Book One)

He's everything she didn't know she wanted. She's everything he thought he could never have.

The last thing I expect when I walk into The Hawkeye Club is to fall head over heels in lust. It's supposed to be a rescue mission. I have to get my baby sister off the pole, into some clothes, and out of the grasp of the pussy peddler who somehow manipulated her into stripping. But the moment I see Savage Hawke and verbally spar with him, my ability to remain rational flies out the window and my libido takes center stage. I've never wanted a relationship—my time is better spent focusing on taking down the scum running this city—but what I want and what I need are apparently two different things.

Danika Eriksson storms into my office in her high heels and on her high horse. Her holier-than-thou attitude and accusations should offend me, but instead, I can't get her out of my head or my heart. Her incomparable drive, take-no prisoners attitude, and blatant honesty captivate me and hold me prisoner. I should steer clear, but my self-preservation instinct is apparently dead—which is exactly what our relationship will be once she knows everything. It's only a matter of time.

The truth doesn't always set you free. Sometimes, it just royally screws you.

AVAILABLE AT ALL RETAILERS:

books2read.com/SavageCollision

Tortured Skye (**The Hawke Family - Book Two**)

She's always been off-limits. He's always just out of reach.

Falling in love with Gabe Anderson was as easy as breathing. Fighting my feelings for my brother's best friend was agonizingly hard. I never imagined giving in to my desire for him would cause such a destructive ripple effect. That kiss was my grasp at a lifeline—something, anything to hold me steady in my crumbling life. Now, I have to suffer with the fallout while trying to convince him it's all worth the consequences.

Guilt overwhelms me—over what I've done, the lives I've taken, and more than anything, over my feelings for Skye Hawke. Craving my best friend's little sister is insanely self-destructive. It never should have happened, but since the moment she kissed me, I haven't been able to get her out of my mind. If I take what I want, I risk losing everything. If I don't, I'll lose her and a piece of myself. The raging storm threatening to rain down on the city is nothing compared to the one that will come from my decision.

Love can be torture, but sometimes, love is the only thing that can save you.

AVAILABLE AT ALL RETAILERS:

Books2read.com/Tortured-Skye

Stone Sober (**The Hawke Family - Book Three**)

She's innocent and sweet. He's dark and depraved.

Stone Hawke is precisely the kind of man women are warned about—handsome, intelligent, arrogant, and intricately entangled with some dangerous people. I should stay away, but he manages to strip my soul bare with just a look and dominates my thoughts. Bad decisions are in my past. My life is (mostly) on track, even if it is no longer the one to medical school. I can't allow myself to cave to the fierce pull and ardent attraction I feel toward the youngest Hawke.

Nora Eriksson is off-limits, and not just because she's my brother's employee and sister-in-law. Despite the fact she's stripping at The Hawkeye Club, she has an innocent and pure heart. Normally, the only thing that appeals to me about innocence is the opportunity to taint it. But not when it comes to Nora. I can't expose her to the filth permeating my life. There are too many things I can't control, things completely out of my hands. She doesn't deserve any of it, but the power she holds over me is stronger than any addiction.

The hardest battles we fight are often with ourselves, but only through defeating our own demons can we find true peace.

AVAILABLE AT ALL RETAILERS:

books2read.com/StoneSober

Building Storm (The Hawke Family - Book Four)

She hasn't been living. He's looking for a way to forget it all.

My life went up in flames. All I'm left with is my daughter and ashes. The simple act of breathing is so excruciating, there are days I wish I could stop altogether. So I have no business being at the party, and I definitely shouldn't be in the arms of the handsome stranger. When his lips meet mine, he breathes life into me for the first time since the day the inferno disintegrated my world. But loving again isn't in the cards, and there are even greater dangers to face than trying to keep Landon McCabe out of my heart.

Running is my only option. I have to get away from Chicago and the betrayal that shattered my world. I need a new life-one without attachments. The vibrancy of New Orleans convinces me it's possible to start over. Yet in all the excitement of a new city, it's Storm Hawke's dark, sad beauty that draws me in. She isn't looking for love, and we both need a hot, sweaty release without feelings getting involved. But even the best laid plans fail, and life can leave you burned.

Love can build, and love can destroy. But in the end, love is what raises you from the ashes.

Tainted Saint (The Hawke Family - Book Five)

He's searching for absolution. She wants her happily ever after.

Solomon Clarke goes by Saint, though he's anything but. After lusting for him from afar, the masquerade party affords me the anonymity to pursue that attraction without worrying about the fall-out of hooking-up with the bouncer from the Hawkeye Club. From the second he lays his eyes and hands on me, I'm helpless to resist him. Even burying myself in a dangerous investigation can't erase the memory of our combustible connection and one night together. The only problem... he has no idea who I am.

Caroline Brooks thinks I don't see her watching me, the way her eyes rake over me with appreciation. But I've noticed, and the party is the perfect opportunity to unleash the desire I've kept reined in for so damn long. It also sets off a series of events no one sees coming. Events that leave those I love hurting because of my failures. While the guilt eats away at my soul, Caroline continues to weigh on my heart. That woman may be the death of me, but oh, what a way to go.

Life isn't always clean, and sometimes, it takes a saint to do the dirty work.

Steele Resolve (The Hawke Family - Book Six)

For one man, power is king. For the other, loyalty reigns.

Mob boss Luca "Steele" Abello isn't just dangerous—he's lethal. A master manipulator, liar, and user, no one should trust a word that comes out of his mouth. Yet, I can't get him out of my head. The time we spent together before I knew his true identity is seared into my brain. His touch. His voice. They haunt my every waking hour and occupy my dreams. So does my guilt. I'm literally sleeping with the enemy and betraying the only family I've ever had. When I come clean, it will be the end of me.

Byron Harris is a distraction I can't afford. I never should have let it go beyond that first night, but I couldn't stay away. Even when I learned who he was, when the *only* option was to end things, I kept going back, risking his life and mine to continue our indiscretion. The truth of what I am could get us both killed, but being with the man who's such an integral part of the Hawke family is even more terrifying. The only people I've ever cared about are on opposing sides, and I'm the rift that could end their friendship forever.

Love is a battlefield isn't just a saying. For some, it's a reality.

AVAILABLE AT ALL RETAILERS:

books2read.com/SteeleResolve

You can find information on the rest of Gwyn's books on her website:

www.gwynmcnamee.com